A Fist Full of Holey Dollars

Sara Powter

Bible Quotes from the King James Version

ISBN: 9781923097407
Paperback edition

ABN 99 768 734 831
Pacific Wanderland Publications
Kincumber, Australia NSW 2251

saragpowter@gmail.com
https://www.sarapowter.com.au

1st edition 2026 printed by Kindle & print
an Amazon Company; available on Kindle Unlimited & in print.
2nd edition, Large print paperback, 2026 Pacific Wanderland Publications
3rd edition, Hard Cover 2026, Amazon USA

Cover Painting
Shoalhaven Valley, New South Wales
1861 (flipped)
Artist *Conrad Martens*
England, Australia 21 Mar 1801 – 21 Aug 1878
https://www.artgallery.nsw.gov.au/collection/works/8956/

Rudi Inset
Andrew Copland (d.1807) By George Watson (1766–1837)
Dumfries Museum and Camera Obscura
https://www.tumblr.com/thesixthduke/104095781279/gentlemaninkhaki-andrew-copland-d-1807-by'

Coins
Holey Dollar and Dump
https://coins.tsbnk.ru/entsiklopediya/inostrannye-monety/ot-funta-k-dollaru-istoriya-monet-avstralii/

Cover by
Beckon Creative
beck@beckoncreative.biz

Cultural Advice
Aboriginal and Torres Strait Islander people should be aware that this book contains names and stories of deceased persons.
Acknowledgement of Country
In the spirit of reconciliation, I acknowledge the Traditional Custodians of country throughout Australia and their connections to land, sea and community.
We pay our respect to their Elders, past and present, and extend that respect to all Aboriginal and Torres Strait Islander peoples today

Australian Historical Novels

(All stand-alone books)

A First Fleet Stories (1788+)

Gentle Annie Soames
The Emancipated Potter
Paternity Unknown

The Hunter to Macquarie Collection (1795-1822)

When Upon Life's Billows
The Saddler's Song
Tuppence to Pass
His Majesty's Pageboy
A Fist Full of Holey Dollars
Far From the Whispering Sheoaks (2026)
Bound Down in Iron Chains (2026)
Buddy's Promise (2027)
Quest for Survival (2027)
Linen Shirts Aplenty (2027)

Unlikely Convict Ladies Trilogy (1792-1840s)

Dancing to Her Own Tune
(co-authored by Sheila Hunter & Sara Powter)
Amelia's Tears
A Lady in Irons

The Lockleys of Parramatta (1800-1901)

Unshackled Lives - *Prequel novella - free with newsletter signup*
Hands Upon the Anvil
Out Where the Brolgas Dance
Diamonds in the Dirt
The Earl's Shadow
Once a Jolly Swagman
Jonty's Journey

The Convict Birthstain Collection (1820-1840s)

No More, My Love
The Vine Weaver
Scotch at The Rocks
Waiting at the Sliprails
Convict Shadows of the Past
In Defence of Her Honour
I Can't Stop Tomorrow
Madeline's Boy
Jam or Marmalade for Tea

Fools Gold Trilogy 1840s- 1850s

The Breeze Gently Shifts
The Silver Thimble
Knots Behind the Tapestry

Sheila Hunter's Australian Colonial Trilogy (1840-1850s)

Mattie
Ricky
The Heather to The Hawkesbury

NOTES about the Holey Dollar.

Arriving in New South Wales in 1809 after the January 26th, 1808, Rum Rebellion—the colony's only military coup—Governor Lachlan Macquarie discovered a severe shortage of coins. To assert control over the NSW Rum Corps, Macquarie purchased 40,000 Spanish Reales, also called 'pieces of eight.' A convict forger, William Henshall, punched out the centres of these coins, and both the outer rings and central 'dumps' became legal tender in September 1813, remaining in circulation for nearly a decade until British sterling arrived in 1822. By introducing official currency and imposing strict tariffs on alcohol importation and sales, Macquarie weakened opposition. With John Macarthur absent in England for most of Macquarie's term, managing the 'exclusives' proved somewhat easier.

The coins' origins and manufacturing process remain uncertain. The account in my story is one credible hypothesis, and I have included all available historical data, though sources are scarce.

Read more of the Holey Dollar story here…

https://www.nma.gov.au/explore/collection/highlights/holey-dollar

https://www.nma.gov.au/defining-moments/resources/holey-dollar

https://coinworks.com.au/1813-dump

Thanks to

my husband, Steve.
Thank you for all your support in my writing.
He's my Alpha reader.

To Roby Aiken
for your patience in correcting my punctuation

and to my Beta readers
Noreen Robertson, Linda Upcroft,
& Anna Marie Leffew
for doing the final read-throughs
and to

Rebekah Robinson for my cover.
by Beckon Creative
beck@beckoncreative.biz

Table of Contents

The grammar and language in this book are Australian English spelling.

KEY

~ - Time passing in the same locality

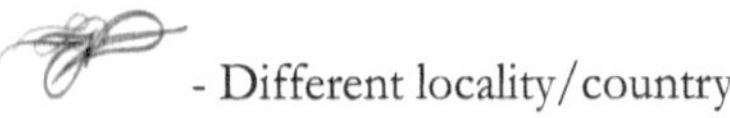
- Different locality/country

1808 Town map and character list at the back.

Chapter 1 Distasteful Duty

Sydney Cove, May 1810

Captain Rudolph Greenwood had been assigned to oversee the convict women again this morning. Of all his duties, this was the one Rudi disliked most.

As he prepared for the day, he pondered the future of the colony under the leadership of the new, pinch-faced Scottish governor. What could this man possibly achieve?

The colony was in a vulnerable and precarious state. Food was scarce, and the surrounding land was largely unproductive.

The European settlement was comprised of convicted criminals, the untrustworthy and corrupt New South Wales Rum Corps, and a few cautious free settlers. On top of this, the settlement's activities were constantly under observation by a suspicious native population.

Rudi wondered what the new governor could do in a land largely populated by such untrustworthy people, many with whom he served —men often more corrupt than the convicts they guarded. He had already had enough of the unruly prisoners. He had arrived with a batch of female felons on the *Speke* in November 1808.

Rudi had been in the 102nd Regiment of Foot when he reported for duty in London. Since the new governor arrived, he had been transferred to the 73rd Regiment. He was waiting for the paperwork to be processed. He knew the long trip back and forth to London took time, so he was not expecting news of its completion any time soon.

His six-month-long journey here had been gruelling, and Rudi had been glad to see the last of the bucking seas. He quickly discovered he was no sailor, but his regiment was the army, not the navy.

He was only here because his uncle had suggested it would be better than what he was dealing with at home. He soon discovered that this was debatable. Did Uncle John not know the hell he was consigning Rudi to?

From the moment Rudi stepped aboard the *Speke* at Falmouth in early May, the only times he was not sick were when he was on land at Rio de Janeiro or Cape Town.

The behaviour of the nearly one hundred female convicts on the vessel was as bad as that of his fellow soldiers. The captain, John Hingson, had no control over the women; his duty was to his crew.

The ship's doctor, Macmillan, was the first to tell Rudi about Governor Bligh. Macmillan had been in Sydney when Bligh arrived to relieve Governor Phillip Gidley King.

King was ill, and his departure came at an unfortunate time. From his last meeting with former governor John Hunter, Rudi knew the colony was unstable and that a mere spark could ignite the New South Wales Corps into rebellion.

Rudi thought back to why he had enlisted. The former governor, John Hunter, was his maternal aunt's brother-in-law. The extended family saw one another as often as possible. Rudi adored the kind gentleman and called him "uncle."

It was his honorary uncle John who had suggested that Rudi enlist in the army, believing it would give him a sense of purpose.

Uncle John knew how deeply Rudi was wounded by his brother Malchus's obnoxious behaviour toward him.

Uncle John understood that the only way for Rudi to find himself, and hopefully fill the void in his heart, was to leave home. In 1800, after five years of clashes with the same military leaders Rudi now served under, Uncle John was recalled from his post as governor of New South Wales and brought back to England. As expected, he was exonerated and swiftly promoted.

Rudi had wanted to know as much as he could about the place he was heading to. He read his uncle's journals. Now he wished he had remained ignorant.

The voyage itself had been reasonably calm compared to the First Fleet voyage in 1788, but after nearly half a year, every day at sea was a sore trial.

Those one hundred and eighty-two days were spent being ill. They were vile. He suffered greatly for the entire voyage and was ill every day. Rudi never found his sea legs, and the stench from below decks was horrific. He managed to appear for duty before finding a spot near a railing to heave his heart out overboard.

By the time he arrived in the colony, his uniform hung from his gaunt frame. He had hated every moment of the voyage, and the dismal sight of his destination only deepened his despair. This hot hellhole was even worse than he had imagined.

The only thing keeping him in this accursed place was the thought that leaving meant repeating the sea voyage. He would never willingly venture out to sea again. That meant he was consigned to his dismal life here in this desolate place.

Rudi had been in Sydney Cove for over eighteen months and longed, every single day, for the cool greenness of England. Yet there was nothing left for him there. His loved ones were all dead, taken in one night by a fire. Parents, most of his siblings, the house and even the staff had perished in a single sweep of the Almighty's hand. Only the gardener was found outside—and he was dead as well. The gardener's elderly father and son were the only staff members who survived. The younger man had been with Rudi, and the old man was at home, ill.

Rudi groaned, anger flaring at the blow dealt to him and his family. How dare God take everything? Only his elder brother remained, spared because he had been visiting his wife's family. They were safe with her relations, but Rudi was not welcome there.

Having inherited the estate, Malchus would likely rebuild the family home into a grandiose edifice. It would never be the same. It would not be the home Rudi had known.

Rudi had been away at basic training and had not had the chance to say goodbye to anyone. The gardener's son had driven him to the base. No, he could not go home—his home was gone. He angrily swiped away an unwanted tear.

Rudi had already endured a summer in this repugnant land. The heat was horrific, yet he had no choice but to don his red woollen uniform coat and report for duty. The relentless heat was inescapable.

The flies were terrible, and he had swallowed more than his share. The creatures were intolerable enough, but then the fires came. His fair skin burned within minutes, the sun blistering his lips so quickly that only smearing honey gave a modicum of relief.

Even the honey here was vile. Unlike the sweet clover honey at home, this local stuff was thick and dark, with an almost tart bitterness. Unfortunately, though it soothed his sunburn, it drew more flies.

The doctor, D'Arcy Wentworth, had told him of the benefits of this dark, sticky goop. Rudi liked the tall Irishman, who understood his dislike of the settlement.

An Aboriginal man named Bungaree had also spoken of the virtues of this dark honey, as well as other local medicines.

D'Arcy had mentioned that the first doctor to arrive with the First Fleet, John White, had befriended a young man named Nanberry and documented many local bush medicines and treatments.

Rudi remembered reading about these in Uncle John's journals and sometimes used the simpler ones, such as the native honey.

After a quick breakfast, he exited his accommodation and walked to the female barracks. Rudi waited for the convict women to ready themselves for their various duties in the colony.

Before his arrival, convict women had been sent to the timber gaol and factory in Parramatta, but shortly before he disembarked, that factory had been damaged by fire. With nowhere else to send the women, they were assigned to whoever could accommodate them. Others were housed in a makeshift dormitory in Sydney, where he was assigned today.

One of his onerous duties was to ensure they reached their designated workplaces each day. He always made sure they were fully clad before entering their accommodation, but one or two would still flaunt their charms to him or the other officer on duty.

He hated this work. He was a soldier, not a nanny.

Some women waited until the overseeing officers arrived before they stripped off, brazenly baring their breasts to him and his fellow officers.

Rudi knew that many of the guards willingly took what was offered. He did not condemn them, for he, too, wished he had a female companion. He had half a mind to find one as a bedfellow, but they would have little privacy even if he did. However, that was not the real reason he held back. He had no experience with women, and although his body cried out for one, he had never sown his seed and had no wish to be laughed at by a felon whore because of his innocence. His friend Lance also avoided such women.

So, Rudi could not take a woman back to his room, and he had no intention of his first act of intimacy being in full view of other felons.

He had kept his inexperience from his fellow officers and had no wish for them to discover it. He knew that if he relented and chose the wrong woman, she would spread the news of his virginal status far and wide, and he would be ridiculed by his peers. No, he would stay well clear of them all.

With a huff of frustration, he swivelled on his heel and left the women's sleeping quarters. He was on guard duty, and although bedding one of them would take his mind off what he should be doing, duty always came first, and today he needed to concentrate on that. He muttered as he left the sleeping quarters. "Damned duty!" Uncle John had drummed that into him. He was also aware that slaking his lusts once would only whet his appetite for more.

As he exited the dormitory, several junior soldiers and another captain were waiting for the women to assemble for muster. Rudi read out their assignments, then handed them over to the soldiers assigned to escort them.

Rudi's duty was over. His eyes turned towards the bay.

After Governor Macquarie arrived, he transferred several officers into his own regiment. As of yesterday, Rudi found himself in the 73rd Regiment. The transfer meant that although he no longer had to stand guard, he still had to ensure the women were secure in their quarters. He had signed up to fight, not to babysit whores.

From the time the First Fleet women were landed on 6 February 1788, they had been targets of men breaking into their quarters to satisfy their lust. He read that on the very day they landed, the poor creatures had not even reached their quarters before being set upon by the men.

On arriving in 1808, Rudi visited Uncle John's friends to deliver mail. That included the Brays at the mill and other friends out west, the Milroys and Osbornes. Uncle John had suggested befriending the miller and his wife, and that was how Rudi met Connie and Nigel. Both had arrived in two of those eleven flimsy ships, as did Colin Osborne, the potter in Parramatta.

Rudi paused in his thoughts. He was gutted when he realised he had contemplated doing to others what had been done to the miller's wife, Connie Bray. She and many of her friends had been savagely violated on landing. She coped with that as well as her severe scars caused by her stepfather. Through it all, she helped others and kept smiling. It was at their house that Uncle John could watch the movements on the magnificent harbour.

Rudi blanched at his thoughts. After confirming the guards were in position, he ordered the women escorted to their daily duties. Once they were gone, he was free until the afternoon muster. He walked off to find solace away from the unruly crowd. He wished his life—and what had occurred—were different. He walked past the old cottage on Bennelong Point and wondered how long it would take to drown if he simply walked into the sea.

He was so hot.

Would drowning be frightening?

Oh, how he wished that cool water would envelop him.

His mind turned over what he had heard in the officers' mess last night.

They said the new governor was a devout Christian. Rudi grunted, wondering how faith could help his leadership. Church had never drawn him; he had little experience with that institution. Yet he believed in God because he blamed that great deity for the deaths of his loved ones.

His parents had been socialites. Though not in the top tier of society, they were well-connected enough to be invited to many second-tier events. Malchus had embraced that lifestyle to the fullest. Church attendance was not something they embraced.

Uncle John had encouraged Rudi to attend church with him, and Rudi had gone to placate the old man.

St John's church in Hackney was a new structure, built after the previous church, St Augustine's, had outgrown its capacity. After they were seated and Rudi had picked up a prayer book, Uncle John mentioned that it had been repaired by a felon in New South Wales, Obadiah, 'Buddy' Jensen. He had lived in the crypt at the back of the cemetery. Years earlier, one of the girls from the crypt had sailed with the First Fleet from this very church. That was when Rudi first learned about Connie, who had been only a teenager at the time.

Rudi met Connie upon arriving in Sydney and delivered a letter from his uncle to the young couple. His heart went out to the beautiful, but scarred, woman and her husband, Nigel, who had been one of her abusers. How could she forgive him for his vile actions? He found that she had. Connie adored her husband, and he her.

Rudi unbuttoned his red uniform jacket, was about to peel off the hot coat, and walk into the water. Maybe drowning would be quicker if he kept it on.

He wanted to end the pain and sense of abandonment when a call from the hill made him turn. His friend Lance had come looking for him.

With a groan, he sighed. "Tomorrow…"

~

Thankfully, the next day, Rudi was on chain gang duty with Tobin, and for once, he didn't mind. Whenever he guarded the female felons, his mind took control of his nether regions. Mind you, they taunted him.

Chain gang duty was hardly pleasant, but it was the lesser of two evils.

Thankfully, no more female transports had arrived since August of the previous year.

He detested this place. He loathed the smell, the heat, the flies, and the people who lived there, except Lance and D'Arcy. The Milroys were also nice, but he didn't get to see them often as they lived in Toongabbie. He hated the loneliness when Lance was assigned elsewhere. He didn't like his peers, and the feeling was mutual. He had heard them call him "Moody Rudi."

How he could be so lonely, surrounded by so many people, was unfathomable. He felt empty inside. Uncle John had used the word "void." He was correct. Today, to make matters worse, he hadn't slept well last night.

This morning, he had an hour before he was required for duty. Lance would have things under control. Rudi wanted to stretch his legs.

As he walked past the salt boilers at the quay, he thought about the past eighteen months and the choices he had made.

Rudi had enlisted, hoping to be sent to war to fight the French, half-hoping he would be killed on the battlefield, but Nelson defeated his French counterpart at the Battle of Trafalgar. Rudi enlisted before he heard about a lull in the fighting. Instead of being sent to France, he was sent halfway around the globe, where he found himself aboard a convict transport ship.

This was not his plan.

Rudi arrived months after the New South Wales Rum Corps rebelled in January 1808. Since then, he had seen George Johnston and John Macarthur a few times from a distance but thankfully had no need to speak to either of them. Uncle John had warned him to stay well clear of both agitators, so he had.

Remembering Uncle John's words, Rudi realised that his anger didn't truly reflect how he felt. Uncle John had warned Admiralty House in London that an uprising was brewing, and they had refused to listen. Uncle John had been livid.

Now, rather than fight in the French War, Rudi was supposed to quell unrest among his peers. When he first arrived, Rudi was ordered to guard the governor, who was under house arrest. For the vice regal man, there was no escape.

Although the coup had occurred before Rudi arrived, the Rum Rebellion, as it was being called, had barely lasted a day before military disorder set in.

Once in charge, George Johnston reassigned many of his soldiers to guard duty of the imprisoned governor, basic jobs were ignored, and the town's filth made it stink.

Rumours abounded about where Bligh had been discovered. Many of the Rum Corps boasted that Governor Bligh had been found hiding under his bed. Rudi had chuckled when he heard that. He didn't know if it was true, but he knew fear, and if the soldiers he worked with were after his skin, he would have hidden as well.

Thankfully, he had not had much interaction with the troublemaker John Macarthur, who had quickly left for London to appear in court with George Johnston and others involved in the coup. Hopefully, they would stay there.

After Governor Bligh was officially removed from his viceregal position, he was placed under house arrest for over a year and later stated he would sail to England. Instead, he went south to Van Diemen's Land. Even in Hobart, Bligh's reputation preceded him. Lieutenant-Governor David Collins of the Derwent River settlement refused Bligh permission to land, and he was forced to remain on his ship for the duration of his stay.

When Bligh sailed for England in March the following year, Rudi was reassigned to oversee the women felons.

On his return to Sydney, Bligh expected to receive all the privileges of the governorship, but Lachlan Macquarie had already replaced him.

Rudi had been impressed that Macquarie did not explode on hearing what the man required, no, that word was too mild: Bligh demanded. The ousted governor returned from his refuge in Van Diemen's Land to find that Macquarie had things under control; he eventually went back to England.

Rudi knew more than enough about Bligh, as he had been placed on personal guard duty again for the man when he sailed into Sydney Harbour in January of that year. The previous governor was supposed to have gone to England the year before, but had not, which was how Rudi became aware of the aborted trip to Hobart.

Only three days earlier, Bligh had finally sailed for London to stand as a witness at the court-martial of George Johnston. Rudi hoped he would never see Bligh again, but wondered if the man would turn his ship around and return a second time.

Macarthur and Johnston had departed soon after the coup, followed by some of the other mutineers. The colony had yet to settle, but most of the troublemakers had been assigned some distance from the main settlement.

Rudi regarded this new, weedy Scotsman, Macquarie, with a

puzzled gaze. He believed that David Collins was another such man. He knew Collins's history after reading Uncle John's journals as part of his preparation for this voyage. David Collins had served under John Hunter as Colonial Secretary before returning to England. In 1803, Collins was promoted and sent back to serve as the lieutenant-governor of the newest arm of the penal colony in Van Diemen's Land.

Rudi shuddered at the demands made by Bligh and the unrealistic requirements demanded by the deposed officer.

By the time Bligh left, Rudi was ready to throttle him. He had been on a rostered day off when Bligh returned, but by then Macquarie already had things well in hand.

Governor Macquarie had only a few weeks' grace before Bligh arrived, as the new governor's ships, *HMS Dromedary* and her sister ship, *HMS Hindostan*, had reached Sydney a few days after Christmas in 1809.

Bligh came hard on their bow waves.

Rudi smiled. In the week before Bligh's return, Macquarie had already ripped the carpet from under the rebels' feet. He rescinded all land grants made between January 1808 and his arrival.

The following week, the new governor announced that anyone appointed to an office of law after Bligh was overthrown would be immune from prosecution for any acts committed while in office.

Rudi chuckled to himself.

The canny Scotsman then announced that he wished for "Union, Tranquillity, and Harmony." Rudi guffawed. As if that would happen, a miracle would be needed. The currency in the colony was rum. How could that be fixed?

Rudi relaxed on the grass and took a deep breath. For once, he was at peace. Moments like this were rare; there was little to like in his new homeland. He had chosen this spot because there were no hovels, shanties, or filth to mar his view or offend his nostrils.

The original farm from 1788 had been in the cove behind him, but like so many other ventures in this stinking, hot land, it had been a dismal failure—too hot, too dry, and the seed had been sterile.

From here, Rudi could sit and dream of sailing away and going home. He huffed again. Even at home, there was nothing for him. He had no land, no entitlements, and little to no prospect of wealth of any sort. His elder brother, on the other hand, was as fit as a fiddle and already had two children, Freddy and Georgie, according to the most recent letter from Uncle John.

Dreaming of home only made him sadder. He watched the

various boats move around the vast harbour and imagined drifting out to sea, never to return. Should he do it?

Rudi lay back in the shade of a tree and closed his eyes.

~

When Rudi woke, his mind was unsettled. Was suicide really so bad? He watched as some boats hauled in nets heavy with fish, while others crossed the harbour carrying passengers. If he were going to do it, he should move.

He saw the small government barge heading to Parramatta. It rarely carried free settlers, but it was the easiest way to transport prisoners and goods to the western settlement. He didn't think it would run until late afternoon today. The river's shallowness at the destination meant the tides controlled the timetable.

He was tempted to strip off his coat and walk into the water. For a second time, he unbuttoned his jacket, ready to walk into the sea. He was sure death would be quick, as he couldn't swim.

Rudi heard the town clock chime six.

He had not realised he'd been sitting on the rocky headland for hours. He had missed the day's duty. He should have been with the chain gang. He groaned.

His stomach grumbled, and he headed back to the barracks for something to eat.

Reluctantly, duty called once again.

~

The remaining hours passed slowly.

No one spoke to him except to issue an order. Lance was nowhere in sight.

Releasing a long huff, he thought, "I hate this vile place."

He had no desire to keep on living. Why had he returned to eat? He should have walked into the bay and finished everything.

After the evening meal, his lonely, lumpy, horsehair-padded pallet bed called. He was weary of everything.

Chapter 2 A New Day Dawns

The chorus of raucous birds woke him as the dawn light chased away the darkness. He was on chain gang duty again today and had much to do before they headed out for road repair. He would need an excuse to explain his absence the previous day. He could be prosecuted for dereliction of duty, so he would claim illness. Well, it was, but in his mind. After tossing aside the blankets, Rudi splashed cold water on his face from his ewer to wake himself properly, then dressed and went to get hot water to shave. His fellow officers greeted him with a nod of acknowledgement in the breakfast room.

Lance said, "Morning, Rudi. Feeling better, did you sleep well?"

Rudi grunted and then pulled himself up sharply. He realised his foul mood would not do. He grimaced a smile and replied, "As much as one ever does in this hellhole, thanks, Lance."

Knowing that the three who shared this small mess room were from a similar class at home, he said, "I willingly admit I miss my feather mattress and hot chocolate in the mornings. The heat and cacophony of screeching birds here does not ease my waking, and I really wish I had a valet." He released a long, frustrated sigh. He moaned, "I am so not a morning person." Or an evening one, either, but he would refrain from voicing that thought.

His peers chuckled.

All agreed.

Lance said, "You're not wrong about the valet. I'm well over looking after my clothing and cleaning my room."

Other heads nodded. For once, they agreed with him over something. That was a first. Rudi cocked an eyebrow in surprise but said nothing to them. He turned to his friend and said, "Hey, Lance, how about we look around for a suitable woman to be our cleaner and housemaid? I'm not talking about anything else, as we're officers and need to set an example for the other men."

The other two men at the table agreed, but Rudi knew they had each taken advantage of an available woman when they wished. They did not use them as maids or cleaners.

Captain Lance Upcroft replied, "I like the sound of that, Rudi, but as the women are locked up until we release them each morning, it may have to be a free one." His mind turned to what might have been if Elise's father had permitted them to wed. Would he even be here? Where was she? He sighed, and thinking of her, smiled to himself as he recalled her beautiful face. He huffed silently, but remained quiet.

Orders for today's duty arrived. His sour mood eased when he learned that he and Lance were assigned together today. They had not worked on the same shift for weeks. Things were looking up. Even better, they were assigned mounts.

Rudi shrugged. "I'm okay with that. Actually, I'd prefer it." He added, "Well, I'm on chain gang duty today, but we'll keep our eyes open for a likely candidate. Even waking up to hot water would be nice."

The other soldiers, including the man who brought the duty roster, discussed how the proposed woman would spend her time, but all agreed she would not be taken against her will. If, however, she wished to offer other services, they would not refuse.

Rudi took a mouthful of tea, so he didn't need to respond. His peers went down in his estimation. For them to wish to abuse or violate a woman just because she was female disgusted him, but he remained silent. Lance also remained quiet.

Rudi poured himself a mug of hot water and went to shave in the wet room. After catching his friend's eye as he left, Lance did the same and went to his room.

Once dressed, they consumed a breakfast of fried eggs on toast with lashings of butter, and the officers went about their duties.

With Rudi and Lance rostered onto the same chain gang, six other soldiers were under their care. They had thirty shackled convict men to oversee repairs to the water-damaged roads.

Lance hoped it was the team he usually worked with.

Thankfully, the roads were not too bad due to the drought. They had managed to repair most of the nearby damage from last year's storms over the summer, but a section about five miles out was their destination today.

Rudi knew that the convict chain gang was supposed to walk to the job, but as they had the big wagon, they would get much more done if the convicts travelled in the vehicle with the soldiers.

The convicts had to fetch their food and drink for the day, then assemble in the barracks' courtyard. One of the orderlies loaded a hamper with food and ginger beer for the soldiers, and they set off at a steady walk. The convicts would remain on foot until they reached the outskirts of town. The wagon also carried rocks and tools for the day's work ahead, but once the main road west was reached, Rudi and Lance made everyone hop on, and they could travel much more quickly. They had done this before, which meant they would accomplish a longer stretch of roadway.

Over the summer, if they had a long section to finish, the men would not be exhausted by the time they arrived. Today, as on most days, they had a mile of road to repair. All wore cabbage palm leaf hats to protect them from the sun.

Rudi was unsure how far the previous work gangs had gone. Once the convicts were set to work, Lance and he planned to have a long gallop to blow away the cobwebs. They would also check the section of road ahead for any urgent potholes that could pose a danger to passing vehicles.

By eight o'clock, the gang reached the previous day's repairs. The day was already getting hot. The convicts were unloaded and assigned to their tasks. Once they hauled off the hamper and the rocks for the pothole repairs, Lance and Rudi gee'ed up their steeds. They set off west, supposedly to check the road ahead. They remained at a trot until they were out of sight, then took off at a full gallop. They were neck and neck when they came to a bend in the road.

Thankfully, they slowed, for when they rounded the bend, they came across a carriage that had come to grief and was tilted at a dangerous angle. The men were able to pull up in time.

A man was on the ground and not moving, so they knew help was needed. One wheel on the carriage lay in bits beside the fancy vehicle. It had hit a large pothole and was shattered; the metal rim was bent to the hub. They realised that the driver had been knocked out as he fell. Surprisingly, the carriage horses were standing quietly.

Rudi hopped off and went to check for passengers. "Lance, there's a lady in here, but she's out cold as well as covered in blood. We'll need the wagon, two soldiers, and two of the strongest men. Can you get them?"

Lance rode around the carriage on his horse. As the horse circled, Lance said, "Consider it done. Is she breathing? I can see the one on the road is stirring. Feel for a pulse on the passenger." He waited while Rudi checked the woman's neck.

Rudi nodded. "She is, but she has a big bump on her head that is oozing blood. The accident must have happened a while ago, as the blood on her gown has already congealed." He paused as he eased his hand from her neck. "Bring Tobin Jeeves, as he's got some medical knowledge."

Lance nodded and sent his steed flying back to get help. Thankfully, they had only ridden for about ten minutes, if that.

Rather than move the woman, Rudi went to see how the driver was.

The man was flat on his back, and his leg looked twisted. His leg was broken at the shin.

Rudi groaned, knowing that this injury could mean he would lose his lower leg. He pulled up the driver's trousers and was pleased to see the bone had not broken the skin. While the man was still unconscious, Rudi moved to the man's foot and straightened it, then pulled and reset the bone as best he could.

The man groaned, but did not wake. At least he wasn't dead.

Rudi looked around and saw a few dead branches nearby. He chose a sturdy, straight one, splinted the injured leg, and tied it to the other limb with the bandages he carried in his saddle bag. He checked and noted that the man was now breathing evenly. The man appeared to have no other injuries beyond a slight graze on his temple.

Long ago, Rudi had learned to carry a few things with him, as he had often been called upon to tend to an injury or two over the years. When they stopped for work, he had forgotten to remove the small medical attachment to his saddle and leave it for Tobin. He knew he had some linen bandages and a bottle of brandy in his saddlebag.

Before Lance returned, Rudi carefully opened the top door of the tilting carriage and crawled into the cabin. Before moving the lady, he checked her limbs by lifting her gown and feeling her legs. He hoped she would not wake while he did so. All four limbs seemed unbroken.

He carefully lifted the woman from inside the lower door and sat, cradling her. He noted there was a pool of congealed blood on the floor of the carriage. He had no idea who she was, but her hair smelled nice, like violets. He had just eased her into his arms when Lance returned and opened the lower carriage door.

His friend said, "Is she still alive?"

Rudi nodded and said, "Yes, but she hasn't stirred yet. I can't feel anything broken."

Lance glanced at his friend. "You checked her legs? Seriously?"

Rudi blushed and nodded. "Well, someone had to, and I had to do it before you came back with them." He nodded towards the other men.

A chuckle escaped Lance's lips. "Fair enough, that's your thrills for the day, my friend."

Rudi would have sworn at him had he not had a lady in his arms. "Lay off, Lance. It needed to be done." He looked down at the sleeping beauty on his lap and said, "Can you help me get her out of here?"

Lance nodded while still grinning.

Between the pair of them, they gingerly eased her out of the carriage and laid her on the grassy verge while they checked to see if she was bleeding from anywhere else but her forehead.

Rudi carefully ran his hands through her blood-caked hair, but could feel no other wounds. She, too, murmured but didn't rouse.

Lance watched as his friend tended to the unresponsive woman. He was impressed by how gentle Rudi was. He expected this terse soldier to be rough and uncaring, but each movement was careful and almost tender.

Rudi looked up and saw Lance's intense gaze on him. He said, "We need to get her back to the hospital, Lance. I have no idea how long they have been outside like this, but the blood she shed has already congealed. This is way out of what I can treat." He glanced up and saw another soldier bending over the driver. "Tobin, is he alive?"

The soldier nodded. "Yes, sir, but he's had a pretty good whack on his head. His skull may also be fractured. We'll need to be careful of his neck and back when we move him."

The two captains swore in unison.

Lance said, "Rudi, you and Tobin will need to cradle them in the back of the wagon, and I'll stay with the crew. Brenton Wright will need to drive you back. He was a coachman in his previous life." He waved the man towards the soldiers and motioned for the felon in question to turn the wagon.

As Brenton turned the flatbed wagon, Lance released the carriage horses from their traces and tied them to the wagon while the others worked on the patients. The group pushed the now-empty vehicle off the road. Minimal luggage had been on the carriage, which was now all stowed on the wagon to lean against and cushion the passengers. There was one case and some soft furnishings from the carriage. Rudi knew from home that there was often a storage area under the seats, where blankets and cushions were kept. He checked these and found a jewellery box under the lady's seat. He collected everything and carried it to the wagon before hopping up and receiving the unconscious damsel onto his lap.

Tobin cradled the driver between his legs, with his head immobilised between Tobin's thighs. Reluctantly, Rudi did the same to the lady. Their heads now rested on the pillows.

Rudi and Tobin were travelling on the wagon, each cradling an insensible patient while a convict tooled the reins.

Lance was left with the four horses. Thankfully, the two carriage beasts had come to no harm except sore mouths from their bits.

Once the soldiers deposited their patients at the hospital, Rudi said he would ensure they returned the wagon for the chain gang. This was not how he expected the day to go, but at least it was not dull.

On the journey back, the conversation was kept to a minimum.

Rudi fell into thinking. For once, he realised he was not angry with everything or everyone. His emotions were in turmoil. He wanted to stay with this beautiful woman, but didn't even know who she was.

The outbound trip was only half an hour this morning, but the return journey was taken at a snail's pace to avoid jostling the injured people.

By ten o'clock, they were entering the outskirts of town. Neither patient had roused, although both groaned occasionally.

Rudi held the woman's head still as they travelled, and each time she moaned, he found himself caressing her cheek to comfort her.

They arrived at the hospital, such as it was, and called for an attendant to help them. Not only did two attendants come, but the principal surgeon, D'Arcy Wentworth, arrived, along with his assistant, William Redfern.

D'Arcy probed Rudi for information.

Rudi reported everything he knew but kept the news of the jewellery box to himself. He would inform the senior doctor in private.

Two orderlies first moved the injured driver inside by rolling him onto a stretcher and then gently carrying the insensible man.

D'Arcy debated where to take the lady. The hospital had no facilities for females, but she needed proper nursing care. He had his own room at the hospital and realised it would be the only safe place for her. He turned to the waiting orderly and said, "Change the sheets on my bed; we'll have to take her in there. It's the only private room in the place." He turned back to Rudi and noticed that the soldier looked anxious, as if he wished to say something. "Rudi, what's wrong?"

Rudi said, "I checked her limbs; they seem fine."

D'Arcy's eyebrows flew up in surprise; then he frowned as he looked at the soldier in shock.

Rudi saw the look he was given. To justify his actions, he said, "Well, I could have brought her here in agony with broken legs like the man, or I could check while no one was around. I chose the latter. I reset the driver's leg as much as I could. I have minimal medical skills, but I am not a complete novice." Rudi huffed with indignation.

The doctor chuckled. "Rest easy, my friend. I know you're not a lady's man, but your tender care of her is a little surprising. Your reputation precedes you."

This comment made Rudi even angrier. "Just because I don't fawn over women and I treat them all with respect doesn't mean I don't like them. I do, but I won't use them to quench my base desires or sate my physical urges." He remained on the wagon with the lady in his lap. He hoped she had not heard their conversation, but it was too dangerous to move her until the orderlies returned.

D'Arcy dropped his voice. "Sorry, laddie, you've been here eighteen months, and your name has not been linked with any woman or convict."

Rudi looked at the doctor in disgust and replied, "And it won't be, D'Arcy, because I will mean my vows when I marry. I saw what London was like, and I was not impressed. My brother sowed his seed with every maid we employed and many of the village girls. Most were unwilling. Just because I don't sow my seed doesn't mean that I will not wed one day, but I will only marry for love, and that has not occurred."

D'Arcy grinned wickedly. "Well, you look comfortable with your current burden. You have not stopped stroking her cheek since you arrived."

Rudi nodded. "It settles her." He didn't know why, but didn't want to let her go. He suddenly remembered the jewellery box. "D'Arcy, I have her luggage and a special thing here." He pulled back the blanket slightly, revealing the ivory-inlaid jewellery box to the doctor.

The convict was still in the driver's seat and did not know about Rudi's find.

D'Arcy pulled a worried face and asked, "Can you keep them safe? There is nowhere here that would be secure."

This meant that Rudi would need to be informed about her well-being, so he grinned and said, "Willingly, my friend."

The two orderlies returned as he spoke, and Rudi eased himself out of the way.

The lady was rolled on her side, then back onto a stretcher.

Rudi watched her get carried inside and realised they would need some nightwear for her. He dug deep into her portmanteau and extracted a lady's night rail and some undergarments. He was surprised to see there was men's attire in the case. He said, "Brenton, stay here for a bit."

Tobin returned as Rudi found what he was looking for. "I'll be back in a moment, Tobin, but get ready to head to our rooms instead of back to the men. We're to keep her luggage chest in my room." He tapped where the jewellery box was under the blanket, then, while the driver was distracted, he grabbed it and stuffed it in the portmanteau.

Tobin nodded.

Rudi followed the orderlies' path, delivering the woman's nightwear and necessities to her, then returned to Tobin and Brenton.

~

Half an hour later, they had unloaded the luggage and were on the road back to the chain gang, with a spare wheel.

Brenton remained silent until now. He said, "Sirs, that was a nice thing to do for them. Do you know who she is?"

Rudi shook his head. "No idea yet!" He looked at the convict driver and asked, "How does Lance know your background? I know no one usually asks about one's past, but I presume you did something pretty bad to be on a chain gang?"

Brenton shrugged. "Not so, sir, but no one believed me that I had no knowledge about a hold-up. I was left much as this driver was, but because I came around before help arrived, I was arrested and charged with being a highwayman. Unfortunately for me, the robbers killed the rest of the people in the carriage, and I was covered with their blood when I checked to see if they were alive, just like you did, sir. The dead were three armed footmen and the squire. I was the only one left alive. As the driver, I had only received a glancing blow." He shrugged. "I was taken into custody rather than treated for my injuries."

Tobin gasped. "They didn't even send you to a doctor?"

Brenton shook his head. "I didn't even get to say goodbye to my wife and children." He released a long sigh. "I miss them."

Rudi frowned and said, "How does Lance know you?"

Brenton's expression was angry. His reply was quite curt. "I've worked with him before, sir." He refused to say any more.

Rudi's brow cocked in surprise. He and Tobin exchanged glances but changed the subject.

Chapter 3 Sleeping Beauty

The mystery lady lay unresponsive for two more days.

Reverend William Cowper's wife, Ann, came and sat by the woman's side as often as possible.

There were no female nurses, so she was called in with Elizabeth Macquarie, who was in town at the time, to tend to the female patient. This mystery woman was obviously of quality, but no one knew who she was.

The two attending ladies changed the patient into her nightwear, and then Elizabeth left her in the doctor's and Ann's care. Ann and Doctor Wentworth sat her up and almost forced her to drink. The woman initially sipped the fluid until they held some sweet lilli pilli cordial to her lips. She drank deeply and then slept again.

Every few hours, the doctor would bring her more cordial. She would semi-rouse, drink, and then sleep for a while.

Ann Cowper was beside her on the third day when her patient awoke. The lady's eyes fluttered and then slowly opened. A murmur escaped her lips.

Ann put down her knitting. "Hello, dear girl. You gave us all a fright, dear." She heard the door open and saw the doctor look in.

Doctor Wentworth asked, "Is she awake then?"

Ann nodded and said, "Just this moment, sir." She covered the woman's exposed nightgown. It was see-through, and her breasts were visible.

When Ann had her covered, the doctor entered and walked to the bed.

The woman's eyes were open and fearful. Although she had not said anything yet, a strange man approached her. She shrank towards Ann.

Doctor Wentworth felt the woman's brow and asked, "Do you

remember what happened?"

The woman tried to shake her head but groaned. She murmured, "No, not really. I was talking to my husband when I was thrown from my seat. Where's Andrew?"

The doctor's eyes lifted and met Ann's. He had told her that the man died earlier that morning. He returned his gaze to his patient. "Who's Andrew? If I may ask?" Was there another person in the carriage? If so, where was he?

The woman said, "He is my husband."

Doctor D'Arcy came around the other side of her bed and took her hand. "Ma'am, so you remember coming to town in a carriage?"

A frown crossed the bruised brow. "Yes, we did. It's fuzzy. I can't remember." She rubbed her temple and groaned. Her hand fell to her stomach. "Oh, yes, I remember now. We were coming to town to see a doctor about our baby."

The doctor gasped. Doctor Wentworth asked, somewhat panicked, "You have a child? Was it with you?"

She tried to shake her head, but it hurt. "No, but we're having one. I have been extremely ill, and Andrew was worried about me." Another frown flickered over her brow. "I remember now. Andrew was driving, and we wanted to confirm my suspicions. Where is he?" She saw the faces around the bed blanch. She began to panic. "Where is he? I want to see my husband."

Ann grabbed her hands. "Dearie, you were in a bad accident, and you were both seriously injured."

The lady's eyes were fixed on Ann's face. "He's dead, isn't he?"

Ann nodded and replied, gently holding her hands. "If your husband was the man driving, then yes, my dear, he has gone."

The lady gasped. "Oh no!" She collapsed back onto the pillows.

Doctor Wentworth noticed the tears welling in the lady's eyes. He came to her side and said, "Ma'am, we thought he only broke his leg, but by the time he arrived here, his head injury was far more severe than was initially thought. He passed away this morning without regaining consciousness." He exhaled and looked at the new widow. He had not realised the driver was this woman's husband. "Ma'am, he is still here as he has not been taken to the church yet."

The lady pleaded, "Can I see him?"

Doctor Wentworth nodded. "After I have checked you and your child, you may. But to be safe, we will take you there in a special chair. We have one with wheels." He turned to the minister's wife and said, "Mrs Cowper, can you leave us for a few minutes, please?"

Ann Cowper said, "Yes, doctor. I will wait outside. Call me if you want me, dear." She moved to leave and then turned and asked, "Dear, may I ask your name?"

"It's Mrs Edwards, Bethany Edwards." The lady added, "Thank you, Mrs Cowper."

Ann smiled that she had caught the doctor's use of her name. She closed the door quietly and waited for the medical man to call her back.

The check on the baby's welfare didn't take long. Doctor Wentworth left to get the wheelchair while he sent an orderly to prepare Mr Edwards' body for viewing. He had the man's clothing in a canvas bag under her bed, as he had discovered a lot of money in the pockets.

Ann had brought a bed jacket for the lady from home, and when he returned with the chair, Ann helped Bethany put it on. She eased her legs from under the sheets and waited on the side of the bed for the doctor's return. The jacket covered her to the waist, and Ann collected a blanket for around her knees. Her dark mane of luscious, wavy hair fell to her waist.

Doctor Wentworth returned with the three-wheel contraption; they eased the injured lady into it and covered her legs.

Andrew Edwards was laid out as though he were sleeping. His hands were crossed over his chest, and his eyes were closed.

His wife gasped when she saw him and his horrific injuries. His skin had coloured and made his face blue with severe bruising. She wept as she realised she was utterly alone in a foreign country. She stood at the side of the morgue table and stroked his beloved face for the final time. She leaned over and kissed his cold lips as a farewell and then clasped his hand in her own. She caressed his cold cheek with her other hand. "Goodbye, my dearest friend! I will do my best to bring our child up as you would wish." She kissed his lips again and then collapsed back into the chair. She wept freely, turned to whoever was standing ready to push her chair, and gave a nod to leave.

Ann passed her a clean handkerchief and walked beside her, holding her hand as they made their way back to her room.

Ann had spoken to her husband, William, the previous night, and they had discussed offering the mystery lady a room for as long as she needed it. She wondered if Bethany had anywhere to go. Now was not the time to discuss that with her, but she would certainly tell the doctor.

Once Mrs Edwards was in bed, the pair settled the now grieving widow back into her room. They left her with a tea tray and some scones, doubting whether she would touch them.

Ann exited with the medic and carefully closed the door behind her. "Doctor, William and I spoke at length about this dear lady's plight. We have a room available at the rectory for as long as she needs it. If she is in the family way, returning to their home, if they have one, would not be advisable."

The doctor nodded. "Mrs Cowper, that would be very beneficial for her. However, you already have four young children to care for."

Ann smiled. "My stepchildren are wonderful, sir. If this poor lady is expecting a baby, she will need some help and moral support." She blushed and said, "We can bring children into the world together."

The doctor's brow cocked, and he congratulated her. Doctor Wentworth grinned. "I wondered why you happened to be at the hospital when she arrived. Were you coming to see me?"

The minister's wife nodded. "I will be twenty-nine when this child arrives, which is very old for a first baby. I am worried. I'm surprised I am hiding my condition so well, as I worked out I am due in about ten weeks."

Doctor Wentworth knew he would oversee Ann's care but would introduce her to a local midwife he trusted. D'Arcy said with a grin. "It will be my honour, Mrs Cowper. When did you say you were due?"

Ann nodded. "Our happy event is about July if my calculations are correct. To say I am surprised is an understatement. It took me some months to realise my condition, and I was well advanced before I noticed. William knew what to look for, having had four children with his first wife, Hannah. I thought I had a tummy bug." She blushed, then giggled.

D'Arcy smiled at the thought of what the clergy couple needed to do to have a child. He shook his head as he walked away.

~

It was another day before Rudi was off duty and had enough time to visit the lady at the hospital. When he did, D'Arcy escorted him to the room and knocked. A lovely melodic voice called, "Enter."

The doctor pushed the door open and greeted his patient. "Nice to see you up on your feet, Mrs Edwards. I have someone here who has been asking about your well-being daily. He is the gentleman who found you. May he come in?"

Bethany nodded. "I would like to thank him."

D'Arcy waved Rudi in. She gasped when she saw the tall, handsome soldier in a red coat. She clung to the chair lest she swoon.

Rudi gasped. His view of the blood-caked lady attracted him

when she was unresponsive. Now, her sad, mauve eyes lifted to him, and she gave him a smile that set his heart racing. Her freshly washed hair was dark and curled softly around her face. His heart skipped a beat, and that had never occurred before. He swallowed nervously.

Bethany walked to Rudi and held out both hands. "Sir, I find myself owing my life to a stranger. You stopped and assisted us when others would have stolen our valuables."

Rudi bowed his head in acknowledgment. "It was the least I could do, ma'am."

She continued. "The doctor tells me you have our portmanteau and my jewellery box."

Rudi nodded. "I do, madam. I only opened your case to get you some attire when you arrived and, later, the gown you now wear."

She nodded carefully. "I'm unsure if you heard, but my husband did not make it. He passed away yesterday." She teared up at the mention of his passing.

Rudi jumped. "I had no idea the driver was your husband. Oh, ma'am, I'm so very sorry." It suddenly occurred to him that that was why there was male clothing in the case. "Ma'am, if there is anything I can do to assist you, please let me know."

Bethany nodded and gave him another smile. "The minister and his wife have offered me refuge until my child is born in the spring." Her hand fell to her stomach. "It was for this reason we came to Sydney. We have been hunting for a farm, but have decided none are suitable for our needs. Andrew grew up on a dairy farm, and there doesn't seem to be any in the colony. He wanted to start one but could not find suitable land or the necessary animals."

Rudi was gutted. His eyes fell to her stomach and then lifted back to her face.

She saw his subtle glance and blushed. She sighed. "Sir, may I trouble you to deliver my possessions to the rectory? I will stay with the Cowpers until I can work out my future. I have no idea what I shall do with myself, as I have no one at home in England. But I'm in no hurry to decide, as I will remain in Sydney until my baby arrives. What I shall do then is a mystery."

Rudi was thrilled that she would remain close. He knew she had to have at least a year's mourning for her husband, and he wished to remain at hand if she needed assistance. "I will deliver your luggage this afternoon, ma'am. Do you have transport from here?"

Bethany shook her head carefully. "Not until my carriage is repaired. Apparently, only one wheel is damaged?"

Rudi grinned, nodding. "With that, I can assist too. We didn't wish to leave the carriage unattended, because it would have been stripped. After we dropped you off here, we collected a spare carriage wheel from the stables and brought your conveyance to town. It is currently in the government carriage house with a new wheel, along with your steeds. They were mostly uninjured, by the way."

Bethany smiled at the devastatingly handsome young man. "You have my thanks again for that, sir, but now I have no driver."

With a cheeky grin, Rudi bowed and said, "I am at your service when I am off duty; however, for the moment, I can assign a man to you when you require. I have recently discovered that he drove carriages in England and drove you here after the accident."

She cocked an eyebrow and nodded. "I suppose that would suffice should I need one. Thank you again, good sir." She turned to the doctor. "Sir, did Mrs Cowper mention if she was to return here today?"

D'Arcy had listened to the repartee and smiled. Rudi's interest in this female intrigued him. "No, ma'am, she did not. However, I do vouch for Captain Greenwood. I've known him for eighteen months. You will be safe with him if you should ever need an escort. He is well known to me, and I assure you he is a gentleman." He smiled and said to the embarrassed officer. "Rudi, I presume you mean to have Brenton drive the carriage if required."

Tongue-tied, Rudi nodded.

D'Arcy said, "If so, then ma'am, you will need to give the captain notice so the driver is available."

Rudi grinned. "Normally, yes, D'Arcy, but I shall reassign him to the stables as I was asked to find a trustworthy stablehand for the town. I am off duty today, so I can harness her carriage and deliver her myself." Rudi turned to the lovely lady. "Ma'am, are the Cowpers expecting you today?"

She nodded. "Yes, sir. Mrs Cowper mentioned that any time after luncheon would be suitable. Again, I am in your debt."

Rudi bowed. "I shall collect you at one o'clock if that suits you?"

Bethany smiled, gingerly nodding as her head still hurt. "Thank you, Captain."

D'Arcy almost had to drag Rudi from the lovely lady's presence. "I have other patients to see, and Rudi, I cannot leave you here alone."

Rudi was almost pushed out of the door. D'Arcy closed the portal behind him and said, "Rudi, pick your chin up off the floor, will you? I can see that you are attracted to her, but she only lost her husband yesterday. I can tell by how she said farewell to him that she loved him dearly, so go easy on her."

Rudi chuckled. "I'm floored, D'Arcy. She's beautiful, but her eyes are so sad. How is she going to cope with being a single mother in this hellhole? She'll be a target for every lusty male in the town. All I want to do is be there for her and protect her. I have no other love interest, and at least I can be her bodyguard when required." He paused and said, "Thanks for the endorsement, by the way." He felt like skipping and shouting with delight.

D'Arcy chuckled. "Just go easy on her. I said when you brought her in that something about her drew you in. Mind you, we had no idea the man was her husband." He rubbed his nose. "I wonder what his story was?" He shrugged. "I suppose we'll find out soon enough."

Rudi smiled and nodded. "You're correct. I suppose I had better go and prepare the carriage. I'll bring Brenton and introduce him to her." He turned to leave and said, "Thanks again, D'Arcy."

He had gone before D'Arcy had time to reply. Rudi's medical friend watched the once morose captain walk off with a spring in his step. His bright blue eyes twinkled with delight. He wondered if it had occurred to Rudi that if he were to make a move on Mrs Edwards, he would be bringing up another man's child. He shook his head and returned to the ward full of injured convicts and a few soldiers.

Brenton was pleased not to be on road repair duty today. He grinned and shovelled out the muck from the stables. He loved the smell of the horses and adored the great beasts. He had just filled the muck trailer and wondered what else he would be asked to do. He thought he would tend to the two new horses and check their injured mouths. He had his head down and was checking their horseshoes when he heard footsteps.

Rudi had checked the barracks only to discover that Brenton had already gone to the stables for the day's assignment. Tobin and Rudi had pumped Brenton for information about his background, from the hospital to the road crew. The more they asked him, the more credible his story seemed. Therefore, Rudi was not surprised to find Brenton checking the two new horses. Most other convicts worked in the local food gardens, but the plants did not grow well in Sydney. Uncle John's garden at Government House had almost died after Governor Bligh had been under house arrest in the official residence.

Lance had taken out another team to repair the next mile of the road. Rudi discovered that Brenton was now permanently relocated to stable duty at Lance's behest.

Rudi had planned to drive Mrs Edwards' carriage the short distance to the Cowper's place and walk back. With Brenton here, that could change. Rudi leaned on the stable gate, watching the convict tend to the beasts' welfare.

Brenton had already placed some liniment on the injured lips of the two new horses and was running his hands down the lead horse's fetlock. Brenton looked up to see that he was being observed. "Hello, captain. Were you looking for me?"

Rudi nodded. "Yes, are they up for an outing?"

Brenton's nose screwed up. "Only somewhere short. Has Mrs Edwards been discharged from the hospital?"

Rudi's brow cocked. "How do you know who she is?"

A chuckle emanated from the stall. "Captain Lance may have mentioned it, sir. Are we to take her to the reverend's place?"

Rudi roared with laughter. "Is there nothing you don't already know?"

The horses all started at the sudden noise, and Rudi apologised. The horse Brenton was working on gave a sideways shuffle.

Brenton grinned but remained silent.

Rudi said, "Sorry, Brenton. I should have been more sensitive to your position. Are you injured?" For a convict, this man had confidence in his work.

Brenton was stunned at the moody officer's enquiry. "No, sir, I am used to similar beasts and their actions."

Rudi spoke more quietly this time, saying, "I presume Lance mentioned that Mrs Edwards was to stay with the Cowpers?"

Brenton nodded. "I figured that is why I was not assigned to a gang today. I have checked the new carriage wheel and all the tack and shafts. All are in good order. Only the wheel was damaged. They must have hit it at speed, as it almost exploded. I've never seen a hub cracked before. For it to have thrown the driver, I'm guessing he was in the middle of a conversation with his wife as the communication hatch was open. It would be the only reason he was not watching the road near a corner."

Rudi nodded in agreement but had no idea if he was correct. "We are to collect Mrs Edwards from the hospital at one o'clock. However, I will also need your assistance to load her portmanteau, so have an early meal and come to the officer's rooms at half twelve." Rudi didn't wish to befriend the convict, but then again, aside from Lance, he hadn't wanted to befriend anyone here. He turned to leave the felon but said, "Brenton, I have offered your services to her as a coachman if she requires you. This means that you will no longer serve on a chain gang."

Brenton gasped. "Truly, sir? What will I do between times?"

Rudi shrugged. "We don't have a proper stable hand, and you seem to know the work; how about that? I can have you assigned here permanently." He was about to walk off when he turned and asked. "Can you read? As that would be a great help."

Brenton nodded. He felt like hugging the surly captain. "I'd be delighted, sir. Truly, I would. May I rearrange things here and do the tack? The stables need a loving hand."

Rudi nodded and walked off. With the Macquaries living in Parramatta, there was little need for a full-time stablehand. Having Brenton available to everyone would be good. It also meant that messages could be sent to have mounts readied when required. He smiled to himself.

~

The carriage pulled out of the government stables behind Government House at a quarter to one. From there, they travelled west of the town to the barracks and collected the blankets and pillows that Rudi had taken from the Edwards' carriage. They loaded the portmanteau from Rudi's room. Rudi said, "I shall ride in the carriage until we collect our passenger. Then I shall join you."

They arrived at the almost derelict timber hospital at Dawes Point as close to the appointed time as possible. D'Arcy met them at the door with Bethany Edwards in a wheelchair. She had been ill again that morning, and the doctor had rechecked her. She was light-headed, but that was expected.

She was about to stand and greet her steeds when D'Arcy all but chastised her. "Ma'am, I assure you the horses are fine." D'Arcy beckoned Rudi, who had hopped out of the carriage. "Rudi, can you deliver her directly to Cowpers' place down near the Tank Stream? She has been unwell since you departed. I want her to rest this afternoon, and I will call on her tonight."

The patient folded her arms in frustration. "I can hear you, you know, gentleman." She said with a huff. "You are both as bad as my husband was. I do not like being fussed over. I am merely carrying a child, not dying. Illness and lightheadedness go hand in glove with my condition. I will survive, you know."

The doctor said, "That may well be true, madam, but you have suffered a great loss and also had a head injury. There can be side effects from both."

She huffed again, stood quickly, and nearly fainted.

Rudi was beside her and caught her. "Ma'am, permit me to see you to your carriage." She nodded, and her arm snaked around his neck.

Behind her back, D'Arcy gave Rudi a silly grin.

She was gently placed inside the carriage and settled on her seat. Her reluctant murmur of "Thank you" made him smile. He replied, "Any time, my lady."

She started. "I have no title; please do not inflict that upon me."

Rudi chuckled as he settled her. "Consider it done, ma'am. I shall ride on the top with Brenton." She nodded. He shut the door and said through the window, "The box that was under your seat is in your portmanteau. I did not open it." He turned to walk away, intending to climb up onto the driver's seat with Brenton.

She called to him. "Sir, it's only a short distance; please ride with me." She relaxed onto the luxurious, soft, familiar squab seats and waited for him to climb in.

Rudi gave Brenton instructions and then followed them. The carriage dipped as he entered, and he took a seat opposite her. He wondered what she wanted.

D'Arcy watched the strange interaction between the two and waited, watching until the carriage drew away from the front of the hospital.

Bethany initially ignored Rudi until the hospital building was gone from sight. She leaned towards him and tapped his knee. "The doctor mentioned that you checked me for broken bones before moving me from the carriage. For that, I thank you…" She paused and waited until he gave her his full attention, "…but if you ever lay a hand on me without my express permission again, I will bring every lawman down on you until you plead for mercy. Do I make myself understood?"

Rudi nodded. Was she serious? Did she think he was going to molest her? He swallowed nervously and wondered if he should react. However, he replied with a meek, "Yes, ma'am." He gave her a wry smile, unsure whether she was angry. He knew she was in mourning for the loss of her husband, but he still intended to be on hand if she needed his assistance. Was she that unreasonable? Rudi turned and looked out the window at the passing squalor. His mind was in turmoil, as was his heart. Not that it was broken; he didn't know this woman. He had rescued her, but know her? No, he didn't know her at all. Her past was hidden from him. He stole a glance and noticed a beautiful smile on her lips. Their eyes met, and he froze.

She said, "I mean it, sir. I am recently widowed and am carrying my husband's child. I have much to sort out and will have no innuendo or taint applied to my name. I may well need your assistance, but I am no convict wench to manhandle or cheap woman to approach. We may well be thrown together by circumstance, but I wish to make myself totally clear about this. Doctor Wentworth said you are a gentleman. The fact that he trusted you with my possessions speaks volumes, but I loved Andrew. He was my life. Please remember that."

Rudi was even more stunned. "Ma'am, I would never do anything to harm you or your unborn child. I will make myself available to be your bodyguard or escort, should you require either, as you should never be seen about this town alone. Please, promise me that. D'Arcy knows me well and entrusted me with your things as you were sleeping in his room. Anyone had access to them there. I am not a rogue ladies' man, ma'am. He questioned me about that on the day I brought you in. However, I do not trespass on what is not mine to touch. My lack of reputation where women are concerned is because I respect your gender, ma'am, not because I'm not attracted to them. He said you can trust me because you can; nothing more, and nothing less."

She gave a nod of understanding. "Fine, I just wanted to make myself clear. That is all. I understand that I will need a male around me for certain things and one who will respect my time of mourning. Even Andrew would not permit me to go anywhere alone. I have no intention of making long-term decisions until my baby is born. I will stay with the Cowpers for the moment, but how long that will be is undecided."

Rudi found words spilling from his lips. "Ma'am, I am at your command. Send word if I am required."

A frown flittered across her brow. "You are not to presume anything from this, do you understand? I am a widow of less than a week."

Rudi nodded. He sighed with relief. She wasn't banning him from her presence after all. "Yes, Mrs Edwards, I understand fully." A smile hovered on his lips. "This is no place for a woman, any woman, to be on her own, be she convict or free, married or single. All females are fair game to the unscrupulous so-and-so's who inhabit this filthy mire of a town. I might add that not all of them are convicts, either. Trust no one." The carriage eased to a halt, and Rudi realised that they had arrived. "May I assist you down?"

She shook her head. "Possibly, sir, as there is no wheelchair here,

I may need your assistance." She gave a shy smile and added, "But I'll see how I do."

Ann was outside waiting for them, and four small faces appeared behind her. Bethany presumed that these were William Cowper's four children from his first marriage: Henry, Thomas, Mary, and Charles. They ranged in age from a toddler to a lad of about ten. Bethany was familiar with their names from Ann. She smiled. Ann had confessed to her that she had married William Cowper only six months after his first wife died. His first wife, Hannah, and Ann had been much the same age, and he needed a mother figure for his children. He had already been offered the position of assistant minister out here before Hannah died. As Ann was nearly thirty and unwed, she agreed. She had never expected to have her own children.

Bethany hoped to stay until her baby was born, but if Captain Greenwood was right, living on her own would not be feasible. What to do? She sighed. Those were decisions for the future. For now, she had to get out of the carriage without collapsing. Her legs were still weak. She was thankful for the strong gentleman waiting for her. She may have to rely on him far more than expected. She eased herself forward and went to put a foot on the step of the carriage. A wave of nausea washed over her. "Sir, I may need your assistance after all."

Rudi reached out his hand, and she shook her head.

She said, "I may need a lift, sir. Do you mind?"

Rudi didn't mind at all. He shook his head, biting his lips to stop a big grin. She was feather-light and a delight to hold. She only came up to his shoulder, and even though he was aware that he was tall, she was of a diminutive height. He swept her up in his arms, careful to cover her legs and hide them from view.

Ann shooed the children away and led the way to her guest room.

Rudi carried his burden up the steps into a delightful room overlooking the recently cleaned Tank Stream. He gently placed his lovely burden on the side of the bed, then bowed and went to retrieve her luggage.

Brenton had already unloaded her case when he returned. They carried it upstairs for her. Rudi assured her that Brenton would be at her call if required. The carriage and horses could remain at the government stables for as long as needed. Bethany was to settle in and heal. Rudi took his leave and bade her farewell.

Chapter 4 A Lady in Mourning

Word spread throughout the colony about the tragic demise of the young husband, leaving a beautiful young expectant widow.

The day after Bethany's release from the hospital, Andrew Edwards was buried in the burial ground near the military barracks. Many attended the service even though they did not know the deceased man, but they wished to catch a glimpse of the supposedly beautiful widow.

Rudi was on hand in case she required his assistance. She did, and leaned on his arm, but it was more for protection.

D'Arcy stood on her other side, protecting her from view.

Her veil was dark enough to cause the leery men to groan as they could not see her face. The roads were lined with sightseers who wanted to know whether she was as pretty as others said she was and if she would consider remarrying quickly. All the lustful men were out in force.

Rudi was on hand for Bethany. He remained attentive but did not encroach. He had borrowed the wheelchair from the hospital for the service. Although Bethany attended the church service, she refused to go to the graveside because the ground at the cemetery was too uneven for the wheelchair, and she had no intention of being carried. She insisted that Andrew be given the last rites before he was buried. William did that for her before his body left the morgue room.

Rudi remained close enough to beckon if she needed his aid. She had no intention of supplying the township with any gossip. Rudi returned her to the rectory after the service and left her to mourn her beloved husband. He handed her one of his handkerchiefs shortly before he carried her to her room. She thanked him with a beaming smile.

~

It was three weeks before Rudi saw Bethany again. In the interim, he had been on chain gang duty and had little chance to think about the sick lady. However, he was amazed that thoughts of ending his life had not resurfaced.

There had been an escape by one of the road crew, and, as it had occurred under his watch, Rudi spent days tracking the absconder with the aid of the Aboriginal man named Bungaree. The skill of this fellow astounded him. He followed the native man's path through the bush, and Bungaree pointed to broken twigs here or a crushed leaf or toadstool there. There was rarely dust that showed foot or bootprints, but Bungaree followed the felon's path as quickly as if the track was lit with lamps.

They had camped in the bush for two nights before the escapee was arrested. On the first night hunting for the convict, Rudi had not expected to remain out overnight. Stupidly, he had not brought supplies other than a water bottle. He carried his musket and had accidentally picked up dumbbell shot instead of ordinary shot. These double-balled pellets would tear the felon in half should he be required to use them.

Bungaree had his spear and a strange, partially flat, curved stick tucked into his belt. As they entered a clearing, Bungaree saw a small wallaby grazing on the waving grasses. In an instant, he had extracted the flat weapon and thrown a spear with it with a flick of his wrist. The lethal implement twisted as it flew silently across the grass and hit the joey in the head, killing it instantly. With a yelp of delight, Bungaree took off on foot and reclaimed his weapon and the animal.

By the time the sun reached the horizon, a fire had been set in an open area, and the animal was placed in the flames to burn off the fur. Once done, Bungaree pulled it off the fire, spread the coals and let the fire cool a little. He then placed the wallaby back on the coals. Every ten minutes or so, he turned it, and by dark, their meal was ready to eat.

The entire posse was well-fed, and they slept with their feet near the fire to keep warm.

The next night, Bungaree fed the group with water birds. He noticed a flight of ducks land, and he slipped quietly into the pond and sank under the water with hardly a ripple. One duck, then another, was pulled under the water. With no sound, Bungaree moved back to the edge of the waterhole and emerged with five drowned ducks in his hands. He encased these still feathered birds in mud and set them into the coals of the fire. Once again, they ate like kings. They were slightly gamier than roasted fowl, but delicious.

Connie had told Rudi about two children, Nanberry and Abaroo, who had lived in town the year after they arrived. They were the two children who had survived smallpox and lived with the settlers from the First Fleet. Abaroo lived with Reverend Johnson and his wife, and Nanberry with Dr John White. Their knowledge helped save the starving Europeans who had come to live in the new land. Bungaree was another such man, but he was from a tribe farther north.

Unexpectedly, while Rudi was daydreaming, Bungaree yelped with delight and pounced on the hiding felon. When his work was done, he jabbered something unintelligible to Rudi as he slapped his back with glee. His payment would be a few coins, an item of clothing and a month's food ration. Not only had their people been decimated by disease, but their hunting grounds were shrinking as the towns expanded. The help had gone full circle. The settlement now provided food to various tribes.

It was this last item that brought Bungaree such joy. His tribe was from the northern side of the next river up the coast, and their small clan had been crippled by smallpox soon after the First Fleet arrived. Over twenty years later, the remnants of the clans were slowly multiplying again, but food supplies and hunting grounds were diminishing as the settlement grew. The supply of European food eased hunger but did not adequately replace their prior access to their traditional food sources. The hungry settlers had almost cleared the foreshores of shells, and the tribe had to search further afield to eat. Therefore, each commission to hunt an escapee brought prosperity to his people.

Bungaree was a loveable larrikin, and Rudi enjoyed any time spent with him. This native man had travelled far more than Rudi, having spent time with Matthew Flinders exploring the coastlands and finding areas to expand the penal settlement. He spoke English well and was willing to act as an interpreter when required. Rudi met Bungaree's wife, Cora Gooseberry, and was impressed by her support for her husband's interactions with white settlers. She had an infectious giggle, often heard. Though more often than not, she would shake her head at some misunderstanding, and she would simply walk away.

With the felon now in irons, on return to the gaol, the prisoner would be put to work on the treadmill or breaking rocks. He would be marked never to be released. Rudi felt sorry for the felon, but he could have had an easy life; however, this Irishman chose to stir up trouble. Rudi had wondered what they would eat if they had another day in the bush, but he never found out, as the felon was captured soon after dawn. They made it back to the road by noon, and the prisoner was in irons in gaol by nightfall.

Rudi was itching to see if Bethany was all right.

~

By the end of June, Bethany had fully recovered, but as Ann was now heavy with child, she was unable to care for her four stepchildren and run the rectory. Bethany stepped in. Her own condition was hardly showing, and even though she was fatigued, she cared for the four children and entertained them.

Henry and Thomas, at ten and eight, were set school lessons. Mary, at five, was given a slate with letters and numbers to learn, and Charles, although only three, was shown how to hold the chalk and had to trace letters on his slate. The Cowpers had two maids, a cook, and a gardener to help around the house and prepare meals, so Bethany only needed to entertain the children. Her lightheadedness had resolved; although her feet swelled badly, she was able to walk regularly. Usually with Rudi attentively close.

Due to her condition, Ann remained close to home, but Bethany often walked with the children along the foreshore. Her soldier shadow was never far away.

Rudi realised that to see Bethany without compromising her, he would need to start attending church. He swallowed his pride and joined the Cowpers at the nearly completed church building. The original church was burned in 1798, and then a storm hit the partially rebuilt replacement structure. It had taken ten years to rebuild until Governor Macquarie arrived. He fast-tracked the construction.

~

July finally came, and so did William and Ann's baby. D'Arcy Wentworth and a midwife came and attended the minister's wife for the birth.

Bethany intended to stay close, but Ann's screams of pain distressed the children. The four little ones came to her in tears at the shrieks of agony that their stepmother emitted.

Bethany sent for Brenton, and he took them all for a long drive. She had the cook pack a small picnic of boiled eggs, bread, butter, and fruit, and they headed up to the headland to watch the ships in the harbour for some hours.

As the sun set, Bethany loaded the children back into the carriage to return home.

William Macquarie Cowper was born on July 3rd and was a fit

and healthy young man.

Ann was well and had survived the birth. She was up and on her feet within days.

Bethany knew all this was ahead of her, so she listened hard to what Ann needed. From sunning her private areas in the morning to sitting on a soft pillow to ease the pain in her nether regions, even salt baths helped with the healing.

The two women drew close, and for the first time since Bethany lost her husband, she found purpose and some peace. What was worrying was the rate at which her stomach grew. She rested when she could, but with five small children in the house, exhaustion frequently overwhelmed her. However, the children kept her from dwelling on her dire situation. She was alone with no family in the world. She knew it was no use going home as she had nothing there, but what would she do?

~

Winter hit with vengeance. Rudi was frequently occupied with his duty. The rain came and washed away much of the main road at the creeks. Road gangs were multiplied, and days were long in the cold weather. Some mornings, the ice in the puddles would need to be dug out before any repairs could be made. However, this made patching the holes less messy.

Rudi and Lance recruited more soldiers and flatbed wagons for the side roads. Reassigned convicts from the brick pits were sent to do the work. Their duty was to keep the main Parramatta Road in good repair. With these additional resources, they could reach the most affected areas more quickly.

~

Each winter storm, and there were many, washed away more sections of the road. Rudi and Lance were kept occupied and away from Sydney, often for nights at a time, as they camped out.

Rudi was overseeing one of these road crews when Lachlan Macquarie passed by with his guards en route to town. Rudi had not noticed who was in the carriage until he heard his name called.

The heavily accented voice yelled, “Greenwood! Come hither.”

Rudi swivelled and realised the governor had called to him. “Sorry, sir. Did you want me?” He saw Captain Mark Duffy, Lachlan’s personal guard, the driver, beside Joseph, with Mark’s stepson, Josh, as the groom on the back. Rudi nodded to Mark, as he was another of the few men he liked. One of his predecessors, Crispin Milroy, lived at Toongabbie, and he had been Uncle John’s security guard. Rudi had spent the weekend with the Milroys.

The Scottish governor beckoned him.

Rudi motioned for another soldier to take over his guard duty. He came to the side of the carriage, and Lachlan threw open the door.

The Governor gave Rudi a lopsided smile. "Hop in, soldier."

Rudi did and seated himself opposite his boss. "Yes, sir."

Lachlan cleared his throat and said, "Tell me, how often do you need crews to fix these roads?"

Rudi's brow creased. "Sir?"

Lachlan asked again, "How often are road crews required to do repairs on the roads? Daily, weekly, monthly?"

Rudi shrugged quite rudely. "All of those, sir, depending on the weather. Our teams can service a mile of road per day, even if it's badly potholed, and more during dry periods. After rain, the roads need a lot of work, but the struggle to keep them safe is constant. Lately, we've camped out to complete longer distances."

Lachlan sat relaxed, arms folded, legs outstretched, and feet crossed. "How do you suggest this be solved?"

The abrupt question was shot at him. Rudi shot back in jest and said, "Unless you can cobble all the roadways or pave them somehow, the repairs will be never-ending. However, I don't see that happening any time soon. Proper culverts or bridges across the creeks would help significantly. Even gravel on the surface would assist."

His boss's bushy black eyebrows flew up in surprise, and then he roared with laughter. "Greenwood, I realise you have been busy with the road crews, but do you ever read the paper?"

Rudi knew he blushed. He disliked reading the banal writings of the Sydney Gazette. It rarely carried any decent articles, so he usually only ever skimmed it. "Not really, sir; I don't get a lot of free time for pleasure."

Lachlan chuckled. "You should, you know. It's where I post instructions to the community. However, that being said, I ask because, in March of this year, I appointed Reverend Samuel Marsden, Simeon Lord, and Andrew Thomson as trustees for managing the new turnpike roads. As you will have heard, all government vehicles will be exempt, creating funds to implement your suggestion." Rudi nodded." I have added tariffs on imported alcohol, which will contribute to the construction of a new hospital that D'Arcy Wentworth is overseeing. However, once this is built, funds will be redirected to road maintenance and other projects. Money is required to repair or replace the thoroughfares, including cobbling the worst road sections and constructing bridges. I am on my way to ask Wentworth if he's interested in collecting the funds when the turnpikes are constructed. That will be next year sometime. The reason I ask is that I want you to work with them as an advisor on this road, as I know you work well with Wentworth."

Rudi was stunned. "Me, sir? What would you like me to do?"

Lachlan had hardly moved. "There are obviously sections of the road that will require more work than others, and who better to know where those are than the repair crews. I need these marked on a master map, and then D'Arcy can assign priorities to the most-needy sections. He will also be working with them, in his role as chief of police."

"Oh!" Came the embarrassed reply. Lance mentioned something, but Rudi took little notice. "I can do that, sir. I know which areas need repair after every rain. I could colour-code them or list them in order of urgency. The culverts or bridges would need to be first."

The governor said, "I like that; do that as well." Lachlan gave another one of his lopsided grins, followed by a long sigh. "If you have any ideas for curtailing forgery, let me know. If only colour coding the promissory notes were as easy." He sighed. He noticed Rudi's puzzled expression and chuckled. "Read this week's paper, laddie. We're experiencing issues with forged four- and five-pound notes. So much currency leaves our shores, and we are once again low on coinage. Solve that for me with a colour code, and I shall give you a land grant."

Rudi had heard Lance discuss the problem with the other officers in his cottage. He shrugged. "Make your own coins, sir. All the inns seem to have their own tokens and prefer to accept them rather than home-brewed alcohol. Make a unique coin that can't be used offshore."

Lachlan sat up with a jerk. "How, we don't have a mint?" His frown made his brows meet, and a furrow formed. "We would need steel dies, a forge, and a master craftsman. Do you have any suggestions for that?"

Rudi knew some of the convicts were forgers and said, "I have no idea how coins are made, but some of the convicts here are charged with forgery. Metalworking smiths or even blacksmiths might know. I'm sure you have access to the records to check whether any of those are in the colony. Someone has been making the tokens locally. If not, I'm sure one will be sent here sooner or later."

Rather than answer, Lachlan let down the window and called to his guard. "Mark, join us, please." Lachlan liked this soldier. His usual bodyguard, Henry Antill, was busy elsewhere. Mark Duffy had become Henry's backstop but had also become a friend. The fellow's size was enough to dissuade anyone from interfering with the viceregal carriage.

The very tall Captain Duffy joined Rudi on the seat opposite. "Yes, sir. How can I help?"

Lachlan relaxed and folded his arms again. "Do you know off-hand if we have any metal forgers in the colony?"

Mark glanced at Rudi, then back to Lachlan. "Ahh, no, sir, not off-hand. Should I?"

Lachlan shook his head. "Not yet, but Greenwood has just devised an idea to solve the forgeries and finances. We're going to make our own coins, Mark."

Lachlan's grin made Mark chuckle.

Rudi was stunned. "You mean that you will do it, sir? It was just a throw-away idea."

Lachlan's deep chortle made Rudi smile. "Well, laddie, your throw-away idea fell into fertile soil. It will take time, but I think it will solve everything." Lachlan's gaze flicked from one captain to the other. Both young men were in the prime of their lives. He presumed Rudi aspired to a promotion. He smiled and said, "Greenwood, you will oversee your idea's production when we get it sorted."

Rudi was stunned. "Me, sir? Why?"

The governor chuckled. "Why not? You came up with the idea, so it will be your baby. Someone has to do it, and it was your brainwave. It will take time to arrange, so don't expect this to happen overnight. Give it some more thought, and look around for a suitable coin and also a building we could use. Come and see me tonight as I'm staying in town."

Rudi's eyes flew open. "Tonight, sir?"

"Yes, tonight! Think about it while you're on guard today, and run your preliminary thoughts by me. Mark will join us. I'm not sure if you know that Josh is Mark's stepson and my groom. I trust him, so you can send messages with him." He gave the soldier a nod and a small salute.

Rudi knew he had been dismissed. He moved to leave, and the governor added, "Eight o'clock sharp, Greenwood."

Rudi nodded. "Yes, sir," and hopped out of the carriage smoothly.

Lance joined him and intended to pump his friend for information as soon as possible.

Rudi and Lance stood watching as the governor's carriage headed towards Sydney.

Lachlan's young groom, Josh Callan, knew Rudi well. The lad

waved from the back seat as they rounded the bend, and then the carriage was gone.

Lance turned to Rudi and asked, "What was all that about?"

Without turning, Rudi replied, "Potholes initially, but I think I just talked myself out of chain gang duty for a while."

His friend's incredulous look made Lance frown. "How so?"

Rudi explained and repeated the relevant parts of the conversation. "He wants to see me tonight. I'm to have a proposal of sorts ready about a new coin." Rudi's eyes had not left the dust ball that was blowing over the tops of the sparse scrub. "How can I do that, Lance? It was a throw-away comment about making our own currency."

Lance chuckled. "How about we chat about it while we watch over the crew?" He pulled out a pocket notebook and a small pencil. "First, we need a forger. I'm sure the governor will come up with some names, but Brenton and I were chatting about a chap named Henshall who was done for forgery. He was a metal plater and cutler in England. They were assigned together for a while when Brenton first arrived last year. Henshall might be a place to start. Brenton said he's shifty but not a hardened criminal. If not, he may even know someone who could do it. Phil Tindale is a free settler and a blacksmith, accompanied by his wife, young son, Tom, and daughter, Caroline. They may also help. Next, you will need a venue."

Rudi knew of a place. "How about the rooms under the government printer? George Howe, the printer, has an empty basement. I happened to be down there a few weeks ago as he needed some paper moved, and I had to take a dozen convicts along to do the work. The basement was too damp to store newsprint paper. It should be both safe and dry enough for coin production."

Lance frowned. "You mean under the factory and print shop in town? The town is riddled with felons. It would need to be secured. However, it's within view of the official residence, so it should be safe enough, I suppose."

Rudi nodded. "Yes, but the basement can be easily secured. Tindale could fix that with a grill and locks. The room is lined with sandstone blocks rather than brick, so you couldn't even tunnel into that area. We would need only one big grill gate and a guard. There is only one door in or out, and it's underground, so there are no big windows. If we papered the small window, no one would even be able to see inside. It would work well."

Lance shrugged. "I haven't been in there, but if you have, you would know."

Rudi grinned stupidly. "Then all we need is a suggestion for a coin, something different and unmistakably ours. I don't think we could actually make the blanks as we don't have access to the metal, a foundry or a forge, let alone a coin press, but some existing ones could be overprinted." He put his hand in his pocket and pulled out his fist full of coins. The eclectic currency selection included British, Dutch, Indian, and Portuguese currency, each with varying denominations and sizes. However, he also had one large Spanish Real silver coin. "If the governor could source some of the larger Reales, they could be overprinted, making them worthless outside our country." He looked at the Spanish coin and added, "I wonder if we could do a two-for-one and punch a smaller coin out of the middle?"

Lance had not taken his eyes from Rudi's face. "Do you mean to use another country's money and re-stamp it? Couldn't you cut a silver piece of eight into triangular sections? Other countries have done that."

Rudi's shoulders lifted in a shrug. "I have no idea, but if you say Henshall is a metalworker, he would know what can be done. I only have to present my suggestions. I have no idea what blanks or coins the governor will be able to find, if any. But I know I rarely have any of the same country's currency in my pocket, and it's because any coin is accepted in this God-forsaken land. This is worth five shillings in any country, so they often are taken away by sailors. We need a coin that is worthless offshore. I presume he will want something unique. Hence, the idea of not just clipping this Real into pieces of eight."

Lance nodded; he shoved his hand into his pocket and pulled out his selection of coins. He looked at the unusual collection and said, "I know grog and rum are both now illegal as tender, but I also know many still use various-sized kegs and flagons for bartering. Bligh attempted to outlaw it, but it remains in use. I hope this governor can resolve that issue. Your idea may well do the trick."

Rudi and Lance pocketed their eclectic wealth, but as Rudi did so, his fingers touched the edges of the large silver Spanish coin. He pulled it out again. *Dei Gratia 1796 Carolus IIII* was stamped on one side, and *Hispan Et Ind Rex* RPR on the other. He mused, "I wonder if they would need to be remelted or just over-stamped?" He knew this coin was dated 1796. He presumed there were other years they were minted. He would check the next one he received. He smiled as he noted the different way the Roman numerals were written as IIII instead of IV.

Lance did not hear his friend's query as he had already walked off. Rudi shrugged and shoved the coin into his pocket again. At least he had some ideas to present to the governor tonight.

Chapter 5 A Holey Good Idea

Winter 1811

At eight sharp, Rudi stood at the front door of Government House in Sydney. His breath clouded as he spoke. The front guards let him pass. When he knocked, Mark opened the door. "I hope you have come up with more ideas, as the governor won't let this scheme of yours go. He's been on about it since we met you." He helped Rudi remove his overcoat and hat and hung them on a coat hook near the door. Mark brushed something from his friend's uniform lapel.

Rudi grinned. "Lance and I have a few thoughts jotted down." He had brought a few larger coins that could possibly be used, but that decision was up to the governor.

Mark led the way into the office. Lachlan was standing in front of a roaring fire, warming himself. The fire was built up in an attempt to ease the chill in the high-ceilinged room.

The cold outside had penetrated Rudi's jacket. His fingers were numb, so he flexed them to restore circulation. He had forgotten to wear his thick leather gloves.

Lachlan said to both soldiers, "Come and thaw out over here, lads." He moved aside to let them both join him.

They enjoyed some banal chatter about the cold snap and how quickly it had hit before Lachlan moved towards his desk. "Let's get down to business. Your idea, Greenwood, has taken root, and I was wondering if you have had any more thoughts about it?"

Rudi nodded and asked if he could show them. Lance must be acknowledged for his input. "I do, sir, but I had help."

"Of course, you can show us. That's why you are here." Lachlan pointed to the two chairs on the other side of his desk. "Fire away, laddie." Now thawed, Mark and Rudi seated themselves.

Rudi dug out his plan. He had transcribed Lance's notes and added to them. He had also swapped a few of his smaller coins for any other large coins from fellow officers. He pulled out six more penny-sized disks. "Sir, Lance Upcroft and I put our heads together after you left." Rudi spread out the stack of large mismatched coins and confidently explained his ideas.

Lachlan listened without interruption. His face was incredulous at what he was hearing. "Could we do that?" He looked at the collection of coins and tokens. He reached out and picked up the sizeable Spanish Real. "This would be big enough to counter punch over the printing, and it seems thicker than the locally made tokens or even the thin copper pennies from home. I don't suppose you know any forgers? I have not had a chance to look over the convict records." He put his hand on a giant ledger beside him. He looked at his guard and then returned the coin to the others.

Mark shook his head. "I don't, sir."

Rudi swallowed and added, "Captain Upcroft did mention there is one possible man, but I have no idea of his record, skills or background. Lance said he's a metal worker and forger. If so, he could be just the man you want. Brenton Wright, the new stablehand here, was transported with him, and they arrived on the *Alexander* in 1806. I spoke briefly with Brenton, who assured me that Captain Upcroft's statement was accurate. Sir, William Henshall should possess the necessary skills to perform any required work. Brenton also mentioned that at his second trial, Henshall provided evidence about other forgers and, for his second conviction, received a reduced sentence in return for his assistance. He sounds shifty, but not a hardened crook. He's not keen to return home, as he'd be lynched."

Lachlan gazed at the man opposite him. "You have done all this already? I suppose you have even thought of a place where he could work."

Rudi nodded with a grin. The governor reclined in his chair, folding his arms as they talked. "Well, go on! I'm listening."

Rudi dug out another sheet of paper. It was a roughly drawn map. "Sir, under the government printer is an unused basement. It is stone-lined and has only one entrance, making it secure. A new grill gate and security guard would be all that is needed. I was down there moving out the newsprint paper for George Howe a few weeks ago, as it was too damp for the new paper. Mind you, the moisture may have been caused by the lightning strike earlier this year. However, a coin press or other machinery would be unaffected by dampness. There is no leak; it's just cool and damp." He paused.

Lachlan rolled his hand in a sign to keep talking. So, Rudi

continued. He reached out for the Real. "Sir, rather than just using an existing penny or even this silver Real, you would only have a single reused coin; however, if you punched a smaller coin from the centre, then you could have two denominations. It's why I chose this one." He tapped the Spanish Real. "Sir, this coin is silver, thick and large. It should tolerate some tough handling without splitting. I think something called annealing can stop that. Henshall would know. As I said, it is big enough to cut a smaller coin from the centre, should it be possible; thus, two for the price of one. However, I have no idea where you would source blanks for these or similar. If you used a locally produced token, such as that one from the Liverpool Arms, I'm sure it would crack. It's cheaply produced, made of copper, and thin, so forgers could also duplicate it. However, they couldn't access the more expensive Reales to make their own coinage."

Lachlan chuckled. "You astound me, Greenwood. You threw me a comment, and I challenged you to follow through. Now you have a potential solution to our biggest issue in this penal town. If only England had sent a large amount of currency, we would not have had this alcohol problem. That should have occurred with Governor Phillip in 1788, but there was much that was not added to that voyage. There was a shortage of ammunition, food, and clothing, among other things. Hunter brought many necessities, but again, no coins. Currency was the least of their worries, as this was only ever supposed to be a penal town. Food became the priority after they settled. The Webb brothers, from the First Fleet, brought the first still in the late 1790s. Thomas Webb returned with that after going to England to collect their pay. Others copied it, and then local grog production quickly became a currency. Much of this happened between Governor Phillip's departure in 1792 and John Hunter's arrival three years later. I had the story from them myself. Admiral Hunter had forewarned me, but I did not realise how severe the problem was until I arrived. You amaze me, laddie."

Rudi sucked in his breath at the governor's mention of his uncle. To cover his astonishment, he shrugged with embarrassment. "Lance Upcroft helped, sir."

Lachlan nodded. "Good! You give credit where credit is due. I presume Upcroft would be willing to oversee this project with you? Presuming, of course, that I can source some coins and get this Henshall fellow, or someone similar, to work out a way to strike these disks."

Lance had mentioned his jealousy at being left out of this meeting; therefore, Rudi was sure of his assistance. He replied, "He would, sir."

Lachlan nodded again. "Good, then leave it with me. This won't happen overnight, but we now have a beginning." He turned to Mark and addressed him. "Mark, find out where this Henshall is and see if he can do such work. Don't mention why we are interested yet."

Mark grinned. "Will do, sir."

Lachlan released a long sigh. "Greenwood, if we are to work closely, as we will, I prefer informality. I gather you know Mark and call Upcroft by his Christian name; what is yours? Something unusual if I remember; Ruben, Randolph, Rupert…"

Rudi couldn't believe the governor, his commanding officer, wished to know his Christian name. "It's Rudolph, sir. I hate it, but that's parents for you. It's not as bad as Malchus, that's my brother's name. I prefer Rudi. I believe its root history is Germanic and means fame, glory, or honour. However, the 'Dolph' bit means wolf. I have the temperament to fit that part of the moniker and the grey eyes to match." He gave a wry grin. "Moodiness is my greatest fault."

Lachlan chuckled. "I'm known as a dour Scot, so I can relate to that. Lachlan means 'from the land of the lakes', but my island, Mull, is certainly full of inlets, not lakes. Mark knows my temperament well." His black, bushy brows raised then knitted, and he glared at his security guard.

Mark chuckled. "It's all bravado and bluff, Rudi. Everyone was betting that Sir couldn't rein in the exclusives, and he has. Your suggestion will pull the rug out from under their feet, so you have earned our support. However, you may well have made enemies of them. I believe that Macarthur's cronies will hate you, so try not to cross them."

Rudi relaxed. "I'm here to serve, sir." He thought back to his deep depression of only a few short weeks ago. He had hated it here. He had few friends, little responsibility, and a tedious, dead-end job. Being permanently moved from guarding the flaunting women was fabulous. The prospect of overseeing this new project and Mrs Edwards' appearance in his life had changed everything. Bethan… he had called her that once by accident, and she liked it. He smiled. Yes, Bethan meant the world to him. She didn't seem to mind him using it as a pet name for her.

Lachlan stood, placing his hands on his desk. He pushed himself up and said, "Well, gentlemen, we have a way through this mire of forgery, illicit grog and underhand transactions. I think there is little more we can do tonight, but should you get any more 'throw-away' ideas, please tell us." Both captains also stood, and Rudi took his leave.

Mark assisted him with his overcoat, and Rudi turned to exit with his hat in hand. Mark said, "Thanks, Rudi. If this works, it could turn the colony around. Keep it mum for the moment. Only discuss it with Lance in private."

The chill hit Rudi as the front door opened. He nodded and departed. His breath clouded as he said good night. He saluted the guards and set out to return to the barracks on the other side of the small valley. The air was crisp, so he buttoned his coat all the way down and pulled up his collar. He stuffed his gloveless hands in his pockets, then picked up his pace to keep warm. He took the pathway past the rectory and planned to cut across the footbridge over the Tank Stream leading up to the barracks. This was the most direct route back to his quarters. Rudi was so excited about the prospect of a change in duty that he didn't notice his surroundings. As he neared the creek, he heard hushed voices and wondered who was out on such a cold night. He had reached the small bridge at the Tank Stream when he recognised a familiar voice. He knew it belonged to the soldier who worked at the orphanage. He disliked him intensely. Rudi knew the children were terrified of both this man and the matron. There was no evidence of foul play to justify arresting either of them. He was about to call a polite greeting when his world went black.

Unbeknownst to him, he had surprised some unscrupulous scoundrels who were moving some illicit grog from one of their hiding places to a safer venue. The voice of the crook beside the man who hit him said, "Cor, Dennis, it's one of the captains from the chain gangs. What if you've killed him?"

Dennis Scriven was employed to oversee the orphanage. He abhorred the screaming female brats that he was in charge of and ensured that they were petrified of him. He wouldn't have minded if they were a bit older, as he could have used them to slake his lusts. But these girls were too young for his liking. The good thing about being stationed on the foreshore was the access to the bay and the hiding place for the illegally imported spirits.

Occasionally, like tonight, they had to empty the outside storeroom because another shipment was due at any time. He needed somewhere bigger, but where?

Dennis swore. "Can't be helped. Greenwood knows who I am as we're in the same regiment. He'll think he's been robbed, so we must strip his pockets." He motioned for one of the men to empty Rudi's pockets.

~

Dawn broke, and the raucous screech of the birds woke Bethany. Something upset them this morning, as they were making an excessive noise. She rolled over and felt ill again. Morning sickness was expected to last only a few weeks, not months. She made it to the chamber pot before heaving up the contents of her stomach. She relieved herself after throwing up. Having a baby was tiring. The chill of her room made her reach for her dressing gown. She dragged it on and went to rekindle the fire in her room. The big log she had added just before she slept had burned down to coals. A section was still hot. She ran her fingers through her luxurious, dark, wavy locks and pulled out a few loose strands. She rolled the hair around her fingers into a loop and poked the pulled-out hairs onto the coals. The hair caught alight instantly. She stoked the kindling around the remains of the log, and the room warmed up quickly. She held out her hands to warm them and realised that the birds' cries were much closer than usual this morning. She moved to the window and peered into the gloom of the morning mist. She saw the birds dive-bombing something near the footbridge over the creek.

She waited as the fog lifted and realised that it was a person. She was about to move away, thinking that it was a drunk, but she caught a glimpse of a red uniform coat poking out from under a familiar overcoat. Rudi wore a dark red soldier's coat despite being promoted to captain in the governor's regiment, and his overcoat was not government issue. It was unique in the colony as it was an expensive, woven wool. She gasped. It was him.

Bethany quickly dressed and went to investigate. She donned her walking shoes, overcoat, shawl, gloves and muff and went through the kitchen door. She walked to the garden gate and let herself out, then followed the pathway across the large vegetable garden to the creek through the back gate. This was locked, but she knew where the key was kept and had grabbed it on the way out of the kitchen.

Her quarry was only a short distance away. The man was face down on the grassy verge near the footbridge. She knelt in the dewy grass and felt for a pulse at his neck. Thankfully, it was strong. There was no smell of alcohol on him, but there was blood on his head. Even that was only a small area. His uniform hat lay next to him. The red she saw was where his overcoat had been pushed aside. Tucking his arms down beside him, she rolled him over and gasped in horror when she confirmed who it was. "Rudi, Captain Greenwood, can you hear me? It's Bethan, Rudi, wake up." She stroked his cheek. He stirred but did not wake. Her unborn baby objected to her position, and it kicked. Knowing she could do nothing herself, she removed her scarf and wrapped it around his face for warmth. She then put his gloveless hands inside her muff. No one was around, so she knew she had to return to the rectory to get help. She awkwardly rose to her feet, pulled his coat over his legs, then turned tail and quickly walked back. Her growing stomach stopped her from running.

Delia Gordon, the cook, met her on her return. A maid and Fred Morgan, the gardener-cum-footman, were in the kitchen too. "Mrs Gordon, Mr Morgan, we need help. Rudi, Captain Greenwood, has been injured and is lying near the bridge outside. We need the doctor and some men to bring him here. Send help quickly, please." With word now given and help coming, Bethany grabbed a few blankets from the linen press and returned to Rudi's side as fast as possible. Molly Marchant, the upstairs maid, arrived in the kitchen as Bethany went out the back gate. Molly was issued instructions to inform the mistress and prepare for the possibility of a patient. Fred Morgan had already left to get Doctor Wentworth, who lived only across the creek from them. He would find someone to help bring the officer into the house.

Bethany knew her body heat would warm Rudi, but she could not lie on the ground and take him in her arms. She drew him into her lap, as he had done to her only a few months ago. She could feel the ground's cold seeping through her gown, but their position meant that Rudi was now resting between her legs and not on the cold earth. The blankets covered him completely. He moaned and started moving, trying to fight the weight off him.

She said, "Rudi, lie still. You are safe." Bethany felt his cheek and realised that her shawl was now somewhat bloodied. She slid her hand to the back of his head, where she had seen a dark patch earlier, and found it was bleeding again. His skin was now warm to the touch, whereas it had been cold earlier. She released a long sigh. Hopefully, she would not need to wait long for help. She stroked his cheek and tried to stir him. "Rudi, wake up. Captain Greenwood, can you hear me?"

Rudi stirred. He could hear Bethany's voice, but he was unable to move. His arms felt heavy, and his body seemed to be pinned to the ground. He couldn't even turn his head. Something soft and warm surrounded his face. His eyes were heavy. Why couldn't he open his eyes? Why couldn't he move his hands or turn his head? It was too hard to fight. He surrendered to the warmth enveloping him. He had felt so cold, and now that had gone. Darkness overcame him, and he succumbed to the need for sleep.

Bethany's concentration was entirely focused on Rudi. "Don't die, Rudi. Please, don't die on me. I need you." She caressed his cheek and then pulled away her hand. Realising what she had said. Her feelings for this man were overwhelming. Surely, it was far too soon after Andrew's death for her to fall in love? Footsteps approached, and Bethany looked up and saw Doctor Wentworth crossing the footbridge. "Doctor, it's Captain Greenwood. He must have been here all night." Her hands still rested on his cheeks, holding his head still.

The doctor looked worried. He made her remove her hands, and he checked his eyes, then D'Arcy smacked his cheek quite hard. "Rudi, can you hear me? Rudi, wake up."

Rudi stirred. Something had hit him. He heard his name and detected a sweet aroma. It was Bethany's violet scent. He smiled. He liked violets. He liked Bethany as well. He groaned. Who had hit him? Why? He surrendered to the overwhelming tiredness again. He sighed and relaxed. Ahh Bethan… He smiled.

Bethany saw the slight smile on Rudi's lips. "Did you see that doctor? His lips moved. He'll be all right, won't he?"

The doctor caught a hint of panic in her voice. "I won't know until I check him over. You did the right thing by keeping him warm."

William Cowper arrived through the back garden gate. "Bethany, D'Arcy, what has occurred?" He fell to his knees beside the soldier.

The widow said, "It's Captain Greenwood, William. I can't rouse him."

William nodded. "Molly has a room prepared for him. Rudi will be better with us than at the hospital. D'Arcy, can you have him carried in through the back garden?"

The doctor nodded. "Thank you, Reverend. I was hoping you would offer him a bed as the hospital is full of chest complaints. He would be much better cared for here than there."

Lance, Brenton, and Tobin arrived as he spoke, with Fred following. Rudi started fighting against being manhandled.

Bethany stroked his cheek and said softly, "Rudi, you are safe. Let us care for you." Her voice soothed him, and he quietened.

The four men rolled Rudi over, slid the blankets under him, and carried him into the house, cradling him in the blanket sling as carefully as if he were being taken on a stretcher.

Lance and Rudi were off duty today, but Lieutenant Tobin Jeeves had to take the chain gang out. He needed to return to do the morning muster, and Brenton was due at the stables, but he remained to assist in getting Rudi stripped and into bed. The reverend brought one of his own nightshirts, and Rudi was soon ensconced in the guest room next to Bethany.

Lance checked his friend's pockets. No coins. While alone, he said, "Rudi, you've been robbed." Rudi heard but didn't reply.

Ann fed her baby and settled the child back into the crib. Molly and Fred were tending to the needs of the other four children. Fred was accustomed to acting as a valet to the older boys and the minister. Molly looked after Mary and little Charles. They dressed the children and ushered them downstairs into the kitchen for breakfast while the patient was settled.

Mrs Gordon had cooked them 'dippy' eggs for breakfast, and there was a plate full of buttered toast fingers to eat these with. Being a weekday, Fred and Bethany usually had a few hours of classes for the three older children. Today, Fred suggested he take the four of them out of the house while the doctor tended to Rudi. Molly needed to be on hand to make the beds and available to bring items for the patient.

The morning muster was about to start, and once it was over, Fred would let the boys kick a ball around the parade grounds at Hyde Park. They were not usually permitted to attend this spectacle in person, but they had often watched the assembly from the upstairs windows of the guest rooms.

Once Rudi was settled into the big feather bed, Brenton left for work at the Government House stable yard. No sooner had he arrived than the senior guard abused him for being late. Brenton explained. "Sorry, sir, but Captain Greenwood was set upon last night, and we have just taken him to the minister's house. He's not come around yet."

The guard was shocked. "You mean Rudi? He was here last night talking to the governor."

Brenton shrugged slightly. "I don't know about that, sir. I was called early this morning to help Captain Upcroft and Lieutenant Jeeves to move Captain Greenwood into the minister's guest room. He's in a bad way, sir. He still had not stirred when I left. The doctor was still with him."

Mark had opened the front door and overheard the conversation. "Did you say Rudi is injured?"

The convict nodded. "Yes, Captain Duffy. I think he must have been out there all night. Captain Lance said he didn't come home last night after he had been called to a meeting somewhere."

Mark was stunned. "He was here until about nine last night. He must have been attacked on the way back." He paused and asked, "So, he's at the minister's place, is he, not the hospital?"

Brenton shook his head and then nodded. "Doctor Wentworth doesn't want him there. He said there's a chest problem sweeping through the patients. He'll stay at Cowpers' if that's all right."

Mark nodded. "Yes, yes, that's fine. I'll go and let the governor know about Rudi." He turned on his heel to go. He spoke to the other guard and said, "Gerald, Brenton knows Greenwood well, so he's not to be in any trouble for being late. He was only following orders."

The guard saluted and returned to his position at the front door.

Brenton grinned as he walked off to the stables at the back of the large garden. He liked his new work. He would be happy if only his wife and children could join him. Lance said he would write to them on his behalf. Hopefully, Lance's brother would cover their fare out here. He wanted the governor to know about the captain, but he had been unsure of how to tell him. Walking past the front of the house instead of the usual rear pathway had done the trick. Rudi Greenwood had changed of late, and the moody, bad-tempered soldier was gone. The captain often stopped and asked about his day. Brenton was fully aware of what was different, but he wondered if the captain recognised that change in himself. The man was in love. He chuckled as he entered the stables and opened the large doors to flush out the stale air.

Back at the rectory, although now in bed, Rudi lay still and pale. The fire had been built up in the room, and a wrapped hot brick was placed at his feet. Ann hovered nearby as Bethany waited at the door. She had only ever seen Andrew naked and was unsure if she should enter the unmarried man's room.

William needed to leave to do the morning service, and he left D'Arcy stitching Rudi's head. Ann was called away to tend to her children, and D'Arcy called Bethany to hold his patient still. The gash needed three stitches, but it had now stopped bleeding. She moved away once the treatment was done. No sooner had D'Arcy tied the last knot than Rudi started moaning. He was trying to push off the heavyweights, which crushed his body and impaired his breathing. He felt like he was drowning. His feet hurt, but the more he struggled, the more the bands constricting him tightened. Why did his feet hurt? They felt like they were burning. He moved them and discovered that the sheets were cool to the side.

D'Arcy said to Bethany. "See if your voice calms him. It did before." Bethany did as he asked and came to Rudi's side. He had managed to get an arm out from under the blankets. She clasped her fingers around his. "Rudi, it's Bethan. Can you hear me? Squeeze my hand if you can." He gave an imperceptible squeeze, and she nodded to the doctor. "Rudi, you need to rest and heal, but first, can you take some warm tea?" Again, he squeezed her hand gently.

D'Arcy poured some tepid tea from the pot Molly had brought about twenty minutes earlier. He said, "Rudi, I need to sit you up to drink." He eased his patient up and helped him drink a full mug of tea. Once consumed, D'Arcy said, "Sleep now, my friend. You are safe and warm."

Rudi's eyes were still closed, but he murmured, "Hot, too hot," and he tried to push off the blankets. Bethany took off the heavy feather quilt and removed the brick. Rudi relaxed. She said, "Sleep now, Rudi." She released his arms from under the layers of bedding. Ann returned and stood watching.

D'Arcy said farewell to the ladies and headed off to work. He'd missed breakfast and knew he had a full day. He had to check in at the hospital and had his magistrate's duty this afternoon. Thankfully, William Redfern had taken over most of the hospital work.

As he entered the kitchen, Mrs Gordon pointed to the kitchen table, where a large plate of bacon, eggs, sausages, and three slices of buttered toast were laid out next to a jar of marmalade. He grinned his thanks and tucked into the delicious treat.

Ann, Molly, and Bethany alternated in watching their patient for the next three hours. He was restless but didn't appear to be ill.

Bethany had just dozed off in the armchair in Rudi's room when a noise from the bed stirred her. "Thirsty!"

She came to his side. "Captain, are you awake?"

A smile hovered on Rudi's lips before he opened his grey eyes. "You called me by name earlier. I remember smelling violets, and I knew you were close."

Bethany chuckled. "I wondered if you had heard that slip. I shouldn't be so forward, unlike you, Captain Greenwood." Her giggle was delightful. It was uttered with great relief.

Rudi smiled. He turned to look at her. Her mauve eyes held a hint of blue today. The slight movement hurt, and he groaned. "You can be as forward as you like, Mrs Edwards. I don't mind at all." To wake and find her beside his bed almost made whatever happened to him worth it.

Bethany heard soft voices. Ann joined them. "Are you up to some questions, captain?" Rudi sighed with frustration. He wanted to speak with Bethany alone, but that would have to wait. He wasn't going anywhere for some time. He was as weak as a newborn babe. "I suppose so. Who's here, ma'am?"

Ann rose as her baby cried. "The governor and Captain Duffy are in the sitting room. Are you up to seeing them?"

Rudi was still trying to focus his eyes. "Yes, that would be fine." He was about to say more when he realised he had to keep knowledge of their plans under wraps. "That's okay!" He relaxed, forgetting Bethany was still there. Her soft sigh made him turn to her. "Can we speak later? I need to see them alone." Bethany nodded, rose, and exited. Mark was waiting outside the room with the governor.

The two men entered, and Mark closed the door behind them.

Lachlan took Bethany's seat, and Mark stood at the foot of his bed. Lachlan didn't beat around the bush. "What the heck happened, Rudi? Did you make it home last night?"

Rudi tried to shake his head, but it still hurt. "No, sir, I only made it as far as the bridge. I heard Dennis from the orphanage speaking with someone, but I couldn't tell who he was talking to. Then my world went black." He remembered stirring in Bethany's lap, but he didn't realise that at the time.

Mark growled with anger. "So you have no idea why they hit you?"

Rudi said, "No, Mark, no idea at all. I was out cold before I heard what they were discussing. I think I heard Lance say they took my coins, so I have been robbed. There aren't many of those Spanish Reales around. Thankfully, I left the sheets of paper and the map with you. Mark, check my pockets, please."

Mark did as requested. He shook his head. "All empty."

Lachlan blew out his lips at the reply. "Another blooming puzzle to unravel. They could be smuggling, but I do not know if they are a fringe group for the exclusives. George Johnston and Macarthur's friends are widespread throughout this town. Once we implement your idea, that will clip their wings severely." He put his finger to his lips.

Rudi gave a wry grin. He had no idea how long that would take to sort out. He checked to ensure he wasn't naked and struggled to sit up.

Lachlan chuckled. "Don't look so down in the mouth. I checked the records after you left last night and discovered Henshall is out in the Hawkesbury area. We're heading out there next week, and we'll sound him out." Knowing he could learn no more, Lachlan stood and walked to the door. "Take time to recover, Greenwood. You'll be busy once this takes off. Rest while you can." He left.

Mark followed, turning to give Rudi a wink at the door. "Respect her, Rudi."

Chapter 6 The Picnic

Once the footsteps faded, Bethany appeared in Rudi's room. "Is there anything you would like?"

Rudi grinned and said, "Some of your time before we are interrupted again. I wish to say thank you for coming to my aid." His eyes fixed on her violet ones. "I heard you, Bethan. I heard you begging me not to die." She smiled, and his heart did a flip. "I promised that I would not make the first move, but let me say, I'm shuffling closer, just so you know. I want to be near you, but you must tell me when you are ready." He heard Ann approaching as the baby was crying. He said, "You shouldn't be in here alone, Bethan; it will compromise you."

She chuckled. "You forget, I'm a widow in mourning, not an unmarried girl. I am also expecting my dead husband's child. There's not much you can do to me, Rudi." Ann didn't come. She turned away to the baby's room. Bethany dropped her voice and said, "Rudi, give me some time. That's all I ask. It's only been a few months since Andrew died. I loved him dearly, but he's gone. I know I will need to remarry, as I have no other option. I have nothing to go home to, so I must make a new life here. I quickly learned that what you said about being a lone woman in this town is far too true. Time is all I require, Rudi. Can you wait?"

He caressed her hand. "For as long as is necessary, Bethan." All thoughts of suicide had fled the day he rescued this beautiful woman. She drew him, but it was deeper than mere beauty. She glowed with an inner contentment. Rudi wanted what she had, but had no idea what that was.

~

Spring was a welcome arrival. Rudi's head took two weeks to recover fully. He was put on light duties, which meant he didn't need to sit out on the cold wagons and guard the chain gangs on road repair. Rudi had been brought in as a security guard for the governor when Mark and Cathy's baby son, Gideon, was ill. Rudi loved this job as he used the time to get to know his superior officer.

D'Arcy left Rudi's stitches in for ten days, and the scar was itchy. He winced every time he combed his hair. He had enjoyed his fortnight-long respite at Cowper's place as Bethany made time to spend with him daily. Until her year of mourning was ended, Rudi had no intention of asking to court her, but he mentioned his intentions to her. Keeping her safe until the baby arrived was the biggest problem. Two other officers had already made vile comments about bedding her. One ended up with a bloodied nose when he mouthed off too close to Rudi. His automatic reaction had been to raise his fist. Somehow, Bethany discovered that he had risen to her defence. Her only reaction was squeezing his hand, and she murmured her appreciation. Rudi was frustrated. Her condition was making her front heavy, but she wasn't due for weeks.

A celebration was planned to mark the official announcement of William's position. It had been delayed since the August notification. However, in the first week of September, the Sydney Gazette finally reported the nomination of William Cowper as the first assistant chaplain. Robert Cartwright had been named the second assistant and would be placed in Windsor, not Sydney. It was now official. William was thrilled. A picnic luncheon was planned for September 7th at Parramatta behind Government House. Bethany was considering not attending as she was due the following month. Ann was well after the birth of their son, William Macquarie, but he was known as Macquarie, and the children shortened it to Mac. Bethany was keen to join them but realised a carriage journey at eight months along would be out of the question. After church, Bethany swallowed nervously and asked her protector, "Rudi, would you come with me if I could catch the boat?"

Rudi chuckled. "Need you think otherwise? If you are keen to attend, I shall willingly be your escort." Her smile was heart-warming.

~

The ferry trip to Parramatta was considered too dangerous for the children, but Bethany was determined to go to the picnic and travelling by water meant a smooth ride. The ferry times for the sloop were suitable, as the high tides occurred in the early morning and afternoon. They had time to make the journey, have a picnic and return before the tide was too low. The Macquaries were hosting the celebration in the Domain Garden at the back of their Parramatta home, and the Marsdens, Cartwrights, and Cowpers were the honoured guests.

Bethany and Rudi hoped to go for a walk alone, but her feet were too swollen to go far. Rudi strolled around the grassy area and escorted her to the nearby privy outside the ramshackle Salter's dairy building. This area was closer than the government residence, which was located farther down the hill. As they strolled in full view of everyone, Rudi managed to converse with her privately. "Bethan, did you know that the Macquaries are moving back into Sydney for a while? They will expand the existing facility here by constructing additional staff quarters. They will still stay here occasionally until most of the building is complete. Until then, they will reside in Sydney. I thought you would like to know."

Bethany smiled. "It's not every day that the governor's lady helps one undress and put to bed. Although I wasn't aware of that until much later. Ann told me. I like Elizabeth very much; she has no upper-crust attitude that makes me uncomfortable. She often comes to talk to Ann and me when we are at an event like this. I like that about her." She paused and glanced at him. Her mouth opened to say something, but closed again.

Rudi said, "Bethan, it's me, and we're alone. Say what you wish."

She nodded. "I'm frightened, Rudi. I can't stay with the Cowpers for much longer. I feel I have already overstayed my welcome with them, but I have no direction. I have no idea what to do, where to go, and I am unsure…" She glanced at him again.

Rudi was delighted. "About me?" He finished her comment.

She nodded, then shrugged. "…or us, in actual fact. Amongst other things. I'm supposed to wait a year before entering a courtship, but here, Ann tells me things are a little different, less rigid, so six months is adequate. That is up. I have a month until I'm due." They had just walked behind a large tree and were hidden from the view of most of the celebrating group. She rubbed her very large stomach.

Rudi turned to face her. "It would be my greatest pleasure if you would court me. I promise to bring your child up as you and Andrew planned. You don't need to do this alone, Bethan. I intended to propose as soon as it was deemed suitable, but, as I have already said, that has been my intention since soon after I met you. Even before I knew Andrew was your husband."

Her face lit up. "Courting. Yes, Rudi, I would like that." She lifted her face to his, hoping he would kiss her. "May I ask, how long is 'deemed suitable'?"

He chuckled and brushed his lips over her cheek. "Bethan, I have a confession to make, one no one else knows. I have never kissed a woman or been with one in an intimate way. When I marry, I will make my vows in earnest. I may be a soldier, but my reputation for moodiness is one reason I made few friends. I have been called 'Moody Rudi' more than once. I don't drink or carouse with them. Therefore, I will not even kiss you yet. The timing for our engagement is in your hands. I will ask the question, but you may have all the time you need to answer." He dropped to one knee behind the tree and asked for her hand in marriage. "My dearest Bethan, I would be honoured if you would, at some time, consider my offer to become your husband."

She gently tugged him from his position and pulled him close, regardless of who might see. Her head hardly came up to his shoulder. But she felt so safe in his arms. "I will willingly court you, Rudi. You will get just a one-word answer when I am ready for the next step."

He kissed her forehead. "That is all I ask, my dear."

They emerged from their cover with a lightness in their hearts. "Bethan, I will hunt around town for a house for us. I have the means available and will arrange for Brenton to move in. He will still need to complete his work at the government stables, but I can reassign him where needed. Do you have any preference for where we live? I may have to build from scratch if there is nothing suitable." He glanced at her to gauge her reaction. "I can also request to have some other house staff. The *Canada* arrived last week with over one hundred female convicts, and we have nowhere to send them. For now, they remain on board. Would you be averse to having convict staff? Molly is one, and I think Mrs Gordon came out as a convict. We will need a nursery maid, and I know some of the convict girls are pitifully young, but many have younger siblings at home."

She giggled. "Why would I mind, Rudi? If these girls need a safe placement, then can we take more? I can train them as maids and teach them to read and write; then, they will be able to rise above the mire of their current status." She gave him a coy look. "Are you that sure of my answer?"

Rudi chuckled. "Should I not be? Would you have permitted me to court you if you didn't like me a little?"

She shook her head, and the dark curls around her face bobbed enticingly. "I like you more than a little, and I shouldn't."

Rudi looked surprised. "Why? We are not doing anything wrong."

She huffed. "No, we aren't, but I should be in full mourning for Andrew. Ann and William are still paying the price for marrying so soon after the children's mother, Hannah, died. I have no idea if they knew each other before her death, but the speed of their nuptials would have raised many eyebrows at home. It's just as well he's a minister." She paused. The baby gave a big kick. "Ouch, little one, that hurt." With her back turned to the crowd, she took Rudi's hand and placed it on her stomach. "Rudi, this child will need to know about his or her father. I will not deny it that knowledge. Andrew must always be part of their life. You must be aware of that."

Rudi was astonished by the child's vigorous movements. "Of course." The baby kicked again. He asked, "Does it hurt? It seems to be kicking quite vigorously." He felt the tiny lump and realised it was a foot. He knew that his hand should not have been placed so intimately on her person. She was so large that he had seen her rest a teacup on her belly.

She saw the awe on his face. "Sometimes it keeps me awake at night, but often it's active when I'm tired. Talking of which, I need to put my feet up. I've been so tired, and carrying this extra weight around hurts my back. It aches constantly, particularly all day today."

They rejoined the picnic in time for the celebrations to be officially acknowledged.

~

An hour passed with much laughter and conversation. It was a perfect day for a picnic, and even the children were well-behaved.

Ann sidled up to Bethany and said, "You were a long time on your walk to the privy, my friend."

A blush crept over Bethany's face. She nodded. "He asked to court me officially, and I said yes."

Ann gasped. "Really? You are serious about him then?"

Bethany nodded. She caught his eye across the group. "Yes, very serious. He also asked to marry me but told me not to reply until I was ready." She broke eye contact with Rudi and turned to Ann. "How soon is too soon after Andrew's death? Ann, I ask you because you had to make that decision yourself. Please, my friend, I hope you don't mind me asking, but I can't stay with you forever."

Ann giggled, ignoring the question. She said, "Rudi was such a surly man before he met you. He was known as Moody Rudi. I don't even think I saw him smile. Only Captain Upcroft and D'Arcy could tolerate his company." She paused and glanced across at the captain. He had not taken his eyes off Bethany since she sat down.

Bethany sighed. "I heard that from everyone, including him, but there must be a reason."

Ann frowned. She knew his story. "Dear, have you discussed your faith with him yet? Until you came, I only ever saw him in church when he was ordered to be there. I would hate to think of you being unequally yoked with a non-believer."

Bethany shook her head. "No, we haven't. It's why I didn't say yes directly. It's a conversation we need to have."

Ann saw the children returning and knew they were about to be attacked by little people. "Don't leave it too long, dear girl, or it may be too late to pull out."

With the children's arrival, Ann was occupied by their demands.

Bethany turned back to look at Rudi and frowned. Did he truly lack a strong faith? Had she misread him? Bethany moved away and took a place on a rug overlooking the official house.

Various conversations were going on around her, but she was deep in thought about Rudi. She jumped when she felt someone beside her, then smiled when she realised who it was.

Rudi approached and asked to join her. She nodded but didn't smile. "Bethan, what's wrong? Did Ann say something to upset you?" He wished he could bring her comfort, but he was not even permitted to touch her in public.

Bethany shrugged. "Maybe, I'm not sure."

Rudi's heart sank. "Have I done something wrong? Should I not have approached you yet?"

Bethany sighed; the time had come. "No, it's just that we have not had one critical conversation, and the outcome will sway my decision." She inhaled, frowned and released a sigh. "Rudi, in all this time we have known each other, you have never mentioned your faith. Okay, admittedly, neither have I because I try to live it. I don't blame God for Andrew's death, as I know it was not His doing, but something you mentioned made me worry. I feel something bad happened to you, and you blame God."

Rudi's gaze was fixed on hers, but when she said that, he blanched, then replied, "How could I not? Who else could I blame? He let my family die in the fire. He could have saved them, but He didn't."

Bethany's heart sank. She was stunned at his outburst. "Rudi, don't you know God at all? That's not how He works."

While keeping his voice low, he said, "Oh, I believe in Him so that I can blame Him. How else can I explain everything that happens?" Rudi's eyes tore away from her. He was feeling angry for the first time in quite a while. "Other than me, the only member of my household who didn't die was my brother. Everyone else, man, woman and beast, died that night." He sighed angrily. "If God didn't do that, then who did?" Rather than wait for her reply, he jumped up and walked away. If the truth were told, he stormed off in anger, seething with hurt and loss. The hurt of losing his family never eased, but for a while, he had forgotten his anger at God. Even when he went to church, it wasn't to find God but to see Bethany. Everything of late had been for her. She was a beacon of light in his dark, lonely world. He wandered away from the gathering and along the top of the cliff overlooking the river. He stood next to a fallen tree and sat at the far end of the large log. The idea of jumping off the cliff swept across his thoughts. For her to reconsider accepting him because of his lack of faith in God completely threw him. Why wasn't she angry that God had taken her Andrew? Why? What had drawn him to her? A pretty face? No, there was something more. He turned and looked back at the gathering. Reverend William Cowper was walking towards him. He groaned. He knew he was in for a grilling. He had managed to avoid a deep conversation with the religious chap all the time he was holed up at their house, but after Bethany's comments, it was time to face the music. He refused to stand as he should when the minister approached. He ignored the man's arrival.

William came and sat in silence next to Rudi. They watched the various birds swimming on the stretch of water in the river below. William dropped his head in prayer. Rudi had seen him do this before and wondered how it could possibly help.

They waited in silence, neither prepared to say anything.

Eventually, William took a breath to speak, but Rudi's words almost exploded from his lips. "God killed my family; how am I supposed to love a deity that took all whom I loved? How? Tell me… How?" Rudi almost shouted the last word at William.

William's answer floored him. "God didn't do that, Rudi, sin did."

"Sin! How can sin do anything? It's inert." The respectful captain in him was well buried. He felt like a confused child, and he wanted to weep on his mother's lap, but she was dead. Dead and burned alive whilst she slept. What hurt more was that his brother laughed at his tears. That was why Rudi had left all he knew and come here. There really was nothing left for him in England except Uncle John, but he was the one who had suggested he enlist. Even he didn't want him near.

William's following soft words were like a balm. "Sin is why we are here in a penal colony; sin is why bad things happen. Sin is why sickness, death, fires, floods, storms and tempests of other sorts occur, Rudi. God didn't make the earth like that. God didn't make sin; we did.

We are all sinners; only some of us here are in physical irons, but we all need to repent for our wrongdoings." William inhaled, then released a deep sigh. "Are you prepared to listen? Until now, you have fought about coming to church, but even going to church does not make you a believer, does it?"

Rudi shook his head. He'd been there each week since he met Bethany. He was no closer to belief than when he started going. He nodded, "Go on." He was close to tears at the thought that Bethany might turn him down due to his lack of faith. He could at least listen. The well-known depression was seeping over him.

William's quiet questioning eased his hurt. "How much do you know about God? Do you know the bible stories? Adam and Eve and so on?"

Rudi shrugged and said, "A bit. What have they to do with sin?"

William smiled. "Everything, Rudi, that's where it all started. Do you remember the story of the Garden of Eden and how the snake offered Eve the forbidden fruit?" Rudi nodded. He had been to church often enough to know the basics.

William relaxed and said, "Well, the snake was Satan in disguise. Up until then, God walked with Adam and Eve in the garden. They were naked and knew no evil. When God made everything, all this beautiful place we live in, He made it perfect. No storms, sickness, earthquakes, floods, fires or famine. The Bible says He makes all things good; good as in absolutely perfect." William saw Rudi turn to face him, but he didn't pause. "God didn't include those bad things on earth when He made it, as he supplied the land with moisture in dew and fog. He didn't need to create storms, fires, or floods because His creation was in balance. When sin entered the world through Eve's action of eating the fruit, the world went out of kilter." William took a breath and saw that Rudi wanted to say something. He put his hand up and said, "Later. Let me finish." Rudi nodded.

William continued by saying, "However, Eve's action was not the first sin. Everyone thinks it was, but the first sin was committed directly to God by one of his own angels, named Lucifer. We now call him Satan or the Devil. When he sinned against God, other angels agreed with him, and one-third of the angels were banished from God's presence; they became the demons. Satan was banished from heaven, bringing the turmoil and sickness with him. Even then, mankind still loved God. Sin entered our world when Adam and Eve disobeyed God's only rule."

Rudi couldn't help himself. "Only one rule? I could cope with that."

William shook his head. "None of us could, just as they couldn't, Rudi. We are all sinners and fall short of God's will for us. As you obviously don't know the full story of Eden, I shall summarise it for you. When God created the Earth, He made Adam and Eve perfect, but He gave them one rule: not to eat the fruit from the Tree of Knowledge, or they would die. They could eat from the Tree of Everlasting Life or any other tree, but they chose not to. The fruit the snake offered Eve was from the Tree of Knowledge. She knew it was wrong, and she challenged the creature. Satan lied to her, saying that they wouldn't die but would have their eyes opened to things they didn't currently understand. As with many of his lies, he was partially right, but that is also why God said not to eat it. Death would come later, but it would now involve pain. Well, the punishment for their action was to be cast out of the Garden of Eden. That also blocked them from access to God, or so they thought. God still watched over them, but they still had Free Will."

William paused and sighed, saying, "It was that same Free Will that started all this trouble, as God gave the angels the same gift of choice." He turned to Rudi and said, "We still have Free Will, Rudi. Every decision we make is a sample of that. We face decisions from the moment we wake up to the moment we fall asleep. Many of them affect others."

Rudi nodded. He understood that all too well. "So how does my Free Will make a fire start that killed my family? I wasn't even there."

William smiled. "You weren't, but that doesn't mean anything. Bad things that happen are not the responsibility of any one person. Humankind as a whole, are sinners." Rudi frowned.

William asked, "Do they know how the fire started? An accident or, as they say, an 'act of God'? Which is wrong, by the way!"

Rudi gasped. "It was presumed to be a lightning strike during a storm." He angrily swiped away a tear. "They had no chance of escape. So much for not being an act of God, eh?"

William nodded, and this surprised Rudi. He said, "Rudi, storms didn't happen before our world turned against God. As I said, the earth is out of kilter. So don't blame God, blame Satan. It's more like an 'act against God'. Jesus, who is God's son, could control the storms, but even He didn't cause them. We are all responsible for our own actions, and that also includes working together to protect others. It's why Ann and I are here. In a way, it's why Andrew and Bethany came as well. We are to teach others God's rescue plan. They hoped to employ young convict girls to work in their dairy. That will not happen now, but that was how they planned to help; anyway, that's beside the point: back to our world. Long ago in Eden, God promised a way back to Him; that is, through Jesus's death and resurrection. Jesus is God's rescue plan. Only by following Jesus's teachings can we find that peace with God and, therefore, ourselves. We each need God in our lives, and we are empty if we don't let Him in. One day, when Jesus returns, everything will be restored to its original, perfect state, as God first created it. The storms will cease, sickness will be banished, floods, earthquakes, fires, and famine will all be gone, as will death. However, in the meantime, we must learn to live in a fallen world. We must stand firm and be forthright in our faith." William turned to look directly at Rudi. "I feel that emptiness in you, young man. I have been watching you since we arrived, and I can see that you are discontented with everything. It's not just about you finding your niche in life, but you are searching for something you have already discarded. Yes, I know you blame God for the death and destruction of your family, but it goes much deeper than that. I think it's why you have been drawn to Bethany; you see in her what you need. You are seeking to fill the void in your life, but she won't be able to do that for you. God can. He can heal you in a way no other love can."

Rudi gave him a single nod. The minister was right. He felt empty, but could God fix that? "How can I fill it then? I know enough about things to know I've lived a good life, but even that is not good enough for God. I'll never be perfect. How can I live up to a perfect God? Nothing I can do is ever good enough. I've always fallen short of every expectation. My brother loved rubbing that in." He couldn't believe that tears were welling in his eyes again. "I'm a nothing to God, sir. Why should He bother with me?"

William smiled. His gentle words hit home. "We are all 'nothings' without God, Rudi. Yes, me too. You must not only believe in Him but also ask for forgiveness and try to follow the path that will lead you to Him eternally. Remember, believing is not enough. Satan believes in Him and knows God much better than we ever will, but we have something that he will never have. God has promised a way back to fellowship with Him, like the pure relationship that Adam and Eve had in the Garden of Eden. It's not only about saying 'yes' to Him; we need to live our lives with our eyes focused on Him. We must keep the Free Will option front and centre as every decision is down to that choice. If you need help deciding, ask yourself, 'What would Jesus want you to choose?' If you think He would be happy with your decision, then that's good. But if you feel uncomfortable knowing that God would be displeased, then walk away, son."

Rudi nodded while wiping his eyes with the heels of his hands. Everything he had thrown at God was wrong. He was wrong. "I can't walk away from Bethany, sir. I want her in my life; no, I need her. She is my compass. I can't do this alone anymore."

William put his hand on the soldier's shoulder. "None of us can do this alone, Rudi. We all need God as our crutch and mainstay. I freely acknowledge that when Hannah died, I fell to bits. I had already been offered this position and was eager to accept, but then my wife fell ill. Everything came to a halt. I had four children who needed a mother, and I needed a wife. I had no choice but to trust God. Then I met Ann. A mere six months after I buried my beloved Hannah, I remarried. Eyebrows were raised, believe me. Rudi, I had no choice but to trust God and that He knew better. The children adore her, and now we have little Mac. I never expected to be here without my Hannah, but that was not God's plan. Bethany never expected to be here without Andrew to protect her, but that was not God's plan. Death took them both." William took a deep breath and said, "Fine, so what do you do now? You have a decision to make. First transfer that hate and blame from God to Satan. Focus on God's love for you. He only wants you to be the best you can, and He will help you with that if you ask Him." He saw Rudi nod. "Bethany knows her mind, and I overheard your conversation before you walked away. Her decision rests with you and your next move. So, young Rudi, your future is in your hands." William turned and beckoned Bethany. She slowly made her way towards them.

Rudi didn't realise she was coming. He was still deep in thought and had no idea that he would soon need to decide which way his life would turn. Rudi nodded to William and said, "I need the void in my life gone. It's eating me. Before I met her, I was angry with everything, but she oozes peace and tranquillity." His head dropped as he said. "She's too good for me." After a few moments, Rudi smiled at William. "I'll need lots of help. Transferring that hate will be easy, even if the hurt remains. If you say all this is true, then I'm willing to listen and learn. Will you help me?" Rudi looked at the minister.

William grinned and nodded towards the picnic area. "Yes, of course, and I won't be the only one." He said, "Be honest with her. Tell her about your family, about what happened and the cause of your anger. She will understand. However, she will not respond to your proposal until you are man enough to show your weaknesses and prove your faith. She will also refuse to marry you if you cannot be her equal in faith." He stood to leave. "You have taken the first step; let her walk with you on the path of life. Do you remember the story of Job, where all his family died under similar circumstances to yours? Well, she may well be the first step to the beginnings of your new family. Trust God, Rudi. He loves you, even more than Bethany does."

Rudi gasped at that thought. He sniffed away the last of his tears, then stood and watched William as he walked away. As his lady love came to his side, Rudi offered Bethany his hand as she arrived. They sat together in the sun, and Rudi revealed his past worries. He repeated much of what he had told William. He admitted his anger at God and his error in doing so. He fell silent, hoping she would say something.

She did. "I need a man who will be a Godly leader for my children. One I can look up to and be tolerant with me." She didn't intentionally flutter her eyelashes, but her violet orbs glazed with unshed tears. "I need a man to rely on, Rudi, a strong, Godly one. Can you be that man?"

He grinned and nodded. "I will learn to be, Bethan." He paused for a while before he turned to the lovely lady and said, "Bethan, I meant what I told William. You are my compass, but I now realise it was because you pointed me to what was missing in my life. God shines through you, but I need you beside me to find my way. William said that my life mirrors Job to a point. I know that he also lost everything but never turned away from God. I hope that is true, as Job regained all he lost and more. I said I wouldn't bother you with my attention. But I think a three-hour courtship is plenty long enough." He dropped to one knee and said, "Bethan Edwards, will you do me the honour of becoming my wife? I need you near me to learn about God and how to live life to the fullest."

Bethany stroked his cheek as he knelt before her and said, "I'm still not going to answer you yet because I need to be sure, Rudi. We have time. I'm not saying no, but don't rush me. As to growing together, yes." She sat rubbing her back. "Will you walk back with me?"

Rudi's heart sank. "Yes, of course."

Bethany could tell he was upset. "Rudi, don't go sulky on me either. I don't need that at the moment." She didn't intend to tell him that she wasn't feeling well. All the walking wasn't helping. "Can we go home, Rudi? I want to rest." She leaned heavily on his arm.

Rudi took her hand and said, "I'm so sorry, Bethan. I will endeavour to be the man you need. Let me try?"

She nodded. "For now, just take me home. I want you near me if that's any consolation." For Rudi, it was. His face broke into a big smile.

Chapter 7 The Ferry Ride

By the time they returned to the picnic, D'Arcy Wentworth had arrived at the gathering and mentioned that he would return by boat as soon as it came. Bethany's face lit up. The rest of the picnic party intended to stay for some time. As soon as he ate something, D'Arcy was ready to leave.

Lachlan had Mark's stepson, Josh, harness the governor's small carriage to drive the expectant lady down to the government wharf with her two male escorts.

D'Arcy had spent the day at the small military hospital, where he was checking on a convict patient with a broken leg. That building was in an even worse condition than the Sydney one. As he had been at work, he had his medical bag with him. William offered the tired doctor a seat in the family carriage, but D'Arcy didn't feel like taking a noisy trip home. A peaceful trip on the sloop sounded delightful.

He was tying up loose ends so he could concentrate on the construction of the new hospital in Sydney. He wasn't sure that packing the foundations with rubble was a good idea, but he was no builder. He knew all his spare time would be spent tweaking the design before he was content with the flow of the workspace on the wards. He needed a break from stress before returning to Sydney. The last thing he wanted was to be stuck in a carriage with a gaggle of screaming children.

The steam-powered, sail ferry arrived, and the three boarded.

D'Arcy took a deep breath of the slightly salty air and relaxed.

Rudi settled Bethany in the small cabin and let her rest in peace. She mentioned she wanted to have a nap. Rudi left her lying down and joined D'Arcy. The two men walked to the stern and watched the crew work the sails and ropes.

Rudi felt like weeping. "I proposed, D'Arcy, and it didn't go as planned." Rudi couldn't meet his friend's eyes, so he dropped his head.

D'Arcy liked Rudi. His worldly innocence was quite telling, and the young man had no idea how much that appealed to women. He knew of his nickname, and he chuckled. "Love never goes as planned, my friend. Trust me, I know." He paused and thought back to England. He loved Jane, but she was oh-so-young. He sighed and said, "I never intended to have a romantic attachment with Ann Lawes, whom I rescued from an abusive husband. However, she has just given birth to my son, George. I've kept the news quiet, but the word is now out. Rudi, if you love the girl, be the man she needs you to be."

Rudi blew out his cheeks. "This afternoon, William challenged me about my faith, and I had to admit my antipathy towards God. Then he explained about sin. I've never heard faith summed up how he did, and it makes sense." He paused, thinking deeply. "Bethan won't accept me until I have proven myself to her, and I have no idea how to do that to myself, let alone prove my faith to her. She's asking the impossible."

D'Arcy threw his hands up and said, "I believe in God, but don't ask me more. I've seen the Catholics and Protestants fighting all my life in Ireland. Now, Marsden is continually on my back to get married. I'm tempted now I've found Ann, but… well, she is already married." He shrugged. Was the service he underwent in England with Jane valid? They had not used their real names. "Am I the marrying type? Even if I were, Ann's husband is still alive. We can't even call our relationship a common-law one."

The ship rounded the last of the mangroves and headed back to Sydney down the expansive bay. It had taken an hour to reach the end of the narrow section of the waterway and the mangrove line at the entrance of the Parramatta River because there was no wind and the small boat floated downstream with the receding tide. They were under sail, but the boilers were just being stoked.

Rudi went to check on Bethany a few times, and on each visit, he saw her asleep in the small cabin. She had her feet on the bench seat, and she looked peaceful. He paused, gazing at her, overwhelmed by his adoration for this diminutive girl.

The boat was now passing through the shallows near the area they called Kissing Point. At low tide, this area was impassable.

Rudi was halfway back to D'Arcy when the boat jerked and then stopped.

Pandemonium broke out on deck, with the crew running thither and yon.

The sails were dropped and furled, and the steam engine cut. The small vessel was stuck fast on the sandbanks at Kissing Point and going nowhere.

D'Arcy spoke to the captain while Rudi checked on Bethany. He almost ripped open the cabin door when he saw the bench empty.

Bethany was on her hands and knees on the floor, and she was groaning in agony.

Rudi came to her side and dropped to his knees beside her. "Bethan, were you thrown from the seat? Are you injured?"

She shook her head and was breathing deeply. "No, Rudi, the baby is coming. I've been having pain for nearly an hour. They started soon after we left the town jetty. I've been sleeping between pains." Another groan escaped. She spoke through clenched teeth. "Get the doctor, Rudi."

Rudi didn't want to leave her. He said, "But…"

Through gritted teeth, Bethany said, "Rudi, I need the doctor now."

Rudi ran. "D'Arcy, the baby is coming. It's too early. She's not due for a month."

D'Arcy swore; so much for a peaceful trip! "Fine, come on. Thankfully, I have my bag with me, but please ask the captain if he can boil water or if he has any clean fabric, such as towels, sheets, or linen, to wrap the child in. We're stuck fast and not going anywhere until the tide rises."

D'Arcy collected his medical bag from the wheelhouse and made his way to Bethany.

Rudi saw the captain at the bow, looking over to see how shallow the water was. He delivered his message and asked all the crew to stay well away from the cabin. He then joined D'Arcy, who had just washed his hands and doused them in neat alcohol. He reeked of rum.

They walked into the cabin to the expectant mother.

Before they entered, D'Arcy said, "You won't like what you hear, as she will scream a lot, but I'm going to need you with me for this. If you want to learn to pray, now is the time."

Rudi was a bundle of nerves. He nodded.

As they made their way into Bethany, a groan sounded from the cabin.

Bethany was still on her hands and knees. "Rudi, help me up. I need to stand up, and I can't."

Rudi went to her aid while D'Arcy dug out his medical equipment.

They managed to get her to her feet.

D'Arcy said, "Bethany, have you removed your drawers yet?"

She looked horrified. "No, of course not."

D'Arcy chuckled, "Then that must be the first thing you do."

She was horrified. "Why?"

D'Arcy laughed and explained, "You are having a baby, dear girl, and that's where it will appear. The way it got in there is how it comes out."

Bethany nodded, then turned to Rudi and blushed. "Don't you look, Rudi!"

Rudi turned around, and she lifted her skirts and untied the string of her drawers. The fine white linen pooled around her feet.

D'Arcy held her while she stepped out of them. Thankfully, the boat was not rocking.

Tears flowed down her cheeks. "This is not how it should be happening. I wanted to have Ann with me and… and…" She wept bitterly.

D'Arcy gave Rudi the all-clear to turn around, and another contraction hit as he did so. Bethany almost collapsed into Rudi's arms.

He pulled her against his chest for support.

She screamed in agony, but it was muffled against his shoulder.

D'Arcy said, "When this contraction has passed, I need to see how close you are to delivery. Remember to breathe deeply through each pain."

Bethany nodded against Rudi's shoulder.

Rudi whispered encouragement to her as she leaned against him. Then, out of the blue, words flooded into his mind. He was overwhelmed with a massive feeling of peace and said, "Dear God, we need you more now than ever. We need you to help Bethan get through this birth, and please God, keep her safe for me. Sustain her and give her strength. Show me what she needs. I need her so much. I need you too."

Bethany pulled away a bit and looked at him, stunned. "You prayed!"

Rudi grinned. "I did, didn't I? Shouldn't I have done that?

She smiled in reply. "Yes, you did and 'Yes', Rudi."

His eyes flew wide open. "You mean Yes to my earlier question?"

She giggled. "Yes. Yes to everything. I love you."

Rudi felt like shouting with his delight, but he kissed her brow instead.

D'Arcy grinned almost wickedly. "Congratulations to you both, as I presume you have just become engaged?"

Both nodded, grinning.

Bethany reached up and kissed Rudi's cheek.

Rudi wished he could kiss her properly, but at that moment, another contraction hit.

Her knees went weak.

D'Arcy said, "That was quick, Bethany. That was less than five minutes apart. I really need to see how close you are to delivery."

Once that contraction passed, they managed to get her on the bench seat, and D'Arcy lifted her skirts to check how dilated she was.

An expletive escaped D'Arcy's lips. "Sorry, Bethany, but you are nearly ready to deliver. That was very quick. Have you been having contractions all day or general back pain?"

She nodded. "Sort of; I have had back pain since this morning. Was that labour pain?"

The doctor nodded. "For a very few, my dear, but your contractions are very close. Normally, a first labour is lengthy. Plus, most births are extremely painful." He looked around the cabin and saw a small coopered garbage bin behind him. He tipped the few items out and passed her the bin. "You will need this in a few minutes."

No sooner than he uttered the words, Bethany grabbed the bin and vomited.

Rudi held her to stop her from toppling over.

D'Arcy said, "Action stations, everyone. Bethany, you will soon feel the urge to push. Do not fight it. You will need to take a deep breath and push as hard as you can. Rudi, follow my instructions precisely. Sit on the bench with your legs apart. Bethany, position yourself between his legs, facing me and then squat down. Rudi will wrap his arms around you and support you as I catch the baby."

He arranged them as he wished, with a folded towel under her and then sat cross-legged on the floor at Bethany's feet with a pile of clean linen dish cloths next to him.

As Bethany was now squatting, D'Arcy hoisted her gown up and prepared to deliver a child. He was in full professional doctor mode.

Bethany was in such pain that she didn't care who saw what. "Rudi, don't drop me. My legs are going to give way."

D'Arcy said, "This will hurt, Bethany. Scream if you wish. Most women do. Let Rudi give you his strength; rest against him and relax when you can. Don't fight the pain. Breathe through it. Mouth open and breathe deeply."

She nodded.

D'Arcy looked up at the white face of the new fiancé and chuckled. "Just don't pass out, Rudi. She needs you more now than ever before."

Rudi nodded and whispered encouraging words in Bethany's ear. "I'll pray you through this, Bethan. We can do this together."

Bethany nodded. "I can't do this without you beside me, Rudi." She took three deep breaths and said, "D'Arcy, I need to push."

With that, she groaned and pushed.

D'Arcy said, "The head is out; another big push, my dear."

It took two more groans and pushes before Bethany felt a big whoosh between her legs, then relief.

D'Arcy held the child aloft and smacked it.

The cry of a newborn infant broke the silence in the cabin.

D'Arcy grinned. "You have a son, Bethany."

The three watched as the child turned from a limp grey to a healthy, squirming pink.

The cord was still attached to Bethany, pumping life-giving blood into the baby.

When the cord finally lay flat in D'Arcy's hands, he tied a string around it and cut it. He reached out and grabbed a clean towel from the pile the captain had supplied and swaddled the newborn baby in it. Rather than hand the baby to his mother, he said, "Stand up and give your legs a rest. There is more to come, and this bit really hurts."

Bethany was horrified. "It hurts more than that? Blooming Eve! God told her she would need to travail in pain to give birth. Now I understand what that meant."

D'Arcy chuckled. He'd heard many comments after a birth. That was the first time for that particular one.

Rudi stood her up, and then D'Arcy handed Bethany her son. Rudi still had his arms around her, ensuring her legs did not give way. He pulled her back against his chest. "What are you going to name him, Bethan? I wondered if you wish to call him Andrew?"

Bethany pulled back the towel, partially covering her son's face. "Would you mind? Andrew and I always wanted to name a son after him, but we were going to use it as a middle name, so he would have his own identity. However, with Andrew gone, he was Andrew James, so I think that would be nice to name him after his father, but I would like to add Sydney for where he was born."

Rudi's hands were still around Bethany, resting on her stomach. He felt a movement similar to the one Bethany had let him feel when she let him feel a kick. His eyes flew to the doctor's face. "D'Arcy, give me your hand." He placed his friend's hand on her stomach. "Does the afterbirth move?"

D'Arcy shook his head. "Bethany, give Andy to Rudi and let me check your stomach."

Rudi helped her sit and then took the child from her. She lay back on the couch, and D'Arcy carefully felt her stomach.

D'Arcy prodded and poked, and his fingers pushed into the side of her tummy. "Bethany, Rudi is correct." He took a deep breath and said, "My dear, you have another baby in here. It appears that you are having twins. I'm sorry I did not pick this up earlier."

The newly engaged couple gasped.

Rudi then chuckled. "It looks like the story of Job has happened again. God has given me not only you, but a ready-made family as well."

Bethany was weeping. "Twins? How am I going to cope?"

Rudi came to her side. "We will cope, my sweet. We will be an instant family. I hope you have more names picked out."

His smiling face reassured Bethany.

D'Arcy interrupted. "Bethany, if you can stand and walk a bit, then it can help the other baby turn. It's got lots of room now, so it should spin around quickly. You may need to bend over and relax your stomach."

For half an hour, Bethany and Rudi walked around the tiny cabin.

Although the tide was rising, the sloop was still stuck fast. Thankfully, that meant the deck was not rocking or rolling.

D'Arcy said, "Bethany, you will need to feed Andy, and that should get things moving."

Ann had shown her what to do, but having two men with her was embarrassing. Thankfully, the gown she wore had a ribbon tying up the front. She untied this and pulled down her dress. She wasn't wearing a corset as it didn't fit over her stomach.

D'Arcy draped a length of clean linen over her shoulder to cover her breast, then showed her how to let the baby latch on. They turned their backs to give her some privacy.

Andy seemed to know what to do, and he sucked hard.

After five minutes, the pain started again. "Ouch, that hurt!" She put her hand to her stomach. "I can feel the other one moving."

D'Arcy helped Bethany lie down, then felt her stomach and said, "The other baby has turned, so it shouldn't take long now." D'Arcy relieved her of Andy, who had fallen asleep and handed him to Rudi. He said to Bethany, "Doze while you can."

When another contraction hit less than ten minutes later, D'Arcy checked her progress and said, "You're nearly ready again, Bethany."

Twenty minutes later, after a series of close contractions, Rudi lay Andy on the bench between the piles of clean linen. He then stood Bethany before him and wrapped his arms around her, as he had done earlier. She squatted, and three pushes later, Bethany was holding her daughter.

This baby was tiny and needed a smack to breathe.

D'Arcy checked her over and said, "She's small, but she seems healthy." Once freed from her mother, the doctor wrapped her in another clean towel. Andy was still asleep.

Rudi remained holding Bethany. "A pigeon pair, Bethan. What about her name?"

Bethany smiled as he looked at the beautiful little girl she now cradled. "We had chosen Amanda for a girl. It means 'worthy of love' or 'lovable'." Bethany blushed and said, "We were going to do the names alphabetically. The next one would have started with B. Something like Bertram, Boyd, Brian or similar. Maybe I should name her Belinda, but I never liked that, and I don't want two Bethanys in the house."

Rudi chuckled. "Were you planning on twenty-six children? I might need a promotion to afford that many."

The three of them laughed.

D'Arcy said, "Feed Manda, and this will hasten the two afterbirths. They will hurt, Bethany, so I give you fair warning. These are attached to you, so it's a different sort of pain. It's more like a cut as they are attached, but the babies were not. Plus, you have two to deliver."

Bethany nodded. Once again, she covered her breast with a square of linen cloth and fed her newest baby.

Silence reigned for about fifteen minutes as she fed. By then, her second baby had fallen asleep as well, and Bethany wished she could, too. She was exhausted.

The boat began rocking as the tide had risen. Manda stirred and gave a small cry as she was put next to her brother. With the sloop's first movements, the first pain of the afterbirths arrived.

Bethany had cried out with the births, but this was a sound Rudi never wished to hear again. Her scream cut Rudi to the core. All the while, he prayed and whispered encouragement to her.

Manda stirred at the noise and started to cry.

Rudi caressed her cheek, and she settled.

Although they were painful, the two placentas were delivered without difficulty. D'Arcy placed the afterbirths in the bin she had used earlier. He asked, "Will I keep them and bury them on shore, or are you happy for them to go overboard?"

Bethany didn't care. "Throw them over, that's fine."

D'Arcy padded her nether regions with a towel. He settled Bethany to rest while Rudi soothed his soon-to-be stepdaughter.

D'Arcy felt sorry that Andrew would never meet his children, but he took comfort in knowing that his name would live on through them.

The little girl was soon rocked to sleep again, and Rudi placed her beside her brother. He had plenty of experience cradling children, as he had many younger siblings, all of whom had died in the fire.

Bethany relaxed on the bench seat. Rudi covered her with a blanket and ensured she was comfortable.

The three members of the Edwards family were soon asleep.

D'Arcy drew Rudi aside and out of the cabin. He gently closed the door and said, "Well, you mentioned that you needed to prove yourself. I think you just did. You were there for her at her time of greatest need. I know you have some form of faith, as something must have motivated you not to play around as many other men do. You and Lance stand out from the crowd."

Rudi shrugged. He had believed in God, but he did not wish to admit that it was more a belief in a higher power, one he could yell abuse at. He refrained from sowing his seed, unlike Malchus, believing his brother caused enough trouble by doing precisely that with their maids. Now, all that had changed. William's words just made sense. The fact that he prayed when Bethany was in pain spoke volumes. Previously, he would have cursed God for causing her pain.

The doctor looked over at his young friend. "Rudi, I value your friendship, as you are not here to feather your own nest. Many others are out for what they can get. Unlike you, I was here during the Rum Rebellion and found I could not walk an impartial line. I chose the side that would further my career. At least I still care for my fellow men and women, and that saved my neck. Some others here are not that fussy. The new governor sees that in me and trusts me somewhat."

They stayed chatting at the railing. The pair had not even noticed that they were now well off the sandbar.

The sails had been hoisted, as the winds were behind them, and the steam engine was puffing away; they were soon nearly halfway home.

D'Arcy and Rudi remained outside the cabin, on hand in case

Bethany needed them.

She slept on.

As they neared the wharf, D'Arcy explained, "She will bleed for about six weeks. So, do not plan any outings or functions during that time, or even a marriage for that matter, as you would need to delay your wedding night if you do." His startling blue eyes looked deeply into Rudi's face. "Rudi, she will need you more closely now than ever. The loss of her husband will often overwhelm her. Melancholy can eat away from within. Be there for her, but do not push her. Her emotions will be raw." He paused before adding, "Expect that she will withdraw her acceptance of your proposal due to her having twins."

Rudi knew that as well. He nodded, but his heart dropped.

D'Arcy continued. "Watch her. Be understanding. Comfort her, but be aware that she may sometimes push you away. Her emotions will already be in turmoil after the unexpected birth of two babies. Expect tears and laughter; however, consider asking for permission to marry her sooner rather than later. That will give her security, and that is something vital, not just for her, but also so she does not become a target for other lustful men. She will need to settle into a routine quickly. This will give her something to look forward to."

Rudi was somewhat overwhelmed. Less than six hours ago, he mustered the courage to court her. The proposal had not been planned, nor had anything about this relationship. Now, he was to be a stepfather to twins. Thankfully, he was comfortable around babies. He turned to his friend, saying, "To say I am out of my comfort zone is an understatement, but I intend to be whatever she needs." A wonderful feeling washed over him. He smiled, "D'Arcy, I love her. I would do anything for her." He gave a long sigh of contentment.

D'Arcy chuckled softly and replied. "I know you will, my friend. You will be a wonderful husband and father."

Chapter 8 Double Delight

1810

When the ferry finally reached the jetty, William, Ann, and Lance were waiting. The vessel was four hours overdue, and everyone was concerned.

Brenton had arrived at the scheduled time to drive Bethany home, but the small steam sloop didn't come. He parked at the top of the hill so he could see the Cowpers' carriage when it arrived back.

When William said the ferry service had left hours earlier than they had, he went to find Lance.

When the sail of the little ship finally turned the point, all were relieved.

The waiting friends discovered that although only the three passengers departed from Parramatta, new passengers arrived mid-trip.

The crew tied the vessel securely to the berth, and D'Arcy appeared on deck with both babies in his arms. He called William on board and handed him a baby. The other, he carried to Ann and gave his precious bundle to the surprised young minister's wife.

Rudi appeared, carrying Bethany; her arms were wrapped around his neck, and she gazed adoringly at him.

D'Arcy hastened back on board and assisted them down the wobbling gangplank. He said with a grin, "Well, that was an eventful trip. First, we had an engagement, then twins. I won't forget bottoming out at Kissing Point in a hurry, as that's where it all occurred. At least these two didn't scream much." He returned for his medical bag and apologised to the captain for the mess in the cabin.

The captain waved him away with a grin and sent two crewmen to attend to the aftermath of the double delivery.

D'Arcy had mopped up most of the mess with the remaining towels.

Congratulations ensued from all.

Rudi carried Bethany to the carriage, where William, Ann, Lance, and D'Arcy joined the newborns.

Once seated, the babies were introduced to everyone.

Andy and Manda were still asleep, but they were stirring as they needed food.

Ann was due back for Mac's feed and planned to sit with Bethany to ensure that she knew how to latch the babies to her breast properly.

Brenton had precious cargo on board and carefully drove up from the Cockle Bay Wharf at walking pace. He eased the carriage to a halt outside the rectory and waited patiently.

Lance joined Brenton on the driver's bench seat, and they headed back to the stable yard.

Lance said, "Well, that's a thing that I bet the ferrymen won't see repeated too often. Rudi tells me they became engaged just before the babies arrived. That will be a challenge for him."

Brenton nodded. "It will, Lance, for them both. I have twins myself and know the challenges they bring. Feeding them will be the least of their worries. It wouldn't matter so much if they slept at the same time, but they won't." He sighed. He missed his family so much.

Lance said, "Tell me about them, my friend. How many children do you have? I haven't seen you much since we left school."

Brenton was the son of Lance's father's estate steward. They were educated together and remained best friends throughout their boyhood.

Lance enlisted and left for a year. When he returned, he made an offer for a girl, which her father refused. Elise was fifteen, and Mr Price told Lance that she was too young. He returned to duty to wait for her. When he returned home on leave to propose, the Price family had vanished.

Brenton said, "The children? Other than the twins, three more; the eldest, Joey, was ten when I last saw him years ago, and the girls were one when I left." Brenton wished there were some way they could join him. "The middle two boys were five and seven when I last saw them." Lance had not yet offered to write to his brother, and Brenton refused to presume on his friendship.

Lance was one step ahead. "Brent, would they come if we sent the fare? Rudi said you can be assigned to him when he finds a house. If so, would your missus be interested in working with them? Here, married women can still work."

Brenton's face lit up. "Oh, my word, she would. We still write when we can. She's been ironing and cooking for the minister, as he's not married. Our little tackers also usually pull their weight. They do the chores around the home and… Oh, Lance, could that even be a possibility?"

"I can but ask for you, Brent, but I know other spouses have joined their husbands or wives out here." Lance paused and asked more about his home life. "Do you own your own place, or are you renting?"

Brenton slowed the carriage down and let the horses walk. "We had rooms on the estate I worked on. She left there when I was arrested. Carol, that's my wife's name, wrote that she had rooms with my cousin, but I don't know how long they can stay there. I inherited some money, so they should have enough to live on for some time. Can I write to her immediately?"

Lance shrugged. "Sure, why not? We should have thought of this before, Brent. She will probably be given a land grant as a free settler." He paused and looked at this gentle giant of a man. "Your arrest could be a Godsend for you all: a new start and a life where you are a landowner. However, let's get them here first. I'm happy to sponsor her for the fare. I believe it's £10 for the family to join you."

Brenton's weathered face broke into a beaming smile for the first time in a long time. "Lance, you don't know how much this means to me. Carol is the only girl I've ever loved, and it broke my heart daily thinking I'd never see her again." He flicked the reins, and the horses picked up their pace. He sat up a little straighter and was smiling. Even the use of his childhood nickname was music to his ears.

They were soon turning into the government stable yard.

~

Meanwhile, back at the rectory, Rudi carried his new fiancée into her room and settled her on the bed.

Ann then banished him. Ann and Molly tended to her bloodied clothing and, fifteen minutes later, had Bethany in bed, decently clad in her night attire.

While Ann was settling their mother, D'Arcy used the kitchen scales to weigh the babies. Andy was just shy of six pounds, and Manda was a shade over five. She was small, but healthy.

Carrying both infants, D'Arcy entered the bedroom and showed Bethany how to position two pillows and feed both babies at once. Although they were tiny, they were both healthy.

D'Arcy suggested keeping them in a warm, darkened room for at least another month.

The clothing Bethany had for her baby would be too big for these tiny bodies, so all they could do was wrap them warmly in flannel swaddling.

The twins fed and went back to sleep quickly.

Before Bethany slept, she wanted to see Rudi.

Although it was not usual, this situation was not either.

William permitted Rudi to enter her room unchaperoned.

Bethany held out her hand to him.

Rudi came to her side. He realised that she wished to say something. "Yes, my sweet?" His words were questioning, as was his frown.

She patted her bed, and he sat down beside her.

Bethany inhaled deeply, then spoke softly. "Rudi, I feel I have put you in a difficult position. I agreed to marry you, thinking that I was having one baby. Having an instant family thrust upon you is unfair. I am willing to retract."

Though D'Arcy had warned him, Rudi jumped up in horror and blanched. "No, you can't, Bethan! Oh, Bethan, my dearest love, I need you so much. I want you all. I told you I would honour Andrew and ensure the children know all about him; I will hold to that. Please, don't cast me aside on the happiest day of my life. Please, my love." He fell to his knees beside her bed and buried his head in the sheets. His shoulder heaved with his sobs.

She reached out and ran her fingers through his thick, dark locks. "Rudi…"

He blinked as his eyes were filled with tears. Interrupting her, he pleaded. "Bethan, I love you. I will love these tiny mites, too. Just give me a chance. I won't fail you, I promise!"

Bethany was stunned by his passion. "Rudi, it's more of me failing you, my love." She cupped his cheek and noticed it was wet. "Are these for me?" She thumbed away a tear.

Rudi shrugged, nodded and admitted they were. "They are more for the thought of losing you. Please, Bethan, I need you all in my life. You do not understand how knowing you and loving you has changed me so much, and all for the better. I need you to teach me about your faith."

She said, "If you're sure…" She held out her arms to him, and he almost fell into them.

His face lit up. "Sure! I've been sure for weeks, but I thought it was far too soon to approach you. Please marry me. I need you to teach me about God. I need it all, and I need you, all of you. It's like God is restoring the loved ones I lost in the fire."

"Then, yes, because I need you too." She knuckled up his chin with a hooked finger, leaned forward, then kissed him on the lips.

The small peck sent shockwaves of desire shooting through his body. He gathered her into his arms and said against her hair, "Thank you, God! Thank you so very much for bringing her into my life." He breathed deeply, inhaling the scent of violets from her hair. "I love you so much."

She moved away from his embrace slightly.

He thought Bethany was pushing him away, but she drew his face down for their first proper kiss.

Although short, Rudi was in seventh heaven.

Bethany opened her lips and gave him his first lesson on how to kiss properly. Ann walked in without warning and giggled.

They fell apart, guilty of such inappropriate activity.

Ann said, "She's just had two babies, Rudi. There's not much you could get up to anyway. You're already engaged, so it's not as if William would force you to marry her."

Bethany relaxed against her pillows. "I need to sleep anyway. Rudi, come and see me whenever you can, and we'll discuss dates. I think you will need to get permission from the governor, won't you?"

Unabashed, he nodded and grinned. "I shall put a request in for that immediately. The sooner the better." He leaned over and kissed her forehead.

~

By the end of September, the Macquaries had completed their move back into Sydney and settled at the crumbling official residence in town until the extensions in Parramatta were complete. The house in town needed replacement because it had been hastily erected in 1788, but there were more urgent needs than a new governor's second residence. The viceregal family already had a lovely home in Parramatta that John Hunter had built. It was this abode that was being expanded to accommodate additional staff and include official guest rooms.

The roof of the original official residence in Sydney had been re-shingled a few times, so it no longer leaked. They hoped to stay for only a few months.

News of the eventful ferry trip spread quickly through the barracks. The crew had passed on all the juicy gossip.

Rudi's face now more often showed a smile than his previous usual grimace or frown.

~

Two Weeks later

Before Rudi knew it, he found himself at Government House

again.

On the last day of September, Rudi was leaving the rectory after seeing Bethany and the twins when Brenton halted the governor's carriage beside him.

Lachlan dropped the window and said, "Off to anywhere important, Greenwood?"

"No, sir, I'm off duty, so I've just been to see Bethany and the twins." Rudi grinned. They had grown so much in the two weeks since they were born.

Bethany was already up, occupied with teaching the Cowpers' children. They had not yet discussed wedding dates, as he needed to obtain permission to marry. However, the twins' baptism had been arranged for that Sunday. He was to be a godparent to both infants.

Lachlan said, "Good, hop in. I've been meaning to have a chat, and now is as good a time as any."

The carriage dipped as Rudi entered. He nodded to Mark and took a seat beside him.

Lachlan gave him one of his lopsided smiles. He said, "First, congratulations on an eventful engagement. It's not often you get presented with a ready-made family. I suppose that brings me to one of the reasons I have kidnapped you. Your letter of permission to marry is sitting on my desk. Can you come now and collect it? Look after her, laddie. You've both had enough loss in your lives so far."

Rudi sucked in a gasp and frowned. Who had told him?

Lachlan chuckled at his shock. "Don't you think I found out who my officers were before I arrived? However, I failed to mention that I met your brother through John Hunter. Yes, I also know that you have a connection with him. I noted that you made no claim on him when I mentioned him last visit. Let me say I understand why you chose to sail halfway around the world rather than accept a single groat from your remaining sibling. I'm sorry for the loss of the rest of your family."

Rudi realised none of his friends had betrayed his confidence. He released a sigh of relief. "Sir, Malchus and I have always had issues." Rudi almost choked while voicing the understatement. "His name means 'ruler', and I've always said he lauds it over everyone like a king. I don't miss him." He gave the governor an embarrassed look.

Lachlan nodded. "I can understand that. However, you are about to become stepfather to two newborns. You are currently living in the barracks, but women are not allowed to live there. I presume you have thought about that?"

Rudi nodded. "Yes, sir, I'm hunting around for a house, but I may need to build one before we can marry."

Lachlan's brows shot up. "You have brought funds?" He smiled.

Rudi nodded but didn't elaborate. "I have, sir."

The governor liked this young man and noticed a change in him since the picnic, if not earlier. He had become both softer and yet more confident. With a nod of acknowledgement, Lachlan said, "Knowing your next project, I presume you would wish to be at hand. I have a suggestion, but let's discuss this privately."

Brenton was still a convict, and they all knew he could overhear conversations in the carriage.

The three alighted, and Rudi waved to Brenton and young Josh, who was sitting beside the older man. The boy obviously adored his role as a groom and companion to the middle-aged governor.

For Brenton to be driving the carriage meant that Joseph Bigg, Lachlan's usual driver, was sobering up again. No one said anything, but Brenton was often seen at the reins while the governor was in town.

Lachlan made his way indoors with the two captains hard on his heels.

Rudi presumed they had more information about his suggestion.

No sooner had they seated themselves in the office overlooking the town than Robert Fopp, Lachlan's butler, brought in a tea tray. He poured each man a large mug of the strong black brew, handed them around, and departed.

Lachlan took a sip, put it down, and then walked to the window. "While that's cooling, let me update you. However, before I do, Rudi, I wish to ease your worry about what I know about you. None of your friends here has spoken out of turn. Mark and his wife will both confirm that I thoroughly investigated the backgrounds of all my officers. I knew more about them than they knew about each other. They didn't meet until they were in Portsmouth, and they were married in Cape Town, but I already knew where they came from and their history in London. As you were already here, I had to learn more about each and every officer who awaited me and whom I could trust. John Hunter volunteered information about you. You have a champion and an enemy; as I said, I met them together. Your brother was not impressed with the Admiral's endorsement of you."

Mark nodded with a grin. "Cathy's and my accents are the same, as we both grew up in the Rookeries in St Giles, London. So, we both came from the seedy side of London. Young Josh, too."

Rudi gasped. He knew that area as an unsavoury place to walk through, let alone live. He had never been there. Although stunned, he tore his eyes from Mark and turned back to Lachlan. He was astounded but managed to keep his mouth closed.

Lachlan continued. "Because of your contact with John Hunter, I discovered your family died under tragic circumstances, well before you said anything. Through your brother's gift of the gab, I also know your grandmother left you £100. I presume they are the funds you have access to?"

Rudi nodded. He smiled, knowing their grandmother knew he would receive nothing as the second son. "Sir, she knew I would inherit nothing. She rectified that by leaving me £100. She also left the five younger children £20, but when they died in the fire, that money reverted to me, not to Malchus. My brother was livid that he received nothing from her at all." Rudi shrugged with a grimace.

Lachlan smiled and said, "Rudi, after I saw the admiral, I asked him to tell me more about the accident. I have recently received his reply, and more information has been uncovered. Your gardener had been checking everything outside the house after a storm passed. He spoke to a passing patron at the inn who had seen him outside. He must have tripped or fallen, and his oil lamp dropped. That lamp caused the fire. He was the first victim, not the last."

Rudi was on the edge of his seat. "Really, sir? It wasn't an act of God?"

Lachlan shook his head and turned back to the window, looking at the building down the road. His guards outside had moved away, so he said, "Laddie, I know why you came here. That's why I'm trusting you to oversee the new mint works. John Hunter spoke very highly of you, unlike your brother. The admiral's endorsement is enough for me." He turned from the window and looked at Rudi, then said, "Now, to other things. We have a new future for you to plan. Hopefully, you will permit us to help."

Lachlan took his seat at the desk and tested the temperature of his tea. He drank deeply and then explained, "Mark and I visited Windsor and found Henshall. He seems perfect for the role, and while there, I interviewed him unofficially and learned how to punch a hole from the centre of a disk. He informed us that there are two possible methods of achieving this. The first option is a screw press, and the second is a drop hammer press. I have no idea what either of these machines does or how they work, but that is our next step. I have already put out feelers for suitable coins, but so far, nothing is available; however, none of that was unexpected. As you say, annealing may be required at some stage, but that will depend on what coins I can source.

Hopefully, I will be able to find some silver Spanish Reales, and as Henshall said, silver will be easiest to work with. A letter for funds has already been sent. Now we must wait."

Rudi glanced at Mark and noticed the grin on his lips.

Lachlan saw and continued. "What I want to speak to you about today is accommodation. We have investigated the basement you suggested, and I feel it is suitable and secure. However, I need someone who is almost on-site. The new house adjoining the Government Press is vacant. Although George Howe would like to move from his rooms above the factory, I will offer you the large house instead. There is a smaller residence diagonally opposite the surveyor that he can have, rather than needing to move later. It's still better than where he is now, which is in the small flat above the print shop. It will fit his growing family. However, I have also earmarked a large vacant block between his new cottage and James Bloodworth's residence for you. It's large enough to build whatever you want and close to where the mint will be. The land is free, but the materials for the house must be purchased. I can arrange convict labour, as I have crews that can build simple structures, such as a house. However, you will need to join a queue for their use."

Rudi gasped and was about to speak.

Lachlan put his hand up to stop Rudi from interrupting him.

Mark sat beside him, grinning.

Lachlan continued. "With a wife, as she will soon be, and two children already, your need is greater. I need you to be available when we start minting, so I require your presence on-site before we enter production. I do not wish you to be seen entering or exiting the building, so we shall keep the work quiet for as long as possible. The other consideration is that you will need staff. Captain Upcroft mentioned that Brenton Wright has a wife and children at home whom he wishes to reunite with. There would be room for them in the staff quarters at the back of the house and more for indoor maids."

Rudi looked at Mark, then back to the governor. "But sir, I'm a nothing; nothing special at all."

Lachlan chuckled. "Cowper said that you said the same thing to him. Before God, we are all special. You know the bible story about Job?"

Rudi nodded. He had read it again recently.

Lachlan continued after acknowledging that nod. "You also lost everyone and everything you held dear, but you didn't turn to crime; you didn't lose your temper except maybe with yourself. Rudi, you would no more hurt someone or betray me than you would hurt Mrs Edwards. Apparently, you didn't even hurt your obnoxious brother."

Rudi shook his head. Ignoring the comment about his brother, he replied, "I would never harm either of you, sir."

Lachlan smiled and responded. "I know you wouldn't, but laddie, I am surrounded by those here trying to feather their own nests at the expense of everyone else. I'm endeavouring to change that. Lance Upcroft is another I am trying to find a niche for. I shall keep my eyes open for somewhere special for him. The convict assignment roll is his current temporary placement. Eventually, he will be working with you when we source coins. I'm also familiar with his background. I admit I was not aware of his connection with Brenton Wright. School friends, in case you don't know."

Rudi knew, but smiled as he didn't know what else to do. He was overwhelmed that all this had fallen at his feet. Had he taken his life as he planned, none of this would have occurred. Bethan would be put at risk and... He paused in his thoughts and thanked God for Lance's interruption that afternoon and the dinner bell the following day.

Lachlan signed a document and handed it to Rudi. This was their permission to marry. It was not folded, so Rudi read it and smiled. "Thank you, sir. I don't suppose you'd be interested in giving the bride away. William can't do both roles."

Lachlan chuckled. "I'd be delighted. Now we're in town. Mark knows my busy days, so you may discuss the dates with him."

Lachlan opened his desk drawer and pulled out a bunch of six-inch-long keys. "These are for the house. I have kept one set for security. The dwelling is yours from today. You will need to furnish it, but I think Andrew Edwards has some furniture in storage. I shall allocate four girls from the *Canada* for you. They are young and need a safe place fast. They will be given their allocation of convict clothing and a blanket, and I'll include some horsehair mattresses. They can move into the house tonight, as I need to get these young girls out of their current location as quickly as possible. Mrs Edwards should know all about managing staff. Oh, and I will assign a guard to patrol the printer's building and the house until you move in." He turned to Mark. "Mark, can you arrange for the girls and their goods, as well as the Edwards's possessions in storage, to be delivered to the house, as well as a guard?"

Mark made a note and nodded.

Rudi took the iron keys and gazed at them. "Sir, I am beyond words. I deserve none of this."

Lachlan put a caring hand on his shoulder. "None of us does, Rudi; that's what makes it nicer. I grew up poor, and I empathise more with them than with the wealthy. Go and have a look at your new house. Do you need a lift back? I suggest that while only the convict girls are there, you do not take up residence until after you marry."

Rudi shook his head. "Thank you, sir, I won't. You have done more than enough. Far more, sir." He looked at the large iron keys in his hand. One day, he would build a house for Bethan. But for now, he was given one at no cost. He looked up and realised he needed permission to tell her of his new job. "Sir, may I tell Bethan why we're being given this living? She will ask."

Lachlan nodded. "Of course, but ask her not to speak of it. William and Ann already know, as I often run things by him, since he sees and hears things happening on and below ground level. He won't break his vow of confidentiality, but he can provide general information. He fully endorses this project, by the way. So you can talk to them. I asked him not to say anything to you until your house was fully furnished. Please ensure that no one else is listening. Especially the children, as they don't realise the importance of loose lips."

Rudi nodded and left on cloud nine. Diagonally across the road was his new house. He had watched this being built and wondered who would live there. To discover it was for him, no, his family, was astounding. He stood outside the official residence, looking at the lovely two-story home across the road. He would be the governor's closest neighbour. He would start his family here before he built their own house. He felt slightly guilty about arranging for Lachlan to give Bethany away without consulting her, but William would need to perform the ceremony. He pocketed the bunch of keys. He decided to wait until Bethany could accompany him to see their house for the first time. She had not mentioned any furnishings, but he had not mentioned his inheritance either. They had much to discuss. He hoped she would be happy.

As he had no other plans for the day, he walked down the hill again to the rectory. He knew William would be free, and he would first mention the wedding to him as he would perform the service; at least, he hoped he would. He knocked, and Fred opened the door with a chuckle. "You can't keep away, can you, Captain?"

Rudi grinned. "I have good reason to visit often, don't I?'

Fred nodded and said, "Mrs Edwards is still in class, but the reverend is in his office."

Rudi said he'd see William first.

By noon, the men had compiled a list of a dozen possible dates to present to the bride and Mark. Surely, they would find a suitable one.

As the children had finished their lessons for luncheon, he went to see Bethany. He heard a baby cry and footsteps that he recognised overhead. Knowing she would need to feed both babies, he went to help change them before she fed them. Ann would not permit him to stay while Bethany breastfed, so he arranged to speak to her after afternoon tea. He knew how to care for both little ones, as he had often assisted his mother with his younger siblings. Holding the babies was a delight. It was something he was both comfortable and familiar with.

Manda was so tiny that he was frightened to touch her, but Andy reminded him of his youngest brother. Phillip had died in the fire at the age of only three, but Rudi often changed him. He gave Bethany a tip before removing his soiled napkin. She had already caught a golden shower once. A cold, damp cloth on Andy's stomach usually did the trick. Manda never showered anyone, but she was a wiggler.

By the time he left a few hours later, he had a selection of dates and an invitation to return for dinner that evening.

Bethany blushed when he mentioned the early dates, but shook her head and whispered. "Can we make it after the end of October, preferably early November, as my bleeding will have stopped by then?"

Rudi nodded and grinned. D'Arcy had explained to him that she would bleed for six weeks after the birth, but he had not understood that would preclude any intimacy. The fact that she wanted to be that close, if not intimate, with him was a delight. They settled on three dates in early November that would suit them. Hopefully, Lachlan would be available for one of them. He had mentioned another trip scheduled for mid-November, so the early dates would be preferable unless they wished to marry without the governor present. Thankfully, Bethany was delighted that Lachlan wished to give her away.

Dinner that evening was a delight, as usual. Afterwards, Ann and William made themselves scarce while Rudi told Bethany in detail about the meeting. "Dear one, we have a house, but we need to furnish it." He saw her jump.

She clasped his hand and said, "Oh, Rudi, I completely forgot. Andrew sent over our possessions, which was another reason we were coming to town, as we had been told they had arrived. Our things must have been placed in storage somewhere." Her face lit up in excitement. "Most of this furniture is from my parents' house. When they passed away, I inherited it, but we didn't wish to live in that house, so we sold it. A lot of Papa's furniture went with the sale. We used the money from my house to come here, but we kept some of the more sentimental pieces. The big four-post bed was my Mama's bed. Rudi, I'm so sorry. I had completely forgotten about our furniture. I know that Andrew also placed some funds in his bags. I have not even looked through the clothes he wore, as I can't bring myself to do that yet, but the doctor gave me his fob watch and money clip, so I have about ten pounds on me. Andy will get those items, but we can use the cash for whatever we wish. The clothing Andrew wore had more money in the pockets, but I have not yet emptied them. The children will have needs as they grow, and I can purchase whatever they need with that money."

Rudi was thrilled about the furniture for them. Even more to hear that the majority of the inheritance was hers, not Andrew's. He would leave it to her to decide what she wished to purchase for Andrew's children. He was just as content to buy what they needed as long as they were happy and healthy. He wanted Bethan to be happy. If that was what it took, that was fine.

It had not been intentional for her to hide this windfall from him, so he decided to tell her about his inheritance. "Bethan, I'm not wealthy, but I received a small inheritance from my grandmother of £100. However, when my five siblings died, as per my grandmother's stipulation, their money came to me rather than being shared with my elder brother. Sweetheart, I have £200 to build our own house, but I have saved another £25 from my wages."

She fell silent for a while. "Rudi, Andrew left me quite well off. If you had looked in the jewellery box, you would have seen far more than gems. The lower layer contained our funds. There is £300 in there and more in his luggage. So it seems we will be quite comfortable. Andrew intended to buy our farm here with this money, only to discover that land was still being granted rather than sold. However, he found no land suitable except an area behind Government House in Parramatta, and Mr Salter would not sell his dairy to us."

"Did you not wish to live in your parents' home?"

She shook her head.

After a long sigh, she admitted, "It was not a happy home, Rudi. Andrew rescued me. I was the only child of the union, and Papa always blamed Mama for that. Papa died soon after we were married, and Mama moved out the next week. She came to live with us. Andrew managed a large dairy farm, and we lived in a cottage on the premises. Mama was only there for six months when she died. Papa had made her life a living hell, but somehow, she kept me safe. We were not wealthy enough to entail the estate, so I inherited everything. I wanted nothing to do with my childhood memories except my faith and Mama's bed, where she often snuggled me. Her room was all that kept Mama and me from collapsing under Papa's authoritarian rule."

She glanced at Rudi; he reached out and drew her to him. She continued, "I only went back once, and that was to choose which things I wished to keep. All of them were either mine or Mama's. Andrew sold the house, along with everything in it that we didn't want. We even brought the kitchen utensils from home. Mama and I did much of the cooking ourselves as Papa refused to hire more than a couple of maids, a gardener and, of course, his own valet. That horrible man was as mean as Papa, so they suited each other."

She shivered. "Rudi, once we marry, I'm perfectly content for you to take all this money and use it as you wish. I would ask that some be set aside for Amanda's dowry and an equal amount for Andy's needs. Andrew would have wanted that."

Rudi drew her into his arms. "I would have done that anyway, my darling love." Rudi kissed the top of her hair. "My sweet, we shall start our own memories here in this lovely house. If you have any ideas for the design of our new place, let me know. For the moment, we will start our married life in the house the governor wishes us to live in."

Unbeknownst to Bethany, Rudi intended to order more furniture for the rest of the house, but he would see what was in storage before that occurred. He knew there was a ship leaving for Batavia in the next week or so, and another for India soon after.

Chapter 9 A New Beginning

Ann offered Bethany two beautiful, linen, pulled-thread, embroidered baptismal gowns for the twins' Baptism the last week in October. These gowns had been what William's first wife, Hannah, had made for her children. One had been worn for Mac's Baptism a few months earlier, where Lachlan and Elizabeth became Mac's Godparents.

Bethany wanted her babies baptised before she remarried, so they would have Andrew's surname in the register.

Ann already had two baptismal gowns Hannah had made; she had not cut up her wedding gown. She never intended to wear it again, but had brought it from England to cut up for a baby's Baptism gown, unaware William had brought everything of Hannah's.

The offer of the Cowpers' gowns had come about because Bethany was about to cut into her lovely flounced wedding gown when Ann walked into the room. She was aghast at what her friend was about to do. Ann snatched it from her and carried the armful of what looked like lace, downstairs.

Bethany followed, and she looked flustered.

Ann said, "Rudi, Bethany wishes to cut up her first wedding gown, but I think she should wear it again. This creation is far too lovely to hack up."

Rudi fingered the lace. He knew very little about ladies' attire, but could see that this gown was of the finest quality. He watched as Ann held it up. The row upon row of ivory coloured lace fell into place, and he gasped. Rudi made the final decision. He said, "Bethan, I only have my soldier's pay, and it's not huge. That gown is incredible, and I think you should wear it for the wedding rather than chop it up for the babies. No one here will have ever seen the like of the beauty of this dress. Ann says she has two baby's robes they can wear."

Bethany came to his side. "But Rudi, what will people say?"

Rudi chuckled. "I don't care, my dearest. It's none of their business. I wish to state here and now that if you married in a convict's drill gown and calico apron, I would be happy. Why waste money on another frock when you already have a perfectly suitable dress there in Ann's hands? In that outfit, everyone will be unable to tear their eyes from you. Please, dear one. If it still fits, sweetheart, please, feel free to wear it."

Bethany shook her head. "But it's almost white, and I'm now a mother."

He cupped her face in his hands and said, "Tie some pretty ribbon on it, dip it in tea, although I'd rather you didn't do that. I don't care what you wear, my sweet, as long as you turn up."

She giggled and nodded. The loving look on her face made him catch his breath. "Fine! I will wear it, and don't worry, I will be there."

Rudi heaved a long sigh of relief. "Good, as I'll be there really early."

After much discussion with Rudi and Ann, Bethany agreed to wear her exquisite, multi-flounced lace gown from her first wedding.

~

A couple of weeks before the wedding, Lance had arranged for four convicts to move the heavy items out of storage. The house still needed more furniture to fill it, but the storage area held a disassembled large bed, two large wardrobes, two matching tallboy chests of drawers for their room, a valet stand for Rudi's uniform, and a bedroom armchair, amongst other items. Accompanying crates contained numerous kitchen implements, including a complete set of pots and pans, kitchen cutlery, and a canteen of silver table cutlery, plus a crate of household linen. This included soft furnishings and items for a sitting room.

Other crates contained dairy items that were not unpacked. Lachlan had expressed a desire to establish a proper dairy industry one day, so Rudi thought they might leave these items for him to use. They intended to have only one cow for their house if they could find one to buy.

The four convict girls from the *Canada* were a delight. They ranged in age from fourteen to eighteen. The two youngest girls occupied themselves while the work went on inside. All four girls had younger siblings at home, and all had been convicted of theft, mostly for stealing food; however, the eldest one had also stolen money from a gentleman's pocket and was caught.

The girls, in order of age, were Daisy, Ivy, Vera, and May. They unpacked the soft furnishings as fast as the men carried them in. They were told not to touch the various portmanteaus of clothing, as Bethany wished to do that herself. One case contained her own baby clothing, which her mother had made, along with other sentimental items.

Until they married, Bethany could only be at the house while the furnishings were arranged, while Ann and her children were there. They remained until the last wagon load was brought into the house.

The four new maids began unpacking after Bethany pointed out which crates would be used. An upstairs spare room contained crates and trunks that the girls were not to open.

~

The following week, the men reassembled the bed in the master bedroom. Even the feather mattress was in perfect condition. Bethany had been worried it might have gone mouldy, but there were no marks on it.

Ann and Bethany made up the big bed a week before the wedding. They used a set of linen sheets and a patchwork quilt her mother had made for her.

Bethany unpacked two cases of her clothing into one of the vast wardrobes Rudi had purchased locally for their room. The others were placed in two other upstairs bedrooms.

Rudi had returned Andrew's garments from the hospital the day he collected Bethany. She had not even glanced at the draw-string canvas sailcloth bag since he had given it to her. Now, Bethany removed the valuables from Andrew's pockets and from under the false lining of his shoes, then handed the cash to Rudi. She refused to keep these clothes for Andy as his father had died in them. William could give them to someone in need.

Rudi ensured she knew where the money would be kept and told her to use it as she wished. "This is your pin money, love. Buy what you want with it." He would not be an overbearing husband who demanded ownership of everything. That was not his way; at least, it was no longer his way. All thoughts of ending his life were gone. He had too much to live for now.

While Andrew and Bethany travelled around the new settlement farm-hunting, they left most of their personal possessions at the hotel, where they had intended to stay on the fateful day of their accident.

They had slept on the floor of their carriage while they had hunted for a farm. The pillows and blankets had been all they had taken for bedding. All that had been moved to the Cowpers' place when Bethany left the hospital. Rudi and Lance collected it and took it all to their new home. The bulk of Andrew's possessions were now piled up in the spare room to be sorted after the wedding or whenever Bethany felt ready to do that job.

Bethany knew she should go through the two cases of Andrew's clothes, but there was no hurry to do this. She had yet to decide what to do with them.

Eventually, she decided to keep some items for the twins and to give the rest away to the needy at church. Sorting the massive amount of chests would take time. Most of the contents were household items.

~

Only days before the wedding service, ensuring Rudi was close by, Bethany finally went through the bulk of Andrew's clothing. She wanted this job done before they married. She intended to give William the bulk of his attire to give away. However, she decided to give Brenton his oiled, multi-layered overcoat because he didn't have one. He needed it to stay warm and dry while driving in all kinds of weather. This was a top-quality frocked driving coat, and Andrew may not have died if he had been wearing it. He had been her best friend for most of her life, and she missed him. She knew Rudi already owned an overcoat, and it was even better quality than this one. She took a deep sniff of his coat and could still catch the scent of his sandalwood shave soap. He was gone, and she had to start again.

She turned to Rudi, who was watching from the door. "I would give this to you, but I could not stand to see you in it. I hope you don't mind."

Rudi shook his head. He saw her loving action, and his heart sank. Would she ever love him like she had loved Andrew?

She missed the wave of melancholy that washed over him.

He said, "I have one, Bethan. You give it to whomever you wish."

She nodded and replied. "I'd like Brenton to have it. Andrew would have liked it to be put to good use."

~

On the tenth of November, Rudolph Greenwood not only took a wife but also became a stepfather to two adorable, nearly three-month-old babies.

The wedding day arrived as one of those glorious spring days where the sun shone, the birds sang, and there seemed to be little trouble in the colony for once.

Lachlan and Elizabeth stayed in the carriage at the front of the church until the bulk of the congregation had seated themselves. They did not wish to draw attention from the bride and groom.

Ann and Elizabeth both offered to be Bethany's attendants for the ceremony, and Bethany was delighted.

Brenton was to bring her to the church, where Lachlan would meet her outside.

Lance and Rudi were already inside with William.

Rudi's brow was beaded in perspiration from his nerves. Today, he would be able to kiss Bethany as he wished. They had stolen a few quick pecks and even one longer one after she had the babies, but he had not encroached since then. As he waited, he thought back over various recent conversations. He meant his words to D'Arcy that he intended to keep his vows, and that meant before his marriage, too. He would honour her no matter what that entailed. Bethany would need to teach him everything about the act of marriage, as he knew nothing about intimacy between a man and a woman. That was an embarrassing discussion that had occurred only the previous week.

Thankfully, she was forthright enough to say, "Rudi, I had a very happy and fulfilling first marriage. I will also teach you how to make this one the same. I fully intend to enjoy being with you. It's why I wished to wait until we could have a real wedding night." She had blushed.

Today, her words washed over Rudi all over again as he stood in front of the church waiting for his bride. He felt himself flush scarlet at the memory of that loving, but somewhat inappropriate, conversation.

She was thrilled that he knew nothing. She confessed that Andrew had not even kissed her before they had wed. He smiled at her embarrassed confession.

Interrupting his reverie, Lance dug Rudi in the ribs. He said, "Gosh, look! Turn around, Rudi. You need to see her."

Rudi turned and gasped. All his nerves fled as he saw the glow from her almost white gown lighting the entire church as she stood at the entrance of the building. He could not see her face as she was silhouetted against the spring sunshine, but the white gown reflected the light, brightening the interior of the new building. He saw Lachlan take his place behind her just outside the church entrance.

Elizabeth and Ann handed her a posy of native spring flowers and then took their places to precede her down the aisle. Ann started the procession, with the First Lady following her, serving as Matron of

Honour, as was fitting for her position in society.

Rudi's gaze was fixed on Bethany's face. She walked so smoothly that she looked like an ethereal figure floating towards him. An angel, his angel. Rudi was astounded that the viceregal couple had not only assumed the roles but also offered their staff to prepare a wedding luncheon at Government House.

Last week, he was presented with his long-overdue new regimental uniform. His red coat and white trousers of the 102nd regiment had been replaced with the new light red fitted jacket with the gold and white trim that reflected his rank as a third-year captain for the 73rd regiment. He now had two gold epaulettes on his shoulders instead of just one, as he had served for more than three years in his current position. His new regimental colours were yellow, not green. He had not shown Bethany, as it was to be a surprise.

Mark had brought his uniform down to the barracks three days earlier and handed him his official transfer papers that London had now endorsed. He was one of the one hundred soldiers from the 102nd Regiment not to have been returned to England after the rebellion. Some of the regiment left in May and were sent to serve elsewhere, many in Ceylon or India.

Now, he knew why he had been chosen to stay, and it was because of his relationship with John Hunter and his uncle's endorsement. That meant a great deal. However, as he had not been involved in the rebellion, he was given an automatic transfer into the arriving 73rd regiment under the new commander, Lachlan Macquarie. Lachlan had worked his way to the top rather than buying a commission.

The authorities had overlooked Rudi's documentation while dealing with problems in London, so he had never received his new lighter-red officer's uniform or his black trousers.

Mark also wore two gold epaulettes on his red jacket, indicating that his promotion had been approved, as he had previously been entitled to only one. He had transferred regiments before leaving London.

Rudi wondered whether the governor had found Lance a new position, but he had not heard anything. He knew he was still receiving some funds from his father.

As Bethany progressed towards him, he smiled. He saw her gasp in astonishment. His old dark-red coat was gone, as were his uncontrolled temper and hatred of everything. He felt like a new man, washed clean, inside and out. He now regularly wore a smile and was often heard laughing. From today, his life would begin again. He was determined to be everything Bethany needed in a husband and father for her children. She had even caught him humming when they walked with the babies who travelled in a wicker basket on a four-wheeled frame.

Bethany and Lachlan walked down the aisle behind the ladies. Rudi's grey eyes met her mauve ones, and both smiled. She was taking so long to reach his side.

Finally, Lachlan delivered the bride to her groom, took his own wife's arm, and they sat in the front pew.

Ann stood next to Bethany, ready to hold the posy of flowers.

William began the ceremony, but Rudi and Bethany hardly realised they were getting married.

Neither listened carefully, and they were surprised when they were pronounced man and wife so quickly.

The service was soon over, and both knew they were married for better or for worse. Rudi knew his life would be better, and he was determined to make hers good. Would he ever measure up to Andrew, though? Rudi looked down at the beautiful woman beside him.

The small peck he intended to give her was not what Bethany wanted.

For the first time, Rudi kissed his wife as he wished.

She threw herself into his arms and drew his head down for a long, earth-shattering kiss.

Lance's chuckle eventually broke them apart.

Rudi pulled away but said, "I love you, Mrs Greenwood."

Bethany hid her face against his shoulder. She had just kissed him silly in front of his boss, the First Lady and all their friends. She giggled and whispered, "Sorry," but she gave him a big, loving smile.

They signed the register and then led the way out of the church. As the bridal couple emerged, a rousing cheer echoed through the town.

Brenton had snuck into the back pew to watch but was now at the door of Bethany's carriage. There was an old boot tied to the back of the carriage for luck, and to wish the couple fertility and prosperity.

They were to lead the procession up the hill to the official residence for the luncheon. Only a dozen were on the guest list, but word had quickly spread of their nuptials, and many of the town's residents were outside awaiting them. Everyone loved a wedding, and no matter who the bride and groom were, the well-wishers cheered them as Brenton drove them away. Moody Rudi had married the widowed beauty. Everyone was stunned by the change in the previously dour man.

The luncheon was a delight, but Lachlan and Rudi did not extend the proceedings.

Rudi fully intended to carry his wife across the threshold, then directly up the stairs and lock out the world until the babies needed them. Bethany had important lessons she wished to teach him, and he wished to learn them as soon as he could.

~

Their new house had a room perfect for use as a nursery. Bethany currently had both babies top-to-tail in a cane basket.

Rudi was delighted to buy the nursery two cots and other items. However, his first purchase for her as an engagement gift was a pushcart so they could walk with the babies in the cane basket.

This was a very unusual engagement present, and Bethany had chuckled delightfully. He had also bought her a lovely sapphire ring along with a wedding gold band.

Because her hands had swollen, Bethany removed her first wedding ring before the twins were born and had stowed it in her jewellery box. Amanda would inherit this when old enough.

As a wedding gift, Rudi purchased two low-armed rocking chairs for Bethany: one was upholstered for their nursery, and the other was wooden for the elevated covered back verandah outside the babies' room.

Bethany was delighted when she saw them the day before.

The week the maids moved into the house, Bethany asked the four new girls to sew curtains from a bolt of fabric Rudi had purchased.

They could all sew, which gave them something to do while awaiting the new family's move. Rudi chose a thick, royal-blue gaberdine for the babies' room because it kept out light, cold, and heat. As this and their bedroom looked out onto the government printers' building, he also purchased a bolt of white cheesecloth to use instead of lace or voile curtains for privacy. There was enough fabric to cover all the windows, including those in the girls' rooms. Every window opening was screened with dark-dyed cheesecloth.

By the time of the wedding, even Brenton's quarters had window coverings.

The new house came with oil lamps suspended from the ceiling that could be lowered for lighting. Each elevated lamp lit up the entire room. However, the whale oil smelled terrible, but that was all they could buy.

They often used cheap, but dimmer, tallow-dipped rush-wick candles instead and placed them in the spare glass chimneys from the lamps.

Rudi had ten days off for a honeymoon, and during that time, Brenton moved into the quarters above the stables.

Lance had finally revealed to Rudi that he had known Brenton since they were boys. They lost touch when Lance enlisted, and Brenton married soon afterwards and moved away.

When Lance found his childhood friend here, he did what he could to protect him. Driving the wagon for the chain gang was the best and safest job he could find for his friend. He still had to fill the potholes, but it was preferable to breaking rocks or working in coal or brick pits. Transferring Brent to the stables had been wonderful.

~

The newlyweds spent the ten days of blissful marriage settling into their new abode. The twins were now in a routine of sorts. The cots were pushed together so they could hold hands through the slats.

Brenton was delighted with his new digs.

Two days before Rudi needed to return to work, he helped Brenton and Lance move George Howe into his new house.

The printer was delighted that Lachlan had signed over the freestanding cottage to George. He was now a landowner. Something he never dreamed possible. Admittedly, the block was tiny, but it was his. The widower, George, and his common-law wife, Elizabeth Easton, along with their five children and George's sons from his previous marriage, shared the cottage.

Shortly before the move, George postponed the evening classes he ran. He usually held these classes from half past five to half past eight a few nights a week. He put his education to work making some money for his family. Once they settled, his school would restart.

~

Unbeknownst to Rudi, one more move was yet to occur. Lance was permitted to move into George's old flat above the printer.

That done, he received orders for his new position. Lance was delighted. He had his own room and space. He would eat his meals next door at the Greenwoods' house with Brenton.

The captain of the *Canada* brought word that another convict transport would arrive before Christmas. Lance had been permanently promoted to oversee the processing of new convicts rather than filling in for Geoffrey Gilmore. Their friend, Geoff, had his promotion to major finalised. It had taken years for the documentation and uniform to come from England. Lance now had a small office near the docks. He was to work under Geoffrey's watchful eye. His first job was to find placements for the hundred women on the *Canada*. Lachlan was making room for whoever commanded the new group of convicts. Hopefully, whenever the next ship came, it would bring more of Lachlan's regiment.

~

On December 16th 1811, a sail was sighted. All was in readiness for the arrival of the new officer in charge of this load of felons, whoever it was.

Lachlan was delighted to discover that this ship, the *Indian*, carried the ship's surgeon's wife, Mary Evans, and their children, and they were planning to stay in the colony. However, she did not come alone. She employed a maid who had five children. They, too, were planning to stay.

Unbeknownst to everyone, Brenton's wife had found a way to reunite with her husband at no cost to anyone. Mrs Evans' passage was free, and provision for staff was included in her passage. However, at home, she had none.

Carol Wright heard of Mrs Evan's plight and begged to come with her. Therefore, the Wright family was already on its way before Lance drafted the invitation letter. It would have gone out on this very ship.

Along with these two women, seven of the soldiers' wives accompanied their military husbands. Five more children were among them. Carol and her children willingly cared for all the young ones on the journey.

Lieutenant Richard Lundin was the officer in charge of the twenty-eight privates, one corporal, and one sergeant who oversaw the transportation of the two hundred male convicts. Much to his delight, he was allocated Lance's old room at the barracks.

Joseph Bigg had taken Elizabeth Macquarie to visit Ann Cowper for tea in the smaller carriage, so Brenton was on chauffeuring duty for the governor. When Lachlan arrived at the wharf to meet the new arrivals, Brenton drove the big carriage to the dock.

Lachlan and Mark exited the vehicle and walked towards the longboat.

From across the water came a familiar voice for Brenton. "Papa, Papa, we're here. Papa, we all came."

Another young masculine voice called, "Daddy."

A familiar lady's voice met Brenton's ears. "Brent! We've come."

Brenton thought he was hearing things. He froze, then turned toward the convict ship and saw Joey standing on the foredeck, waving with both arms. His family were here. Tears flooded his eyes. He swiped them away and saw his beloved Carol arrive next to his sons. All the familiar faces appeared around them. He sighed with relief. They were all still alive, and they had come to join him.

Lachlan turned to look at his motionless driver. "I gather your family found a way to join you. My long boat can bring them ashore, and you can drive them home and then return for me."

Brenton grinned and nodded. "Thank you, sir. Much appreciated." He wiped away more tears of joy.

Lachlan chuckled. "Upcroft's new housemate may arrive this afternoon, so your household will soon be busy."

Brenton hitched the reins to the rail and moved closer to wait for his family to land. He knew D'Arcy must have already given the all-clear to come aboard, or Lachlan would not have been here yet. That was the usual procedure: medical clearance before the governor's inspection.

Carol and the children soon descended the rope ladder and came ashore. Brenton's heart was thumping so hard that he could hardly breathe. Their luggage could be brought up later.

On stepping foot on the dock, Brenton swept Carol into his arms. He kissed her passionately, ignoring the shocked faces of those watching. Both were weeping, and the children clustered around their parents.

Even twelve-year-old Joey didn't seem to mind his parents' public display of affection. It had been years since he had seen his father, and he had shot up to nearly his father's shoulder.

The twins were now three, and Brenton could no longer tell them apart. They did not remember him, but the excitement was infectious.

The three boys hugged him tightly.

Brenton clung to Carol and kept saying, "I'm so sorry. I'm so very sorry." He felt a firm hand on his shoulder and looked up to see Lance.

The officer grinned at the happy reunion. "Are you going to introduce me to your lovely lady, my friend?"

Lance was on duty but had not yet received the all-clear to board. He had to arrange placements for the newly arrived convicts, but he was not needed for the moment. D'Arcy had sent word to him that the *Indian* carried nearly two hundred male convicts. These were relatively easy to place compared with the women.

Once the introductions were done, Lance left his friend for his reunion. "See you all tonight at dinner."

Brenton nodded. He was still dazed.

With Lance now heading out to the ship, Brenton loaded his family into the carriage and drove them the short distance home. Their large flat was situated above the stables, but was very similar in size to their cottage in England.

An original upstairs tack room had been converted into another bedroom, giving the family three sleeping rooms and a living room. Kitchen facilities were minimal, with only a single hob stove.

Bethany hoped the new arrivals would eat with their family, so they had not installed a kitchen.

Hopefully, Brenton's boys would be willing to help with the vegetable garden for the expanded household.

Lance usually ate with them, as did the four young maids who also served the family.

Bethany hoped to find a cook, but she and the two older girls shared the cooking. She was exhausted as she was still nursing the babies.

Bethany had not long put the quickly growing babies to bed when she heard voices out in the mews at the back of the house. She looked out and saw Brenton kissing a lovely blond-haired woman, and giggling children surrounded them. She realised that his family had arrived unexpectedly.

She called Daisy, the oldest of the maids, to keep an ear out for the twins should they wake, and then she went to meet the newest members of the house. Rather than walk straight up to them, Bethany hung back until one of the children noticed her.

The oldest lad tapped his father on the shoulder, drawing his attention to her presence.

Brenton released his wife and beckoned Bethany. "Mrs Greenwood, this is my wife, Carol, and the children are Joseph, called Joey; Alfred, who is Fred; Herbert, who is Bert; and the twins are Jemima, called Jemma, and Charlotte, called Lottie. I can't tell them apart, so I never know which is which. Carol, this is Mrs Greenwood, and she and her husband, Captain Rudi Greenwood, are friends of Lance."

Bethany welcomed the new family and invited them in for tea as Brenton had to return to the dock.

They had nothing to unpack yet, so they all welcomed tea and the use of a privy.

Bethany said, "I'll make tea. Children, there are oat biscuits in the tin."

Carol was stunned when Bethany put the kettle on the stove and made tea for them all. "Ma'am, do you not have a cook?"

Bethany chuckled. "Not as yet; we manage as best we can. I have four young girls living in the staff rooms; if I had a cook, one of the girls would need to leave. We originally had a couple of convicts in your loft, but we reassigned them so Brenton could move in. Hence, the vegetable garden has gone to seed." She sighed. "I'm so tired after feeding my twins that it's nearly killing me."

Carol gasped. "You have twins, too, ma'am?"

Bethany nodded. "They are nearly four months old, and I'm exhausted. I wouldn't mind if they slept simultaneously, but I get one off to sleep, and the other wakes."

Carol chuckled. "I know that all too well. Our little ones did the same. You would think that identical twins would eat and sleep at the same time." She shook her head.

Bethany smiled. "It's just as well that I love them so much. They are all I have left from my first husband. Rudi and I married only a month ago."

They sipped their tea while the children devoured a pitcher of pink lilli pilli and wild honey cordial.

Carol smiled. "Ma'am, I may have a solution. I was an assistant cook at the big house where Brenton worked. It was how we met. Once we were married, I had to leave. I was wondering what to do with my time when I came, and was planning to find work. For Brent to have a place for us already is wonderful, but I'm not one to sit and twiddle my fingers. The children can tend to the garden as they did at home." She swallowed nervously. "Ma'am, would you permit me to be your cook?"

"Firstly, please call me Bethany." Bethany was delighted. "Really? Would you do that? Lance lives next door, and he joins us for meals, and we're expecting another man to join him soon. Oh, this is truly wonderful."

~

By the time Brenton returned with the governor, Carol and the children had made the beds in their rooms with Bethany's spare linen, and the hob fire was cleaned out and ready to be lit again if necessary, which was unlikely to be soon in this overwhelming heat.

The temperature in the upstairs room was now oppressive, so Carol opened all the windows and louvre coverings and took the children into the big house to prepare a meal.

With so many mouths to feed, she needed to see what the pantry had to offer. She planned to help with cooking that night and insisted that the children do what they could to help. So, Joey took them outside to the neglected vegetable garden and started weeding it with his siblings.

They were told to watch for spiders, snakes, and ticks. Thankfully, it was too dry for leeches.

Carol cast her trained eye around the pantry and noticed how few items there were. She saw a slate and jotted down a list of questions to ask, and wondered what the local markets were like.

Bethany had gone to tend to her children, and their cries drew Jemma and Lottie inside.

They washed their hands and went to meet the babies.

The three-year-old angels instantly fell in love with the two now dark-haired cherubs.

Bethany had just fed them, and she usually needed to stay with them to keep them from screaming the place down. However, the girls' arrival meant they were occupied.

Each older twin gravitated toward a little one, and the four children sat, playing with rattles, until the babies drifted off to sleep on the floor.

Bethany released a sigh of contentment. She flopped back into her chair and smiled.

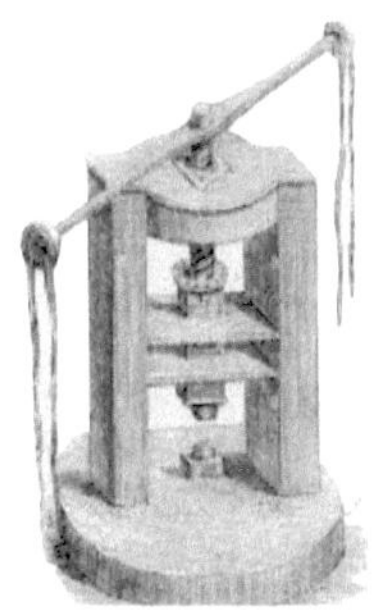

Chapter 10 Holey Possible

Christmas came and went, with the extended household running like a well-oiled capstan. Rudi was delighted to wake each morning with his beloved Bethan snuggled to his side.

Brenton's three boys tended to the vegetable garden as if they were old hands. The twin girls occupied the babies, and the maids worked in the house and stable quarters.

Lance was delighted to see his old friend happily settled, but one face had yet to appear. Although he had been expected to arrive earlier, William Henshall was still out working on the Hawkesbury River area near Windsor. Lachlan and Mark had not mentioned what he was doing, but they decided it was not much use to bring him in until they had something for him to do.

Rudi and Bethany began sketching designs for the new coins. They had various options, and Lachlan would need to approve the final design. Not knowing which large coins they could source, they created designs for each type. Of course, they were aware that Henshall would need to tweak the pattern to fit. They added a few dots to make them harder to copy. Silver darkened with age, so they all knew that some unscrupulous crooks could forge iron versions. Anti-forgery marks were imperative.

They found another forger in town who had been arrested for manslaughter but had been sent out as a felon instead of being hanged. He was not considered trustworthy, so Henshall was still the preferred option. Under the guise of research, Rudi questioned the local man about how he had forged the coins. It turned out that he had made his own coin dies, and he and his brother had a small furnace, from which they produced their coins from scratch from melted-down silverware, which was why they had taken so long to be caught. Their coins had been made from molten metal rather than existing coins, so his information was not as helpful as Rudi had hoped. They had no access to valuable silverware or even a sufficiently high-temperature furnace to melt such metal. As yet, the colony lacked the necessary raw materials to make silver coins, so that was not an option. However, the felon's tongue was loosened when he had a few drinks under his belt, and he freely told Brenton, Rudi and Lance about drop hammers and punched coins instead of using a screw press. They needed to determine what these machines were and which one would be better suited for their project.

It was finally time for William Henshall to be let into the secret. He would move in with Lance and be assigned to work in the family vegetable garden while awaiting the project's start. While he bided his time, he could experiment with machines and methods, not to mention the various coins they now had at their disposal.

Behind the scenes, Lachlan had been writing letters and asking for permission to source approximately £10,000 worth of foreign coins, provided he could find some. His hunt had already begun.

~

William Henshall arrived from the Hawkesbury area shortly before Easter in 1811. He had no idea why his placement had been changed. He was even more surprised when two captains personally escorted him to the governor's office from the convict barge. His previous escort needed to return to Parramatta. Henshall had not been told that he was now to live in town, only that he had been reassigned. He had been issued instructions to clean up before he arrived and had bathed at an overnight stop in Parramatta gaol and wore the new allocation of convict clobber he had been issued.

The meeting at Government House found him seated in a hard, straight-backed chair, surrounded by three intimidating military captains and the governor. He was decidedly uncomfortable, both physically and emotionally.

Lachlan relaxed at his desk while twiddling his fingers. Smiling inwardly, he watched the convict in front of him grow increasingly uncomfortable. After releasing a long sigh, Lachlan smiled. "Well, Henshall, I think today may well be your lucky day. You see, we need your metalwork skills, and by we, I mean the colony. Before I say more, I need you to swear that what we speak of in this room will not leave it. You may only discuss it with these men. As a reward, I will rescind the remainder of your sentence and reunite you with your family out here, should you wish. How do you say?"

William jerked upright. "You would bring my wife and family out here at no expense to me?"

Lachlan nodded.

William was astounded, "…and rescind the last of my time?"

Lachlan nodded again. "If you keep mum about our project, then yes."

William grinned. "Deal, sir, and I don't even know what you are asking me to do. I would do anything to see my family again. Time served is beside the point. I would serve it again if I could have my family back. I can't ever go home, so they would need to relocate here."

Lachlan leaned forward. "Fine, then you know what is at stake. If word of this leaks out, all bets are off, as I know only those in this room and the minister know of our plan. Should word spread, and you, sir, will end up in the Newcastle coal mines on a pick and shovel, unlikely to see the light of day or your family again."

William nodded. He was all ears, and his eyes were as big as saucers.

Lachlan unfolded some of Rudi and Bethany's drawings and placed a Spanish Real on top. "We need money, and I mean currency, and the only way we can do it is to make our own."

William released a long sigh and grinned, then said, "And…"

Lachlan gave one of his elusive smiles. "And, sir, as I said, we…" waving his hand around the others in the room. "…we need your expertise." He glanced at his three officers, who were all nodding. "Are you willing to work with us? I will also throw in a land grant at the end of this project."

William almost jumped out of his seat. "Free land and my family? Absolutely, sirs! I am thrilled to be part of this. May I ask what ideas you have?" He was itching to get his hands on the paperwork the governor had in front of him. He managed to contain his enthusiasm, but his fingers were twitching.

Mark noticed and chuckled. He said, "William, we are right at the beginning. Rudi Greenwood, next to you, had the idea and will oversee the project. Lance Upcroft, to your right, will be on-site with you. It's why they escorted you from the ferry. One loose word out of place and this colony could erupt. That rebellion would sit firmly on your shoulders."

William gasped. He knew the knife-edge the colony sat on. The Rum Rebellion had taken years to come to a head, but it had not fully cleared the air. Rumblings were still occurring, but for the moment, with Macarthur still away, things were quiet.

Lachlan eventually pushed the documents closer and said, "Here, this is what we have thought so far."

The governor finally gave William what he wanted. William pored over the pages while the other four men sat watching nervously.

Lachlan stood and paced the room while the felon read.

When William reached the final page, he sighed.

Lachlan spun around and asked, "Is it doable? Will it work?"

William grinned and picked up the Spanish coin. "I think it will, sir. But can we get these or similar?"

Lachlan sank into his chair. "Ah, yes, well, that's the issue. It may not be these exact coins, but something comparable and in silver."

William scratched his head while thinking. "About this small coin. I can't see how we would punch them neatly. I don't think you could use it unless you heat, re-press and mill the edges. Otherwise, they would have a sharp edge. Can I have a bit of time to think about it?"

Lachlan gave him a reluctant nod.

William looked at the governor and said, "Sir, you have thrown me a corker of an idea, but it's not that straightforward. Newly minted coins are not made of pure metals. To do this, the equipment may have to be quite hefty. And if I am supposed to make them, where will you store them until they are all done? You can't just have them dribbling into circulation. I presume you will have a date in mind?"

Lachlan shook his head. "Not yet, as we have no idea how long it will take to access the needed coins or how long you will need to re-mint them. We don't even know how many we will need or can get." He sighed with frustration. "I don't know if we are talking weeks, months or years."

William flipped over to the pages that Bethany had drawn. These featured the designs. Rather than reply to Lachlan's comment, he asked, "Sir, do you know about annealing?"

Lachlan nodded, then shook his head. "Sort of. I know what it is, but I don't know how it relates to coins. Rudi mentioned something about metal cracking."

William nodded. "Yes, sir, so we'll need a small forge or kiln. For the press, will it be possible to source a selection of larger coins so I can experiment with them before we find a suitable coin to buy? I expect the hole will be the easiest to do, but the dumped bit from the centre will be bent, and it may even buckle the remaining ring. It can be reheated and semi-minted. If so, I can then mill an edge on the outside. Once the centre has been punched out, we can do something similar to the centre of the newly holed disk with a milled cylinder roller."

Lance and Rudi thought they would need a furnace to anneal the small coins, but they had not yet determined how to do that. There was one small area of the wall where a flue could be installed to vent an internal, oven-like forge. It wouldn't need to be big, as the coins would need to be re-stamped while still hot. To cover the flue installation, a fireplace would need to be installed in the printery upstairs.

Lance mentioned their idea, and saw William frown.

William said, "Sirs, until I see the venue, I'm blind to your information. I have no idea how much room I will require or what the facilities are like. Depending on the floor material, I can't determine the size of the machinery we can use. Would it be possible to see the venue at least?"

Lachlan placed his hands on his desk and stood. "I thought you'd never ask. Let's go and see it now. One thing I would like to remind you of is that outside of this room, there is no mention of our plan. Just call it 'the project'."

The three officers accompanied the governor and the convict out through the front door and down the road to the government printing office.

The eclectic group appeared to be heading toward Rudi's house, but after walking along the side of the building, they entered unseen through the back door of the printing room next door. This led into a corridor, and at the end, instead of turning into the printing press.

Lance opened a locked timber door that led to the basement. Before heading down the narrow stairs, he lit two oil lamps, handed one to Lachlan, and held the other high.

The confined room was almost pitch-black, with no uncovered windows, only a paper-covered, barred vent. However, this was necessary for their purposes.

Once they had all negotiated the wooden steps, Lance handed his lamp to William. He needed to look around the room.

William paced out the room, then estimated the ceiling height at about eight feet.

Once he had looked around the vast space, he said, "This will do nicely, sirs. A decent hammer press drill is about seven feet high, and although you can get smaller ones, they would not be adequate."

In his mind's eye, he turned around and placed the various bits of equipment he would need.

Looking at the governor, he said, "Sir, as to storage, there is no vault, and a large safe could not fit through the doorway. That opening would need to be widened anyway to accommodate the drill, and the wooden steps will need to be replaced with stone ones to support the weight of the machinery and blanks. A gently sloping stone ramp would be better."

Lachlan nodded. He assumed the narrow access would require work, and he knew he had to arrange a grill door for this room. He wondered who would make that. An idea came to mind. He knew of a young, free-settler blacksmith who had arrived early last year and thought he would speak with him. Phil Tindale brought his wife and two children. They initially settled in town, and although they still owned the house on Pitt Street, Phil moved his wife to Parramatta, where he built a new forge. He had been asked to make some special hidden hinges for the extension of the government house out there, and Lachlan had seen the quality of the young man's work. It was superb. His young son, Tom, worked with him.

There was another blacksmith at Castlereagh, but he liked Phil, and having a house in town could provide good cover. The man was also a regular at church, so he knew he was a believer.

As this thought occurred, he asked, "William, for the machinery needed, could a blacksmith make what is required, or would we need to purchase a new press? I have a man in mind to make a grill for a security door, and he might be skilled enough to construct a press."

William nodded. "If you're thinking of Phil Tindale out at Parramatta, he's got the required ability, sir. His young lad, Tommy, also has the makings of a skilled craftsman. The dad is a nice chap. I've had him make a plough for the farmer I was assigned to. He made it from my drawing, and it was brilliant. Phil even improved my design. If he can make that, then the press will be simple. He would need some hefty pig iron to make the frame. It would not be pretty, but it would work. Dolly it up by applying a coat of stove blacking to prevent rust; that should do the trick. I will also need high-quality, refined steel to make the coin dies. Once annealed, the hot disk and small coins would need to be struck on both sides by the steel dies, for a total of four dies. They wear out, so I'd need replacements for each. That would entail another press." He fell silent for a while, then said, "Is there somewhere we can go with some light? May I add, sir, I've never done anything like this before, and therefore, my ideas may not work."

Lance suggested they head upstairs to his rooms.

The small sitting room would suit, and Lance could show William his new abode.

The felon had not yet been informed that he would be living on-site. He would soon have a Ticket of Leave, which would allow him the freedom to be at large in town.

These rewards could be rescinded if he didn't toe the line.

Lance led the way out of the dingy basement and up the outside staircase to the residential accommodation on the top floor.

Rudi locked the basement door and followed his friend's path.

Lance opened the flat's door and ushered Lachlan into the sitting room.

Once everyone had arrived, Lachlan said, "Tell him, Lance, and show him his room."

Once inside, Lance said, "William, come with me for a bit."

William obeyed, somewhat nervously.

Lance pointed to a bedroom and said, "That's my room." He kept walking and opened the door of the front bedroom overlooking Hunter Street. "This is your room. We're now housemates, my good fellow, so I'll be on hand to keep an eye on you." His words sounded strict, but he grinned. "Pick up your chin, laddie. The governor has more for you. Come along!"

William gasped. This huge room was lovely. His family could fit if required.

Lance led the way back to the small sitting room and took a seat, saying, "I think he likes it, sir."

Lachlan watched William's face as he entered on Lance's heels. He chuckled. "William, do you understand the trust that we have in you? And yes, we are all aware of your history. I have something else for you, as you will need a little more freedom than you currently have. This is a Ticket of Leave authorising you to be unescorted in the course of your work. Step out of line, and you will forfeit it, be shackled by nightfall, and be forced to walk on a treadmill the following day. One step, one wrong word, and the next riot will be on your head. So stay sober. Better still, no drinking until the project is complete."

William's hand was shaking as he reached out to take the parchment. "Sir, I am overwhelmed and honoured to be given such responsibility. I will do my best to serve you. The rewards are all for my benefit, and it is well beyond my comprehension to disobey any of your instructions. Oh, sir, my tongue is running away with me."

Lachlan grinned. "I might add, you have not asked me how many coins we need. I'm hoping to be able to source about fifty thousand Reales, and if so, you will be busy for some years."

Everyone but Lachlan gasped.

Rudi said, "Sir, will we need that many coins? That would be over one hundred thousand separate coins."

Lachlan nodded. "That's my aim. I need to stop the rum trade, and this new currency is the only way to do that. However, I have no idea if I can even source a quarter of that amount."

He turned to William and said, "I need to ensure you can do the work before I start finding the coins."

William noted that the governor had pocketed the Spanish coin as they left the office. "Sir, may I have another look at the Spanish Real?"

Lachlan dug it out of his vest pocket and passed it over with a flick.

The polished silver coin flashed in the afternoon sun as it crossed the room.

William caught it with a slap between both hands. He wished to test for hardness. "Sir, do you mind if I bite test it? It may, and hopefully will, dent. I need to know how much silver it has in it."

Lachlan motioned for him to continue.

William bit the coin, testing its hardness and inspecting the tiny tooth indentation. He grimaced and said, "Oh, sir, these are hard. Many of these Spanish coins contain gold content. That makes them easy to work with. I think this coin is nearly pure silver. It is much harder than gold. I don't think a screw press will work unless the coins are annealed. That will cause many issues, as I am unable to regulate the heat. I can't have a large fire down there because there are no open windows. Fire needs oxygen to burn, hence the use of bellows. I will need an intake hose from outside to bring in air. A small flue will not be adequate."

Lachlan sighed. "Darn! I will ask Tindale if he will come and talk to you when he's in town next. I'm sure he will have some ideas about how to make this all work. Fine, we will need a chimney, a flue and an air intake of some sort."

William put his hand up like a schoolboy. "Sir, there is one thing I will need, and that is four coin dies. If these…" he shuffled through the sheets, "…these drawings are what you want, then I will need to engrave the dies for both sides of each coin, as each coin will need two dies: a head and a tail. These could take weeks to complete, and I may need a few attempts to get them right. I would also need a milling roller. This would be to finish inside the hole and the edge of the small dump." He flipped over the coin and checked the design. He looked at the governor nervously. "Sir, I am a metal plater and cutler, not a professional minter. I will do my best, and if I can work with Phil Tindale, we should be able to work out something."

Lachlan nodded. "Fine; in the meantime, do what you can on

designs. These may be too intricate. Run them by me before you start the dies. Modify them if you must, but keep to something similar. Until this project starts, you are to work next door in the Greenwoods' vegetable garden with the children there. You will eat with them, so the more food you grow, the better you eat. You will no longer get convict rations since you have your Ticket. You are also to lay off the grog completely. Drinking loosens the lips, and drunks speak out of turn."

William gave a bow of agreement in response.

With a sigh, Lachlan stood. He didn't trust this man at all. "Remember, one loose word, and you're back in Windsor or moved to Newcastle, and your Ticket will be torn up forever. You will serve your term of confinement in the harshest possible way I can find. All the other offers will be rescinded. If your family is already here by then, I shall forbid you to see them." He turned to look at Mark, "We have other appointments, I believe? We had best leave."

~

It took Phil Tindale a month to arrive with his wife and children. Phil had to shut down his small forge while he and his wife took a few days' break at their home in Sydney. He had come to collect some raw material for his blacksmith's forge, but refused to leave his wife and children alone in the western penal town. This was like a mini holiday for the family.

Although only eleven, young Tom was a strapping lad, but he was no match for a villainous escaped convict. While his father checked his new cargo of pig iron for his forge, Tom guarded his mother and sister in their Pitt Street house.

The Tindales had a lovely house in Parramatta, built slightly above his forge, so Phil was always at hand for his family should they need him. Visitors had to pass his smithy workshop to reach the house. However, the Sydney house was larger. If Tom eventually took over the forge, then his sister, Caroline, could inherit the Sydney home. That was for the future, but he wanted to ensure his children were well cared for. Having heard he was invited to meet with the governor and Henshall, Phil put two and two together and realised something was afoot. He knew William Henshall to be a small-time silversmith who made cutlery and the like. For the governor to seek his input as a blacksmith, he narrowed the options to a few ideas. He wondered whether the plan was to make coins. He knew currency was desperately needed. He was one of the smiths who made copper tokens for the inns. But even copper was a rare commodity in the colony, and most of it was hammered into tubing for stills.

Amongst this delivery of iron, Phil discovered a single length of toughened steel that had accidentally been included in his last shipment of raw material. He knew that this special steel was needed to make the dies used in coin production. He cut off a six-inch length of this and smoothed the end in his forge so this could be etched as a test for stamping a coin. Phil wondered if the jeweller in town would sell him some more engraving tips, as they were not something a convict could purchase, but they were often used in his line of work. He smiled at the thought. He nodded to himself as he walked.

Having seen Henshall's plough drawings, Phil knew William was a skilled craftsman who could easily engrave a design on the end of this chunk of metal.

With a slight spring to his step, Phil made his way to the large residence on the hill. He was greeted by the guards who had crossed their muskets to bar his entrance.

One guard demanded, "Who goes there, sir?"

Phil drew himself up and said, "I am Phillip Tindale, blacksmith, and I am here at the governor's request." The guns moved aside.

Another soldier must have been waiting just inside the door as it opened. "Come in, please, Mr Tindale. We have been waiting for you."

The tall officer ushered him inside and closed the door behind him. He then led him a short distance down the hall and knocked on the door. A call of "Enter" was heard, and the officer opened the door and ushered Phil inside the viceregal office. Phil followed the officer and saw the governor with his nose to some paperwork.

The officer said, "Tindale is here, sir."

Lachlan looked up and said, "Wonderful! Mark, please send someone across the road for the other three men." Lachlan turned to the blacksmith and said, "Take a seat, please, Tindale. All shall be revealed shortly. If you don't mind, I shall finish this screed while we are waiting."

Phil sat as instructed and wondered whether his assumptions were correct. He relaxed and looked around him. Something was definitely afoot, and he was certainly not in any trouble. He prayed silently as he looked around the timber-lined office.

A short time later, voices were heard approaching. Mark tapped on the door and opened it. He did not wait for permission to enter.

Phil knew one of the men was the convict William Henshall, but he did not know the other officers. He smiled. If Henshall was involved in the discussions at this stage, then it could only be something vitally important.

Lachlan was about to start discussions when another knock came. He sighed in utter frustration at the interruptions and called again, "Enter."

The butler brought in a fully laden tea tray with two plates of cake and biscuits. He poured a mug of the hot, sweet brew for all six men and then, with a bow, departed.

As soon as the door closed, Lachlan said, "Right, gentlemen, before we get down to business, I shall introduce you all. Henshall, like it or not, you will be Bill for the duration of our discussions as we have another William in our team, although he's not with us today."

Captains Mark, Rudi, and Lance were introduced first, and Phil gave each a polite nod as they were seated. When it came to Henshall, Phil gave him a slight tilt of his head as befitted his convict status. Phil had already met this man, so he knew him. He said, "Hello again, 'Bill'."

William grinned at the familiarity. However, he disliked the name, Bill. On the ship out, all convicts on his vessel had been banned from calling each other by name. As they were shipmates, the term 'mate' became common amongst all convicts. It was a term well known in his part of England, and it seemed that many of the felons on board knew of its usage. At least Bill was a little more personal, and he realised this was to avoid confusion. He knew Phil was a free settler, so he had never used the familiar slang term *mate* for him. Being called Bill was almost as bad. He swallowed a comment that he should not have even thought.

Lachlan opened his desk drawer and pulled out a sheaf of papers and three large coins. "Tindale, I shall bring you up to speed. Rudi Greenwood, sitting on your left, came up with a possible solution to our alcohol problem. We need local coinage, and since we do not have the mineral resources to make our own blanks, we have discussed reusing some larger ones. I know they have done something similar in the West Indies. The five shillings that Governor King assigned to the Spanish Reales' value here make them tempting to steal and take with departing sailors, as their value is higher in other countries. Many of the coins King previously had access to have since been traded with those leaving the colony. Therefore, we need a unique coin that holds no value off our shore."

Phil nodded. He was fully aware that much of the existing coinage departed on the ships with those returning home or with sailors heading to foreign shores. He nodded in understanding, realising that the governor had not finished.

Lachlan continued. "Currently, we have locally made cheap tokens made of iron, tin or occasionally copper, issued by specific inns and stores that are worthless elsewhere." He paused and gave a smile. "I gather you may have had a hand in minting some of those yourself?"

Phil nodded. "It's not legal currency, so I made simple copper or iron disks and imprinted the inn's name on them. Some wished for a picture, so I etched some into the plates." He shrugged. He had checked that he was legally permitted to make these before he started work, but that was some time ago. "I hope that is not a problem?"

Lachlan nodded in understanding and continued. "No, no, that's fine. I'm not worried about that. However, nowadays we also have British coins circulating alongside Dutch guilders and ducats, Indian mohurs and rupees, Portuguese johannas, and, of course, various Spanish coins. As I said, much of this coinage comes and goes in the colony due to trade with visiting merchant ships. That is where you and Henshall come in. Mary Reibey's store deals with most currencies."

Phil glanced at the felon and smiled. His guess was correct. A glint of excitement lit his eyes.

Lachlan saw the glance and smiled. "Tindale, no, I shall call you Phil as the others are all on first names. We've had a few months' head start on you, but we have made very little progress so far. That is why you are here now. You know metal and the smithing of such materials. Bill is knowledgeable about the finer points of metalwork, but we have no trustworthy master minter in the colony who can work on this project. One is a murderer whom I would not trust in a room full of armed soldiers. He's more likely to sell his mother than tell the truth. You two hopefully have the skills we require."

Lachlan looked at Phil's gentle smile. He liked a man who held his questions. He noticed how relaxed the blacksmith was as he sat and how at ease he was. This man oozed tranquillity.

Lachlan continued. "These are the coins we have narrowed it down to. What we hope is that, instead of just defacing an existing coin, as in the West Indies, we punch a small disk from the centre and make this our own unique currency, rather than completely remelting and minting it from scratch. This will also mean we get twice as many coins from the original currency. You are here because Bill can punch the holes out and do the work, but we need a machine to do it. Do you have any suggestions?"

Phil leaned closer and said, "May I…" pointing to the coins.

Lachlan nodded and handed him the three large coins.

Phil knew each well, as they had often passed through his hands in payment for a smithing job. "Sir, I feel that the Spanish Real will be the most suitable for your purposes. These are predominantly silver and should withstand the pressure you will demand without much annealing to punch the centre dump. The melting points are all high except for lead and tin, but they are not suitable metals for working with. People bite-test gold and silver coins because counterfeit coins are often made of lead and coated with a layer of precious metal. Lead is soft and dents easily. Gold does too, but not quite as easily. If you bite hard enough, silver can dimple, but iron and steel do not. Silver is the next coolest metal, melting at about 1700°F; gold melts at 1900°F, and copper melts at a similar temperature. Steel is by far the hottest, but we have no hope of reaching those temperatures in a small internal forge. I can't even do that in Parramatta. You need specialised high-grade coal as fuel, and we have none. It reaches a temperature just below 3000°F, which is needed to soften steel, let alone melt the purified metal. However, you only need to heat the metal to orange to make it malleable. I understand these Reales have different silver percentages depending on the year minted."

Lachlan's brow cocked. This man knew his metals well. He was the correct choice. "So, disregarding those other coins as well as the inn tokens, presuming we can buy some Reales, how would you suggest we proceed?"

Phil turned to Henshall. "Bill, do you have any suggestions? You are more used to fine metals than I am."

William said, "I was thinking of a hammer press rather than a screw press, but that will only remove the centre. He's right about cutting the centre dump. Imprinting the dumped section sufficiently to obliterate the existing patterns requires heat. I can't see how we can get around doing that without annealing them to imprint the small disk and emboss the now-holed large coin with the new value."

Phil nodded. "The heating point for liquifying the silver is 1700, but you do not need to liquify it, only soften it to take a new pattern, which is quite deep. So, I'm thinking a shade over 1100 would do it. If so, a simple hammer press will be sufficient to stamp a single dumped disk when two men work together. To centre it correctly, you would need a special cavity, and you could quickly drop in a coin and press it on both sides while it's hot."

Phil looked at Bill, thinking hard. "You know, I have heard of someone using a homemade hand crank coal forge to soften metal for jewellery work. If you do only a few at once, then that should work perfectly. However, I am not sure where you would find one. If you have a few men working with you, it should give you time to punch six to eight coins before the next lot is hot enough. It would be long, laborious, and very hot work, but I feel that would be the best way to do it without making many errors."

Lachlan sat up and asked, "Could you try to make a press like that for us? Word will spread if we start looking to buy something, even the hammer press. We're doing everything on the quiet for now."

Phil grinned. "I could have a try. It wouldn't be pretty, but it should work. Small bellows could be handmade. I know for a fact that we have no specific bellows makers in the colony, as I had to make my own. I could make a very small set, but I would need high-quality tanned hide, not kangaroo. George Ellis may have something I can use. He even has some tanned African hides. They may work."

Lachlan added, "Do you want to try your hand at making the hammer press, as well? We shall also need some steel dies to punch the design while they are hot."

Phil chuckled. "I'm one step ahead of you, sir. I guessed why I was called in when I heard William Henshall would be here. I brought something with me that I thought he could start on." He dug into his pocket and pulled out the shiny shaft of hardened steel. "I had a thought about etching in the design. The jeweller in town is a friend of mine. I have purchased diamond-tip engraving tools from him because I often engrave items for clients. Even my new stirrups and the like bear my mark. Therefore, no one would be any wiser if I purchased more diamond engraving tools."

Bill gasped. "This is forged steel. I will need this stuff to make the die for each side." He fingered the shiny chunk of metal lovingly. "How did you get this?"

Phil nodded and said, "I have one single length of this metal. It was included by accident in a shipment of pig iron with my last order. I call it a God incident, as I didn't order it and have never been sent any before. This is a sample for Bill to practise on. I can cut more and will set it aside for this project. I presume six-inch lengths are suitable? I can't get my forge hot enough to liquify it, so I thought it would work for a coin die. I presume you have a design in mind?"

Rudi nodded. "Yes, we have agreed on a crown for the centre dump with New South Wales and the year on one side. The reverse will be stamped with fifteen pence. The holey coin will be worth five shillings. It will be stamped in a narrow ring around the hole. Bill has the design. He said something about making a milling wheel, but I'm not sure what that does."

Phil nodded in understanding.

Lachlan smiled at Mark and Lance, who, up until now, had remained quiet. "Upcroft, I can see you have been thinking hard about something. Spit it out, laddie."

Lance shrugged. "I'm just wondering what we will call our new currency. The English have pounds, shillings and pence, but do we want that? It may have that value, but the Indians have rupees, the Dutch have guilders, and so on. What about our new currency?"

Mark chuckled and said, "We've all been calling the big coin a holey coin; what about a 'holey dollar' and the small one a 'dump', as Phil just mentioned? Again, it's what we have called it when we talk about the punched-out section, but is there a reason they can't be pence and shillings?"

Lachlan chuckled and shook his head. "The Holey Dollar and Dump it is then, but with the previously agreed value of fifteen pence and five shillings. They will also be part of the English currency system, but only for our shores. Terra Australis, or as I now call it, Australia, is a different land, so we will be different. Mind you, I dare say the currency will get its own name once it's released into the community. What do you say, gentlemen?"

Rudi frowned. He wondered why the dump was fifteen pence instead of twelve, but he shrugged and nodded. All eventually agreed. None was prepared to argue the point with the governor.

They were all keen to be part of this unique project.

Lachlan's hands almost banged on his desk. He stood and said, "Fine, gentlemen. We have work to do. Bill, start working on the first die once Phil sources the engraving tools for you. Work only in your living quarters, as no one is to know what you are doing. Phil, we will be working closely with you. Most of you should use first names, as you share common names, and overheard conversations will not reveal our project." All nodded.

Lachlan continued. "Phil, can you get on to the drop hammer press as soon as you get home? Then, try making a small hand-crank forge if you can. The bellows will be part of that; see George Ellis about sourcing higher-quality leather. Let me know if you need assistance at the forge. Send me the account for whatever you need. As the mint room is enclosed, that step may need to be done elsewhere until we can install the flue, vent and chimney." He blew his cheeks out and paused before adding, "And while you are all busy, I must find someone to sell me some Spanish pirate treasure. Not a small ask, given that I have no funds to do that. I have no idea how I will pay for them. I intend to submit the account to Admiralty House in London and let them pay rather than the British government. They know I have been repeatedly requesting coinage; still, none has been sent for our use. This will force their hand." Again, everyone nodded. Lachlan said, "Gentlemen, dismissed, but Phil, stay a moment, please."

The other men stood, and Lance, Bill and Rudi departed. Mark remained in his position at the office door and waited for the outer door to close. Lachlan pointed for Phil to be seated again. "Henshall is gaining his freedom to participate, but you are here as a free settler. What recompense can we offer you for your contribution?"

Phil grinned. "Nothing financial, sir; however, pointing a bit more work my way would never go astray."

Mark realised what he meant. He turned to the governor and said, "Sir, when you moved here, the stables out there started shoeing their own horses. They found a farrier to do it, and although they purchased the shoes from Phil, that didn't help much." He turned to the smithy beside him. "I'm guessing there was a fair slump in demand because of that?"

Phil nodded and said, "More than a bit, sir." He sighed sadly. "I have a wife and two young ones to support, and the cash flow has been somewhat restricted of late. My Tom will be an excellent smithy one day, as he can churn out nails and small jobs faster than I can. However, I need to educate him, and I can't afford a tutor. I want our daughter also to be literate, and I don't know of a way that will happen if work doesn't pick up."

Lachlan's face lit up. "George Howe, our government printer, runs a night school here, and Rudi's coachman has three boys who are being educated there. Rudi's wife, Bethany, gives them lessons during the day, and then they go to George for Latin, and so on. If you're interested, your boy could board with the Greenwoods four days a week when classes are held, then go home to you the rest of the time. He can travel with my dispatches."

Phil's face lit up. At home in England, Tom would have been sent to school three years earlier, at age eight. This would mean he was still at home half the week. He said, "I'd like that, sir. I'd like that a lot."

Lachlan replied, "Let me run it by Rudi, and I'll get back to you. I'm out at Parramatta next week. We will come and see if you have any ideas for the challenges I have set for you."

Phil bowed and departed with a spring in his step.

Chapter 11 Rudi's Home

The Greenwood household was chaotic at the best of times, and the arrival of another mouth to feed added to the delightful mayhem of the happy household. The youngest twins were about to turn one.

Andy needed constant supervision because he was a climber. He could crawl over any barrier they erected to contain him. However, he regularly ended up out in the garden with the older boys. Spiders were a constant problem, and he almost picked up a big, black, shiny one.

Thankfully, Joey saw it and jumped on it first. Manda was an angel compared to her adventurous brother. Manda had the five-year-old twins, Jemma and Lottie, to keep her occupied.

Carol and Bethany quickly became firm friends and relished living in the expanded community.

Lance and Bill also joined the household, and young Tom Tindale stayed for four nights a week. As he was twelve, the other boys followed him everywhere. He adored being the pack leader. The vegetable garden was in full production, with everyone helping when available or needed for harvests.

Meal times were a sight to behold, but also full of laughter.

The long table around which the household ate also served as the venue for Bible study. Although the study was directed at the head of the household, Ann Cowper, Bethany, and Carol sat and listened, knitting, while William Cowper and Rudi talked.

Brenton usually joined his friend in the flat instead of staying to listen with Carol and the Greenwoods. However, for the past few weeks, the three men chose to remain in the warmer kitchen.

William started this gathering soon after Rudi and Bethany married. One night a week, the table was cleared after dinner, and the men talked in the sitting room until all the children were asleep. The maids did the dishes while the mothers put the children to bed.

Then the adults would retire to the warm kitchen, and William would open his Bible and answer any questions that had arisen for Rudi during the week.

As they now stayed to keep warm, Bill Henshall, Lance, and Brenton sat through the study. They listened without interrupting.

The men could all leave if they wished, but they remained and sat quietly in the warm room, drinking tea. The conversation was lively and often engaging.

Bethany and Carol knitted, but stayed to listen to William and Rudi talk.

Tonight, Ann joined them. Their son was asleep, with staff monitoring all the children. The four girls were welcome to join the discussion, and usually they did. Soaking in the knowledge about faith.

The minister's words were mainly directed at Rudi, who drank it all in like a thirsty man.

William gave him ideas for putting what he was teaching them into practice in the colony. He asked, "How did one 'Visit me in gaol,' as Jesus instructed, when one lived in a penal colony?" Everyone was essentially living in a prison settlement. They had already fed the hungry, clothed the homeless, and provided shelter to those in need. It was challenging to determine what else they could do. Working on one needy person at a time was all they could handle. Taking on the four young maids was a start for Rudi and Bethany.

Brenton glanced at his friend and shrugged.

Lance cocked an eyebrow in return.

Bill saw and smiled. The discussion was over his head. He didn't understand, nor did he wish to. His eyes dropped to the full mug of hot chocolate he held. This treat was a luxury he had never had before. This drink was even better than ale. His mind focused on what was before him. A smile licked his lips, unnoticed by everyone else in the room.

Rudi observed his friends' subtle actions and explained his lack of knowledge to Lance. "I never went to church willingly as a child, so I knew nothing about God except to blame Him when things went wrong. Our parents and my eldest brother were socialites, but they didn't go so far as to observe the tradition of Sunday worship. When most of my family died in a fire, I turned to the only being I thought was responsible and blamed Him for everything. That, of course, was God. Even the local magistrate called it an 'Act of God'."

Brenton nodded, but Lance frowned. "What changed?"

Rudi continued. "When on the picnic out at Parramatta, on the day the twins were born, everything came to a head."

Lance looked at Rudi and said, "But what happened? You were never religious before. Don't get me wrong. I believe, but it's never been front and centre in my life, but I believe in God. I've noticed a significant difference in you and your attitude since the middle of last year. Brent and I had religion rammed into us at prep school."

Brenton nodded and rolled his eyes. "More than a lifetime's worth."

Bill gasped; neither man had let on to him that they had known each other for so long. His gaze flicked from one man to the other. That explained a lot.

Rudi nodded. He gave a wry smile. "I was faced with looking at things head-on, and I didn't like what I saw. As you know, Lance, I was moody and angry most of the time, and I knew no way to fill the huge void in my life. You know my nickname, Moody Rudi. Well, I could see no way out of the mire my life had become. I had no purpose." He paused, dropped his head, and lowered his voice. "I blamed God for everything bad that happened. I didn't know of any reason why I should remain alive, so I contemplated arranging that. I wondered how fast I could drown if I walked out into the bay. I had even unbuttoned my jacket when you arrived. I don't know why I did that, as the woollen jacket would have made me sink quickly. Two days later, I met Bethan."

Bethany inhaled quickly. He had not mentioned that he was so depressed.

Rudi mouthed, "Sorry," then continued. "Months later, the reverend made me sit and listen. William explained that sin was not God's will, but rather a result of our choices. Those choices have made this world a bad place to live. We all let things slide if we don't wish to become involved. We keep choosing sin and not God's way. I've tried to change my attitude toward things. That, in turn, changed me."

Lance's nose screwed up. "You were that down? I had no idea, Rudi. I'm so sorry that I did not realise how depressed you were."

Rudi said, "I was. My void was more than just a spiritual one, but it's gone. I had this emptiness that alcohol, people, work, duty or food could not fill. I had no idea why I felt so lost. I tried them all, even before the fire broke out. My Uncle John tried to tell me, but I didn't want to listen. Bethan was the one who first showed me what I was missing, and she wouldn't marry me until I faced myself. When I did, what I saw was unpleasant. The relief was like I had stopped banging my head against a stone wall. After William's talk in Parramatta, it was as if the blinding scales had fallen off. A single comment of his made the difference. He said, 'Shift the blame from God to Satan.' I had been punishing myself for surviving and my family dying, but blaming God. I had done everything to myself to cause pain and didn't know how to stop. William called it survivor's guilt." He turned, and his gaze fell on his beloved wife. "I could see in Bethan a light that drew me to her. She didn't blame God for Andrew's death. She somehow glowed, as though she had an inner light. It is not just that she is beautiful, which she certainly is, but her inner goodness shone through. She possessed a strength I couldn't understand, but I desperately wanted it for myself. Yes, it was like she glowed." His eyes remained locked with hers. He saw her smile. "When I lost my family, I fell to bits and turned to the bottle. My Uncle John encouraged me to enlist, but I thought he was shunning me, too. A recent comment from someone who met him made me wonder. When Bethan lost Andrew, who was her security, her beloved husband and her friend, she thanked God she did not lose the children she was carrying. She didn't blame God for the tragedy, as I did. She thanked God that she had not died. She thanked Him that we had found her, not bushrangers or felons who would have stolen everything and worse. She challenged me to look deep into myself, and when I did, all I saw was ugliness and emptiness. I realised that life was not about myself, but others. It was like I was clinging to a sinking boat rather than a life buoy. It took only a few words from William to show me how very wrong I was. From that moment, it was as though the void slowly started filling. I begged God to forgive me. What astounded me was how quickly it happened. It was like floodgates had opened. I had found a firm footing and suddenly, everything finally made sense."

Rudi still gazed lovingly at his wife. "Hours later, when I saw Bethan in such pain while she was having the babies, my first thought was to pray. Only a day earlier, that would never have occurred. Over the following months, we prayed often. Now, every morning we start with a prayer, and every evening we spend time together discussing our faith. Before we married, William and Ann led us in prayer and study; it's why we meet here now. William and I often talked for hours in his office. After Bethan and I married and moved here, we held our study here to avoid disturbing the babies. As we were a majority female household, I couldn't leave her unattended. William has other male staff."

William nodded. "Understanding sin and how it affects us all is vital to finding peace within ourselves. Once we realise that when we feel far from God, it's not Him who has moved but us, we can rectify it. We are all imperfect, and God is still working on us."

Brenton shook his head. "I'm a convicted felon now, sir. Why would God bother with someone like me?"

The minister chuckled. "Brenton, we are all sinners. Your supposed crime is recorded in a book. That does not make us holier than thou. That's what Rudi meant. We all have a God-size void in our lives that only God can fill."

Bill Henshall grunted. "Huh? How?"

William took a deep breath, releasing it as he spoke. "Okay, I'll start from the beginning as I did with Rudi. Do you all agree that God created the heavens, Earth and all we can see?"

The women's and Rudi's heads nodded immediately.

Lance, Brenton, and Bill all shrugged but nodded reluctantly.

Lance said, "We are told so, but we have no proof."

William chuckled and said, "We are sitting around a rush-wick candle. Wave your hand near it and make the flame move."

Lance did and frowned. "And…"

William smiled and asked him, "Did you see the air that moved the flame?"

Lance shook his head. "No, sir!"

William continued, "But you know it moved; you saw it happen. God is like that. We can't see the air we breathe, but we know it's there, or we would be dead. We can't see the wind, but it blows the trees and grasses, and we see the damage it can cause when it's too strong. We don't know what causes the wind to move or why it stops, but we acknowledge that something unseen drives these events. God created that power, and Jesus demonstrated His power when He calmed the storm on the Sea of Galilee. Jesus *is* God. He didn't make the storm; he stopped it. He didn't cause sickness; he healed it. Our disobedience brought death, but Jesus brought the dead back to life."

All were in agreement this time. His logic made sense.

William gave a single nod. "Fine, we'll start with presuming God does exist, as if He doesn't; some great being is responsible for the balance of everything, the bible says that is God. The world would be even more chaotic without God's ordering hand, and in a way, that is what happened. We see that things have changed from God's perfection. That is, and was, caused by sin. It was not just our sin but sin in general. Sin destroyed the perfect world God made. Sin put everything out of balance. No floods, fires, famines, sickness, death, earthquakes, or storms existed before Adam and Eve sinned. There was no theft, murder, or other crimes because that was not how God made us. After that first sin, when Lucifer, who tricked and tempted Eve to eat the fruit from the forbidden Tree of Knowledge, we have been cut off from close access to God. Since then…" He paused, looked around at the men's confused faces, and said, "Think of it this way. Sin, Judgement, and Grace, then repeat time and time again over millennia. We are all descendants of Adam and Eve. Each of us has fallen victim to a temptation of some sort. Theft, lies, immoral thoughts or actions, cruelty to our fellow man or woman. All sorts of things are sins. Bethany and Carol came because of their husbands. Bill and Brenton came as convicts, Rudi came out of anger, or escape, and I don't know about Lance, but Ann and I felt called to be here, but I am not sinless, and neither is my beloved Ann. None of us is, even if we claim to be innocent of the crimes we are accused of. There is not one sinless person in existence, let alone here in a penal colony. Not even the governor. No matter where we are in the world, we are all still sinners. I might add that every one of us will need to stand before God on Judgement Day and answer for every word, deed or action we did or didn't do, including the king and the governor. The Exclusives who cause so much strife in this penal settlement must answer for their sins. This is recorded in various places. Matthew chapter 12 verse 36 states, '*But I say unto you, That every idle word that men shall speak, they shall give account thereof in the day of judgement*.'"

Bill, Lance, and Brenton shuffled their feet uncomfortably.

William sighed again and said, "That's what the instruction to 'visit me in gaol' means. That is a way we can all help our fellow man or woman. They are our neighbours, all the people here: black, white, convict and free, rich and poor, male and female."

Lance said, "I'm here as this is where I was ordered to go when I enlisted." He shrugged.

William smiled as the soldier had missed the point. "Fine, but do you seek out the weak and abuse them or try to place them safely? You now assign convicts. Do you send the young and scared ones to bullies or put them on harsh assignments?"

Lance's head shook, but he frowned.

William continued, "Do you thrash the convict men on the chain gangs to within an inch of their lives or give them a lift on the wagon so they are not too tired to do the work required?"

Lance shook his head again, then nodded in agreement and smiled. "I try to ease their lot in life, sir."

William nodded. "Have you ever told a small lie? There is a fine line between following orders and dominating, but there is always a way to be nice. Lance, you have a reputation for being kind but also just. I get to speak to the prisoners in the gangs; they always prefer to work under you as you listen and care. Rudi, you're the same. That's what Jesus meant by helping your neighbours. However, that's getting off the topic. Where was I?"

Bethany smiled. "Sin, judgement, and grace, William."

The minister nodded and smiled. "Fine, let us return to the Garden of Eden. After Eve gave the forbidden fruit to Adam, both were guilty of disobeying God's only rule. Adam knew what the fruit was and still ate it, knowing that he disobeyed God's only order."

The three new men gasped.

William continued. "Yes, they were given just one rule and broke it. Today, we have hundreds of rules and break many of them every day. God did not *want* to cast them from the garden, but they broke His rule and were banished. That is cause and effect. Cain was born to the banished couple as a result of sin. We don't hear of them much after that, except that they bore more children. Sin was already in each child that was born. Cain killed his brother Abel. Generations later, Abraham didn't trust God enough and slept with Sarai's handmaid, Hagar, and she had a son, but that's not what God promised him. David sinned with Bathsheba; Noah sinned by getting drunk; Lot sinned in Sodom; Moses murdered, fled, and then claimed God's miracles as his; and many others did something wrong. All those who came after them sinned, as do we. We all sin; that's a fact! Only one man was perfect. That is Jesus. From the king right down to the youngest convict, we all need to repent, and God will forgive us. But we are not banished from God, as back in the Garden of Eden, He promised us a way back to Him. We also have many examples in the Bible of people who repented and had their lives completely changed. Jonah comes to mind. Two more examples are in Jesus' bloodline. Ruth left her people and eventually married Boaz; they were the ancestors of King David. She was a foreigner. She slept at Boaz's feet before they were wed. Even back then, she should not have done that."

The ladies gasped. They knew the consequence of such an act would thoroughly compromise her.

William nodded at their astonishment, then continued. "And then there is Rahab from Jericho. She was a prostitute, and she was also in Jesus' bloodline. There are others, too. As I said, David slept with Bathsheba, who was married to another man, and then David had him killed. He was later forgiven after repenting. If these women and David can have their sins wiped clean, then so can we. It's that same sin, judgement, and grace thing over and over and over through time. 'Man sins, God judges us and then He forgives us'. God gave us a way back into fellowship with Him."

Carol's needles stopped clicking. "That's through Jesus, isn't it? I recall that you mentioned it to us last week. I know that Jesus is God's son, and His death wiped away our sins and unlocked the door to God. I have always believed in God but never understood how it all fitted together."

William nodded. "Jesus's death was only part of it. We all still die an earthly death, but Jesus rose again, defeating that. He came back to life through His resurrection, conquering death. But by doing so, He defeated Satan once and for all. Jesus's resurrection smashed the locked barrier between God and mankind. Satan doesn't realise he has already lost that final battle."

Bill frowned. "So if we are sorry, why are we not free?"

William chuckled. "Ahh! Cause and effect. We each must pay for what we have done and continue to do wrong. They are the consequences of our choices. Those same consequences of sin have also separated us, humans, into tribes and now races. In the Old Testament, following the story of Noah, the people were instructed to repopulate the world. They didn't. They remained in the one place and tried to reach God by… how?"

Brenton said, "They built the tower of Babel."

William nodded. "They did, but what occurred?"

Bethany paused her knitting and said, "They were struck with many different languages."

William and Ann both nodded.

Ann said, "And to this day, there are people and tribes in the world being discovered whose languages are unintelligible. There are writings in Egypt and even Scotland that cannot be read. Those different language groups drove the people apart and scattered them throughout the world. Even the natives of this land don't all speak the same language. The Aboriginals from the north of the harbour speak differently from the local ones."

There was some discussion about the various European languages for a while.

Rudi then said, "So if they had not disobeyed God back then, we would all still speak the same language?"

William shrugged, but nodded. "That's what the Bible tells us. Honestly, I am unsure of many things, but I trust God, so I do not need to know them. In essence, that is what you can call a red herring."

Rudi grunted. "A coloured fish, sir?"

William chuckled. "Yes, a dried one, in fact. It is used to distract dogs from hunting hares. It's a distraction that is designed to throw you off the scent. Some discussions are like that. For instance, did Creation really take only six days, or six eons? This is similar. Noah's Ark is another; did it happen? They are red herrings. But know this… God loves us! That is a fact. Not only does He love us, but He also wants each of us back in His fold. That's what Jesus' parable of the sheep and the shepherd means. We are each that one sheep that wandered away from the flock. Jesus is our shepherd who will bring us back. One wandering sheep is as valuable to the shepherd as the rest of the flock. Therefore, we must follow Jesus's teachings." William lowered his gaze into his mug and said softly, "Believing alone is not enough."

More gasps echoed around the quiet room.

William shook his head. "No, even Satan believes in God and Jesus, but he will not be saved because he will never repent and ask for forgiveness. He has lived in the presence of God and still rebelled. We can only be saved by believing that Jesus, God's own son, died and rose again and, by doing so, He destroyed eternal death. We must acknowledge our sin, then we must ask God for forgiveness; that is called repentance. Satan will never do that, and therein lies the difference. If we are genuinely repentant, God will forgive us. Jesus died for us so that we might live. His death and resurrection wiped away our sins. Thus, we gain access to Eternal Life again."

Bill asked, "Every sin?"

William nodded. "Yes, Bill, every single sin, but that does not mean there are no consequences. We still must pay for what we have done. Life and the laws of mankind still mean there is cause and effect. However, we must strive to live as Godly a life as possible. As I said, we must all stand before God on our Judgement Day and answer for our sins. Be they forgery, fornication, drunkenness, lust, murder, theft, lying, immorality or any other sin. All are equally sinful for free settlers, convicts and exclusives alike, and we each must repent. Only then will we be forgiven. Churches are full of sinners, but when we meet Jesus, He changes us. As Lance remarked about Rudi's change, it's noticeable."

A wave of sadness washed over Bill. "But, it's so hard."

William nodded. "It is, but God never promised us an easy life. However, God promised to be with us every step of the way. We are never alone, nor ever will be. We only need to ask. Think of it as a door with a handle on the inside only. God knocks, but He can only enter our lives if we open it from the inside. He will never force us to make that decision. That is what Free Will is. We must choose to follow Him. Every decision we make can only have a yes-or-no answer. 'Yes, it's God's way,' or 'No, it is our way.' It is the same Free Will that God gave Adam and Eve so long ago. He has never taken that from us. It's also why each of us is here. Lance could have deserted. Rudi signed up because he wanted to leave England, etcetera. I know for a fact that some of the soldiers and free settlers deserve to be in irons themselves, but they have not been caught. Some of the early military personnel were actually pulled from county lock-ups and paid to guard convicted felons. Men like Brenton did no crime, but he still must serve time because of the lies and sins of others. Life and mankind are not always fair… but God is. Injustices will, and often do, slip by unpunished here on earth, but those people will need to answer for their crimes to God on their day of judgement. That is why we must not judge people for ourselves. We may not like their behaviour, and we often suggest a way for them to change, but we must not judge them."

More gasps circled the room.

A cry from upstairs saw the four girls leave. Two went to tend to the children, and Vera and May went to bed.

Ann nodded.

William shook his head. "More often than not, people judge themselves unknowingly, unaware that they are often worse than those they criticise. Leave their punishment to God. He will do a far better job at it than we." He looked around the room and smiled. "We are all one family. God's family, and we must behave as such. Whether we are wives, convicts, soldiers, or ministers like me, we are made in the image of God. When we mess-up, we are not just harming ourselves, but also others. Our children learn from watching us." His eyes circled the gathering and landed on Lance. "Lance, you are the only one here with no little ones of your own, but you still hold a responsibility to be an example for the convicts and orphans that you are responsible for. Bill, Brenton and Rudi, you are fathers, albeit Rudi, they are Bethany's children, but it is your responsibility to be a good example for them as they grow. If I asked each of you, would you wish your daughter to grow up and marry a chap like you, it would make you think twice, wouldn't it?"

All four men nodded. Each knew the shame and embarrassment of failing their own standards.

Rudi may not have slept around, but for some time after the fire, he had rarely been sober. He also knew that contemplating ending his life was wrong.

William softly said, "Be the man you wish your daughter to marry. Think hard about that."

Rudi thought of his parents and their disappointment with Malchus's behaviour towards his siblings. As he left to enlist, his mother's words to him were, "Be kind to the young ones, son. Set an example for them to follow. Love your brothers and sisters and always look out for them. Should anything happen to us, I feel Malchus will not. Don't doubt your value or run from who you are." He had not stayed to be with his brother; he had fled, leaving him to his own greedy devices. Once again, Rudi felt conflicted. Should he have stayed? He reached out for Bethany's hand and drew her to him as he sat next to her at the table. He whispered, "I promise I will do my best, sweetheart."

Ann gazed lovingly at William.

Bill thought about his wife, and Lance's eyes dropped to his lap. Where was Elise?

Carol caught Brenton's eyes across the table and smiled. She had chased him halfway around the world. They had a much better life here than they ever had at home; plus, she loved the warm climate.

Bill looked at the three couples and sighed. "Well, that comment has given me something to think about. I haven't been a good example for my little ones, and I feel like I've been given a chance to make something of my life. The governor said he'll bring out my family if our project works."

Brenton nodded.

Some time ago, Lachlan had told them about what the household was working towards. The governor called Brenton for an interview a week after Bill arrived. He realised that living in the same house as the others, but not knowing what they were doing, would make things awkward. The women were also brought into the picture. Though the girls were only told the men were working on a special project for the governor. As a driver, Brenton would also be required to collect items, including the chests of coins upon arrival and the machines from Phil Tindale. When the minting started, Brenton was to work with Bill when available.

Brenton was astounded that his life had completely turned around. He would also be granted land as a reward for his silence. As an employed estate manager, his father had no funds to buy land for him. His elder brother would inherit any wealth the family possessed, but there was very little of that. Brenton had always loved horses, so he befriended the viscount's groom and gained skills at the reins as he grew. Becoming a coachman had been a natural progression, but when his boss died, that position would have evaporated anyway. For him to now be involved in such an important project was beyond his wildest dreams. A slow grin settled on his face.

William looked at him and said, "What's so funny, laddie?"

Brenton chuckled. "Nothing really, sir; I was just thinking back over the last few years. I've gone from the coachman for a squire to a felon, and now to be involved in this project. Well, sir, it's only a greater hand that could manoeuvre us all here and set us to work together to rip the stuffing out from under the feet of the group who dare to call themselves 'the Exclusives.' Dare I say I think it's funny?" He looked across to his wife almost guiltily. "Carol, I will try my hardest to be the husband and father the reverend has challenged me to be. I know you have a strong faith, but I will now support you as I have not done before. I am sorry."

Before Carol could reply, the town clock struck nine. Hearing it, William said, "Oh my, it's late. I have a service at seven tomorrow morning." He stood to assist Ann to her feet. "We really must away. Think well on what I have said tonight, chaps. Next time you have a big decision to make, consider the result well." He draped Ann's shawl around her shoulders, grabbed his hat and coat, and they took their leave. Lance and Bill also left without another word. They had much thinking to do.

Carol and Bethany did the dishes and set the porridge to soak overnight. Rudi and Brenton brought in wood for the morning fire. They also drew buckets of water from their tiny new well and refilled the hot-water fountain on the hook above the fire. Another bucket was left outside on the step so everyone could wash without having to draw water. Carol and Brenton departed arm in arm, and the household soon settled down for the evening.

Rudi watched them leave. Life with friends in their extended household was a delight. Bethany smiled at him. Their bedroom was their only totally private area. Rudi was looking forward to retiring there with his bride.

Bethany snuffed the remains of the tallow rush-wick candles.

Rudi was waiting for her at the internal kitchen door with a cheeky smile on his lips. She came to her husband's side and led him out of the warm kitchen and into the quiet sitting room rather than their bedroom upstairs. Standing before the dying fire, she turned to him. "Rudi, all that talk about you being a great father, and well, they are my children, not yours. You are wonderful with them, but they are not of your flesh."

A flash of worry crossed Rudi's face.

She took his hand and placed it on her stomach. "My wonderful, darling Rudi, heart of my heart and my beloved, this one is yours."

Rudi was astounded. This diminutive woman had brought him faith, love, and contentment, but now she was to give him his own blood family. "Truly, my love?"

Bethany nodded.

The knowledge that they were to have a child of their own was overwhelming. Rudi realised that his eyes were burning, his emotions were bubbling over, and tears were trickling down his cheeks. He gave a sob of happiness before he wiped his eyes with the heels of both hands, then drew Bethany into his arms. "I can't believe that we are to be parents." He sobbed against her neck.

She nodded against his shoulder. She felt his tears seep into her gown. After a few moments, she pushed him away a little. "There is more I wish to say to you, and it is for this reason we are here and not in the bedroom. Rudi, I married Andrew because I had known him all my life. He was my best friend from when we were little, and he was kind and generous. As I said before, my home was not conducive to happiness, Andrew proposed, and we fled as soon as we could. Knowing my father's character, our minister married us without my father's permission. We thought he would follow us, but Papa had an apoplectic attack and died when he realised I had run away. I am the cause of his demise."

Rudi gasped. She had never revealed the details of her previous marriage, and he had not wished to probe.

She moved to the settee and held out her hand to Rudi. He followed and took a seat beside her. She said, "I am telling you all this because I want you to know how I loved Andrew. Rudi, yes, he was my husband in every sense, but in reality, he was more like a brother to me. I wanted children, and he was the only means of begetting them. I mourned him, but not in the same way as if I lost you. You, my darling, beloved husband, are the man I always wished to fall in love with and live happily ever after. Yes, I will tell the twins about their father, but it is you whom I love with a great passion. I am so glad I did not know you when Andrew was alive, as I was drawn to you from the moment we met, well, at least when I awoke." She giggled.

Rudi had hardly recovered from the news that he was to be a

father, and now this. "You mean I'm not second best?"

She shook her head. "No, had I not been married to Andrew, you would have been my first choice. He saved me from an undesirable situation at home. My father was a cruel tyrant who beat both my mother and me."

Rudi nodded. She had said that before. He had even seen a few scars on her back that her father had inflicted with his cane.

Bethany said, "With Andrew gone, we had no impediment but time. That is why I pushed you away a little. I was petrified that I would succumb and permit you liberties that I should not even be considering. I had to keep you at arm's length for my own safety. I wanted nothing more than to run away with you. When I found you collapsed outside the Cowper's house, I nearly died myself. I thought I had lost you as well. I sat cradling you as I would have done anything to keep you safe. However, I had to be seen to be mourning a beloved husband for society's sake. When in reality, I felt like I was mourning a brother, while getting to know the man who already held my heart."

Rudi turned to face her.

She shuffled closer to him on the couch, then continued. She placed a loving hand on his cheek as she spoke. "From the moment you visited me in the hospital, my heart was yours. It was why I was so strict with you in the carriage on the way to Ann's place. When you carried me to the carriage, I wished it could have been for hours, not minutes. I did not really need your assistance to alight, but it was the only way I could wrap my arms around your neck and breathe in your heady scent. Rudi, I love you as I have never loved anyone else. This child I carry is a love child. One born of our deep love and not duty. Can you understand the difference? This child will be special."

Rudi nodded and drew her onto his lap. He was far too emotional for words. His heart was whole for the first time in a long, long time. The void was filled entirely.

While holding her close, he whispered, "I truly feel that I am like Job from the Bible. He lost everything, and then it was all replaced: his wealth, animals, and family. I read that only his possessions were duplicated, as his family awaited him in heaven. That means we have about five more after this one, my love." He chuckled.

Bethany groaned but smiled. "You don't have to carry them, Rudi. It hurts, and so does the birth. I hope I won't be stuck on a sandbar this time, though." She lifted her face to his.

They shared a long, loving kiss.

After a while, Bethany said, "Mind you, I managed two the first time."

Rudi drew away a little and said, "I suppose, due to your condition, we can't have intimate relations until after the baby is born?"

Bethany moved provocatively while still sitting on his lap. "Actually, dear heart, I want it more often. I craved it through my last confinement, but Andrew was gone. It's why you were so dangerous for me to be around." She kissed him again. "Much more often, Rudi, so let us go to bed. I'm certainly not tired. Are you?"

"No!" His one-word answer was enough.

Rather than push her from his lap, Rudi swept her into his arms and carried her upstairs.

They had their lives in front of them, and with Bethany's revelation, it would be a wonderful life. Rudi was off duty tomorrow, so he planned a sleep-in for them both.

Sadly, that did not happen.

~

When dawn came, a howling cry came from the twins' room before the dawn chorus by the native birds.

Andy discovered that he could climb out of his cot.

Manda was still smaller than her brother and could not yet manage the feat.

Andy was going to be a holy terror.

By the time Rudi and Bethany had donned their clothes, Andy had toddled to the door and was knocked over when Rudi burst inside the nursery.

The door hit him in the mouth, and his teeth were pushed through his lower lip.

The baby's bloodcurdling scream woke the rest of the household.

Rudi grabbed him and started panicking.

Carol had been in the kitchen stoking the fire. She raced upstairs in her dressing gown and saw the baby boy's state. There was a fair amount of blood, and she saw Bethany's near panic at seeing her baby injured.

Carol took the screaming baby from his arms. She dismayed Rudi by saying, "Sir, you are making things worse." She held the screaming child out to his mother. "Bethany, hold Andy while Rudi gets some ice. The bucket outside is frozen this morning, sir, and it's just what we need."

Carol pulled Andy's lip off his teeth, flicked the baby on the nose, and made him giggle. "Well, young Andy, you certainly know how to wake everyone at once."

Picking up a clean flannel napkin and handing it to Bethany, Carol settled the baby with his mother and drew Rudi downstairs. "Sir, if he sees you panic, then he will panic. It may look bad, but babies bleed a lot and often for little reason. Some ice in his little hand will stop his lip swelling, and by tomorrow, you will hardly realise he even hurt himself."

Rudi was gutted he'd hurt the child. "But it was my fault, Carol. I hit him with the door."

Carol chuckled and said, "And the next time, it could be Bethany, or me, or even Manda's fault. Accidents happen to children, and it's no one's fault. It would not have occurred if he had not climbed out of his bed, so you could say it's his own fault. It is a consequence of his own actions. Never show panic in front of a child, even if it's bad. Your calmness will ease their stress and make the consequences easier to deal with. It's why you see us laugh if one of ours does something. It's not because we don't care, we do; but it's because we love them, and it's how we teach them to cope. We will not always be there to rescue them."

Rudi nodded. He realised he was covered in Andy's blood. "Thanks, Carol. Did Bethan tell you we are having our own later this year?"

Carol nodded. "I picked it last week. She's still feeding the twins, but since they're on solids, the feeds aren't as frequent. She should be due in about November. Just as well we are all on hand to help, as you will have three under two, and that's a handful at any time."

Rudi sank into a kitchen chair. He was overwhelmed at how the morning had started.

Chapter 12 Unexpected Arrival

D'Arcy had monitored Bethany throughout her confinement, and, aside from her swollen feet, all was well. The baby had a strong heartbeat, and everyone, including D'Arcy, expected that she had a couple of weeks to go. D'Arcy checked her last night and gave her the all-clear to go about town, including to church.

Bethany had been having minor spasm-like pains for two days, but D'Arcy wasn't worried about them. Once more, her back ached for those days, and as last time, her feet were severely swollen, but she was nowhere near as large.

On Sunday morning, the expectant parents decided that the short trip to church would be fine, as Bethany had not been experiencing any labour pains and her back was not sore. How wrong the doctor was! In the middle of William's sermon, everyone heard a gasp quickly followed by a groan of agony.

Lachlan and Elizabeth were sitting in front of them, and they turned to see what was wrong. Bethany's look showed that her time was not just nigh; it was here now. The baby was coming, and it was coming fast. Her waters had just broken, and a massive contraction hit at the same time. Rudi scooped her up into his arms, and Ann led the way into the vestry, as this was the closest exit. They didn't make it further.

D'Arcy was a few rows behind them and followed them out. This time, he had no instruments.

Bethany said, "I need to be sick. Rudi, I'm not going to make it home." He handed her a coopered pail used to carry flowers, and she vomited.

D'Arcy saw Rudi was sheet white. He said, "Rudi, we've done this before. You know what to do." He grabbed his arm and squeezed hard. "Lad, I need your help again."

Rudi swallowed, nodded, and gently sat her in William's work armchair. He helped remove her drawers, and these were all they had to wrap the baby in. He turned to the minister's wife and asked, "Ann, can you find a cloth of some sort? Some hot water would be good. It's too far to go home for them." Knowing that Elizabeth Macarthur's house was almost next door to the church, Ann hurried out to find the required items. With the vestry door now closed, William hastened his sermon and intended to dismiss the congregation quickly. The last thing Bethany needed was an audience to the birth pangs she was suffering. Her anguished cries were audible through the heavy, closed door of the vestry.

As Rudi had done last time, he prayed for her through the birth. Whispering encouraging words as she laboured in pain, his prayers now had more depth. She tried hard not to yell too loudly, but failed.

William concluded the service quickly, and Lachlan and Elizabeth sent away all the convicts and those who did not know the couple well. Many refused to leave. Carol, Brenton and the maids had the twins.

Lance and Bill stayed nearby in case they were needed.

Before Ann arrived back with the water, a scream echoed from the vestry. At the sound of this, conversations outside stopped.

They saw Ann returning with a bucket and an armload of linen.

Bethany's cry was followed by another, followed by the soft sound of a new voice. All heaved long sighs of relief. At least the baby was alive. All were now expecting one more cry of pain as the afterbirth passed.

It finally came. The infant Greenwood was born on October 22, 1811. Like its half-siblings, its birth was eventful.

D'Arcy emerged grinning. "Mother and child are both well; a new angel has been born today. Rudi will tell you the name shortly. Brenton, can you please bring a conveyance to the vestry door? I don't care whose it is, but she can't walk home."

Lachlan nodded for their carriage to be used. It was waiting at the hitching rail. Rudi loaded his precious cargo into the luxurious conveyance and walked from the vestry to the waiting crowd. "It's a boy named Benjamin Phillip Gabriel Greenwood, and he will be called Benji. Benjamin means son of my right hand. We added Phillip and Gabriel because of where he was born." He wasn't going to explain that Phillip had been his baby brother's name.

Rudi was congratulated. Then he apologised to William for messing up the vestry and the church. "I must get her home, but thank you, everyone." He hopped into the Macquaries' luxurious carriage.

Ann had lined the carriage seat with towels, and Bethany cradled their newborn son, who was crying.

Brenton pulled up at their home only minutes later. Rudi carried his wife and son into their home. He was on cloud nine.

The first thing Bethany wanted to do was to feed the tiny newcomer. While she did this, Rudi carried the baby basket into their room and gathered flannel napkins and a larger square of flannel to swaddle the baby. He unbuttoned the back of Bethany's gown and left her to slip off her dress and pull on her nightgown. After nearly a year of marriage, he planned to clean her up himself. He filled a bucket with hot water from the fountain on the stove and returned to wash her.

By the time she was clean, the others had returned from church.

Rudi returned to their room and stood watching his son sleep. He had his mother's dark hair, but the little boy had a square chin, just like his. He stroked his cheek, and the tiny child reacted by smiling. Rudi knew it was not an intentional smile but merely a reaction to his touch.

Unlike the last labour, Bethany was not exhausted, as it had been so quick. The household members entered the room one by one and met the new occupant without touching him.

Bethany waited until the last of them left before she beckoned Rudi to her side. "I can't believe that this one came so fast. I told D'Arcy I had back pain for a couple of days and the occasional cramp. He told me it was normal. Then, in church, it all happened at once. Once again, you were there for me to lean on, and I knew I would be okay. Rudi, I need and love you so much." He kicked off his boots, and though still fully dressed in his dress uniform, Rudi lay down beside her and drew her to him. Sleep would become valuable with a new baby to care for; they stole an hour while they could, knowing Carol and the girls would care for the twins.

Their son's soft cry woke Rudi. He kissed his wife long and passionately, then said, "I'll get him." Rudi rose, changed his son, and brought him to his mother for a feed.

While she was busy with Benji, he went to get more warm water so Bethany could wash again. His entry into the kitchen saw him swamped. Unbeknownst to him, Lachlan, Elizabeth, Mark, Cathy, William, and Ann came home after the service. They had all waited patiently, eager to see the baby. This child would probably be the only baby actually born in the church. Adding the name of Phillip after the church and Gabriel as a little angel born in the sacred building caught the imagination of the entire congregation. This child would belong to everyone.

~

Six weeks after Benji's unexpected birth, he returned to the church for his baptism. This was scheduled for the regular morning service. Lance, William, and Ann were asked to be the baby's Godparents. Thankfully, the morning service went without incident.

As the Macquaries were at the service, they were invited to the Greenwoods' house for morning tea. Once there, Lachlan waited until the children had been either put to bed for naps or taken outside by the maids. Bill came in for a mug of tea and was called to join the gathering. Mark and Cathy were given the morning off duty, and Lance and Rudi promised to escort the governor and his lady home.

Lachlan said, "I will update you about our project while we are together. Mark knows, so that's why he's left. I have heard from England, and we have approval. I don't know much more, but our project can proceed with London's blessing. I am in the process of working out payment for the new coinage, but Bill, I need to know how you are faring with the four dies and other items that are needed." He did not mention that he had the full £10,000 that he requested to spend on sourcing the coins. He had also heard a whisper of where to buy them and had already placed the order.

Bill smiled and nodded. "I have all but finished the first efforts with Phil Tindale's steel. I will need a thicker-diameter metal to punch a hole in the Holey Dollar, but the Dump ones are nearly finished. I have no idea how long the steel die will last, but I was hoping to do a test run with some local currency. I may try to get Phil to soften some steel and spread the lip of two chunks to widen it for the larger disk. I'll need to work around that."

Lachlan said, "Has Tindale finished the required machinery?"

Bill shrugged quite rudely. "I still only have a hand-held punch to make test ones, but that's only part of the process. I tried using a cheese press I found at the store, but it didn't work. I can't do thousands of imprints with a hand punch. I need a mechanical device, as Phil suggested. I gather you have not heard from him," he added, "sir" as an afterthought.

Lachlan sighed and shook his head. "Well, we still have time, but I'll see what coinage we can muster up locally. If we know the required pressure, or even if the central disk needs to be reheated for stamping, we must have all that sorted out before the bulk of the cargo arrives. Are the steel lengths suitable for milling the edges of the dump and the centre of the Holey Dollar?" Bill nodded. Lachlan saw and continued. "I expect our consignment to arrive in a single shipment and hope it will include many thousands of coins. We certainly need the coinage here. Yesterday would not have been too soon for the colony."

Silence fell for a while. Lachlan glanced around the room and asked, "Have the built-in iron chests for the storage been completed? We need thick locks or a large safe on either side of the room. One for the new arrivals and two for the completed coins."

Rudi had undertaken this project with Lance, and they were still trying to keep the idea under wraps. "Sir, Lance and I have nearly finished the brick casing of the storage chests, but we can only work after the printer is closed. Phil is making a purpose-built set of padlocks for each chest and has cut the iron sheeting for the inside linings. Only you and I will have the keys."

Lachlan nodded. "Do you need more bricks? I presume these will be externally encased in more iron so a mallet cannot shatter them?"

Rudi smiled. "Yes, sir! The insides will also be lined with iron. That is the only way we could work out how to secure them. As Phil can't weld them on site, they will be bolted together internally using thicker iron angle braces. The entire thing will then have a cast-iron-reinforced wall on the outside."

Bethany joined the group after feeding the baby. Benji was asleep again, but in her arms. Lachlan nodded acknowledgment of her arrival. He released a long sigh. "Sometimes, I wish we already had it done. Bill, I assume it will take about three months to re-mint all the coins."

Bill had just taken a large mouthful of his tea, and the comment directed at him made him choke. The tea sprayed over his lap. The ladies gasped collectively. Bill wiped his lips. "Oh, ladies, sir, everyone, I'm so sorry." He wiped his mouth and said, "Sir, three months? I doubt that I will get many done in that time. Even with the assistance of these three gentlemen, I doubt that we would get it done in under six months, but probably longer; hence, my inappropriate reaction."

Lachlan groaned. "Never mind the tea. Do you mean it will still be about a year until they are all done?"

Bill nodded. "And we don't have the base coins and are yet to perfect their manufacture."

Bethany raised her hand, unsure if she should speak. Elizabeth Macquarie chuckled. "We're not in school, dear. Speak up."

Bethany smiled at her friend and said, "Sir, could they not be released in batches? It will take time to swap the new currency for the old and also get the population used to the new coinage."

Lachlan's brow cocked in surprise. "You mean that instead of a single release date, we should do this in increments?"

Bethany nodded. "I was thinking of three-monthly releases and an initial limit on how much anyone can swap at once. Shopkeepers will need the coins immediately, and if you issue the pay to the soldiers in new currency, it will filter through more quickly."

Lachlan nodded and grinned. "Any other brilliant ideas?"

Bethany blushed. "Well, you will need an official exchange rate chart. We are familiar with the unofficial value of many common coins. However, I suggest that tokens issued by public bars and similar establishments be declared null and void as of a specific date. Using alcohol as currency would also need to be prohibited as of the same date. The tokens were made for local use only, so I suggest you enforce that for a period, then outlaw them completely. I would give everyone three months to convert to the new coinage. However, international traders can continue exchanging currency if they arrive after the deadline. The warehouses and stores can do that. Residents will need a cut-off date or pay a higher exchange rate fee."

It was Lachlan's turn to cough a choke. "You mean… Oh, I love that. The military and the Exclusives are the ones who still trade in local grog." He chuckled. "Rudi, I think your wife is wonderful."

His raucous laugh made everyone smile. Lachlan turned to his beloved wife and said, "Elspeth, she's absolutely *braw*, is she not?"

Elizabeth reached out to her husband and said, "Yes, dear, it is a good idea." Then rolled her eyes at the Scottish word. "Lachlan, Bethany and I discussed this earlier, and I mentioned that we still had a problem with illicit alcohol. Her idea would solve several issues. As some Exclusives do not live in town, they may miss the cut-off date. I suggest a much higher exchange rate for any surrender coinage after the deadline."

Lachlan's toothy, lopsided grin appeared. He nodded. "Any assistance on that front is good." He sighed. "I know there are still smugglers at work, but no matter who I put in charge, they draw a blank. Dennis Scriven is at the girls' orphanage, ostensibly to monitor illicit imports. He's never got anything to report." He shook his head in disgust. He noticed Rudi frown and said, "Laddie, spit it out."

After a glance at Bethany, Rudi sighed. "Sir, the night I was attacked, I mentioned that it was Dennis's voice I heard. If he was supposed to be on duty catching smugglers, mayhap you need to investigate him a little deeper. If grog is still coming in and he's implicated, that could explain much. Especially if he is pleading ignorance of any cargoes."

Lachlan jerked upright. "You mean he could be part of them? Governor Hunter found that his own private scribe, Nathaniel Franklyn, was the front man for the grog trade. I should have thought of that. Easy money is a temptation for a man as corrupt as Scriven. That never occurred to me, but it could well be why he has never got anything to report. I might assign a few more soldiers to watch him and the shipping."

Rudi glanced at Lance. They suspected who Dennis's friends were, but had no firm evidence. He knew the orphanage had once been used to store illicit imported grog, but surely he would not use the cottage in the back yard there again, would he?

Rudi said, "Sir, rumours and innuendo are not good enough. We have discussed the possibility of military involvement, but he has many friends still in the force. He volunteers whenever the regiment is asked for a duty watch. We all know that grog of all sorts is still being brought into the port. The orphanage was used when Governor King was here to store the illicit imports. Some legally comes from Van Diemen's Land, but much of it arrives illegally from many other ports. Whalers bring in some and sell the stuff, but the volume in the inns' retail is far beyond what tariffs are paid. D'Arcy told me of the rise in drunkenness when certain ships arrive, and I figure there must be a connection." Everyone nodded.

A frown creased Lachlan's brow. The drunken state of the residents in town was dire when a ship full of cheap rum and other spirituous liquors arrived. Even the price rise of the stiff tariffs did not stop many thirsty men from abstaining from the mind-numbing brew. No woman was safe once such men got a belly full of the illegal hooch. Wives and convict staff were abused and often needed medical treatment.

Rudi exhaled, then said, "Putting together the various bits of information, some of this grog comes in convict ships from England, but they are few and far between, as we've only had five in the past fifteen months. I'm wondering if most of it comes in with the whalers and passing traders. Even ships arriving with food likely carry some in their cargo. Bethany's idea of making the tokens null and void will stop those who have them from being able to buy directly from the ships, as the only currency they will have left is the new coinage. As it will be obsolete overseas, onshore smugglers will not be able to use it to purchase anything, and ships will not accept it as payment. Once the three-month moratorium ends, may I suggest that you select only one shop to exchange old coinage for the new currency, and keep a record of who receives it? The more it is regulated, the harder it will be for anyone to flout the laws."

Carol, Bethany, Ann, and Elizabeth excused themselves and went to prepare a meal for everyone. Rudi purchased half a hogget for the festive meal, a luxury few of them had ever experienced in the colony. With nearly twenty to feed, the meat was roasted alongside a plethora of homegrown vegetables, including pumpkins, parsnips, and potatoes. For dessert, a dish of apple cobbler was served with a thick, creamy custard. May kept her eyes on the food while the other three maids attended to the children.

Once the ladies had gone, William said, "Sir, I have an idea about your project. I occasionally get a silver Real in the collection box, and although I'm not prepared to outright donate it for destruction or practice, I would be willing to swap it for coins of similar value. If not, please return it to me in the new currency. I need the funds to support my work and feed the hungry." William noticed Lachlan's facial features registered his disdain. "Sir, I know that you supply food for the convicts and those 'on-stores', but once a convict's term is up, they are no longer eligible to receive food. The women, in particular, have little option but to sell the only thing they have: their bodies. This practice, I abhor. Ann and I do what we can for the poor souls, but they are often starving. Meanwhile, the usually drunken soldiers have free access to what they want, and there is nothing for those who cannot find work. Mayhap, that is something else you could consider. The rich free-settlers do not need free food. Nor do the military with their own farms."

Lachlan groaned. He interrupted. "There are so many needs, and I'm only one man." He looked around the room at the eclectic collection of men and smiled. "I have a strange collection of friends: a convict or two, a blacksmith, a minister, and a few trusted soldiers." He chuckled. "As I have not heard a whisper of our project outside our group, I know that word has not yet escaped the confines of our residences. I'm sure D'Arcy would have mentioned something. This is good. William, you were saying something before I rudely interrupted. How many of these Reales do you handle?"

William smiled. "At least one a week, often more if a merchant ship is in. Some whalers are particularly generous if they have had a successful voyage."

Lachlan nodded. "Good, good, then I shall give you ten shillings instead of their value of fifteen shillings, plus I will give you free access to government food for the poor women. That shall alleviate your financial burden. I wish you had told me about the urgent need sooner. I am sheltered from such goings-on in the town. Henry and Mark are sometimes like mother hens. I need a man who can infiltrate the felons and report back to me. Now, back to the problem at hand." Lachlan turned to Bill. "Henshall, try not to destroy too many of these Spanish coins. I understand that silver has a lower melting point. Phil explained everything, but once the holes are punched out of them, they are worthless until we release the new currency. Hence my reluctance to let you keep any duds or mis-strikes."

Bill nodded. "Sir, even one coin would be wonderful to start with. I need to determine the optimal striking force to cut the hole neatly and the pressure required. Then they must be annealed to imprint the value and remove the existing crown. Yes, the dies are done, but until I try them out, they could be destroyed by the first few strikes of my hammer if the metal is too strong. Phil tried his new small hammer press on iron disks, but not with a real coin." He mopped his brow. "Sir, much could go wrong with this, and I'm a cutler, not a master minter. Give me a fork tine any day, and I'm happy, but I've never done anything like this before."

Lachlan chuckled. "Laddie, none of us have. We're all going in blind. You and Phil at least know where the problems could arise; you are both leaps and bounds ahead of us."

Bill nodded. "As long as you realise that I'm way out of my comfort zone with this."

Lachlan nodded. "So, how many coins are you thinking about?"

Bill scratched his head. He had not given any thought to test coins. "I really don't know, sir. Ten at a minimum, twenty or so to get it right. I'm not even sure I can centre them properly at this stage. I need to make some form of block to seat them into." He paused before adding. "There is at least one more machine that we will need. Once the small coin is made, its edge must be milled to prevent clipping. That's adding the little ridges around the outside. This will also smooth out any rough edges from punching, while preventing the coin from being clipped or defaced. We should do this to the inside of the holed coin as well, but that might be too difficult, as it would mean another machine."

The governor turned to his chaplain. "Get us what coins you can, William. Phil should be able to make any required machine, and Bill will test the first few coins. We'll have to work with what we have and make do."

The minister nodded. "I will do my best, sir, and willingly accept the offer of the swap's value. May I visit the stores tomorrow as we have some urgent needs?"

Lachlan waved his hand. "Of course. Don't wait for any coins to come in—access what food or clothing you need from stores. I shall send a note when I return home. Have some food parcels made up, but I strongly suggest that you only make them with the poorer-quality foods and nothing luxurious, or the greedy will be beating a path to your door."

William's chuckle was heard by all. "You don't need to tell me that, sir. I only give them the flour with weevils and the meat past its usable age. They are still appreciative of what they receive. Even the bruised, unsaleable vegetables from the markets are given to me for the orphanage or the poor. They will eat what they are given if they are hungry."

Lachlan frowned. "The orphanage is fully funded. Why do they need more?"

William shrugged and put his hands up in resignation. "No idea, sir, but they are always crying poor, and the little girls look like walking skeletons. We make them clothing in our ladies' group at church, and send around food."

Lachlan looked at Rudi's face, but the young man didn't see, as he was looking at Lance. Lachlan said, "Spit it out, you two. Have you heard something?"

Rudi shook his head. "It is more of a thought than a fact. Sir, if Dennis Scriven is suspected of smuggling, then the money for their goods must come from somewhere. It may explain why the girls in the institution are malnourished. They are often seen running wild, especially on market days, when many stallholders report stolen produce. The funny thing is, it's nearly always immediately edible food that's taken, so they are obviously hungry." He glanced at Lance and continued. "Sir, I willingly admit that I often looked away if I saw one of them taking food. Sometimes, we would even pay the stallholders for pilfered items. Many stalls also give the children bruised food. Sorry, I didn't think to report it, but I realise it is now just another piece of the jigsaw."

Lachlan nodded. "Well, that's a problem for another day. I'll need a bookkeeper to check the orphanages' record-keeping. In the meantime, I'll see Phil on Thursday to check on his progress. I will add another milling machine to the requirements. Young Tom can travel back with us in the coach for this trip. He gets on well with Josh, and they can sit on the top together." The conversation turned to Tom Tindale and his schooling. He was doing exceptionally well, but all he wanted to do was return to the forge and get back to the anvil. It seemed blacksmithing was in his blood.

Chapter 13 Pirate Treasure

Nearly one year later, 1812

Benji was ten months old, and incredibly, he was already walking. He followed the other children around as often as possible. More often than not, he walked to his cane basket and fell asleep while the other children were digging in the garden, playing outside, or eating. Caring for this happy child was easy.

When Bethany fed him, he kept eye contact with her as he took his fill. His tiny fingers would wrap around her thumb, and he would cling tightly.

Rudi adored his son, and through him, his bond with Bethany grew even stronger. She was a wonderful mother, and the reason Rudi worked hard. If Rudi were off duty, he would come into the room while she was feeding and watch the exquisite picture they made. Benji had inherited his mother's violet eyes, but rather than dark hair, he had snowy-blond locks. The shock of dark hair his son was born with had long since fallen out.

Rudi chuckled. His siblings had been similar. They each had fair hair until they turned about seven, when the dark, wavy hair began to appear.

~

One day in early September, Rudi was watching his wife and son when he said, "Bethan, I thought I knew what love was. I loved my family. I adore you and the twins, but then this fellow arrived. This is a whole new level of love. You told me as much, but I never quite understood. He's half you and half me. I can see he has your eyes and my chin; I can see some of my parents' and siblings' characteristics in him. This astounds me as they will never meet." He moved closer, and Benji reached for Rudi's hand. He grasped his father's finger in his chubby digits and held it tightly.

Bethany smiled benignly. "When I held the twins for the first time, my heart was like jelly. They were so tiny I was afraid I would break them. From the first day on the boat, you were a natural with them. I was in awe of how confidently you held Andy." She glanced at him and said, "Rudi, the twins were not of your flesh, but you still love them. This little angel is ours. Bone of our bone and flesh of our flesh."

Without releasing his son's hand, Rudi moved closer and slid his arm around his beloved wife. "If you had known me before the carriage accident, I would have frightened you away. I was dour, surly and hated every moment of being alive. I had no particular job and felt as though I had virtually no purpose in life. The evening before I met you, I considered ending my life. I was a token soldier, reluctant to draw the next breath. For the second time that week, my jacket was unbuttoned, and I was ready to walk into the sea and end the misery. Then Lance arrived. Bethan, I have never even fired a shot in anger. Yes, I have felled a kangaroo, but that was to eat. Then I met you. Even during your time of great loss, D'Arcy saw my reaction to you. He had to nearly drag me away from your bedside that first day in the hospital."

Rudi leaned over and kissed her gently. The violet scent that she always wore filled his nostrils. "I love you more with each passing day, my sweet girl. You brought me purpose, faith, and something to look forward to each morning. Even if we only have these three cherubs, that is enough."

Bethany's face fell. "Oh, really?"

Rudi's brow furrowed. "Why, love?"

Bethany chuckled and leaned against her beloved husband. "Well, you see, I think Benji will have another full sibling in about March. I thought you might like that."

Benji had just dozed off, and his father's shout of delight made him bite Bethany. Bethany pulled him off her breast and said, "Ouch!"

Benji's face screwed up, and he let out a bellow.

Rudi chuckled. "Sorry, love. I'm delighted, that's wonderful. March, you say. Fine, then from the beginning of February, you will be confined to our home. I'm just letting you know, as I want no repeat births in church or the ferry."

Both of Benji's parents chuckled.

The infant pulled her breast back into his mouth and suckled. Unbeknownst to him, his parents enjoyed a long, deep kiss while he continued to slake his thirst.

~

Three weeks later

Rudi had taken a last-minute shift, filling in for Tobin on a road gang. Today, they were working on the road to Parramatta again.

It was early in the morning of September 26th 1812; a sail was sighted on the horizon. Though the flag was raised on Flagstaff Hill, no one knew if this was a merchant vessel or another convict transport. Lance wondered if it carried Rudi's long-awaited furniture order from the east or possibly the coins. As this ship approached from the north rather than the south, it was presumed not to be a convict transport.

It was the *Samarang*, a sloop-of-war commanded by Captain William Case, which had come from Madras in India. However, the captain was unaware of what he carried. He just knew the chests addressed to the governor were heavy. For all he knew, it could be crockery.

As the senior medic in town, Doctor Balmain was in Parramatta; therefore, D'Arcy needed to board and check all persons on the new vessel. When he asked about their cargo, he was informed that it was a heavy personal delivery for Rudolph Greenwood and Governor Macquarie. He had no idea what the cargo was, but knew the numerous bulky items were addressed to the two men. D'Arcy was pleased to hear that Rudi's long-awaited consignment of furniture was on board. D'Arcy's departing long boat took the two messages back to shore while he finished his inspection. D'Arcy also sent Brenton a message about a mysterious cargo from Madras for Lachlan and Rudi. Rudi's sizeable consignment would need Brenton to bring the big flatbed wagon.

An hour later, after D'Arcy finished his crew check, a few crewmen had coughs and were ordered not to disembark. On heading back on deck, he was surprised that neither of the Greenwood household men had arrived to meet the ship. He checked to ensure that his messages had been sent with the longboat.

The captain assured him they had been.

Sure enough, D'Arcy saw Joseph arrive with the governor, but there was still no sign of Brenton, Rudi, or Bethany.

Lachlan came on board and discovered that his cargo consisted of chests containing the long-overdue Spanish coins. Everything was ready for production to begin, and he was delighted that, at long last, they could start making the coins.

D'Arcy had no idea what the cargo was, but he saw that the governor was happy.

Captain Case handed the governor the keys to the chests, and Lachlan delightedly accepted them. He dared not open them in front of this surly gentleman or the doctor, so he decided to oversee the hold's unloading personally. As Lachlan received the keys, he said, "Greenwood is on road gang duty, so I shall ensure the delivery makes it to his house." He ordered the ship to dock rather than to be unloaded into longboats. Losing the chests overboard would be a disaster, but he used Rudi's large consignment of bulky furniture as an excuse.

After realising this vessel carried his valuable cargo, Lachlan remained on board, guarding his pirate treasure with a grin firmly plastered on his lips. He sent word for Brenton to bring the biggest wagon he could find. He had been re-shoeing the governor's stallion when the message arrived.

D'Arcy wondered what was in the cargo but dared not ask. He left his boss to oversee the freight. He departed to resume his other duties. The items were all to be delivered to the same address, so most people thought they were all for Rudi.

Captain Case from the *Samarang* was a surly gentleman who demanded payment from a newly arrived vessel as recompense for the private consignment. He had places to be, and the sooner he could restock and leave port, the better. Although he was unaware of the actual value of his cargo, he knew the governor was pleased to have it. He was even more delighted to see a coastal trader, the *Estramina,* drop anchor nearby. When he discovered it was filled to the brim with baskets of black coal, he knew he could use it as cargo for the return trip.

Lachlan waited until his chests were on deck before disembarking, then watched until he saw them stacked on the dock before overseeing them being loaded onto Brenton's wagon.

Once the precious cargo was on land, the governor commanded the captain of the *Estramina* to transfer one hundred baskets, each containing a hundred-weight of coal, from one vessel to the other.

With the cargo emptied, the *Samarang* moved away from the dock. After some negotiation, the captain was delighted that Governor Macquarie arranged for the coal ship to be brought alongside the sloop-of-war and load its cargo into his hold.

The *Estramina* had come from Newcastle. She was a colonial vessel and coastal trader under the captaincy of the young Edward Watson, son of the harbour master in Sydney. He was new to the job, and his much more experienced father, Robert, stepped in to oversee the cargo transfer. Harbour Master Robert Watson was ordered to board the trading vessel and ensure the transfer of the cargo was completed with the shortest possible delay.

Lachlan wanted the *Samarang* gone from the harbour before loose lips spread the word about their heavy cargo. The coal transfer on water solved that problem. Rather than wait on the dock, the governor disembarked, presuming his orders would be carried out without fuss. He hoped the *Samarang* would be gone by morning.

Brenton arrived quickly with an empty flatbed wagon to collect the Greenwoods' items, and Lachlan took him aside to explain what else had arrived.

Joseph Bigg was at the reins of the governor's closed carriage, and he refused to help carry the weighty chests, pleading a bad back.

Lance appeared, and he and Brenton heaved the chests onto the flatbed wagon. The chests were loaded first, and Rudi's new furniture was placed on top to disguise the cargo. The wagon was covered in canvas for the short trip up the hill.

With the chests now safe, Lachlan left the dockyard with Joseph. He ordered they pause and wait for the wagon.

Brenton drove directly to the stables of the Greenwood residence, with the governor now following behind the wagon. Brenton knew how heavy his load was, so he drove carefully up the bumpy roads from the dockland lest the axles break on the old wagon and his load be tipped over.

No sooner had the two vehicles left the dock than Robert Watson and John Ballard, the sailing master of the *Samarang*, came to blows over how Ballard weighed the baskets being transferred on board.

For some unknown reason, rather than weighing what was already in the basket, which was known to be the one hundred pounds as requested, Ballard levelled off the top of one coal basket, which, of course, meant that it weighed a scant measure. Rather than the hundred pounds of coal, it now weighed eighty. Edward Watson had no idea what to do and turned to his father for help. Before Lachlan had even arrived at his home, the harbour master and sailing captain clashed.

When Robert Watson boarded the *Samarang* again from the *Estramina*, Robert was clapped in irons.

~

D'Arcy did not wait to see what the cargo was; with William Balmain away, he had things to do. On returning to shore, D'Arcy thought he might as well return home for a meal before he had to go on duty at the hospital. Goodness only knew when he would get home again. He was turning into the mews at the back of his house when a moan caught his attention. It was not one of pleasure but one of pain. Dismounting and flicking the steed's reins of his gig over the hitching rail, he went to investigate. He followed the sounds and walked towards the scrubby bushes that lined the Tank Stream. He saw a clump of rags and moved closer to investigate.

It was Daisy, Rudi's oldest maid, and she had obviously been beaten and probably violated by the torn state of her garments. He ran to her side and said, "Oh, damn!" After quickly checking her over for more severe injuries, he gathered her into his arms and carried her to his gig. He would take her to her home rather than to the hospital. He knew he really must do something about a female ward, but there were few female patients. Convict women were treated in their quarters.

With his passenger now leaning against him, he eased his small carriage out of his yard and headed up the hill to Rudi's house. She was rousing. On arrival at the front of the house, D'Arcy was met by two more panicked maids.

May said somewhat accusingly, "Oh, thank goodness, Doctor. Couldn't Daisy find you? We thought you'd be here an hour ago."

Ivy and Vera then saw the state Daisy was in.

Ivy asked, "What happened to her?"

D'Arcy shook his head, "What do you mean? Has something happened? Daisy has been attacked and most probably violated. Where's Carol and Bethany?" There was no sign of Bethany, and this was unusual.

Ivy screamed, "Oh, no!" And ran to her friend's side.

Vera explained softly. "Daisy went to get help. The mistress has collapsed in her room, and she's bleeding. We think she's lost the baby. Carol is with her."

D'Arcy lifted a wobbly Daisy from the carriage and carried her into her room. He said to Ivy, "Clean her up, and I'll see to Bethany. I'll be back in a tick." He headed upstairs to see the original patient. He thought, "What a day!"

Carol was hovering around Bethany's bed. There was a pool of drying blood on the floor and a bloodied gown at the end of her bed.

D'Arcy drew Carol aside and told her of Daisy's attack.

Carol left to attend to the maid, while D'Arcy remained and checked on Bethany.

Bethany had been hanging the wet washing, nothing too arduous, when violent pains had hit low in her pelvis.

Daisy heard her cry and went to get Carol, but it was too late. A gush of blood while she was trying to change made Bethany scream again. Carol came to Bethany's side and sent Daisy to get the doctor.

Bethany had indeed lost the baby, and she was in shock. She had been four months along and had minimal sickness with this confinement.

All that trauma had occurred over two hours ago. They wondered why Daisy had not returned with a doctor. Any doctor would have been welcome, but none came.

Bethany overheard D'Arcy telling Carol about Daisy, and she struggled to rise from her bed. For the young girl to have been attacked was horrible.

D'Arcy growled at his patient. "And just where do you think you are going, my dear?"

She said, "Daisy needs me."

D'Arcy shook his head. "Rudi and your children need you more. Carol and the girls can cope with the situation downstairs. Daisy's sore and bruised, but she will live. I'll see her in a minute. If she falls with a child from the attack, we'll cope with that later." D'Arcy knew this was all too common in this hellhole of a penal town.

Bethany collapsed back onto her pillows. She nodded weakly. "Oh, the poor girl! She had a bad enough time on the ship out. Did you know that she protected the three younger girls? She forbade the crew from using the girls carnally and protected them the only way she could. She is emotionally damaged enough from that. Now, for this to occur to her is downright cruel." Bethany sobbed at the horror her young maid had to endure. "D'Arcy, what can be done to stop men abusing women and girls in such a way? Before I left the hospital after Andrew died, Rudi warned me never to be alone." She was lying in her bed, mourning the loss of her own child, whilst praying that Daisy would not conceive one.

D'Arcy fell silent. He thought back to his meeting in England with the beautiful young Jane. She was only fourteen when they met. She was too good for him. Years later, she still held his heart. He had no answer for Bethany and said as much. He did what he could to protect the girls, but he had taken one woman as his own bedfellow. Although his current partner, Mary Ann, whom he called Ann, came to him for protection, it quickly became intimate. Initially, she was his housekeeper after her husband, James McNeal, disowned her. That man had since left the colony with their son. D'Arcy's relationship with Ann developed quickly, and she gave birth to their son less than a year after her arrival at his house. She was currently expecting their second child.

William Cowper had read him the riot act, but D'Arcy explained that it was impossible to marry Ann because she was already married, and James would not release her. Unable to take her son with her, she had fled from her husband in fear for her life. All D'Arcy did was to protect her. He sighed and thought about procreation as he worked.

Bethany watched the emotions play over their friend's face. His startling blue eyes looked sad. "Are you all right, D'Arcy?"

He jumped at her question and replied, "Sorry, yes, I was just thinking about my own sticky situation with Ann at home. She is carrying our second child, and with the loss of yours and the hope that Daisy does not conceive, I was thinking about conception and procreation. It's the circle of life, but sometimes things get out of our control. I admit that Ann came to me of her own free will, but I did not pressure her to do anything. She made the first move, and I did not rebuff her. On board the *Neptune* on my way here, I met Catherine Crowley. She delivered my eldest son, William, before the ship arrived in Sydney. Three more children followed, but our daughter died when little. Catherine herself died in 1800, shortly before Governor John Hunter departed. All these ladies reminded me of a lovely lass I met in England. Her name was Jane Austen. Had she been older, I may not even be here." He shook his head. "Enough of that! Now, dear girl, back to you. I feel your child may have been implanted too low, and had you not lost it now, you may well have bled to death when it was born. There is no reason you cannot conceive again, but please allow a couple of months if possible. You will need to wait the usual six weeks anyway.

Bethany nodded. She was teary but understood. She wanted to know why he had not come sooner and wondered how to ask. "D'Arcy, was there some emergency? That is other than Daisy?"

The doctor shook his head. "No, Lachlan was fussing over a shipment of something he ordered that had finally arrived. I'm guessing Rudi also ordered lots of furniture from India, as it has arrived on the same vessel. They should be here shortly. I cleared out before it was unloaded, so I have no idea what has come, but it's bulky. Lachlan is overseeing the unloading with Brenton."

Bethany gasped. She knew that D'Arcy was not aware of the project they were working on, so she smiled. She ignored Lachlan's cargo, saying, "Oh, that's good; we might finally be able to use all the bedrooms here."

D'Arcy nodded. "You are to stay in bed all today, as well as tomorrow, if you can. You should be fine to rise then and take things easy. If Benji still has a night feed, give him a few comfort feeds during the day today and tomorrow, as that will help ease the bleeding."

Bethany nodded. "Thank you, D'Arcy. Can you send Carol to me while you tend to Daisy?"

He left with a nod.

Carol appeared quickly. "Yes, dear?"

Bethany motioned for her friend to close the door. Once she had, she said, "I think the coins have arrived, Carol. Of all the days Rudi has to be away, it has to be this one. He is filling in for Tobin Jeeves on chain gang duty. He won't be home until tonight. Can you tell Bill? He will need to be on hand to help unload it."

As she spoke, the sound of vehicle wheels was heard pulling into the back of their building. "Carol, that will be Brenton. They have brought not only Lachlan's items, but also our new furniture. D'Arcy and the girls know nothing about the coins, so get them out of the way quickly. Please let Bill know first if you can. I'm banned from rising." She huffed in frustration.

Carol was torn. She knew she should remain with Bethany, but the good of the colony was at stake.

Brenton had pulled up the wagon at the back entrance. Joseph Bigg paused behind him, and Lachlan hopped out and waved Joseph away.

Upstairs, Bethany shooed Carol away. "I promise I will stay in bed. I'm not stupid. Go and tell Bill. He has to know about the cargo."

Carol nodded, "Promise?"

Bethany nodded. "Yes, I promise. D'Arcy's words sank in. Rudi would be ropable if I disobeyed the doctor."

Carol nodded and fled. She went to speak to her husband and Bill. She appeared and whispered something to Brenton, making him gasp. He nodded and shooed her away. It was not his place to tell the governor of the double tragedy.

Lance had come from the docks with him to help unload.

Unbeknownst to Lachlan, big troubles were brewing at the harbour. He was oblivious to this while overseeing the delivery of the chests to the basement.

After carrying the furniture that was hiding the chests inside, Lance, Bill, Brenton, and Mark, who had appeared from somewhere, took the chests down the narrow basement staircase and stowed them in the new lockable containers that Lance and Rudi had only recently finished. All the while, the governor stood guard at the vehicle.

Just as the last chest was unloaded and locked away safely, and they were about to retire to the kitchen for some tea, before moving the furniture upstairs, a puffing red-coated private arrived at the back of the Greenwoods' house. He informed the governor of the fracas on the ships and that they needed him back on board to resolve it. The man had been sent over from the official residence.

Lachlan sighed with frustration.

Thankfully, as the furniture was unloaded, Brenton took Lachlan and Mark back to the harbour to sort out the mess involving the coal transfer. As Lance was about to climb aboard, Lachlan shook his head and said, "No, Lance, stay with Bill until things are secured. Permit no one entry to the basement." He passed him the key to the grill gate. "Lock it for me, then walk back down to the dock."

Lachlan still had the captain's keys for the chests on him and would only relinquish them to Rudi. They were so well bolted that only hours of effort would pry the locks open.

~

When Rudi arrived home after his shift, the house was in chaos.

Andy charged into his arms, Benji close behind. He swept his sons up and went to the kitchen, where he usually found his wife.

Today, the children were filthy, Manda was screaming, and the five Wright children were fighting. Bethany and Daisy were nowhere in sight. Finally finding Carol in the garden, he asked, "Carol, what's occurred? It sounds and looks like an explosion has hit the house." Having already stopped the older children from fighting, he put his boys down to rejoin the chaos outside. They had made some mud and were quickly covered in the sticky gloop. Ivy was stirring something on the stove, and May and Vera finally managed to drag the children outside to wash up. Of Bethany, Daisy, Brenton, Bill, and Lance, there was no sign.

Carol drew him into the sitting room and outlined the day's events. Rudi's first thoughts were of Bethany, but as he turned to leave, he asked, "Is Daisy all right?"

Carol nodded. "She'll live, but she's confined to bed. Hence, the children's routine is messed up. Go and see Bethany; she needs you."

Rudi glanced inside one of the spare rooms and saw that his new furniture had been dumped in one previously empty room. He would sort that out later. Rudi retreated to the solace of their bedroom. He tapped softly on the door and heard Bethany's call of "Enter."

As soon as he did, Bethany burst into a flood of tears and held out her arms to him. Kicking off his boots, he crawled onto the bed and pulled her into his arms. "My dearest Bethan, are you all right?"

She shook her head against his shoulder. "No, but I will be. I know women lose children all the time. Elizabeth Macquarie has certainly lost a few, but it hurts so much here." She punched at her heart. "And then there's Daisy, and I can't get up and see her."

He allowed her to weep for their loss. He certainly shed a few tears himself. He refused to release her. "Love, what happened to Daisy? Carol said she had been attacked, but she gave no details."

Bethany confessed to sending her for help alone, and that Daisy had been attacked and violated. Bemoaning the fact that she had not even been able to see her caused her to cry again.

Her weeping continued for some time, and then he realised that not only had Bethany's crying ceased but that she had fallen asleep in his arms. Not willing to disturb her, he relaxed. Carol mentioned that the coins had finally arrived, meaning he would no longer need to leave the house for duty. The treasure could wait.

Rudi smiled at the timing. When he most needed to be at hand, he could be. In years gone by, he would have cursed God for the loss of their child, but now he rested in the knowledge that God knew best. Had he been at home, it would have changed nothing.

Bethany had mentioned D'Arcy's supposition of the danger of bleeding during childbirth, and she may well have died had she carried this child to term. He pulled her a little closer, kissed her forehead and murmured, "Thank you, God, for being bigger than my weak faith. Please, make us strong for you." He smiled when he realised he had become the man Bethany asked of him. He had turned to God and thanked Him rather than abused Him. He chuckled softly. He liked this new self. He had not even noticed the change, but he was fully aware that his beloved Bethan was the reason his old morbid self had long since been forgotten. She had led him out of the deep hole that he had dug himself into. He was still ashamed that shortly before meeting her, he had contemplated walking into the sea and floating out with the tide. He was tired from a day in the sun, so he closed his eyes and dozed.

Pounding on their front door woke them both. "Stay there, sweetie; I'll see what's wrong." He padded downstairs and found one of Lachlan's guards on his doorstep.

The soldier said, "Sir, there's smoke rising from the back of the printer's building next door. I can't stay as I'm on guard duty." The red-coated soldier turned on his heel and went back to the front door of Government House. He was one of Lachlan's trusted guards, whom Rudi knew was named Clarence.

Rudi wondered what was going on. Rather than returning upstairs for his boots, he pulled on his gardening shoes and exited through the back kitchen door, where he saw the children weeding the garden. No smoke was visible.

The reported smoke was, therefore, not from the Wrights' rooms or the flat on the top of the printer, but he certainly could smell something.

He wandered around the far side of the building and saw the offending fire. Some idiot had stacked a pile of rubbish against the side wall of the printery and then set it alight. It was only smouldering at the moment, but without swift action, all their efforts could be in vain.

Rather than tackling this alone, he returned to the children and told them to get help. He grabbed two buckets of water, hoping to help dampen the timber. Word of the fire spread, and Brenton, Bill, and Lance soon arrived to help. All the men in the print shop helped fight the flames. The older children and three able-bodied maids set up a human chain to fill the buckets from their well. Carol and the little children manned the well, refilling the buckets.

Within half an hour, the debris's smouldering remains had been well and truly extinguished.

Rudi pulled the pile apart with a garden rake, making it easier to extinguish the smouldering logs.

The exhausted group retired to the kitchen. Dinner was eaten, and finally, the house settled down for the night.

Lachlan set a guard to walk the perimeter throughout the night. This was changed every four hours, the same as the guards on duty at his house. The fire provided Lachlan with a perfect excuse to station a guard on the government printing premises. So, even the fire turned out to be a Godsend.

Though exhausted, Rudi lifted his eyes and gave thanks for that too.

Word spread about the wilful lighting of the printer's building. As this was the only means of public communication in the settlement, many were angry at the attempt to destroy the facility. They expected a guard to be placed at the building, and it was.

Rudi smiled when he heard about this. God had even paved the way to ensure the building's security. It would have been hard to explain the new guards without this incident. He chuckled to himself and went to take Bethany a mug of tea. She would be permitted to rise tomorrow.

Chapter 14 Punch Drunk

1812 Sydney

Bethany and Daisy were back on their feet only days after the coins arrived. While Bethany and Rudi mourned the loss of their baby, Daisy had weeks to wait before she found out if she had conceived. She had been attacked by three men, all of whom she could identify. They were arrested and each given one hundred lashes. Two of her attackers were soldiers, who were Dennis's friends from the orphanage.

Bethany and Daisy did not know what to say to each other, so they hugged, wept, and hugged some more. In this case, words could not heal, but actions did. Each knew the other was fully loved, supported and cared for. They would both survive no matter what happened.

Living in a penal colony was hard. Life was precious, and people and children died often.

~

At the end of the first week of October, Daisy shouted with delight. Her monthly flow had arrived, and no child would come of her violation. Her life settled back into her usual activities.

Bethany often sought her out for a hug and a quiet word.

Tears were never far away for them both.

Life in the house settled back into normalcy.

~

As a reward for Bill and to encourage the new master minter, Lachlan handed Bill his Certificate of Freedom. It was dated a fortnight before the coins arrived, but the task ahead of this man was mammoth.

Bill accepted the document, not realising what it was. Unfolding the parchment, he realised he was now free. Tears blurred his vision, and he lifted his face to the grinning governor. "Thank you, sir. Thank you so much. You have no idea what this means to me. I intend to go on the straight and narrow, and this project has made me realise how much you have to cope with." He tucked the document under his arm and rubbed his eyes with the heels of his hands. An undignified sniff followed, and then he grinned.

Lachlan muttered under his breath, "You don't know the half of that lad." Then he said chirpily, "You will earn it, Bill, even before you start the huge task ahead of you. You know this is only part one of the deal, and it can still be rescinded should you forget yourself. Never forget that, so stay sober. You still can't leave the colony, but that is partially for your own safety. As you said, you would be lynched if you returned home. I hope that you take the openings that will come your way." Lachlan did not mention any plans for Bill's family to join him. Letters between countries were slow, and Lachlan had only just received the news that they would be on the next ship, which was supposedly due sometime in February.

Once Bill's family arrived, Lance could return to the barracks or, more probably, to one of Rudi's spare rooms.

Life in the household once again settled down, but now Rudi and Lance had a new purpose.

They were both permanently assigned to home duty and worked with Bill and Brenton. Mark came when he was available. Living on site meant they could be almost invisible. No one saw the three men heading into the basement each day. William Cowper and even Lachlan visited to help when they could.

On the evening the machines were delivered, it was all-hands-on-deck; the equipment needed to be moved into the basement under the cover of darkness.

Mark and Lachlan had come to Sydney to ensure all went well. Mark's immense strength was needed to move the large machines into place. However, only Phil knew what went where. He directed how to bolt the new machine to the new workbench.

Lachlan oversaw the proceedings and ensured no one came near.

External guards were now in place following the fire, but tonight they were told to remain on the far side of the building because a private function was taking place at the Greenwoods.

As expected, word had spread about someone trying to destroy the printer's office. George Howe published a scathing article about the ignorance of the fool who wanted to burn the only means of printing a news sheet and the convicts' Tickets of Leave. This article explained that guards would be present twenty-four hours a day, so their presence raised no questions.

George was unaware that over 40,000 silver Spanish coins were stored in locked boxes in the printer's basement.

Lance, Bill, Rudi, and Brenton were frequently seen visiting the building, raising no eyebrows, as many knew that Lance and Bill lived upstairs and that the building had only one entrance, leading off the small corridor to a presumably empty basement.

Machinery movements and any work requiring hammering were done after the printer closed.

A large slab timber table had been constructed downstairs to mount the press and milling machines on.

As the upstairs printer's room was chilly, a double-storey chimney was installed externally to cover the construction of the fireplace in the basement. This was also done after summer in preparation for the cooler months ahead. Thankfully, George had complained about how cold the printing officers were.

Bill had experimented with his twenty collected coins. Only one coin, the first one, had been a dismal failure. Rather than cut a clean edge, the small screw press, which was found in government stores, did as expected and squashed the central area. Bill discarded that machine and planned to return it to the store.

However, Phil had come to ensure all was in order. When he saw the discarded screw press on the floor, he realised he could use many of the components to make another machine they needed. The large steel screw thread would serve as part of a new milling machine. Phil Tindale quickly converted the screw press machine into a fiddle-arm milling contraption that added ridges to the rim by using a long-rolling sprocket to process twenty Dumps at once. The crank handle could roll a row of coins and mill the outer rim with a ridged edge. The carved steel cylinder could also fit inside the hole and mill the inside edge of the Holey Dollar, removing any sharp bits and finishing the coins.

The coins could also be milled in batches of twenty at a time while the disks were still hot from embossing the new design. Inside the fireplace, Phil also installed a small kiln-like structure that could be heated to the required temperature, but even with an external intake flue and chimney, Bill realised it sucked the oxygen out quickly.

Phil added a special vent in the wall above to provide its own air supply, but the door needed to be open while this was in use, so an additional grille gate was added further down the corridor to ensure adequate ventilation and privacy.

Due to the volume of coins that needed work, they had little choice of venue.

~

Production was necessarily slow, and the expected six months stretched to nearly a year before the first sizeable quantity was ready.

Bill quickly realised that rather than processing a few coins on each machine and completing a few each day, it was much more time-effective to process the re-minting in stages.

Over the winter, the men began working in large batches. They would press out three thousand Dumps overnight while the printer upstairs was closed, then heat-stamp the dropped disks while they were still hot. At the same time, one man used the dies to imprint, and the next milled the edges.

Phil had made a special curved scoop that allowed hot coins to be dropped into the milling tray in a straight row.

Once heat-stamped with the new value and imprint, the Holey Dollars required their centres to be smoothed and milled.

Phil's 'fiddle arm' milling machine needed to be adjusted depending on whether they were working inside the hole or on the outside rims of the Dump. The bow-like movement gave the milling machine its name. Thankfully, the same milling machine could be used to mill both coins. The die only needed to be moved. Inserting it into the centre of the hot Holey dollars was tricky but doable.

Doing it in batches meant there were coopered buckets of half-finished coins scattered around the underground room. As these were essentially defaced, they were worthless to anyone. They were not locked up but were covered with a drop sheet to prevent prying eyes, should anyone appear uninvited.

~

The first small batch of one thousand Holey Dollars and Dumps was finally completed by Christmas 1812. All were dated with 1813, as they would not be released until they had finished enough. However, Lachlan selected a few to send to London. He had been told this was required before the currency was released. The diplomatic bag that month contained a very small, valuable box with a heavy iron lock.

There were not enough completed coins to start the currency transition, but it gave Lachlan an idea of how long it would take to convert all the Reales. He discovered Bill was correct in his estimations. This project would take more than a year to complete.

At the end of the day, punching the centres out of the coins, the men's ears would ring with the sound of the hammer press's thump. However, they still did not pause in their work.

The men stuffed raw cotton in their ears to deaden the noise. They knew they needed sufficient coinage ready by the proposed July announcement date, even though the first release would not occur until September. This was a year after the Reales arrived.

The heating of the coins for imprinting was reserved for the cooler months, as the enclosed room became like an oven during the summer.

Either Rudi or Lance was now working with Bill each day, and the other was on guard duty at the grill gate. Usually, both were there, as no convict ships had arrived for some time.

Mark and William Cowper came to help when they could, but both had other responsibilities.

Even Lachlan wished to have a turn, and although his holed coins were not always in the dead centre, most were punched correctly.

A new template plate that accommodated a larger coin resolved the issue of off-centre stamping, though both new coins still buckled a little. Most of the Holey Dollars were slightly bent from punching out the centre, but they flipped them over to double-stamp the value and 'New South Wales' on them after a second annealing.

Bill had not disclosed that he had added his surname initial to the decoration on both dies, and no one had found the two tiny marks. Initially, these were dots between the words in Rudi's drawings. Even after inspecting the first finished test coins, Lachlan had not seen the two small H's hidden in the design. Bill smiled. What they didn't know would not hurt.

Phil Tindale was a frequent visitor because he often needed to come by to tweak a machine, repair or replace a spring, sprocket, or similar component. He also took his turn at making some coins. Various punching methods were tested over the many months between conceiving the idea and the arrival of the cargo. Although most machines worked to some degree, the hammer press, as expected, worked far better. It gave a neat cut that was easy to anneal, re-stamp and mill the edge. Phil's work was to keep the cutting blade of the dump cutter sharp. This blunted quickly if the coins were not hot enough.

The select group of men worked tirelessly.

They realised that, though noisy, the easiest bit was punching the Dump. This was often done either on the day the upstairs printer was in production or after hours. Sometimes the men worked through the night to mask the sound of the dump cutter.

Each process became more complicated and time-consuming.

To resist temptation, no single person was permitted to work alone.

Bill may have been the brains behind the project, but he was still an emancipated convict. Brenton was still serving time.

The sound of the hand-cranked milling machinery could not be heard upstairs above the whirr and clank of the printing presses, but the Gazette was only issued once a week. So, George Howe was none the wiser about the project underway below.

As the summer heat rose, the pile of Dumps awaiting the next stage grew. The annealing process for the bulk of the coins would begin once the cooler months arrived. This meant that it would be all hands on deck after Easter.

George was delighted that the printers' rooms could now be heated by their new open fireplace. He had no idea that it was only a cover for the forge in the basement.

Lachlan wished he could help more often, but his commitments in town won out. If he had a day to do paperwork, Mark came and turned the crank handles while the others fed in the whole coins. Although Rudi and Lance were tall, Mark towered another five inches over both of them. He was built like a man-mountain and could crank the handle for hours without a break. With Mark's help, they could get through twice as many coins.

Of course, they still had to be finished, but that didn't require much physical muscle, only coordinated processing by the three men.

Chapter 15 The Release Year

Early 1813

Easter came and went in a blur of minting activity.

Bill was already on his third die for the 1813 coins, and he had forgotten to engrave his 'H' on this one. However, no one had noticed so far. All but the last one had his tiny hidden mark.

The Macquaries had returned to Parramatta, but Lachlan was still a frequent visitor. The coin re-minting progressed steadily. Lachlan delighted in sinking his hand into a pile of silver coins. Each had done something similar. After all, this was a pirate's treasure.

As the first cool day's arrived, they fired up the small hand-pumped coal forge. The hammer press was now converted into an imprint press, and the dumps were heated and re-minted with the special template to keep them centred. The first two dies marked 1813 had already worn out during the trial-and-error stage; once again, Bill had hidden his tiny 'H' in the new 1814 design, but he would not use that one until after the official release. The pattern was nearly the same, but it had more pearls on the crown reverse of the dump. The new dies would be used after the first batch of coins had been released.

Once heated and re-stamped, the new small coin was slightly larger than the hole it had been punched from. The Holey Dollar was also heat-imprinted with a narrow ring showing the value on one side and 'New South Wales' on the reverse.

This process still distorted many of the coins, but it made them unique and distinct. This currency could not be used outside the colony and was therefore more likely to retain its value.

Bill already had one gripe. He had discovered that a jeweller was melting down some of the already circulating early Spanish Reales for his jewellery making, significantly increasing the silver's value in the colony. He was unsure what they could do about that.

After Phil enquired of his jeweller friend, he discovered that the coins he was using were older and had higher silver content than the newer Spanish coins they were working with. The jewellers' coins contained about ninety per cent silver, but the ones they were working on were a shade over eighty per cent, making it less likely the new currency would be remelted for artistic purposes, as they had mainly been minted just before 1800, and the jeweller's coins were over a hundred years older.

~

July was drawing near, and they needed one-third of the coins ready for the new currency's first release in three months.

Even Mark was present more frequently over the final month, as he had recently sold out. There had been a concert in Parramatta, and then the Duffys stayed in Sydney for a few weeks before moving to their new post. Mark and Cathy were to take over the new Toll Gate in Parramatta. He was officially here, learning the new routine from D'Arcy, but he spent much time at the mint as he could.

D'Arcy was still none the wiser about their project, and he was often engaged at the hospital.

The announcement day finally approached. With much deliberation, Lachlan asked everyone involved to dinner at the official residence. While there, he read them what he had written. "Friends, and Bill and Brenton, I include you both, too. In God's eyes, we are all equal, convict or free. What I have written is to ensure that there is no muddiness about what I intend to do with this money. Now, settle back as it is over two thousand words long."

Mark gave a good-hearted groan and said, "Sir, this is supposed to capture everyone's attention, not bore them to death." Mark's wife, Cathy, was at the tollgate with her son Josh in charge for the night.

Lachlan roared with laughter. "Well, that would be one way to solve the felony problem. Settle down and listen anyway."

They had no choice but to follow their commander-in-chief's orders.

Listening to the long-winded document took nearly twenty minutes.

The ever-efficient governor had covered every possible base and angle, from exporting the new currency for the silver value to possible future counterfeiting. He missed nothing.

There were a few corrections to make it more straightforward. The one thing no one missed was the actual September 30th date when the coinage would become the colony's only currency.

Lachlan read, "I finish with…

And it is hereby further ordered and declared by the Authority aforesaid, that from and after the Thirty-first day of December now next ensuing, it shall not be lawful for any Person or Persons to issue or negotiated within this Territory any Promissory Notes whatsoever for any Sum of Money under the Sum of Two Shillings and Sixpence; and if any Person or Persons whatsoever, from and after the said Thirty-first Day of December, shall nevertheless issue, negotiate, or take in Payment within this Territory any Promissory Note for any Sum under the Sum of Two Shillings and Sixpence, the Offender or Offenders, being convicted thereof on the oath of one credible witness before any two or more of His Majesty's Justices of the Peace within this Territory, shall forfeit treble the Amount of the Note or Notes so issued, negotiated, and taken in Payment, to be paid to the Informer, and to be levied by Distress and Sale of the Offender's Goods, and shall further be imprisoned in any of his Majesty's Gaols in this Territory for the Space of Three Calendar Months, and till the said Forfeiture be paid.

And it is hereby further ordered and declared that from and after the Thirtieth Day of September next ensuing, the Copper Monies now current in this Territory shall not be a legal Tender in Payment of any Sum of Money exceeding the Sum of Fifteen Pence.

Given under my Hand at Government House, Sydney, the First Day of July, in the Year of Our Lord 1813.

"LACHLAN MACQUARIE."

GOD SAVE THE KING.

By Command of His Excellency,

J. T. Campbell, Secretary.

After adding a few suggestions, Lachlan finally put down his quill and said, "I know I have the final say, but I have a few announcements. Rudi, you will be in charge of the money exchange and will need to report to Commissioner-General David Allen, as he will be in town, and I will be in Parramatta. Lance will be working with you full-time, as he will not return to the convict assignment duty until this project is completed. I am unsure if he will be returned to that when we are done with this. David Allen already has the first small batch of coins and is preparing to exchange them with some trusted shopkeepers. As you can see, John Campbell has been brought into my confidence, as has my aide-de-camp, Henry Antill."

Smiling, he then turned to his driver. "Brenton, this is for you."

Bill smiled, presuming it was a Certificate of Freedom. He

recognised the parchment. He waited for the surprise to register on his friend's face. They were not supposed to receive these documents until the coins were finished. Bill had already received his Certificate of Freedom, but Brenton had only been promised a Ticket of Leave. He already had far more freedom as the governor's second coachman than Bill had.

Lance had been warned about what was coming and made sure he was sitting to see his friend's face. Brenton unfolded the document and gasped. "But, sir, you can't give me this!" He handed the document to Carol. She glanced and also gasped.

What they held was better than freshly minted coins. Lachlan had handed Brenton an Absolute Pardon. Brenton unashamedly wept. The heels of his hands ground into his eyes as he desperately tried to stop the seepage from them. It was pointless as they kept flowing. Finally, he was free. He had done nothing more than help his boss. He cradled him as he died. Carol wrapped her arm around her beloved husband as he openly sobbed.

Rather than address the Wrights, Lachlan turned to Bill. "My friend, I promised you your freedom, and you have earned it, but you committed a crime. With your documentation, you have a fresh start. If you stay on the straight and narrow, you'll have a good life. However, what I just handed to Brenton is different. What he is holding is his life back. His document is an Absolute Pardon."

Bill gasped. "Sir, I freely admitted my crime and am sorry. It's why I willingly reported on the other forgers. I do hope to one day be worthy of such an honour should you ever bestow such upon me. However, I confessed my guilt." He bowed his head in thanks, but he was somewhat disappointed that he had not received the same honour. He was fully aware that he would probably be lynched should he return home.

Lachlan then turned to Brenton as his weeping had subsided and said, "You have this document, as I spoke at length with your good woman. She gave me details of the incident. Over the past two years, I have had enquiries made in England; the last ship brought the reply I have been awaiting. I fully expect this document to be unnecessary, as I believe your conviction will be overturned soon. The highwaymen were captured shortly after your transportation, and they were convicted, and most of them were hanged that week. However, one of the young lads who was brought along that evening to hold the horses finally came forward and told his story. It backs up what you told the court. He did not know you had been charged, or he would have spoken earlier. As a reward, he has been released after already serving more than half of his term. I have appealed on your behalf and look forward to hearing back from them soon. I am all but assured that the authorities will see reason."

Brenton was unable to reply. Words that generally flowed freely were stymied as his tongue seemed glued to the roof of his mouth.

Carol's face shone with her big, beaming smile. She had hoped that was what all the governor's questions had been about. She always believed Brenton was innocent. It was not in his nature to hurt anyone.

Eventually, Brenton finally stood, crossed the room, and held out his hand to the governor. "I am beyond words, sir. I have learned to trust the good Lord that His will be done, but I had no idea this could even be possible."

Lachlan stood and shook his assistant driver's hand. "Had you expected it, it would not have been a surprise. In a way, I'm sorry I cannot issue these to all deserving convicts, but that would defeat the purpose of serving time. I am already walking a fine line, and it's only because I'm confident you will be exonerated that I'm allowing you to receive this now. They are like gold, so treasure it." Lachlan paused, then added. "Brenton, you will need new clothing."

Brenton nodded. "Thanks, sir. I will treasure this."

Lachlan chuckled. "This, of course, means that you both will also require a salary. Bill, your payment will be backdated to the date your Certificate of Freedom was issued last September. Sorry, I forgot to mention that. I shall start you both on the standard wage of a private, even though neither of you is enlisted. Are you happy with this?"

It was Bill's turn to gasp. Was he to be paid? He could start saving for when his family arrived.

Both men nodded and grinned. Neither man expected a salary.

Lachlan paused and cleared his throat. "Now, I have a bit of other unrelated news, but it might interest you all. Rudi, have you spoken to D'Arcy recently?"

Rudi hadn't. "No, sir! Should I have?"

Lachlan shook his head. "No, well, he is so excited as Gregory Blaxland has asked his eldest son, William, to join his expedition to attempt to cross the Blue Mountain range. He has also asked a surveyor friend, Lieutenant William Lawson, from the New South Wales Corps. Do either of you know him?" Lachlan's eyes flicked from Rudi to Lance.

Mark had been asked previously, so he remained quiet.

Lance had run-ins with Lawson, so he didn't answer. They now rarely met.

Rudi replied, "Only from the occasional meetings at church, sir. What I know about him led me to avoid a closer friendship. Before you arrived, he was one of the men presiding over the trial of men like Macarthur. He ultimately sided with the rebel rather than the nominated governor. Not that I was here when the rebellion occurred. I arrived only shortly before you, sir. But, knowing what we know now about the Exclusives…" He left that unfinished and ended with, "Well, let me put it like this. Is it not for this reason we are making the new currency?"

Lachlan chuckled. "I shall stay mum about my views on the Corps, but Lawson is a good surveyor. They have a local blacksmith named Edward Field out near Blaxland's farm at Castlereagh, and he's been preparing the items required for their trip. They also plan to take four convicts and an Indigenous man as a guide, as well as the Irish tracker and bushman, James Burns. I have not been informed who the convicts or the Indigenous men are. I wondered whether they intended to take Bungaree, but he informed me that he would not be going with them. D'Arcy said that Burns and this indigenous man are friends and often explore the passes together. It makes me wonder whether they have already seen what lies beyond the mountains. The beauty of this planned journey is that it's been filling the news sheets with what they hope to find once they cross the mountain range; therefore, our project has been easily overlooked." Lachlan took a deep breath and said, "Anyway, D'Arcy is full of every trivial bit of the preparation, so listen hard and try to sound interested. He still has no idea of what we are doing. It's not that I don't trust him, but he, like Lawson, sided with the Rum Corps for the rebellion. It was for that reason he was not involved."

Rudi nodded. "I really should take the time to read the Gazette, sir. You have chided me about that before. Sorry, sir!" He had the decency to look embarrassed.

Lachlan chuckled and nodded, then continued. "The expedition plans to leave in May and spend at least a month traversing the hills and gullies. If they can get across and find more farmland…" he sighed. "Well, we still need more food, which needs more money. There are too many mouths here now for the limited farmland we have. The rainfall in this region is inconsistent, and crops fail. If they can find suitable land for farming, I will go myself and view it to see if I think it is viable. I presume there will be more tribes in that area, and we must also consider their needs. Bungaree tells me that each tribe speaks a different dialect, so whoever we take will probably not be able to converse with the other groups. In the early days, Arabanoo, Bennelong, Nanberry, and Abaroo – or Boorong, as she is now known, and others were utilised for their interpretive skills. Governor Phillip learned from William Dawes that each tribal group had its own dialect. Dawes recorded many words from the local Eora language. John Hunter recorded Bennelong's Dharug language. Those who lived on the harbour's north side spoke differently from those in the Sydney region. I was amazed to discover that the tribes further north, on the north side of Broken Bay in the Brisbane Water area, where Bungaree is from, spoke a language similar to that of the tribes on the western side of the Nepean, rather than the tribes who lived here. The ones on the Hunter River, where we are excavating the coal, have a completely different dialect again. Bungaree's wife, Cora Gooseberry, is one of the Sydney, or Eora tribe. So their language is similar enough to converse."

Lachlan fell silent. Thinking of how he could protect the natives' lands while still using the pastureland for farming.

William Cowper had remained silent until now. He wished to introduce a new topic, as the conversation had shifted from the coins. "Sir, while we are assembled, I was wondering if you know much about a gentleman named Edward Smith Hall?"

Lachlan grinned and nodded. "If you mean the man who came with a letter of recommendation from Sir Robert Peel about eighteen months ago, then yes. Did you know that Peel is the Chief Secretary for Ireland? He has authorised the Lord Lieutenant of Ireland to appoint additional magistrates in a country in a state of disturbance, who were authorised to appoint paid special constables. Peel wishes to form an Irish Constabulary but has not yet succeeded. One day, I would like to expand the police force here with men who are not in the military. We already have bench police in the rural area and foot patrols in Sydney, but it is not enough." He huffed a long sigh.

Lachlan looked embarrassed as he'd run on too much. He said, "Yes, William. I know him."

William nodded and said, "We had a very interesting discussion about starting a specific charity for the poor. He plans to call it the Benevolent Society. Do we have your approval to go ahead? I freely admit that the demands of the poor have recently strained our budget. Thanks to your generosity, they have food, but clothing and accommodations are still in short supply. There are enough wealthy people here to now subsidise this venture, but he will take the reins and seek those funds so we can further this work."

Lachlan waved his hand as he was wont to do and said, "Yes, bring him and Simeon Lord in for more discussions about this. Smith Hall has a merchant background, but I also wish to discuss other topics with you later. Did you know Smith Hall is a great friend and supporter of William Wilberforce? I think his ideas may well benefit the colony greatly."

He turned to his retired bodyguard and said, "Mark, I know you have retired, but can you get Henry to find a date suitable for the three of them to bring their ideas to me?"

Mark drew out a pad and jotted a note with a graphite pencil he kept in his pocket.

Lachlan watched as Mark recorded the details. Mark may have retired, but he still lent a hand where he could.

Lachlan relaxed in his chair, his hands arched, and looked at Bill. His brow furrowed. He tapped his thumbs together and asked, "Is there anything more we need to discuss before I make my final observation about our little project?"

Lachlan cocked his eyebrow and circled the room with his penetrating gaze. His eyes stopped on Bill and remained there. "Has no one got a single word to add?"

Most shook their heads.

Bill just shook. Why was the governor singling him out?

Lachlan took a deep breath, pursed his lips and exhaled. "Fine, then I will bring this gathering to a close with the acknowledgement of Bill's fine work… except for two tiny letters that Mark brought to my attention."

Bill flushed scarlet and then blanched. Perspiration beaded on his brow. He knew his makers' marks had been discovered. He dropped his chin in shame. He uttered a groan and hung his head.

Lachlan released a roar of laughter. "Yes, my friend, your hidden maker's marks have been revealed. Did you not think we would find it? However, it's taken me six months of checking each batch to see your well-hidden initial."

Bill wished there was some way he could sink through the floorboards. How could he reply? Had he blotted his copybook already? Would his family now not come?

Rudi sat bolt upright. "What do you mean, sir?" He could tell by Bill's attitude that he had done something.

Lachlan chuckled. "Bill, this may surprise you, but I'm thrilled you have done this. It's like a tiny security mark that few will see as an initial. Most will think it is just a dot, as Rudi and Bethany planned.

Please ensure that this is on all the future dies and that it's as well hidden each time."

Bill dragged a filthy handkerchief from his pocket and mopped his brow. "Sir, I'm so sorry. I am so used to leaving my 'H' mark on all my work that I added it automatically to the first die. I added it to the next, but I forgot on the third one." He shrugged with embarrassment.

Rudi interjected, "You did?"

Bill nodded.

Lachlan dug into his pocket and pulled out a few of the new coins, which he offered to the visitors.

All inspected them and passed them around.

William shrugged. He moved into the light to see better. "Well, I can't see an 'H' hidden anywhere. Where is it?"

Bill stood and walked to the minister's side. He pointed out where the two tiny marks were on the coins. "They are in the spray of leaves in the counter stamp design of the Holey Dollar, and also, I inscribed my initial between the words 'fifteen' and 'pence' on the reverse of the Dump. See, that's not just a dot as on the original design, but my initial."

Rudi knew he should have noticed. He grabbed one and peered at it. He still could not make out the initial. It looked just like a dot. It should have been a dot where he and Bethany drew it. "Sir, I am so sorry. I should have noticed."

Lachlan folded his arms and nodded. "Yes, you should have, Rudi, but even I didn't, and I used a magnifying glass to inspect the first coins. I knew there should have been a dot; I didn't pick that Bill had turned that into an 'H'. If it escapes us, then it will serve a purpose. Part of my proclamation was about the illegality of attempting to counterfeit these coins. This will make it nigh impossible to do."

Bill nodded, but he felt terrible. "Sir, I did not put it on all of the dies. I forgot to put it on the last one for 1813. Sorry."

Lachlan's penetrating gaze rested again on Bill. "I will add that the next time you wish to do something like this, run it by me first. I may well have torn up your paperwork over this. Be warned, William Henshall, I am watching you!"

Suitably chastised. Bill nodded apologetically. "Lesson learned, sir. I abjectly apologise. I will not repeat this without permission." His brow needed mopping again, but simultaneously, he was relieved he had been exonerated. His heartbeat slowly returned to normal.

Lachlan was not quite done with his new master minter. "Well, now for the sticky question. When do you estimate they will be completed?"

Bill was on safer ground now. "By the end of September, I think we will have at least two-thirds done by the release date. I hope the last of them will be finished soon after Christmas, and certainly by Easter. I already have new dies with 1814 on them. Once you release that proclamation to the press, we don't have to be so careful about maintaining secrecy, only the security of the bulk of the finished coins. If you can double the guard on the building after publication, then we can have all hands working at once. That will hasten things along."

Lachlan placed his hands firmly on the desk. He stood and said, "Consider it done. It's taken longer than I had wished, but it has been done properly. I wish there were a safer place to distribute the currency, but I shall work that out later. It may well need to be issued from the Deputy Commissioner-General David Allen's office rather than Mary Reibey's store. She does have a vault, but it's not as secure as the basement. Leave it with me."

Lachlan huffed in frustration. He had only three months to resolve it. Bethany's suggestion of paying his military in the new currency meant a pay rise of a few pence to most of them. They would all like that.

Chapter 16 Letters from Home

Winter 1813

The Sydney Gazette carrying Lachlan's proclamation hit the doorsteps, street corners and barracks on July 10th 1813 and caused an immediate stir. Those who could not read gathered around those who could. News spread like wildfire. Many were fearful to voice their delight, but others grumbled openly. Lachlan knew that the officers behind the Rum Rebellion were sure to object.

Despite their underhanded dealings, they still controlled a highly profitable grain monopoly in the colony. This would soon cease.

Thankfully, the ringleaders were still in England and would remain there for some time.

Lachlan had informed Rudi that Macarthur had no return date, but his wife was here, which meant that he would undoubtedly come home when permitted. Elizabeth Macarthur was in no hurry to have her husband back, as she had their farm well under control.

Rudi smiled at what Mrs Macquarie had told him. John Macarthur sent a small flock of purebred Spanish merino sheep to their farm. He issued instructions that they were not to be cross-bred with the Barbary rams. Elizabeth Macarthur did as instructed. However, she did the opposite by crossbreeding her flock of Barbary sheep with Spanish Merino stud rams. They were doing exceedingly well. Where John's small flock would drop a single lamb, and many would die, Elizabeth's stronger Barbary cross ewes would drop three or four lambs, and most lived. These new breed of sheep she laughingly called Australian Merinos. Any lambs that had characteristics like their mothers were sent to slaughter. The next generation was mated with a different Spanish ram from John's pure flock. The colony now had regular access to mutton, as she sold the lambs that favoured the Barbary ewes. Elizabeth's flock had grown substantially, and she asked the governor about obtaining more land.

Although the government pig farm at Rooty Hill was supplying vast amounts of pork, beef was still in short supply. Anna King, the previous first lady's farm, now carried over seven hundred head of longhorn cows, but the population was growing faster than her manager, Mr Hassell, could provide meat.

~

The new coinage was announced a month after Blaxland, Wentworth, and Lawson returned from their exploratory trip to cross the mountains. Their adventurers' journey had taken six weeks, and the first person who heard of their discoveries was, of course, D'Arcy.

After his son, William Wentworth, left to report their discovery to Lachlan with his explorer partners, D'Arcy met Rudi and shared the news that a wide valley had been seen from the top of one of the hills. This new grassland could help address the ongoing hunger problem affecting the colony.

Regular loads of food arrived with merchant ships, but the colony needed to be self-sufficient, and it still wasn't.

This new grassland could be the solution for the colony's hunger. Food was still distributed from government stores, but not everyone was getting a fair share of the available produce.

~

During the hubbub of the explorer's return, another convict ship sailed into the harbour. The *Fortune* brought nearly two hundred additional male convicts. Rudi, Lance, and Tobin were busy placing the new convicts, and Bill and Brenton had to manage as best they could.

Rudi knew that Mark was now permanently at the new tollgate at Parramatta. He would remain there until it was established. Lachlan had more plans for them, but those were for the future; Mark had not mentioned what they were. Knowing there would be repercussions about paying tolls to use the main roads, Mark's size alone was enough to stop most complaints. He had been helpful as a bodyguard because of his sheer size. The fact that the governor liked him immensely was a bonus. Mark mentioned that, to date, only Judge Bent had caused problems, as he considered himself above the law. He would rather travel cross-country to avoid the toll.

Rudi mentioned to the governor something he had heard third-hand. Cathy had told Bethany, who then mentioned it to Rudi. A free settler also made loud complaints about the new tolls; however, Mr

Ardeth was an objectionable weasel of a man, and few took much notice of him. Since Bethany suggested watching the man's wife and daughters at church, he observed that they shrank in fear when he was present. Rudi was livid. He had little time for any man who intimidated a woman in such a way, and Lachlan agreed with him. He would watch the man as they certainly didn't need any more troublemakers in the colony.

~

The afternoon before the official release, Sydney.

In Sydney, Rudi and Lance stood at the door of the exchange office, looking into the street. They had opened to supply some shopkeepers with the new currency.

A letter from home had been delivered to Lance that morning. He had not read it as he wished to relish the news from his mother in solitude, but he noted that it was from her, not his father.

Rudi was full of news about the foundations of his new house. The cellar was already lined, and the second course of sandstone blocks was being laid.

Lachlan declared that the currency was to be known as sterling, the same name used in England. Prior to this, the eclectic selection of coinage had been referred to as colonial currency. The English currency could still be used, but only the official smaller coins.

From tomorrow, all soldiers and government employees would be paid in the new coins, which meant some received a pay rise of a few pence, as the lowest denomination was fifteen pence. It was an easy way to circulate coins throughout the colony. This was also why they needed at least a third of the new money to be minted, as the month's pay demands would consume much of the first issue.

Last week, Brenton, Rudi, and Lance oversaw the delivery of the two full chests of new currency to the Deputy Commissioner-General's new secure room across the road from the government printer's building. These smaller iron-strapped chests were the ones that had initially carried the coins on the ship. They were made of heavy-duty material and bound in heavy steel strapping. The triple-locking system on these was undoubtedly adequate for their purpose.

The two officers bolted the door behind them and walked the short distance home.

The guards on duty moved to stand at the door.

Bill was still in their rooms upstairs. His job was nearly done, and he was hunting around for a home for his family.

Having finally been briefed on the project, D'Arcy was tasked with overseeing payroll distribution this month and ensuring each employee received the correct amount. The small locked boxes for each barrack were already packed and waiting, and the appropriate pay journals were ready for allocation. Each soldier received a slight pay rise. D'Arcy was to leave at dawn tomorrow morning and head straight to Parramatta to see Mark and report to Lachlan.

~

Government House, Parramatta.

On September 30th, 1813, Lachlan was up before dawn. He dressed and was already in his office just after daybreak.

Lachlan recalled the past months of frigid weather. He shivered. Houses in the colony were not built for comfort. John Hunter had built this structure with thick, insulating walls to keep out the heat. But that meant the rooms with high ceilings were difficult to warm in winter.

Today was the day the currency would go into circulation. Would there be riots? He hoped not.

He had initially planned Mark's departure to coincide with the release of the new currency, but because Henry was overseeing the construction of the two Parramatta tollgates, the Pitt Row tollgate opened early in the year. This was due to the need to replenish the government's coffers. With the new coinage, the turnpike roads would generate more revenue to fund road surface construction and repairs, thereby spreading the new coinage further. It had taken four years to reach this stage, but it was finally done.

Lachlan was pleased these plans had reached completion. He thought back to Rudi's throw-away comment and chuckled when remembering the astonishment on Rudi's face that same evening. To think the lad could have been killed before it started made him shiver.

With Mark's departure, Henry Antill returned to his full-time security guard duty and was not fully informed of the project until the week before the proclamation. Charles Whalan was an emancipated convict whom Governor King had initially employed as a bodyguard. Charles had since become a good friend. So much so that Charles was left to guard Elspeth and the official residence in Parramatta, should she not travel with Lachlan. Rather than get Henry's help with currency production, Lachlan diverted his trusted friend to another project. Henry had been overseeing the construction of the toll booth on Windsor Road.

Lachlan and Mark jogged along well, but he was glad Henry would return to his side. They had been friends for a long time, and Henry was Lachlan's confidante.

D'Arcy was working with Henry on the roads project as the tollgates now came under his authority. At Lachlan's instigation, D'Arcy had his fingers in many pies and managed them well. D'Arcy was also working to build the hospital, but it was not progressing as he had hoped. The man was also a magistrate, the police chief, and the toll collection officer for the roads. All of which he was more than amply recompensed. He was good at his work, and people liked him, especially the ladies. His piercing blue eyes were amazing. Even Elspeth had made more than one comment on how mesmerising they were. Lachlan laughed off the comment, but he kept the man at arm's length because of them. When D'Arcy Wentworth smiled at people, few argued. Lachlan chuckled. The debonair Irishman certainly had his uses. D'Arcy's familial connection to Lord Fitzwilliam at home had only been revealed when Bligh had D'Arcy removed from office.

Pushing aside a pile of paperwork, Lachlan stood and walked to the office window overlooking Parramatta. The view now was not the long line of hovels that had existed when he first arrived; they were now brick-and-stone cottages surrounded by market gardens.

The lengthy July edition of the Sydney Gazette, containing his proclamation, sat on his desk. His copy of the day's paper announcing the release of the new currency would be delivered around noon. He wondered how this news would be received, but it didn't spark riots. He fully expected repercussions from the Exclusives and some free settlers, but nothing had occurred so far.

Lachlan dropped his head and prayed for the lads and the work ahead of them. After some time, he lifted his head and gazed outside again. Rudi would need to deal with any significant ramifications. As a mere captain, he hoped he would have the authority to cope with them. That idea planted another seed.

Lachlan sighed and remained at his window. He had so much going on that his left hand hardly knew what his right hand was up to. There were many new roads under construction, a new hospital, and numerous building projects. With a list longer than his arm, the designs he wanted to build were more grandiose than the current builders could manage. The architects he had available were not capable of constructing the designs he envisioned for the towns. He wished he had another lifetime to get everything he wanted done.

A long sigh escaped. He had more convicts to house than he knew where to put them, and few, if any, came with qualifications of any kind, let alone the ability to garden or build. Many were still housed in tents, and others were crammed into the overcrowded convict barracks. Then, there were the three new toll gates on the designated turnpike roads. Mark had thankfully taken over the main Parramatta one to get it off the ground. Judge Bent regularly complained, but he and Mark expected it. He assured the troublesome judge that, if he was on official duty, he didn't need to pay. The men had arrived on the same vessel in December 1809, and Lachlan had his measure soon after boarding. They tried to avoid each other.

Mark had a supply of new coins to get them circulating from today; however, most tolls were mere pennies, not shillings. A larger fee was charged when herds or flocks were moved. The military pay was to be the means by which the circulation of the new coinage would be achieved. If they were paid only in the new currency, they would have no option but to purchase goods with these coins. He wished he had bought some coins in smaller denominations. Mayhap he still could. Any funds remaining from the building projects could be used to purchase additional coins as blanks at a lower value.

The introduction of a new currency and increased alcohol import tariffs would ease some smuggling and alcohol consumption, but not eliminate them. He had not yet thoroughly investigated Dennis Scriven and his activities. That too was on his to-do list.

Thanks to Josh's suggestion, when his sister, Jenny, asked about immoral activities outside a particular pub in Parramatta, that single question sparked further change. Lachlan had issued new alcohol licences. More than fifty drinking establishments closed, and others were placed on notice. They were given a few months to shut their doors.

He was disappointed to learn that one of his trusted officers, Phillip Margate, was returning home. His officer had resigned some years earlier and opened an inn in George Street, Parramatta. The *Bird in the Hand Inn* was somewhere decent people could stay, but Phillip had sold it to the owner of the *Red Cow Inn* next door. It was where D'Arcy chose to sleep when he needed to remain in Parramatta.

A long sigh escaped from Lachlan. Had it not been for that proposed sale, the *Red Cow* would have been earmarked for closure.

Another emancipated man, John Ellison, had been put on warning not to short-pour his drinks. He discovered that this man was distantly related to Charles and John Wesley. Lachlan wondered if the short drinks were to curb consumption. Though illiterate, Ellison ran *The Jolly Sailor Inn* at the government wharf and also oversaw Government Stores allocations. He was fully aware that Ellison and his wife had a safe room for abused and violated women, and he knew that few were aware of it, but he and the clergy did. Ellison ran a clean establishment because he had a large family and didn't like the drunken sailors who wanted to drink themselves into oblivion.

When William Cowper mentioned Ellison's familial relationship with John and Charles Wesley, Lachlan realised that, though this chap was a felon, he was trustworthy. Having met him often, Lachlan liked him. He discovered that the relationship was almost as tenuous as Rudi's to John Hunter. Ellison's grandfather had been brought up by the Wesley brothers.

Most of the drunks in town went to the *Woolpack Inn*. They could relieve whatever need they had there. Unfortunately, that inn was near the entrance to the official residence. Last May, he planted a few five-foot-high Norfolk Island Pines near the gate to add privacy for the official residence. These were from Simeon Lord's gardens. Hopefully, they would grow quickly and screen the house from public view.

The carnal activities at the *Woolpack Inn*, which had previously been done in public, were now outlawed. They, too, had been put on notice to clean up their inn. This drinking hole was first licensed by John Hunter. It was a double-storey building and situated in a convenient position for passing trade, so he had no plans to close it. However, he ordered that all outdoor drinking and other activities be moved into their fenced backyard.

Lachlan was fully aware that more illegal drinking holes had reopened, but they were cleaning up their patrons' behaviour. Flagrant debauchery no longer occurred in the public's view anywhere. He dropped his head and prayed that, somehow, God would supply the men he needed to ease his burdens. He dearly needed a friend who had not come to line his own pockets, someone with a strong faith who had no real ties to the colony. But how could that be? Who could possibly fit that role? He also needed a qualified architect with skills in working with sandstone. He sighed and turned to look at the massive pile of paperwork, awaiting his attention. That view brought another sigh, and he turned back to the window. No one had turned up to work with him and infiltrate the felons. He wondered who God would send and when. How would he recognise such a man?

Lachlan knew he was still unwell from his bad decision in Egypt, where he had contracted a disease from a lady of the night. That fleeting incident had occurred after his first wife died and before he proposed to Elspeth. He was still paying the price for that moment of personal gratification. He rubbed his face and felt the pox marks from the mercury-based medicine he had taken to keep the symptoms away.

He wondered if this medicine was the reason Elspeth kept miscarrying.

He watched as the students arrived at the potter's school down the main street in town. Aggie Osborne welcomed the younger convict girls and took as many as possible. Her husband, Colin, trained future potters in the mornings and educated anyone who wished to learn in their new shed every afternoon. Colin was another of John Hunter's protégés. John had found some educated felons willing to teach the younger convicts. Colin was one of the first people John helped.

Lachlan wondered if he could risk pausing his treatment for a while. It wouldn't hurt to try. They had already lost a tiny, sick daughter, Jane, not to mention many miscarriages his beloved Elspeth had endured. There had been six he knew about. Guilt about his condition often washed over him. She knew of his past but never condemned him.

He turned back to his overloaded desk and knew that looking at it would not reduce the pile of work he had to do. An idea occurred to him, one that would undoubtedly put the egotistical Rum Corp at odds. Most military farmers earned more than he did, and he would boot them off the list for free Government Stores from the Commissariat. William Cowper's comments about the needs of the poor had borne this idea. He would bide his time for the regulatory change, but the thought made him smile. Those men who claimed membership in this exclusive group had a dependent and parasitic mentality. They sustained themselves on the strength of their own egos and others' pockets. He chuckled at the thought of what their reaction would be when they heard about that change. He would work with John Campbell to prepare that proclamation. To date, these men had sold surplus food from stores and pocketed the proceeds. No more! He was determined to clip their wings and burn their sticky, greedy fingers.

With a final sigh, he returned to his desk and added a note in his diary. He could hold this threat over their heads should they cause strife. However, he would enforce it next year anyway. They had three months to conform, and he was fully aware that they would object.

He hauled out his chair and set to work on the pile of paperwork. He wondered how Rudi and Lance were coping with the start of the currency exchange. He set up a new office for them under David Allen's ever-watchful eye, and it had twenty-four-hour guards and more security than he had ever personally provided. Loss of any amount of the currency due to theft would render the project null and void.

The first thing he did was to write Rudi and Lance a note of encouragement to be sent in the despatch box that afternoon. He was confident they could handle most problems that arose.

Long ago, he had detailed exchange rates for the unusual coinage that was likely to be presented. The innkeepers would not be impressed that he had deemed the homemade copper tokens null and void for any purchases outside that particular inn from today on. By Christmas, they, too, would be cancelled altogether for use throughout the colony.

His stomach growled. He smelled Mrs Ovens making a cake that morning and hoped Robert Fopp would bring in a large buttered slice. His stomach rumbled as it was empty. He wished he had a coffee. A beverage he learned to drink in faraway lands. He could do with the strong stimulant effect today. None was to be had.

This morning, when he entered his office, it was not coffee he could smell. His housekeeper, Mrs Betty Eccles, had tidied the pile of documents but ensured they remained in the same order. The smell of the linseed oil and beeswax mixture she used on the window sills had a unique odour when the sun hit it, thus assailing his nostrils. However, she was a brilliant housekeeper. She was rarely in his way and never encroached on his family.

The woman was an emancipated convict who had been confined on Norfolk Island with her husband for some years. Phillip Gidley King first employed her as the housekeeper for the Parramatta residence. As he knew her from his years on the island. King surrounded himself with emancipated convicts rather than military settlers, as he trusted them more. Charles Whalan had been one of King's bodyguards. He still held that position, but now he was a friend. Bligh had lived in Sydney, so Betty remained in Parramatta to care for John Hunter's house. She seemed ageless, and when asked how old she was, her answers varied. Mayhap she didn't know. Lachlan had checked her records, and if she was forty-five at embarkation, as recorded in 1787, then that made her over seventy now. He thought she was probably close to eighty, but she refused to stop working. The maids cleaned the rest of the house, but Betty took pride in personally keeping his office immaculate. After a fourth long sigh, he knuckled down to reduce the stack of mail. He reached for the top document and began tackling the work. The scratch of his quill and the ticking of the hall clock were all that was heard in his office for some time.

~

Release day, Sydney

Rudi and Lance were to arrange the payments in town under David Allen's supervision. People were lined up at the door when they arrived. Tobin and Major Tom Turner were to oversee the resupply of the coins from the stock held in the basement. Though September, their new office had no windows, and the temperature outside was chilly.

For hours, they exchanged numerous random coins for the new currency. At noon, everyone had been served. Rudi and Lance were bored stiff. They had exchanged about five pounds worth of coins, most of which were Dumps. Shopkeepers had already been supplied with the new currency, so they were not the only points of exchange.

Hours had passed since the morning rush, and no one had come to exchange their coinage for over two hours. They had set aside a large amount of coins for Mary Reibey's store for delivery the next morning, before they opened the exchange. If they had time today, they planned to deliver the chest as their final duty. They were cold, hungry, fatigued, and totally bored. The chill September wind kept their new office cold. There was no hob stove or open fireplace here.

In the early afternoon, Rudi saw the familiar figure of the amazing lady walking towards them, and he grinned. He knew her well and wondered if she wished them to discuss the delivery of new coins to her store. Did she want to increase the amount of the currency she had been asked to stock for exchange? Lachlan trusted her with a large volume of coins to be repaid later.

The governor took a liking to this emancipated convict lady in her mid-thirties, much the same age as Lance, but she looked older. Rudi was impressed by her strong faith. She had been widowed only two years earlier, and instead of selling her husband's business, she expanded it. Her seven children flourished, as did her businesses. She expanded her farm holdings out on the Hawkesbury River.

Lachlan's friendship with many emancipated felons had endeared him to many in the colony. From his housekeeper, bodyguard, magistrates and now his banker, Lachlan was installing emancipated felons into positions of trust. Even D'Arcy admitted to Rudi that he had come as a doctor rather than be imprisoned as a highwayman. He had narrowly escaped punishment for his misspent youth.

Mrs Mary Reibey currently ran one of the largest businesses in Sydney. She was considering purchasing more ships to expand her importation business. Although she had just opened a new warehouse on George Street in Sydney, her main warehouse was on the waterfront. Her store often served as the town's unofficial bank. Becoming the only currency-exchange venue in Sydney would draw attention to her Docklands warehouse. She also owned numerous other properties, some of which she had leased to the government.

Rudi wondered how much money she was bringing to exchange today. He frowned. She did not appear to be carrying anything heavy, so it was not foreign coins. A sigh followed; it seemed they would need to deliver today after all. So much for returning to Bethan early. He knew that some larger merchants would need to keep international funds to pay for incoming merchandise, as the new coins would be worthless overseas. Mrs Reibey was one such merchant. That was the entire point of the project, but all local trade must be made in the new currency. There were sure to be exceptions to what they had discussed. David Allen had the authority to make individual decisions regarding such transactions, but he was unaware that Lachlan had already spoken with this well-respected individual. Rudi had explained the need for the chest bearing her name.

Lance ushered in the well-dressed widow and smiled, having only recently heard the story of her arrest. When only thirteen, Mary had been dressed as a lad and arrested for horse stealing. He was still grinning as she entered. Lance bowed politely and ushered her into the secure office. The knowledge of her background made him smirk.

The round-faced, bespectacled lady took the seat shown and wrinkled her brow. "You lads are mighty young to be given such a responsibility as this."

Lance chuckled. Knowing she was only three years older than he was. He replied politely, saying, "Yet old enough to be considered worthy of such a chore, ma'am, as are you. Once this is complete, I will take over convict assignments again."

Rudi laughed, knowing he was seven years younger than the esteemed lady. "How can we be of assistance to you, ma'am?"

The lady still had her thick Lancashire accent. She smiled and said, "I have decided to keep all my odd foreign coins as I need to make purchases from the various ships. However, I need these new coins for customers who buy from my store. That, of course, will need to be only in the new currency." She flicked her penetrating gaze over the two handsome officers. "Would you give the governor a message for me?"

Lance shrugged and nodded. "Yes, ma'am."

Rudi had met her before and wondered what was coming. Her benign smile concealed a wicked sense of humour. She said, "I would have appreciated a little more notice, although I suppose three months should have been considered adequate for most people, it is insufficient for a person with various businesses. Thankfully, I had the cash on hand, but other stores may not be in the same position. As the Dump is worth fifteen pence instead of twelve, this will make calculations downright frustrating. There being twelve pence to a shilling, I thought that would have been an obvious value of the smaller coin." She shrugged. "It's as well he's given us some months' grace, or trouble would have ensued. I have done my best to support 'the project,' as I believe your secret was called. I knew something was going on, but not exactly what."

She glanced at both faces. "People talk to a new widow, and many have loose lips. I put things together when I heard from the jeweller that Phil Tindale had purchased more engraving tools from him after being called into the governor's office. I knew, of course, that William Henshall had been moved into the residence above the printer's office with you, Captain Upcroft. And so I put one and one together and figured that we were getting a new currency."

Rudi chuckled. "Not much passes your keen eyes, does it, Mrs Reibey?"

She shook her head. "No, young man. I work hard at that. It's why my stores have succeeded when others, including my late husband, have failed. I save my pennies and spend the pounds wisely. I listen, learn, and keep my mouth shut. My risks are calculated ones, and I don't keep all my eggs in one basket. Men have learned never to underestimate me. They have also learned never to try to swindle me. I'm sad to say that my faith in God does not extend to men." She nodded with a smile. Lance caught Rudi's eye and grinned.

She continued, "I might add, I expect squabbling in the future. Are you really only going to give three months' grace? If so, I will charge an additional fee for currency exchange after that time, in addition to the governor's rate. That will add to my coffers nicely."

Rudi chuckled. "Yes, ma'am. The Governor warned me about your shrewdness. He fully expects there to be an exchange rate from you and others. Captain Upcroft and I must enforce this. On the morning after the deadline, we will visit your premises. Larger stores like yours will continue to receive exchange currency until the coin stock is exhausted. The official currency is the pound sterling, as in England. However, for everyday use, we now have our own coins. Of course, prices may need to be adjusted, but the value is now set. The government can also purchase products overseas with the exchanged coins in storage."

She nodded. "That is what I had hoped. Regarding that problem group, I fully expect they will push you against a wall and demand a free exchange once your Christmas deadline has passed. From what I have heard this morning, problems may well occur even before then. Be on your toes, gentlemen, with your eyes and ears open. Be assured, I will let you know should I overhear murmurs of unrest. My Thomas and I walked a fine line when the troubles occurred in 1808. We kept our noses out of all the fuss and knuckled down to work. Thomas and Andrew Thompson both worked hard to save people drowning during the 1806 floods. Both men earned the respect of our community. Sadly, Mr Thompson succumbed from the aftermath of a subsequent flood, and my Thomas's health was never the same either."

Rudi and Lance offered their condolences before she continued.

She shook her head with sadness at her loss. "My Thomas was a fine man and a good businessman. Although he borrowed heavily from Robert Campbell senior, he paid it all back and made a tidy profit. When he passed, God rest his soul, he left me quite well situated. I have endeavoured to grow the business in his name. Many expected me to sell up and live a comfortable life, but that's not my way. I have seven children to provide for, so I need to keep working. I saw what the colony needed and knew I could do it as well as Thomas, if not better. I was right." She stood and wandered around the small office. She dabbed at her eyes.

The two captains knew that her reputation as a gentle woman belied the toughness of her business acumen. When Governor Hunter was here, Thomas Reibey only had a small warehouse in town from where he sold grain. However, he also had ties with the East India Company. After the catastrophic Hawkesbury River floods in 1806, he and Andrew Thompson heroically saved many lives. As a reward, Thomas was appointed as a pilot at Port Jackson in March 1809. He had already begun expanding his product lines after additional floods struck. After a trip to India, he returned to Sydney sick, but with enough wealth and stock to pay off his debts and then some. He died in 1811. However, Mary refused to sell up and soon ran the largest store in town, growing faster than her husband's competitor, Mr Campbell. Her business acumen surpassed that of many of her competitors. People knew that the governor trusted her. Now, Lance watched Rudi get won over by the older lady. He wondered how many other younger men had underestimated her.

She returned to the desk and took a seat. She motioned for Lance to sit beside her. "Now, gentlemen, I'm willing to leave this extra money with you as I'm sure the new coinage is weighty. Do you have the capacity to deliver additional coins to my store at four o'clock today? I believe you will close soon. The governor said he would leave a quantity with me to be repaid later, but I prefer to pay up front. I have the first delivery, but this is for more." Mary opened her oversized reticule and pulled out a sheaf of notes in English pounds Sterling. A few were torn, but most were in good or reasonable condition. "£200 is what has already been delivered. There is £100 extra. Please count it. The £20 extra is for me, not the shop, so please keep that separate. I do not wish to carry that much around town."

Rudi was watching humour cross his friend's face.

Lance counted the money, as Rudi counted the £20 for Mary. Lance then nodded. It was all there. He wondered what percentage she would add for a commission for future exchanges.

Rudi said, "Yes, ma'am. We can do this. We close the office doors here at three, so that will be no problem. Do you have any particular place for us to unload?" He was fully aware that they had already delivered two hundred pounds to her. Now she wanted more.

The greying head nodded. "I have a drive-through warehouse, captain, so my customers can load and unload in all weathers. Drive in the rear, and I will shut the external doors for security. My store manager and I will oversee the delivery and the count of the new coinage. I might add I do believe that in the long run, this will be a boon and blessing to our town." She stood to leave. "Until four sharp gentlemen! I shall be waiting." Without further ado, she left.

No one else appeared for some time, so Lance took time to read his letter, then he fell silent. Rudi was busy tallying the books and did not notice the change in his friend's demeanour. Mary was the last visitor of the afternoon, so they locked the remaining coins in the new safe. She asked for £120 more, so Rudi placed the coins he counted into two small calico bags.

The bulk of the new coinage was stored under armed guard in the chests under the printer, where it would remain until needed. The rush to exchange coins was not nearly as busy as expected. Some storekeepers submitted delivery requests rather than come to collect them, but they expected this, especially in outlying towns. D'Arcy oversaw the distribution of currency to those stores while handling soldiers' pay and collecting tolls. This afternoon, Rudi and Lance would travel with Brenton driving, as they did not wish to carry the bags and chest of money through the convict town. They both carried their muskets in case of trouble.

Brenton was in the government stables. He greeted them happily. "Hello, chaps. Any trouble today?"

They had heard him singing as he approached. Rudi said, "No, but you sound mighty happy with yourself. What's up?"

Brenton grinned, dug into his inside pocket and pulled out a letter. "This came with the ship last week. It took a while to reach me as it was in the governor's mail." He folded his arms and smiled as they read the document.

Lance shouted in delight. "It's through! You've been exonerated."

Brenton grinned and nodded. He said, "This has been the second-best day ever. The best was the day Carol said yes to a very important question I asked her. I'm no longer listed as a convict."

Rudi read the document and congratulated him. Remembering why they had come, then he asked, "Can you harness a conveyance of some sort, Brent? Preferably, something enclosed. We three have a large delivery to make to Reibey's store and two other shops."

The three soon headed back to the new office to collect the counted money. Once the storekeepers received the new coins, they were all keen to get home and share Brenton's good news.

Lance was silent, but a smile still lingered on his lips.

Rudi was not sure it was genuine. He had wondered what had happened. Was there bad news from home?

Once the deliveries were made, they returned to the stables and assisted in storing the carriage and brushing down the steeds.

Carol was in the kitchen overseeing the preparation of the evening meal for twenty hungry mouths.

Brenton snuck in and slipped his hands around her growing waist. Carol was expecting their sixth child, but she refused to relinquish control of her kitchen. The four maids could all cook well, but Carol still oversaw the entire process. She spun around and chuckled when she recognised the large and calloused hands. "We should be setting a good example for these young ladies, my beloved."

Rather than reply, Brenton lowered his head and silenced future comments with a deep and searing kiss. Carol responded as passionately. The maids watching giggled while Rudi and Lance looked on in amazement.

Bethany heard the voices and arrived on the scene, followed by a horde of children. She turned and said, "Joey, take all the children back to the sitting room." Her comment made Brenton lift his lips from his wife's now reddened ones. "Sorry, Bethany, but please stay, children. I have something to tell you all."

Bill arrived as he spoke and joined the melee. Rudi and Lance stood at the doorway watching. As before, Brenton withdrew the letter from his pocket and handed it to Carol. His face showed the biggest grin any of them had ever seen.

Carol watched his face and noted his delight. Her eyes dropped to the document, and she read the welcome news. She had always believed him innocent. Rather than squealing with delight, she handed the letter to Bethany, then melted into tears. She walked into her husband's arms and wept on his shoulder.

Brenton said, "Can you read it aloud, please, Bethany?"

Bethany nodded. She skipped all the preliminary bits and then ensured his children were listening.

She read, "*After due consideration and the presentation of new evidence, your conviction has been overturned, and you have been completely exonerated. As compensation, the court has awarded you £50. However, the squire's heir acknowledged that you were merely doing your job as you were paid to do and that the presence of blood on your clothing showed your care for your employer. It was reported that you were found cradling his body in your arms when you were discovered. Therefore, his heir has agreed to pay you your full salary, backdated from the last date of pay, at a rate of £25 per annum plus a wee pay rise.*"

Bethany gasped. "Brenton, that's over £150!"

He nodded and grinned harder. He eased Carol from one arm and dug into his pocket. He pulled out two £100 notes and waved them in the air. "It seems we have enough to buy our own house, love."

Bethany lifted her eyes from the document and met Rudi's. He was standing between Lance and Brenton, grinning so broadly that his eyes sparkled. She chuckled. He had certainly come a long way from the dour man she had first met.

On arrival in the colony, Rudi was determined never to befriend a convict. For months, he chose not to make friends with anyone. Lance had been the first to eat away at his resolve. Brenton had wormed his way into his small group of friends, and then Bill had been thrown at him, but Rudi didn't push him away. William's studies led him to realise that all men were equal before God and that he was unimportant. Rudi grinned at his unusual group of friends. He was genuinely happy.

Bethany watched the smile stay on his lips. She had seen his gaze circle the assembled friends. Today, she had more news to share with him. Their household and family were to increase again.

Once the congratulations had been voiced, Lance slipped out of the kitchen without anyone even noticing. When the excitement of the kitchen had died down a little, Bethany drew Rudi aside. She had waited until today to break the news, as she presumed it would be a difficult day. It had not turned out that way. However, she had already waited long enough to tell him that she was nearly five months gone with child. He had been so busy that he had not noticed her fatigue, illness, or absence of menses. Carol had guessed and ensured that she had not lifted anything, but she knew Rudi had enough stress overwhelming him that he didn't need to worry over Bethany. Carol was only a month ahead of her. The Wrights' child was due at the end of December, and theirs was due in January or early February.

Bethany said, "Come with me, my love." She took Rudi's hand and drew him away from the overcrowded kitchen.

Rudi wished to give her his usual welcome hug, so he willingly followed her up the stairs and into their bedroom. These days, it was the only place they had any privacy. Even their children no longer entered without knocking. Bethany held the door open, but softly closed it after he entered. "Rudi, we need to talk."

Rudi spun around and asked, "Bethan, are you ill?" She giggled, which was encouraging. He pleaded. "What's wrong?"

She said, "My darling love, you have been so busy with work that there are things that you have not noticed."

Her smile made his heart skip a beat. "I'm so sorry, my sweet, but what have I missed?" Had he forgotten and used soap and caused her discomfort again? He looked around the room to see if there were new curtains or a new bedcover. It all looked the same.

Bethany took a step closer. "Rudi, I missed my monthly flow."

Rudi gasped. "What? Are we having another child?"

She nodded, and this time, she took his hand. As she had done the day they became engaged, she let him feel the baby's movements within her. Having already carried Benji to term, he knew he should not be able to feel anything until she was about five months along. "Bethan, how many months have you missed?" He felt a flutter under his hand.

Bethany dropped her head to his shoulder. "Some months, like about five." She hated hiding this from him, but she thought he would guess, as she desired his husbandly duties far more frequently of late.

Rudi pushed her away a little. "Five! Why didn't you tell me? Have I been that unobservant?" He groaned in anguish at his neglect of her.

She could tell that he was terribly upset. "No, Rudi. I hid it from you intentionally. Having lost the last baby at four months, you have had enough stress in your life of late. So, I chose not to worry you about my condition. Carol has been watching me closely, and as we are both carrying babies. Daisy has been fabulous. I always intended to tell you today." Her lashes fluttered. "Are you very angry?"

Rudi's arms slipped around her. "How can I ever be angry with you, my love? I willingly admit that I would have been worried sick about you. Especially up until the four-month date."

She nodded and lifted her face for a kiss. "So, I'm forgiven?"

He said, "Always." Further conversation was not required. They knew dinner would not be ready for an hour and that the four maids would look after the children. "So, that's why I have been required more frequently of late?"

She giggled. "Are you really complaining?"

He choked a laugh. "Hardly, my beloved. Whenever you wish."

She whispered, "Now?" They used the time wisely by officially resting. However, if anyone had listened at the door, the sounds that emanated from their room would have given away their enjoyable activities.

Dinner that night was late because Lance had vanished. He was not in his room, and no one had seen him since Brenton's announcement. No one had even noticed him leave.

As the children were hungry and the meal was getting spoiled, the extended family ate. Carol kept a meal for Lance.

Brenton and Rudi decided to go for an after-dinner walk to see if they could find him. They tried the barracks first, and then, after a while, Rudi told Brenton where he used to sit. They ended up at Bennelong's cottage and the small fort that was built on the rocky point nearby. Sure enough, Lance was sitting at Rudi's favourite lookout. In the dim light, his friends approached and sat on either side of him.

Brenton spoke first. "Lance, what's up?"

Lance reached into his coat and said, "You were not the only one who received mail."

Rudi took the letter, but it was too dim to read. He passed it to Brenton. He also couldn't read the letter, but he recognised the writing. Brenton asked, "Lance, is that your mama's writing?"

Lance nodded. "Father is dead."

Rudi gasped. He had never enquired about his friend's family makeup. "Oh, Lance, I'm so sorry. What happened?"

Lance remained silent for a few moments. He wiped his face with the heels of his hands. His friends did not want to push him to speak. "Mama said Father had an apoplectic attack just after Usher's funeral. It took two months for him to die. I planned to go home and see them all again, but now they are gone."

Brenton gasped. "Usher is dead? How?"

Before Lance answered, Rudi asked, "Who's Usher?"

Lance turned his glazed eyes to Rudi and said, "He was my older brother and Father's heir. Yeah, I know. Usher Upcroft is a mouthful, but Lancelot isn't much better. My sisters' monikers are worse." His head dropped, and he blew out his cheeks. With a low voice, he answered Brenton's words. "Mama didn't wish to tell me, but Ush has been sick for about two years. He had always had weak lungs as a lad, but he went on a trek to Africa before I enlisted and contracted something. He seemed fine when I last saw him. Whatever it was ate away at him until he finally wasted away. He had continual hot sweats, and it eventually wore him down. He kept rallying, and they thought he would pull through, but he died shortly before Christmas. They held the funeral on Boxing Day, and Papa made it through the service, then collapsed when he reached home."

Rudi gasped. "That's horrible, Lance."

Lance nodded, then fell silent. "Sorry, chaps, but I'm not such good company tonight. I cleared out so I didn't put a dampener on your celebrations, Brent."

Brenton slid his arm around his childhood friend. He knew Usher well, and the four lads had always been friends. "Lance, we've been friends all our lives. That won't stop now."

Rudi frowned. "What do you mean, Brenton? Now what?"

Lance answered the question. "Now that I have inherited the blooming title of Viscount Boulderson. Rudi, I have to leave. Mama needs me at home. Brenton's father and brother, Gareth, are holding the estate together."

Rudi recoiled. "You had a title all this time?"

Lance nodded. "Of sorts. I was The Honourable, but now I'm Lord Lancelot. In full, it's The Right Honourable, The Viscount Boulderson. Oh, cor, I must return to the horrible marriage mart and find a wife." He gave a groan of what sounded like agony. "Worse still, I have to marry one of those silly, empty-headed, giggling females that I came here to avoid." He turned to Brenton and said, "Elise was gone when I was last at home, or I would have had that sorted. I have no idea where she is."

Brenton said, "I wish I had heard she was leaving. Sorry, Lance."

Lance gave another groan. He turned to Rudi and said, "Your nickname was Moody Rudi, but I liked dancing, and they called me Sir Dance-a-lot. Elise should have been my Guinevere."

Rudi looked at his two friends. "Who's Elise?"

Lance shrugged. "No one you need worry about. She's gone."

Rudi bit his lip to stop himself from chuckling about his nickname and said, "Cor, Lance, why didn't you say anything? I knew you were upper crust, as few have valets. That was the first time it made me think about who each of us officers was. I figured we were all running from something, but I was so self-centred back then I only cared about my own hurts. All of us had personal staff."

A small ship was towing nets and fishing. They sat and watched in silence until it passed. Rudi thought about Lance leaving. He didn't wish to stay if his only real friend left, but where would he go? A wave of depression wafted over him, but he caught himself. God would already have that sorted if he wanted them to remain friends.

Lance said, "Well, you didn't say your father was the local squire. It's second-son syndrome, Rudi. We all enlisted for much the same reason. We were all born with silver spoons in our mouths. Brent's father is, or was, my father's agent, but his family were once squires before Brent's grandfather gambled it all away. We met at prep school, and then when his grandfather died, Papa offered his father a job and paid for Gareth and Brenton's schooling. Growing up, Brent and his elder brother were our best friends. Elise Price lived next door." Lance paused and sighed. "Rudi, you know what it's like. The heir inherits everything and receives the training to manage the estate. We are brushed aside—unwanted spares. Now, I must go home and try to make sense of all this mess, and I do not wish to leave here. Father never bothered teaching me anything." Lance gave a long sigh and stood up, looking out to sea. "Damn, damn, damn!" He turned towards his two friends in the gloom. "I have no choice, do I?"

His friends both knew he had to go. Neither wished to voice their sadness. Brenton said, "You will go, because we will all do our duty. We have always done so and will continue to do that. Come on, let's go back. You'll be taking letters carrying good news home to Gareth and my folks, so don't be in a hurry to leave."

Rudi said softly, "Trust God has your journey under control, Lance."

Lance nodded and asked his two friends to keep his news to themselves. He would say nothing to anyone until he spoke to the governor. "I've got no choice, do I?" he asked again.

Rudi shook his head. He knew that only news of Malchus's death would prompt him to contemplate a return home. A reluctant "No" was squeezed from him. With two children, the elder son would become the squire.

Chapter 17 The Beginning of the End

At the end of the first week in October, Lachlan arrived in Sydney as another convict transport, *The Earl Spencer,* had just dropped anchor. It carried nearly two hundred more male convicts. All of these men had to be vetted, logged, and placed.

Brenton saddled a horse for his boss the morning after his arrival and passed on a message that Lance needed to see him.

Lachlan's bushy brow cocked and said, "Any hint about what?"

Brenton's nod was followed by, "Yes, but all in good time, sir. He'll tell you himself." He cupped his hands so the governor could mount.

This was the first time Lachlan had seen Brenton since receiving his paperwork, and he congratulated him. Lachlan nodded to the stablehand and said, "I'll see him at the ship." He rode off with his young, armed groom, Josh, hard on his heels. Lachlan had half an hour before he needed to be at the dock, and he needed a gallop to blow away his cobwebs. Josh would trail the governor as usual. He was up on his steed and followed closely. They headed to the large park west of the main town and planned to take a few laps around the racetrack. Josh now carried a loaded pistol in his saddle as murmurs of unrest had reached his ears. Thanks to Mark, he was able to use it.

~

With the cobwebs blown away, Lachlan returned and hopped into the carriage that Brenton had readied while Josh tended to the two sweating horses. Lachlan saw Lance waiting for him on the foreshore. He waved Henry Antill away and gave Lance a few minutes while awaiting the call to board. "Spit it out, laddie. Brenton told me you had something to say."

A wave of sadness crossed the captain's face. Lance said, "Sir, I must sell out. My father and brother are both dead, and I must go home and resume their duty. I was the second son."

Lachlan nodded. "Second son of what, laddie?"

Lance lowered his voice and said, "My father was Viscount Boulderson. I must now take up my onerous duty."

Lachlan's face fell. His face rarely showed sadness. "I'll arrange the paperwork, Lance, though no ships are heading to London for some time that I know about. Most are chartered to go to Madras, Calcutta, or Batavia, and then return here. It could be next year before one comes."

Lance's face lit up. "Actually, sir, the longer I can delay leaving, the better. Brenton's brother and father have things in hand at the moment. His papa is our agent. I want to complete our project before I leave, and I believe a few months will be sufficient. Can you do the paperwork and leave it undated for the moment?"

Lachlan nodded, grinned, and said, "Yes, My Lord."

Lance groaned. "Oh, please, sir, don't start that caper. Firstly, someone might overhear you, and secondly, I'll have enough of that at home."

Lachlan chuckled. "Come for dinner tonight, and we'll chat privately. I have a man I wish you to meet, and I think it may work out well. Oh, and I'm here alone as Elspeth is not with me on this trip. She is unwell." Surprisingly, he grinned. "Did you know she is with child?"

Lance gave his congratulations and slowly walked to the approaching longboat. He assisted D'Arcy out of the boat, and the governor took his place. Henry jumped into the vessel, causing it to rock. This brought a chastisement to Lachlan's lips, but Henry just chuckled.

Henry was far more than just a guard. He and Lachlan had become firm friends when they fought in the Americas, where Lachlan was a captain. Here, the American-born Henry Antill was his Aide-de-Camp, as well as his friend and bodyguard. Lachlan trusted Henry above everyone else. Little occurred that he was not aware of. Henry knew of the new currency project from the beginning, but knew he would not be called in unless required. He knew he would be fully informed when the time was right. He had focused on overseeing the construction of the new tollgates and residences. Although he was not actively involved with the coin project, he knew what was happening. He took over Mark's larger quarters inside the new wing of the official residence in Parramatta and now trailed his long-time friend as a bodyguard.

Lance was kept busy working out where the new convicts would be placed. Over one hundred and ninety-six were on board, and he needed to review each record to verify their listed skills. He tried to keep his mind from what was ahead of him. Few of these felons had any noteworthy talents. One hundred and eight men were serving life sentences, and another fifty-eight may as well have been the same, such were their terms. The only option Lance had was to put them in the various pits. Some dug clay for bricks, some stone blocks, and others broke rocks for the roadways.

Lachlan's building programmes were extensive, but he still required a competent, skilled architect. None had come on this ship.

~

Dinner that night was a cordial affair. On arrival, Henry had both congratulated Lance and commiserated with him. He ate with them, then left Lance with the governor to discuss his news.

Lachlan poured a large finger measurement of his best Scotch whisky for Lance, and they settled back in the sitting room to discuss the situation. Lachlan spoke, wanting a reaction, and got one. "Well, my lord, I do not often sit outranked in this room. I know there are more than a few of you officers with illustrious backgrounds. You all come from the same mould. Brenton is another one. I never asked how you two know each other, but I presume you do, as he's always called you by name. Your comment on the docks infers a friendship of long standing."

Lance groaned at the reference to his new status and nodded. He revealed the long friendship. "Sir, Brent had no prospects at home. His father was born as heir to a squire, but they held no title. His grandfather gambled away everything. Our fathers were educated together, so my grandpapa stepped in to help his family when I was little. We remained close until I bought my commission in the army. In the Navy, as you know, you start as a midshipman and work your way up. That's not what happened to me. Like Rudi, we purchased our commissions as captains. I had hoped to face down Bonaparte, but that was all over bar the shouting by the time I had done my training. I was there to do some tidying up, but I saw no active service as such, so I was sent here. Don't get me wrong, sir, I have loved my time here serving under you, but now duty calls me home. Mama and my sisters need me. My sad duty is to present the girls at court when they are old enough."

Lance groaned as if in pain. "I have to face the giggling debutantes of the marriage mart and then thrust my sisters into it."

Lachlan chuckled. "I know that feeling, laddie. I was actually at a royal function when news of the chosen governor's illness reached me. Sir Miles Nightingall fell ill, and I volunteered before they could think of another candidate. I am here today because I spoke up." Lachlan leaned forward and looked the young man in the eye. "Lance, trust God. He is in control. He will have the right girl chosen for you. Henry is also a strong believer; otherwise, I would not have kept him so close. He said as much to me when I told him."

Lance gave a single chuckle, but he muttered, "Not likely!" If only he knew where Elise was. He would marry her in a heartbeat.

Lachlan noticed a swift look of melancholy cross his face, then vanish.

They chatted about dates and sailing vessels, but left the discussion unfinished.

Lachlan said, "Sadly for you, I have commandeered many of the arriving ships to make a return journey to India or Batavia before returning home. We're in very short supply of building materials, and although we have sandstone in abundance, I still have no skilled men who know its strengths and how best to utilise it. It could be next year before a suitable vessel arrives to take you home."

Lance chuckled again. "As I said on the dock, I'm in no hurry to thrust myself and my sisters amongst the vicious mamas and the piranha daughters. As yet, the girls are not old enough to be presented. Gareth Wright can act as an escort if they need to go somewhere, but they will be in mourning for at least a year. Mama adored my father, so she would not throw off her year of mourning early."

Lachlan nodded and reclined. "I have one more thing to mention. A very young lad has recently arrived from Calcutta, where he has been sourcing tea for his father's importation business in Brighton. However, he's here to inspect Marsden's and Macarthur's wool, amongst others. That is another arm of his father's business. The lad embarked on this trip as soon as he attained his majority. I believe he's been abroad for about a year. Once you have this load of convicts assigned, I would like you to take Marcus around the colony and show him the sheep farms and everything else. Though he's a little younger than you, he reminds me of Rudi. You know, innocent of the world's evils. He keeps himself apart from the rabble-rousing, and I've never even seen him with a drink in his hand. His name is Marcus Ryan, and, like you two, he is handsome enough to make most of the ladies swoon. However, I think he's too young to be looking for a wife as yet. He'll be heading back to London soon to report to his father, so in all likelihood, you will travel together. I suggest that you befriend him as he also is a man of faith."

Lance looked up at that bit of information. "Certainly, sir! It will be good for this land to have an export. I do hope he has seen Mrs Macarthur, as her flock is producing the most amazing fleece. The staple is long, and the finished product is soft."

Lachlan nodded. "He has, and is suitably impressed. However, she doesn't have the main flock on the local farm now."

Lance knew that her husband had demanded that she keep her Spanish Merino flock pure. She had. After five years, her flock had quadrupled. Now she was more than doubling her flock each year. Lance admired her greatly, though he also felt sorry for her. John Macarthur had only spoken to Lance once before he left, but that was to give him a tongue-lashing. If he spoke to an officer like that, how would he treat his wife?

Marsden's flock had much poorer quality fleece, and he was jealous that her flock grew so quickly, but had no idea why. Lance certainly had no intention of telling the rotund, flogging parson about her breeding programme.

Lance realised his thoughts had drifted off on a tangent. He smiled and said, "Sir, I have already assigned most of this lot of convict men to the quarries, as even if you don't have an architect yet, cutting stone blocks will save time when one appears, as we will need lots of them when things are ready. The same goes for bricks. The walls on Rudi's new house are up to the top of the first floor. He is waiting for floorboards, joists, and any other materials needed to install a freestanding floor. The only difference between the house he's living in now and the one he's building is that it will have an elevated eight-foot-wide verandah all the way around the top floor. They have found these wide covered areas wonderful as the breezes cool the house's interior and allow use of the outside area in all weathers."

Lachlan nodded. "I agree. They would be useless in England, but I dearly wish to install some on the house at Parramatta. I have added a covered area at the back because the western sun made the kitchen unusable. I like to sit out there myself as I can't be seen from the passing folk on the roadways. Here, I can sit in John Hunter's back garden, which Helena Milroy created. My Elspeth adores the climbing rose here, and it was that plant that gave her the idea of the perfumed garden out at Parramatta."

Lachlan paused and added, "Did you know that the Milroys' first child is buried under the rose? Helena lost it after some months. It knocked Crispin hard, but it was also the turning point in his faith. He told me, Reverend Richard Johnson's words forced him to see God as loving, not cruel. I can see why Rudi and Crispin get along so well. They are two of a kind."

Lance confessed. "I didn't lose a child, but both Brent and I had religion forced down our throats. William Cowper set me right about many things. It was through that conversation that Brent and I finally saw the difference between faith and religion. I have spoken to Henry sometimes, as I know he, too, has a firm faith."

Lachlan's beatific smile was followed by, "I'd be lost in this role without something to believe in and a trusted friend to pray with. It's why I keep him close. Henry grounds me. He knows all about my past errors, yet he does not judge me." His fingers moved to his pox marks.

They chattered benignly for some time before Lance took his leave.

Lachlan bowed to him before he opened the door. This was indeed a very unusual situation.

Lance said, "Sir, may I ask that things remain as they were? I am me. I am no more worthy of that than I was before. Very few know of the situation, and I intend to keep it that way."

Lachlan chuckled. He had intended to stir the lad up. It had worked. "Very well, laddie, but be assured you can let me know what you need. I shall be in touch when Ryan returns to town. I don't suppose you would mind him staying in your spare room, would you? It will be months before you both leave."

Lance shrugged. "Fine by me, sir. It's your flat. It will allow me to get to know him before we sail."

Lance took his leave and returned to his room.

~

Contrary to expectations, the currency exchange proceeded smoothly over the three-month amnesty period.

Overall, people were pleased to finally have access to an official local currency. This eliminated squabbles over the designated value of various foreign coins, many of which had been clipped, thus reducing their value.

Peace settled in town, although word of a few incidents still reached the ears of those listening. The notable absence from the exchange rooms was the military farmers. Few had come to exchange any sizeable amounts of foreign coins, and Lachlan questioned Rudi about this. Was trouble simmering?

As everyone now advertised prices in pounds sterling and coins were widely available, everyone in Sydney and Parramatta seemed happy.

~

Christmas 1813 came and went in a wave of fires, droughts, storms, and overwhelming heat. The military farmers only had one week left to exchange their funds, but they still had not appeared.

There was no sign of Marcus Ryan, but they knew he was alive. He had sent a message to the governor saying he would arrive in mid-January. Marcus had bought a horse and had ridden through much of the farmland to the south. He was currently residing on a small farm where Elizabeth Macarthur had moved a flock of her Merino-cross sheep.

As Lachlan knew that Elizabeth Macarthur was in Parramatta with their Spanish Merino flock cropping her orchard, only the overseer was in residence on the Camden farm. Lachlan was thrilled that Marcus was checking the quality of the new wool strain.

Bill and Rudi finally finished milling the last batch, and the completed coins remained under guard in the basement.

Milling the final batch of coins had been the last job to complete. All forty thousand Spanish Reales had been processed, and the nearly eighty thousand coins would go a long way to settle the colony. These coins were not for release until later in the year and were date-stamped 1814 with the final die.

The second grill door was triple-locked, and Rudi checked it daily. People now knew where the new currency stockpile was housed.

Lachlan doubled the armed guard. One stood at the gate, and the other three walked the perimeter. They swapped each circuit.

Now that Bill was free, he moved out. He had found a paying job with accommodation and was hunting around for a residence for his family when they arrived.

~

On New Year's Day 1814, Rudi set the cat amongst the pigeons by permanently closing the currency exchange room and refusing to accept any more coins. That afternoon, one of the Exclusives arrived in town to make an exchange. A sign on the door directed everyone to Mary Reibey's store, noting the different exchange rate fee. No exceptions would be made.

During that week, Rudi was accosted on more than one occasion by military personnel seeking to exchange their coins. He shrugged and directed them to the waterfront warehouse. One flung threats back at him as he walked away.

That night, a threatening note was attached to his front door. "You'll keep, Greenwood. Watch your back!" Rudi tore it off the nail, but wanted to show the governor.

Campbell's, Reibey's, and a few other stores were venues for outlying farmers who had missed the three-month moratorium on coin exchange. Mary Reibey's store now held the bulk of the colony's coinage and became an unofficial bank. She would exchange all foreign coins for the new currency. All the inn tokens were valueless, even at the specific inns.

Mary kept a ledger of her coin balance and used the foreign currency to purchase goods from incoming ships. Business was booming for her because the exchange rate was favourable. It was money for nothing for her. As the ships needed to restock, they did it from her store rather than Campbell's next door.

Few other stores had underground vaults to secure funds. This had been excavated from a single large sandstone block. The fortified grill door had an iron hatch and was only accessible from Mary's office. Her office was reinforced with iron grilles on the small window and another grille on the door. Armed guards patrolled the waterfront.

~

A few days after the exchange office closed, the news came that another convict transport vessel was approaching. This ship was the *Wanstead,* and she dropped anchor on January 9th 1814. She carried one hundred and seventeen female convicts.

Lance was back on convict assignment duty with Geoffrey again.

Only twenty-nine of these felons were sentenced to life; most received sentences of only seven years. This made things easy as they could be assigned as servants in the numerous houses springing up in the new settlements.

D'Arcy did the official medical inspection. He found that the convicts were well, and only two had died during the voyage. He gave the all-clear for Lachlan, Henry, and Lance to board and begin the assignment process.

The first man Lance met was the extremely young Captain Guy Manning, who had arrived to command the replacement troops for the colony. As both were the same rank, they waited together until given the all-clear to go below. The handsome young man stood at eye level, which was unusual for Lance. He and Rudi were far taller than most men their age, and only Mark towered above them.

Once Lachlan and Henry descended into the hell below, Guy grinned and instantly endeared himself to Lance. He asked, "Any hints on my new boss?"

Lance nodded a greeting to the passenger and turned back to the new young soldier. He smirked. "Yes, keep your nose clean and have nothing to do with the free settlers or lining your own pockets. He's a man of faith, so if you believe, you will go down well. Stick to the job at hand and be straight with him, and you won't go wrong. Oh, and help the helpless. Don't let bullies overpower your commitment to protecting the less fortunate. Are there any of the girls on board I need to help? Most of these cruises into hell have a few."

One of the female passengers waited on the deck with her convict maid, who held a baby. Guy hoped that Lance could find somewhere safe for this woman. Guy nodded towards the woman and child beside him and gave Lance the names. "Other than Kate over there, Mary Amelia Harlow and Catherine Lattimore are two who behaved well and need a good placement. A safe place for them would be good. I've done what I could, but some of those light skirts below would hump a dog if they were paid. They are a bunch of guttersnipes and light-fingered wontons. These three girls are not. They, along with a few others, need a chance to make something of themselves. I can write a list of who they are." Guy nodded towards the passenger and explained. "Kate Harrison is the other one; she gave birth in Rio de Janeiro. She and her son need a safe place. She's a cut above the rest, so I assigned her to a passenger. I have a feeling she is not what she appears to be. She's certainly upper-class. She says the child is legitimate, but she refuses to discuss her husband. It makes me wonder if she is using her real name."

Lance noted the names. He had two men in Windsor looking for housemaids. "Do the two girls get on well?"

Guy nodded. "Yes, they have been in the same cell block and have become friends."

Lance smiled. "Good, as they will be two doors from each other in Windsor. How about we deliver them ourselves? That is, if you are not assigned elsewhere." He paused and said, "This Kate woman must wait until later. She can bide her time at the gaol with the others. She has a baby, so she will be more difficult to place. I have a bit of sway with the governor, and I might take you and another fellow on a tour of the settlement if he turns up. Interested?"

"My oath, I am," Guy said quickly. "Yes, sir, I'm in if you can wangle it." He heard the governor call his name. "Damn! We have to go."

The men each covered an eye and stood chatting for a moment

longer. Lance looked at the young soldier. He had hardly started to shave. He doubted that Guy would even be twenty. They moved to the open hatch and descended the stairs, uncovering their eye at the bottom. This trick allowed them to see in the darkened deck.

For an hour, they followed the governor as he inspected the convicts and the cargo the ship had brought. The animals that had fed the passengers needed to be taken ashore first. Guy needed to remain on board, but Lance offered him Bill Henshall's old room. At the mention of Bill's name, Guy almost jumped. "Did you say, Henshall?"

Lance nodded. "Why?"

Guy chuckled and said, "Come, I have someone for you to meet." Guy led the way to the passenger deck and knocked on a cabin door.

A woman opened it, and Guy introduced them. "Mrs William Henshall, please let me introduce you to Captain Upcroft, late flatmate of your husband." After a few moments of chatting, Lance had to leave with Lachlan. "I shall inform Bill of your arrival, madam." He bowed and left.

Once on deck again, Lance said, "I should have guessed she would arrive soon. Bill has just found them a place. He moved out only a short while ago." He saw Lachlan and Henry waiting for him and said, "I must away. We're above the government printer. I'll tell you why later."

Guy waved as his new friend's head vanished below the railing as he climbed down the rope ladder. He watched the longboat row ashore and saw Lance in deep conversation with the governor. He turned and waved once ashore, giving the double thumbs-up signal. Guy was delighted. Not only did he have free accommodation that wasn't among the rabble of uncouth soldiers, but he also had a tour guide. If his flatmate knew the governor that well, that could be useful.

~

By the end of the week, Lance had helped Guy move into his rooms above the printer. He discovered the young officer was only eighteen. His age was legal, but only just. He had purchased his commission with his share of the family farm's sale. His little brother, Brad, was living with their married sisters, so Guy divided the family money equally among the four of them. That alone made Lance admire this young lad. The governor also liked the young captain.

Marcus still hadn't shown up, but he had written to say he would be in Sydney the following week. Bill collected his family and settled them into their new cottage. It wasn't much, but it was theirs. The governor had arranged a higher-paying job for him and provided a reference. Then, he warned him that further forgery would result in the revocation of his freedom. Having already been convicted twice, Bill knew this and was determined to remain on the straight and narrow for his family's sake if nothing else. Since news of his involvement in the coin project surfaced, he had gained the community's respect.

Marcus's delay in arriving would give Lance time to take Guy and the two convict girls to Windsor for their assignment. The mail coach was by far the quickest, but that would leave them without transport.

Lance arranged rooms for them in the barracks at the northwestern river town, and they would have a few days' break from the monotony of convict assignment duty. Rudi would do the assignments of the remaining women.

Hopefully, this Marcus fellow would have appeared by the time they returned. Lance wondered what he was like and how they would get on. At least both his new housemates were young.

While Lance and Guy were away, the flat upstairs remained empty. With all the coins now made, Rudi was at a loose end. As Lance was delivering the two young convicts to Windsor, he was covering for his friend on duty, but he knew he would need to be reassigned soon. They may even lose this house, and the new one, although taking shape, was far from complete.

When it was getting towards dusk, Rudi was sitting on his back verandah next to Bethany when he heard a knock on the front door.

They were watching everyone at work in the back garden. He called down to Daisy, who was covered in dirt, "I'll get it. Keep working and watch for Benji; he's just about to climb the back gate."

Rudi moved fast when he heard a second knock. He pulled the door open and saw a young man with one of the kindest faces he had ever seen. There was something about this overgrown boy that made him like him immediately. Rudi drank in his first impression of the lad. "Hello, may I help you?"

The young man smiled. "I hope so, sir. Governor Macquarie sent me. I'm Marcus Ryan, and he said there is a room for me here."

Rudi chuckled. "Sorry, I expected a rough-looking older man, not a young lad. I have no idea why, as he did not describe you. Come in, I'm Rudi, by the way. We certainly have a room for you, but you will be alone for the next day or so. The occupants of the flat eat with us, which is why the governor has sent you here, not there."

Rudi led the way through the hall, grabbing a key off the wall before exiting via the back door and into the garden. He turned and looked up, saying, "Bethan, love, Marcus Ryan has arrived. I'll take him over and get him settled." The lovely lady waved back.

Marcus gave her a bow, knowing that he would be introduced to her later. He heard the children's voices from the backyard, but Rudi did not head towards them. It was fortunate that the governor mentioned this was a very informal household.

Rudi slipped the key into the well-oiled lock and led his visitor up the stairs. The apartment was light and airy, and Rudi led him through the sitting room and to the bedrooms. "Oh, by the way, we're all on first-name terms, that's why I'm Rudi, not Greenwood." He stood in the doorway of the bedroom. "Well, young Marcus, you could have chosen between two rooms last week, but Lance met another soldier, and he moved in here a few days ago. So you're to be in this room. They are out at Windsor delivering some convict girls and ensuring they are safe."

Marcus gasped. "You care about them?" He was delighted about this.

Rudi spun around to face the questioner, then said, "I didn't, but then I discovered God loved me just as much as them. Now, Lance and I do what we can for the younger ones. Assigning them to lustful louts will not benefit them, or us. Plenty of women are willing to warm those beds, and that's their choice. We save every girl we can. This new chap, Guy Manning, seems to have similar principles. He's younger than you as he's only eighteen. The governor said you seemed like a nice fellow, and we are to show you around town."

To date, Marcus had said very little. "This will do fine, thanks, sir." He carefully placed his bag on the bed and turned to his host. "I've been investigating the sheep farms for my father's woollen mill at home. Prior to that, I was in Ceylon, visiting tea-producing plantations. I've been away from home for a year, working for my father instead of taking a grand tour. That was not my sort of thing. However, with the war on, it was impossible anyway."

Rudi chuckled. "A bit hard to go traipsing around Europe with Bonaparte on the rampage." He saw the new resident nod. "Come on, let's go and meet everyone." He led the way back to the sitting room, then paused. He briefly outlined who was who and then led the way outside. He locked the door and handed Marcus the key. "We live in a town full of felons, Marcus. Always lock up after yourself, or you will return to find nothing is left. Even the fruit from the governor's tree gets a guard put on it when it's nearly ripe, so consider yourself warned."

Marcus chuckled. "I will, thank you, sir; I mean, Rudi."

When they walked back downstairs, the backyard was now empty. Marcus realised the children were all heading indoors. He noticed a very expectant lady being escorted by a well-dressed man. A teenage lad and numerous younger children were milling around the buckets of water. Most were washing off the dirt from the garden and getting ready to eat. His stomach rumbled as he had not eaten since that morning. By the time the evening meal was over, Marcus felt at home. The extended family prayed before eating and thanked God for their food. As he did this when at home, it made him comfortable.

~

Three days after Marcus's arrival, Lance and Guy returned. Only then did he discover the full extent of what the two older captains had been doing. Guy was astonished that Lance had said nothing. It was only when the governor visited that the truth was revealed.

The governor turned to Rudi and said, "Well, laddie. You have set the cat amongst the pigeons this time. You didn't tell me that you had refused to actually personally exchange some of the outlying free settler farmers' money." He roared with laughter and explained what he meant to the two astonished men. "Manning, Ryan, these two men who have befriended you are the saviours of this colony, at least in this field. Until Rudi had the grandiose idea of creating our own currency four years ago, we were running out of cash. What foreign coins were brought in left the shores as fast on the merchant ships. Hotels, inns, and drinking holes created their own tokens to serve the purpose, but there were more fights than I could count over the official value of said foreign coins. Then Rudi had his spur-of-the-moment idea to make our own currency. Unique ones that no one else could use. We didn't have a mint, but we did have felons who were forgers. Add them together, and we make these." He dug into his pocket and pulled out a handful of Holey Dollar coins and a few Dumps. As these were newly minted, the silver had not yet blackened. A shaft of sun caught them and flashed as he wiggled his fingers. Lachlan added, "These have been a Godsend."

Guy and Marcus each had some of the smaller new coins. They each pulled out their coin fobs and examined the unusual disks.

Guy said, "You made these, Rudi?"

Rudi hated being in the limelight and said, "Yes and no. My idea was a throw-away comment. I had no idea that Sir would actually do it. Lance streamlined my comment, and Sir set the wheels in motion."

Marcus asked, "But you actually made them. How?"

Lachlan's brow cocked. He waited for Rudi to reply.

Rudi looked at Lachlan for permission to answer.

Lachlan said, "Tell them, laddie. It's no secret now." He shoved his coins back into his coat pocket.

Rudi nodded. "Only minutes after my comment to the governor, Lance and I put our heads together and came up with what you now see. We had no idea how this could come about, let alone know that we would physically make eighty thousand of them ourselves. We were guided by a convict named William Henshall, as well as Reverend William Cowper, the governor, his security guard, Mark, his second coachman, Brenton, and us." Rudi nodded towards Brenton.

Marcus reached for one of each sort of coins from Rudi's hand. He had not seen the larger disk. Marcus said, "Go on, sir."

Rudi did, "Our ears would ring for hours after we had spent a night punching the centres out of the Spanish silver coins. Then we discovered that punching them was the easy bit. The coins were then annealed, meaning they were heated and re-stamped. Lastly, the edges and interior had to be milled to create the ridges along the sides to stop them from being clipped. It was labour-intensive, and it took over a year of almost daily grind to invent the process, buy the coins, mint them and finish all forty thousand. But they are now done, and we have put eighty thousand new coins into the colony. However, most coins used are the Dumps."

Marcus whistled as he passed back the coin. Lance turned to Lachlan and asked, "Sir, what did Rudi do to upset the Exclusives this time?" He knew about the note on Rudi's door.

Lachlan's eyes glinted. He chuckled before replying. "I shall answer that by telling our new friends who the Exclusives are. Manning, you will need to know. Be careful of associating with them." He now looked at Guy and Marcus. "Many of these men arrived in the Second Fleet or soon after, certainly before Governor Hunter came in 1795. After Governor Phillip left a few years earlier, Major Francis Grose took over and began granting land to the New South Wales Corps. This was against the direct order of King George III's edict. All land was to be for the government only. No indigenous peoples were to be harmed, and there were orders for the new settlement to foster friendship and learn from them. That worked fine until Governor Phillip's ship was out of sight in 1792. Over the following days and months, Major Grose decided to carve up the land for his friends. Fights ensued as one got better land than another. This group, along with some like-minded Free Settlers, soon became known as the Exclusives. John Macarthur was only a captain, but he quickly grabbed large tracts of fertile land. His voice was louder than his senior officers'."

Rudi and Lance nodded.

Lachlan continued. "Marcus, you have had business dealings with some of them, so be warned; they will do almost anything to make a profit. Mrs Macarthur is fine to work with, but her husband is currently banished for his part in what is called the Rum Rebellion, in which the military overthrew Governor Bligh. I trust none of them, and neither should you. I'm sure they would sell their grandmother if they could get away with making a profit from the sale."

Marcus paled. "Have I done the wrong thing in discussing contracts?"

Lachlan smiled. "Absolutely not, laddie! I'm only warning you to be very careful in your dealings with them. Dot your 'I's and cross your 'T's. We need an exportable product that will generate revenue for the colony. Wool could well be it. It's why I befriended you. We don't have the climate for tea, but with the help of merchants who own woollen mills, like yours in England, this could be the turning point for this land. Marcus, that is why I encouraged you to visit Elizabeth Macarthur's farm farther south and stay at Mark's new shop. I knew you would be safe with my friends down there and that they would show you the farms in that area."

Lance frowned. "But sir, what did Rudi do to upset them?"

Lachlan relaxed. He looked at Rudi as he answered. "Ahh, well, like Rudi, they didn't read their newspapers. They missed the three-month window for the free exchange of coins, so they must pay the higher exchange rate to Mary Reibey. Had they caught the window, then they would have had more money in their hand. Rudi did as I instructed, and he refused to accept any private coin transactions when he closed the exchange office on the final day of December. I alone can permit where they go. So, they lost a lot of money. You know about the threatening note pinned on the front door. It has been followed by overheard conversations detrimental to Rudi. For now, the coins will remain in the basement of your building, lads. This last lot is stamped 1814, so they could not be put into circulation until this year anyway."

Guy met Lachlan's gaze. "Sir, do you mean that the treasury is under our building? So, I'm sleeping on a gold mine?"

Lance, Rudi, and Lachlan all nodded.

Rudi grinned. "Yes, you are. Call it being on security duty. However, it's more of a mint than a mine."

Lachlan said, "Why do you think your building is so heavily

guarded?"

Marcus chuckled. "And here was I thinking I was safe at the top of a print shop."

Lance said with a sly grin. "Other than the governor's residences, there is no safer place in the colony."

Marcus laughed. He relaxed as his shoulders shook.

Lachlan nodded. "I would agree, but the previous governor may not. I won't say where he was discovered, but suffice to say I ensure the beds are clean underneath them."

Rudi choked on a laugh. "Sorry, sir!" He knew the rumour well.

Lachlan turned to Marcus and said, "Even the church was once burnt to the ground. The felons here have no loyalty to the church, so they got rid of it while Governor John Hunter was here. Mind you, John did not let them beat him. He had just finished the new two-storey grain storeroom. The grain was stored on the lower level, but the top floor was empty. Governor Hunter, as he was then, he's now an admiral, and Reverend Richard Johnson moved the services there that week." He chortled at the felon's actions. "They did not miss one single Sunday service. The chained felons had to sit on the hard floor rather than in pews. The fire occurred on a Monday, so everything was rearranged quickly, and services were scheduled for the following Sunday. As the fire started at the main doors of the nave, Richard Johnson and his friends had time to save his library of books, his robes, the registers, hymn and prayer books, and other church paraphernalia. All those had been stored in the vestry. Temporary seating was hastily made for the free settlers, and services remained there until only a few years ago when the current church was finally completed."

Marcus turned to Rudi. "And all this new currency started from a throw-away comment?"

Rudi, Lance, and Lachlan nodded in unison.

Lachlan chuckled. He explained, "And now Rudi has the Exclusives offside because they have to pay more to exchange their old currency. This fine young fellow would not kowtow to their demands." He slapped Rudi on the back and gave a shout of laughter. "They hate him because they lost hundreds of pounds due to their own egos. He may soon require his own security detail. They wish to lynch him. Mayhap I should send him home for his own safety. I may place a guard on his house as a precaution. No, I will get the current guard to circle your house on their rounds of the printery."

Chapter 18 Fond Farewell

Carol's cries woke Bethany just after midnight on January 27th. Their sixth child was coming, and rather than run up and down the staircase and out to the loft, at Bethany's insistence, Brenton had moved Carol into the house and installed her in the visitor's room only yesterday. Daisy moved in with the children.

It was another uncomfortable, hot, and steamy night when everyone had thrown off all their bedclothes. For four hours, Carol held her cries in. Eventually, she could stifle them no longer.

Bethany dug Rudi in the ribs and suggested that he fetch the midwife and a doctor. He initially thought Bethany was going into labour, but then heard a cry rent through the stillness. "Carol!"

Bethany nodded. "Yes, dear one, Carol, not me. Although I do not think my time is far away, as I had a pain myself a short while ago. I think getting D'Arcy would be good, but Doctor's Redfern or Balmain will suffice." By the time Rudi dressed, dawn was breaking.

Although every window in the house had been flung wide open, the heat was already oppressive. Rudi's black uniform trousers were made of wool. By the time he had them on, beads of perspiration trickled down his brow and his back. He said, "I won't be long, love." He first checked with Brenton to ensure everything was well and then left to inform D'Arcy that he was needed.

Bethany pulled him in for a kiss and said, "Please, be careful."

The two men returned less than an hour later to discover Bethany was also in labour. The morning routine was shattered when the two expectant mothers were both in the travail of labour in adjoining rooms.

Carol was in agony, and D'Arcy realised the baby was breech. He had checked her only days earlier, and the child had since turned again. He asked Joey to wake the three men from next door and send them to get more help.

Fifteen minutes later, Ann Cowper and Doctor William Redfern arrived to help where they could. Rudi and Brenton stayed with their wives, as both had assisted with their other deliveries.

Bethany needed to use a basin only twenty minutes after Ann's arrival. For her to deliver first was no real shock to Rudi, as her other deliveries had been just as fast.

William Redfern remained with Carol as Bethany delivered her baby boy. Like Andy, Davy was small but healthy. He released a lusty cry and didn't need a smack to breathe. Rudi and Ann handed the newborn baby to his mother, and D'Arcy left them to check on Carol.

William had things in hand, and the senior doctor watched as another child entered the world. Catherine Wright came out fist-first, then bellowed. It was inspiring to see how quickly William had managed to turn the baby.

D'Arcy left the second room when he heard Rudi call his name.

Rudi called, "D'Arcy, she's done it again. There's another one."

D'Arcy wondered if she was having twins again, but he could only hear one heartbeat. Admittedly, she was larger than with Benji, but not overly so. He returned to Bethany's room to check whether she was nearly ready for delivery.

She still had a way to go, so they got her up on her feet and walked around the room so the second baby could turn.

An hour later, Elizabeth Bethany arrived. Her older brothers called her "Bet Bet" when they heard her name. Like Manda, the newest baby weighed just over five pounds; her twin brother was a pound heavier.

The two mothers were not the only exhausted ones in the house.

Work at the hospital had been left to the staff. William Redfern returned there after Carol passed the afterbirth. D'Arcy remained and oversaw the well-being of both mothers.

The three babies were healthy, and neither mother was bleeding too profusely.

When Bethany sat in bed after feeding the newest twins, D'Arcy said, "I had a feeling you might be having two again this time. You certainly were not as, shall I say, obvious this confinement, but you had morning sickness for quite a long while."

Bethany nodded, chuckled, and turned to Rudi, saying, "Six down, twenty to go."

D'Arcy almost jumped back in shock. "What? You're seriously planning on having that many children? I thought you were joking when you said that last time."

The young parents laughed at his shocked expression. Rudi explained. "No, not intentionally, anyway. Bethan joked about naming the children in alphabetical order just before the first twins arrived. When we lost the baby on the day the coins arrived, we realised that it would have made it to heaven before us. Since it would have been called something like Charles or Charlotte, we skipped C; hence, David and Elizabeth for these two. Although we should have done A and B for the first two."

D'Arcy chuckled. "Well, if you have them in pairs as you have done, you may well reach that number." D'Arcy gave all the usual instructions for post-birth recovery to both new mothers and then returned to work. He had been hoping for a day off today, but that was not to be.

~

Ten days passed, and both women were back on their feet. With so many willing hands to cradle a crying baby, the mothers rose to feed the child and then returned to bed to sleep. One or another of the young maids was on night call, cradling a baby or two or rocking them to sleep.

Daisy remained in the flat with the older children, while Brenton and Carol stayed in the house because all the babies shared the one nursery. Both rocking chairs were brought into this room and used extensively during feeding time.

They saw little of Lance, Guy, and Marcus, until Marcus arrived, puffing, one morning. "Rudi, Lance wants you at the dock. Another convict ship has arrived, and the doctor has sent Lance a message. He sent me to get you. Can you come now? Doctor Redfern said they had thirty-four deaths on this vessel, and the governor is livid. The doctor won't let the governor on board this time because he's unsure if the convicts are still infectious. Mrs Macquarie is due to deliver her child in a month, and no one is prepared to risk anything. This ship is the *General Hewitt,* and has many sick patients who will still need attention. Scurvy has decimated the felons, but some died from smallpox."

Rudi had been on an early shift and finished at two o'clock that morning. He was hoping for an afternoon nap but nodded. "I'll come directly." There had been a fight in the men's quarters, and he'd been called in to arrest the ringleaders. One of the usual troublemakers was duly manacled and put in isolation, awaiting judgement and punishment. He would likely receive fifty to one hundred lashes, depending on who the magistrate was.

Rudi kissed Bethany and walked to their door. He turned and walked back to her side, dropped his head to hers, and gave her a long, loving kiss. "I don't say it often enough, but you really are the love of my life, and every time I wake and find you in my arms, I know I've been blessed." After another kiss, he forced himself to leave.

Marcus walked with him as he returned to the dock. The young man had ingratiated himself with the harbour master and was learning the ropes of shipping from the deckhand. Hence, he had been nearby for Lance to send. As they walked, Marcus said, "The doctor said amongst this lot are some vile crooks. There has been a litany of diseases among the convicts, but he said some may be what the governor is looking for. I'm not sure what he meant."

Since the youngest twins' birth, D'Arcy had handed convict arrival inspections over to William Redfern. Rudi arrived at the dock as a tall man ushered two young girls onto it. When he turned to face him, Rudi gasped. Half the man's face had melted. He could not help but pause and gawk. He realised how rude he had been, lowered his eyes, and kept walking towards the military offices. The man, girls and some of their staff hailed a cab and drove away. With them gone, Rudi walked to Lance's office on the foreshore. "Hello, my friend, what's up?"

Lance nodded his thanks to Marcus for bringing his friend and almost closed the door in his face.

Rudi realised something was up. "Lance, what's with the strange behaviour? Why are you in here and not on the ship?"

Lance almost threw himself into his office chair. "First, and for the colony's benefit, three architects are on this ship. Two were convicted of forgery, but the other one is a soldier. With them here, the governor will have a good reason to hand over much of the building stress to them. But that's all well and good. Did you see the man with the melted face?"

Rudi nodded. "I did, why?"

Lance was so excited. "Rudi, that's Perry White, he's the Earl of Collingsford. He's here looking for his wife, Catherine. Can you believe that she arrived on the *Wanstead*?" He wondered if she was Kate Harrison, as she was a much better class of woman than the rabble. After leaving the ship, he had only seen her once when he wrote her assignment to the *Woolpack Inn* as a bookkeeper.

Rudi sat forward in his chair. "What? A countess arrived as a convict? How so? What did she do?"

Lance was nearly jumping out of his skin, but Rudi was unsure if it was excitement or panic. Lance said, "I was talking to the captain, Percy Earle, about whether he was going directly home or elsewhere. He's heading to Batavia after leaving here. According to the skipper, Perry's wife, Lady Catherine, caught him hugging her friend, and she intentionally stole something, believing Perry could have their marriage annulled if she were transported. Lady Catherine believed he would never set her aside to seek his own happiness. She wants him happy." Lance's fingers raked through his hair. "I know Perry well, Rudi. I have to keep my head down as he will have no wish to be known. I need you to take over processing this ship. Will you do that? I'll still do the placements paperwork, but Major Tom Turner will take the convict ledger to the house shortly, as I'm sure it will be summoned. I want to stay out of Perry's sight until I can speak to him privately."

Rudi owed his friend so much. "Of course, show me what is needed." He was about to check the books when he said, "Lance, I do not believe this is a coincidence. For this man Perry to be here just as you are leaving. I feel, no, I know God has a hand in this as well. Don't push him away, my friend. Seek him out if you can. Or if not, I can invite him over, and you can chat in private; you may be able to help him."

Lance nodded. "You think so?"

Rudi shook his head. "No, I know so. If he wants to be here in secret, then honour that. He could be the man that Sir has been praying for. One to infiltrate the felons and hear the complaints from the bottom. With his scarred face, he'll almost be ignored."

Lance looked shocked. "Okay, fine, can you ask him over tonight? Tom said he's going to suggest that Perry stay with the governor tonight if Sir hasn't already invited him to do so."

Rudi visited the ship and collected the conviction documentation for all the felons. They spent the morning sorting it out, and they processed the convicts on board quite quickly. Many would be taken directly to the hospital. Until the governor approved, the men had to be placed somewhere. Some would remain on board until they were well, and those who had recovered could be assigned to road gangs, which were less challenging than the pits.

Lance marked the three forgers for transfer to Parramatta Gaol until the governor was informed. They would be available if the governor wanted to speak with them.

By the time they arrived home, Rudi had met Francis Greenway, a felon who was supposedly an architect. He summed him up as a walking ego. The man had been found guilty of forging a document and could not believe he'd been caught. He denied it, of course, but many of the felons did.

As Lance expected, Major Tom Turner had been summoned to Government House and had been given the assignment ledger to take. Geoffrey was off duty, so the role fell to Tom.

Lance knew what he was here for, so he had the volume ready. He had put a dot next to Kate's name. He hoped it would not take long to be returned, as he and Rudi needed to complete the assignment of the new arrivals. He marked the page with a bookmark and wrote three names on a slip of paper for them to check. He was sure it was Kate Harrison, but she had a child. Only two other names were possible: one was Catherine Latimore, whom he and Guy had taken to Windsor, but she was too young; the other was Mary Amelia Harlow, but it was not likely Perry would have married either of these girls.

When Rudi and Lance arrived home that evening, they were summoned to visit the official residence.

Lachlan had some business to do in town, and Elizabeth Macquarie had accompanied her husband to Sydney for a medical check-up with D'Arcy. She had about a month to go before their baby was born, and they were taking no risks. They were to return to Parramatta the following morning.

As Henry Antill ushered them in, Lance heard Perry's well-modulated voice. With a cock of his brow to Rudi, they followed Henry to the sitting room door. Henry knocked and said, "Sir, the two gentlemen you invited have arrived."

Lachlan grinned. "Oh, thanks, Henry." He turned to Perry and said, "I believe you know one of these men."

Perry gave him a lopsided smile. Lachlan turned to Henry and said, "Please usher Lance in to Mr White. Then you may retire for the evening, Henry. I need to see Rudi privately, so we will go to my office."

Elizabeth had retired to her room after helping put their visitor's two daughters, Mia and Lou, to bed.

Perry stood at the entry of the new arrival. He wondered if it had been Lance Upcroft he glimpsed on the ship. If so, he was just the man he needed. From memory, the younger man did not appear to have any faith, but he needed him to keep quiet about his identity. Would he be able to beg for his silence?

As Lachlan exited with Rudi, he sent Lance in and shut the door.

He said to Henry, "I'll be with Rudi for a while, and Lance can look into any issues that arise. You were up at what, three this morning? Go to bed."

Henry nodded. "I will, thanks, sir. I'm dead on my feet."

Lachlan stood and watched his friend leave, then turned to Rudi. "We need to talk. Come!"

Rudi followed as ordered. He was also dead on his feet, but sleep would need to wait. He wondered if this was about the new architect. He sat where Lachlan pointed, surprised it was on the settee rather than at his desk. The talk was obviously informal.

Lachlan walked to a pile of letters on his blotter and extracted one. He hesitated before handing it to Rudi.

Rudi accepted the screed and dropped his eyes to the missive. He instantly recognised the lovely handwriting of his Uncle John Hunter. His capital C's almost curved under the words, and the lowercase D's encased the top. Why had Uncle John written to Lachlan? He looked at the governor and frowned.

Lachlan said, "From the second paragraph, laddie."

Rudi's grey eyes dropped to the document he held. His hands were shaking, so he placed them on his lap. He read,

"*Macquarie, I have enclosed a full letter for my nephew Rudi Greenwood, but it only details what I will now write to you. Having met his elder brother, Malchus, you will know there was little love lost between them. However, I need Rudi home.*

Malchus and his wealth-loving wife, Lavender, were returning from London when his coachman drove too fast. Along with their footman, all four were killed instantly. Being the closest family they have in the area, I was summoned to identify the bodies. It was indeed them. Unfortunately, this leaves the three daughters as orphans. Lavender's parents died last year, so the children are now under my care, and they are with my niece, Penny, and me here in Portland.

I need Rudi and Bethany home to bring up these three little angels. Fredericka, Georgette, and Henrietta were not exposed to their parents' egotistical attitudes as they were entrusted to the staff for most of their lives. Break the news to him as gently as possible. The only benefit is that I will see him more often. I love that boy like a son I never had. Please have him bring me news of the Milroy family and send my love to them. Young Jasper also wormed his way into my salt-encrusted heart."

Rudi realised that Uncle John went on to other subjects that were not about him. He was reeling. He had to go home to England. A groan escaped his lips. That meant he had to face a sea voyage. He sank back into the padded settee. Malchus had three daughters! He blanched, and the full realisation washed over him. He was now the squire. A frustrated "Oh no" escaped his lips. He felt ill.

Lachlan wondered if he would pass out. "Laddie, are you well?"

Rudi nodded. "As well as I can be. Sir, I don't want to go back."

Lachlan took a place beside him. "Rudi, I know you know the previous governor; you never mentioned you were actually related to him. I thought it was an honorific title. Your brother said nothing when we met."

Rudi had the courtesy to blush. "Well, it's tenuous, to say the least. I call him uncle as my Mother's sister is married to one of his brothers. The 'uncle' title is truly honorary because he is much older than Mama was. I adored him as a lad and his adventures. He's more of a loving grandfather to me. It was because of his stories from here that I came. Before I married Bethan, I used to visit the Milroys to learn more about what had happened when Uncle John was there. Connie and Nigel at the mill also often received visits from me, as did the Osbornes in Parramatta. Crispin honoured my privacy, so he never mentioned it to you."

Lachlan nodded. He blew out his cheeks. "Fine! So, now I must lose you as well. At least you can travel with Lance and Marcus. I will admit that I have been worried about murmurs of discontent from the Exclusives about your safety. Two have now put a price on your head. You will be out of their reach at home. For some reason, they think you are responsible for their own error and loss of funds. For the duration of your stay, please be careful." He sighed. "Lance was called here tonight, as the earl mentioned he knew him from home. He only caught a glimpse of him on the ship, but knew him well enough to want to see him. He's probably going to ask him to keep his mouth shut about his title. However, as Lance has his own title, I bet the warning will be unnecessary. I presume he revealed the gentleman's identity to you, as I saw you took his role today."

Rudi nodded.

Lachlan continued. "Well, he's only to be known as Perry White while here. I suppose Lance figured out why he had come."

Again, Rudi nodded. He knew that Perry was hunting for his missing wife, Catherine. He and Lance had discussed it in detail, but the only woman who fit the description had a tiny baby. Lance completed her assignment at the *Woolpack Inn* in Parramatta, where they needed a bookkeeper, and she was qualified. Guy mentioned that she was of higher quality than the rabble below.

Rudi had little care about Perry's search. The stuffing had been knocked out of him. A thought occurred to him. "Sir, my new house! It's finished and only needs furniture. What am I going to do with it?"

The governor chuckled. "Let Brenton have it; I hope he won't leave me, too, as he has nothing at home for him. He has money to repay you for the house. I'll ensure that the government endorses his new business. I'm considering appointing him to oversee a new stable block I intend to build. I believe a luxury coach-for-hire business would bring pride to the colony. He can run it from the new stables I wish to build. In the meantime, he can erect a large stable in the mews at the back of your new house, and I'll watch over them. Rudi, take this and read it." He handed him a sealed letter addressed in Uncle John's handwriting. "Hopefully, this will give you full details of the news you have just received." The letter was from Admiral John Hunter.

Rudi accepted it and stuffed it in his pocket. He was in a daze. "I have to tell Bethan." The governor's words finally sank in. "What new business, sir? Is Brenton starting one up? He has not said anything."

Lachlan chuckled. "He doesn't know about it yet. The town needs a coach service to collect and transport well-paying clientele and their goods. The hackney carriage service is all well and good, but I'll drag this town out of the mire if it's the last thing I do. Brenton will have a government endorsement to start this new venture—even an official warrant if necessary. Perry plans to hire him until he works out what he will do. I suggest you all move into the new house quickly. No ships are leaving directly for London until about mid-year. All the other vessels are heading off to India, Batavia, or elsewhere. So you have about three months before you leave. Decide on the furniture you want and leave the rest to the Wrights. I'll arrange passage for the three of you."

Rudi frowned. "Three, sir? I'm not looking forward to another sea voyage. I'm not such a good sailor, but I will not go without my family."

Lachlan chuckled. "Nay, laddie, and nor would I expect you to, but I meant Lance, Marcus, and your family. However, you will need staff." Lachlan watched for a surprised expression on Rudi's face as he spoke. "Vera and May are too young to remain here without protection. I shall assign them to you for the duration of their term, which is only two more years. They can then return to their home if they wish. However, based on John's letter, Malchus's staff will need to be replaced. Mayhap you can continue your rehabilitation work and drag those two girls' families out of the mire of a squalid life in London. Give them all some training and set them on their feet."

Rudi's face lit up. "Really! We can take the younger girls with us?"

Lachlan nodded. "Although they are now old enough to marry, they will only be set upon by lustful leeches if they remain here. No man has taken their eye, unlike the other two girls. Take them home and keep them safe. All their paperwork will be ready. Two of my guards, Gerald and Clarence, have their eyes on Daisy and Ivy as wives. They will be well cared for, so do not think I don't care about them. Once wed, they may wish to stay with Brenton or move into the flat. They get on well with Carol." He stood and moved to his desk. "I have something to give to you and Lance, but I will do that momentarily. Come, laddie. You have served me well."

Lachlan walked to his office door and said, "Soon you can go home and have a lovely life with your beautiful family. Bethany is a gift from God; treasure her." He carried two more envelopes in his hand as he moved through the door.

Rudi stood and followed him.

They joined the men in the sitting room, and Lachlan pointed for Rudi to sit next to Lance.

Lachlan said, "Perry, I gather you have sorted out your issues, so I will not delve into that, but these two gentlemen have served me well. They were jointly responsible for dual-handedly saving our colony from financial ruin, so I have the great honour of presenting you with these." He handed each of them a lumpy envelope.

Lance flicked his envelope open and saw that it contained various lengths of braid, a chunk of metal on a chain, and a document. He gasped, and his eyes flew to Rudi, not Lachlan.

Rudi pried his letter open more carefully. It contained the same braid items. He opened the document and realised it was a promotion and more. He jumped up and said, "But, sir, you can't do this!"

Lachlan chuckled. "I can, and I have, Rudi. The paperwork is already registered in London, and they sent these instead of new uniform coats for both of you. You are both now of the rank of major. Your uniforms are essentially the same, but you must add one or two gold stripes. There is also a brass gorget for around your neck. I'm sure Bethany or Carol can adjust your jackets. But this is my way of saying thanks for what you have done for me and for this town. Congratulations to you both! This rank is worth more when you both sell out. However, on that note, I believe the regent wishes you to remain on half-pay and be on call for him if required."

Perry watched, somewhat intrigued. He turned to face Lance.

Lance gazed at his paperwork, unbelieving what he was reading. He held a letter from the Prince Regent, who had assumed the throne after his father, King George III, became ill. On his second sheet of paper, the regent expressed his personal thanks for his efforts and stated that he expected to see him at court.

Lance glanced at Rudi and saw that he was now perusing his mail. He heard him gasp and saw Rudi look at Lachlan, who was grinning at him rather stupidly.

Rudi said, "But this other thing. He can't just do that, can he?" Rudi passed the letter to Lance.

Lance read the screed and saw that Rudi had been bestowed a title. He would become Rudolph Greenwood, Viscount Buckridge. He chuckled, and that grew into a belly laugh.

Lachlan grinned, nodded and sank into his armchair. "So now you all outrank me. If you three can't call me by my given name, then no one can. When I woke this morning, I never expected to sit here tonight with three peers of the realm."

He chortled, then explained his mirth. "Do you know that there are currently five princes, two dukes, five marquesses, twenty-eight earls, five viscounts, including you chaps, twenty barons, and over one hundred and fifty lords or courtesy lords enlisted in the armed forces? I am familiar with the figures, as I received them in the latest despatches. So, over two hundred of the nobility currently serve in various roles in the various arms of the military. Quite a few of them are here. You are not alone in keeping quiet about your noble ranks. I have no idea who the princes or dukes are, but I have served with enough of you upper-crust fellows to know you two are far more than just a title."

Perry started as Lachlan's words sank in. "Lance, you're titled too? You forgot to mention that. What happened to your brother, Ush?"

Lance explained that both Usher and his father were dead and that he was leaving on the next ship home to assume the title.

The conversation then turned to Rudi, who mentioned that he would be leaving with him.

Lachlan turned to Lance and said, "Rudi's life is now in danger due to his adherence to my rules. The Exclusives have a price on his head. England is the safest place for him now."

They had several months before departure and planned to catch up again. That meant Rudi was grounded in Sydney. For now, Rudi wanted to tell Bethany about the evening's events and that they needed to return to England.

They made their farewells.

Lance and Perry promised to catch up before departing for England.

When Rudi returned home, most of the children were asleep. Rudi drew Bethany upstairs to their room, where they would not be disturbed.

As it had only been two weeks since the birth, they were unable to be intimate. However, that was not what he wanted at the moment. His mind was on other things.

She sat beside him on their bed and listened. Whatever he had to say had knocked the stuffing out of him.

He inhaled deeply, then came straight out with the words he never expected to utter. "Bethan, Malchus is dead, and we need to return home. I knew he had children, but I had no idea they were all girls. I heard two were Fred and George, but they must have been nicknames. He has no male heir. They are currently under the care of Uncle John Hunter, and although his niece is looking after them, Uncle John has requested that we return home." His hesitant glance showed he wasn't finished.

Unsure of exactly what to say, Bethany took his hand in hers and caressed it. "There's more, isn't there?"

He nodded. "There is. Much more."

He dug into his coat pocket and pulled out the envelope containing the braid and gorget. "Lance and I have been promoted to majors, and we'll both be retiring from duty on half pay rather than selling out. The Prince Regent wants us on a retainer if he needs us."

Rudi handed her the various bits of gold tasselling and edging while holding the brass gorget. "Lachlan asked if you could fix up our jackets?"

She nodded. "Of course, Rudi, but something is eating at you, and it's not what you have already told me. What's wrong?"

He groaned. "Uncle John sent Lachlan a letter containing the details, and I'm sure there will be more information about the situation in my letter, but because the idea of the coinage was mine and I was in charge of the project, the Prince Regent has honoured me with a title." He turned to face her. "Bethan, I'm so sorry, but he has bestowed a hereditary title of a viscount on me." He released a huff and slumped as he explained. "This title fell out of use some years ago and reverted to the crown. Apparently, the old codger who owned it was a cantankerous old man, and no self-respecting female would marry him. Eventually, his housekeeper did, but they had no children. I knew of him but never met him." He groaned again, then sat bolt upright. "Bethan, I do admit that his house is magnificent. It will need work, but it will be large enough to bring in many girls who need our help. Oh, and Vera and May will be the first two. They are to return with us."

She was stunned. "You mean home to England? They can come?"

Rudi nodded. "They can, my love. They only have two years to serve, after which they will be released. Lachlan will do the paperwork, and we are to take it with us. The governor has charged me with helping to get their families out of the mire in which they are living in London. We are to start with them and their family. Lance's friend, Perry, mentioned that a friend of theirs, Elizabeth Fry, is to help the female convicts, so we are to hunt for her in London on our return." He fell silent.

Bethany watched as his expressive face showed concern, worry and then delight.

After a while, he said, "Bethan, if old Viscount Buckridge's house needs repair, that's where we will start. Rather than hire many tradesmen, we shall bring the girls' fathers and brothers to learn the trade under a skilled craftsman." He grinned. "We can do this, love. I can see how God can use us over there as He has here. It will be different, but we might be able to stop some of the young lassies from falling into situations where they end up here."

Unexpectedly, Bethany giggled. The giggle turned into a laugh, and she fell backwards on the bed, trying hard to stop the bubbling delight exuding from her lips. Unable to do so, she pulled Rudi down to her side and hugged him so hard he thought he would pop.

It was her turn to confess.

She moved slightly away from him so she could see his face. "That cantankerous old devil that you so aptly described was my grandmother's elder brother, so I know the house well. I wonder if the prince is aware of my connection. Probably! You are not wrong about it being large enough to house many helpers. However, I refuse to allow anyone to live in the attic bedrooms until they are refurbished. They are inhumane, and his staff were always getting sick as there was no heating. He blocked up the fireplaces in the staff rooms to prevent fuel waste. However, all the fires downstairs were lit, making the place a hot house. He only permitted his staff one thin blanket each for warmth."

She giggled again and said, "Well, Lord Rudolph, it looks like

God has a new plan for us and provided us with the means to help more than we can here."

Rudi drew her into his arms and soundly kissed her. "And do you know something… I never doubted that He would have it all arranged. Mind you, you never mentioned your illustrious background."

Bethany's head shook. "Why would I? I have no claim to it. He disinherited his own sister. We only visited when he was in London, so I went a few times. I met him twice and didn't like what I saw. That was after he married the housekeeper, but Granny was friends with many of the old staff, so we used to sneak in with her and see them. I was a small child at the time."

Rudi drew her into his arms and said, "I should have trusted God more, shouldn't I?"

Bethan nodded against his shoulder and then turned his head for a long and loving kiss.

~

The following morning, Lachlan sent a note, relieving Rudi of duty for the next week. He instructed him to begin arranging to move into the new house. Before leaving for Parramatta with Elizabeth, Perry and his daughters, Lachlan had seen Brenton at dawn and mentioned some changes. Lachlan would now work on organising the construction of a large stable.

Lance knew Perry's wife had been assigned to Parramatta, and Perry wished to collect her as soon as possible. Major Tom Turner was accompanying them with Josh as groom and Joseph at the reins. Perry's staff sat up with Joseph.

Lachlan would not give Perry's wife a pardon, but he would reassign her to Perry. The White's would remain at Government House until they could arrange accommodation.

Perry was the man that Lachlan had prayed for. God had sent Lachlan not only the confidante he needed but the perfect man to infiltrate the felons. Now he could hear what the masses thought, as Perry's face would merge with the scarred felons who lived in the penal town.

~

Only days later, news came that an unexpected merchant ship, the brig *James Haye*, had arrived packed to the brim with goods for the colony. The waterfront stores benefitted from the cargo, and the local jeweller purchased some pearls and dark pearl shells to make buttons and jewellery. However, as impressive as the cargo was, it was the crew who drew eyes. Some of the most remarkable male specimens of humanity were on board. These divine men were divers from the Otahitian Islands, known in Sydney as Tahiti. They had brought a cargo of Pacific Island pearl shells and black and rainbow-coloured pearls, unlike anything anyone had ever seen.

These brown-skinned, half-naked men made many a woman swoon. Initially, they were bare-chested, but the effect they had on the women made Lachlan ask them to cover up. They had tattoos on their arms, legs, torsos, and faces and were fierce-looking, but these man-mountains were gentle giants. All stood at over six feet tall, and they were all good-natured.

These Godly men preferred spending time caring for the orphans in town rather than drinking and carousing. They kicked a ball with the little unloved girls at the orphanage and purchased food and fruit for them.

William Cowper quickly learned that the London Missionary Society had visited their islands and that all the divers had a firm faith in Christ.

At Sunday worship, their harmonious a cappella singing was divine. Many stopped singing to listen to their harmony. The crewmen's singing was so good that the rest of the church would fall silent to listen to the harmony of their strong male voices.

Captain Folger of the *James Haye* informed Lachlan of his intent to depart around mid-year, unless he could source a full cargo earlier. This meant Rudi and Lance had three months to arrange the new house.

As the captain had to source a cargo to fill the last of his hold, Lachlan sent him to see Rudi and Marcus. All the possessions they had acquired would be sufficient to care for the cargo. Bethany wished to take her mother's big bed home, as it would return to the room from which it originally came. On one of the many visits to the viscount's house, Bethany's grandmother had removed her bed. She gave it to her daughter upon her marriage. It would now be returned to its rightful place, only it would become the master bed. The other furniture Bethany had brought would travel with them.

Captain Folger allocated them as much cargo space as they wished.

Marcus sourced as many bales of fleece from Elizabeth Macarthur as he could. This would fill much of the hold, and the Greenwood items could be stored on top. Marcus would have it transported from London to their mills in the north of England.

~

With the move into the new house the following week, they decided to leave the new furniture Rudi had purchased from India. They were taking only the best pieces of furniture Bethany had brought, as they held sentimental value. The bed was flat-packed and left to load along with the other larger items they were taking home.

Rudi wished to take his valet stand as a reminder of the happy days in the colony. It was made of red cedar and was beautifully crafted.

The new teak furniture Rudi had purchased was moved to the new house and would remain with Brenton. The second four-post bed that Carol had given birth in would become the master bed.

Rudi had a lovely local timber desk that he decided to keep, as Bethany had purchased it for him as a gift.

The two rocking chairs would be shared. The upholstered one would be put in their cabin with the baby's cots.

Carol would keep the wicker upholstered one for her baby.

~

On the ship, Vera and May were to share the cabin with the babies. The other three children would be beside them, and Rudi and Bethany's cabin sandwiched them. Next to them, on the far side, was one spare cabin where the small group could sit and chat privately, with another empty room on the far side of Marcus. Marcus was in a smaller cabin next to Lance on the other side of the corridor. There was a small storeroom next to him for excess luggage. No other passengers were booked on this return voyage, so two cabins were converted into an activity room for the children and a quiet reading room for the older children or adults. That left one cabin available for any late-booking passenger. It would also be used as a time-out room if the children were naughty.

The older twins were now four years old, and Benji was nearly three. He was the child that everyone needed to watch. He was an absconder and managed to climb most fences and knew how to open doors. He was known to drag a chair down a corridor to open a bolt that was head high for an adult. How they would manage Benji on the ship was a concern. On top of that, Rudi was worried he would once again be seasick for the entire voyage, as he had been on the journey out.

Marcus eventually solved the problem of ensuring the safety of the three older children. Many of the passengers on his journeys had travelled with infants. He had seen some young ones wearing kapok vests that floated; when a child fell overboard, they would pop up and remain buoyant.

In the interim, Rudi had leather harnesses made for Andy, Manda, and Benji, and took them for long walks while wearing them to help them get used to being restrained.

Rudi had to tug on Benji's lead only once as he nearly ran under a horse. The small boy's fright was enough for him to ask for the harness to be put on each time they left the house. The harness provided Rudi and Bethany with security and peace of mind while allowing Benji to run free.

~

With only a week to move, the household was in chaos as everyone packed and readied for the move to new premises.

Brenton and Carol were to stay in the guest room, as Brenton positively refused to sleep in the master bedroom until after Rudi left.

Risking being lynched, Rudi finally had to drag Brenton to Parramatta to hear from Lachlan that he was being given the house to keep, along with all the other governor's plans.

Lachlan said, "Brenton, part of the deal for your help making the coins was to bring your wife and family out. Well, they didn't need any assistance with that, so this is an easy way out for me. Accept the house and land, and pay Rudi's costs for the house, if necessary, from the money you received as back pay. I will discuss what I would like you to do the next time I'm in town. Rudi knows and will tell you, but I wish to outline how it will work." He waved his hand and dismissed them.

As Rudi reached the door, Lachlan added, "Perry found his wife, Katy. They are currently resting. She is well. He has a son, now named David, that he knew nothing about."

Rudi nodded and dragged his friend out of the room. They walked out the front door and wandered down the grassy embankment towards the ferry. It was due to leave in twenty minutes, so they were in no hurry. Rudi pulled at his arm and asked, "Now, are you happy?"

Brenton had a huge grin plastered on his lips. "No, but if it's going to be given away to someone, I'll use it to rescue more young maids. I insist on paying you the £30 for the building costs and furniture. No arguments, please."

Rudi nodded. "Deal, my friend," Rudi revealed the governor's plan.

Reeling from what he heard, Brenton accepted the offer to become the stable master for the governor and, eventually, to run the viceregal stables while they were under construction. He would become the first top-class carriage for hire in the colony. As such, he could hire whom he wished once they had the governor's blessing.

Brenton was on cloud nine. "I'm glad you're leaving me with two helpers. Daisy will be able to help those who have been attacked far more effectively than Carol or I. Do you know that she told Carol her horrific life started when she was ten? Her father decided to educate her on how to pleasure him while her mother was expecting a sibling. How disgusting is that? Will you try to save her sisters?"

Rudi nodded. He felt ill when he heard the comment. "Oh, Brenton, I had no idea. I'm so glad she's not returning to be near him. The governor stated that one of the soldiers had expressed interest in marrying her. Do you know who it is?"

Brenton nodded. "It's Clarence. He's already asked her, and they have been given permission. She was a little scared to tell you."

Rudi frowned. "Why? We care for them both. Clarence is a nice young man. He also knows of her attacks and background, I presume?"

Brenton nodded. "Yes, and it's why he wishes to marry her. He wants to protect her. Vera told him about their voyage out, and Daisy walked in, overheard his horror, and then she walked out again. He proposed immediately and soundly kissed her." Brenton chuckled. "Gerald is pursuing Vera, but is holding back until Daisy is settled. Both girls have asked whether they can stay with us after they get married. I have agreed."

Rudi knew of Daisy's reluctance to be around young men, but Clarence had often walked the four girls home after church. He had heard Daisy call him "Clay" and wondered whether a budding romance existed. "Brenton, taking those two home would only worsen their situation. I shall tell her that we are thrilled. I wonder if they can wed before we leave. Her room at the house is better than Clarence's at the old wooden barracks." He sighed, then added, "Perry told me about Katy's friend in London. Her name is Elizabeth Fry, and after helping Katy while in gaol. Mrs Fry has decided to do the same for as many other female felons as possible. Girls like Daisy and the other three would have been among those she would have helped. It's what Bethan and I hope to do at home. We won't be in London, and we don't intend to tread on Mrs Fry's toes, but ask if we can work with her."

Brenton said, "What can you do?"

Having dawdled, they arrived at the ferry as the skipper was casting off the ropes. They jumped on and moved to the bow, where they continued their conversation.

Rudi finally answered him. "Quite honestly, I have no idea what we can do, but then again, God will have that all organised, won't He?"

Chapter 19 Fists Full of Happiness

The sailing date for the *James Haye* was pushed back due to a fire in one of the ships anchored nearby.

The *Three Bees* caught fire and burned to the waterline.

Initially, everyone thought it was the *James Haye* due to the angle of view from the shore.

The delay eased the pressure of trying to get everything ready on time. They now had some extra weeks to sort themselves out.

Passengers and cargo booked on the *Three Bees* had to be rearranged.

One passenger took a smaller intermediate-class cabin at the far end of the deck, while the other passengers were travelling in steerage. With no other intermediate passengers, the captain moved the steerage passengers up one deck to fill that area with the extra cargo.

The travellers had another ten days before they needed to board.

Rudi took Bethany and the children to visit the Milroys in Toongabbie. They had visited often over the years, but for this trip, they had mail to collect for John Hunter. The Greenwoods stayed only one night before returning to Sydney.

~

Lachlan waited until the household was settled into the new residence, then came for an unannounced visit one evening after dinner. It was mid-April, and he was due back in Parramatta the next day. He had come to Sydney for the night to attend to a few matters after the birth of their son, Lachlan Macquarie Junior.

Brenton answered a knock on the door and was surprised to see the governor there, unescorted, wearing an oversized, drab overcoat. “Come in, please, sir. I dare not question your activities, but should you be here unattended?"

Lachlan chuckled. "Shh, Henry may hear you and come after me. I have officially retired to bed early." He chuckled and entered.

After checking he had not been followed by any scoundrels, Brenton hurriedly closed the door behind their illustrious visitor.

Lachlan asked, "Is everyone still here?"

Brenton assured him they were, presuming he meant the three men from the flat, as they still came for meals.

Lachlan smiled. "Good! Can you get the maids to take over putting the children to bed, and then gather all the adults in the sitting room? I have something for you all."

Lachlan was thrilled to catch everyone at once. Lance, Guy, and Marcus had not left after their evening meal. He could hear their voices out the back. Guy was to move in with Brenton after the others left.

Bethany and Carol had just finished feeding their babies. The two young mothers hastily handed over the youngest three and went downstairs to join the illustrious visitor.

Daisy and Ivy had managed to get the older children into bed. Vera and May were preparing food for the morning.

Rudi and the other three men had been bringing wood for the kitchen. At Brenton's call, they brushed themselves off and joined Lachlan, who awaited them in the front room.

As they walked in, Lance gave a shout of horror and gave Rudi a hefty thump on his shoulder.

A giant huntsman spider with a dark body and striped legs had crawled out of the wood he had been carrying and crept up Rudi's back. Seconds later, it would have crawled into his hair.

The horrid creature fell onto the floor and wiggled in its death throes.

The men jumped away from the critter. Its legs moved as its final moments of life ebbed away.

Rudi blanched, and Lance pushed him towards a seat.

Lachlan saw the action and said, "I've been here for five years, and those ghastly things still breathe more fear into me than a man with a sabre coming at full charge. I also hate the shiny black ones. I quickly learned never to leave anything on the ground. The snakes also terrify me." He shuddered at that thought. "It's also why every window in our residences has cheesecloth nailed over the openings."

All the occupants nodded. Each one agreed. They had done the same thing to their windows.

Rudi scooped the eight-legged body into the ash pan and shoved it into the dying embers of the fire.

The hairs caught alight, and the creature burned with a pop of its fat abdomen.

After a few moments of silence as they watched it burn, Lachlan spoke. "Well, friends, sorry to gatecrash, but this was a last-minute thing. I have two more people to arrive; then I will tell you why I am here and why I have come unattended."

There was another knock as he spoke, and William and Ann Cowper let themselves in.

Lachlan stood at the fire and waited until everyone was seated.

Rudi could see he was grinning, so whatever it was had something to do with the coins.

Only Bill, Mark and Cathy were missing. Marcus and Guy had no part in coin manufacturing, but they were not asked to leave. Guy had been reassigned as a bodyguard for Lachlan and had arrived for dinner after duty.

Lachlan moved so everyone could see him. "I have come to give you each a small token of my appreciation. Before I tell you more, let me assure you that these are recorded in the ledger and are all above board. I have reimbursed the coffers from my own funds. Mark will receive his share when I see him next, as will Bill and Phil. I couldn't leave them out, as they were instrumental in making our project happen. But you are my friends and I wished us to be together one last time before we part company."

Bethany frowned. "May I offer you refreshments, sir?"

Lachlan shook his head. "As much as I would like to say yes, my minders will soon start hunting for me. So, I must be quick."

He put his hands in his overcoat pockets and pulled out small calico drawstring bags. "I wondered what recompense I could give each of you as a thank you for your tireless work. I had the great delight of plunging my hand into a chest of mixed coins and grabbing as many as I could in my fist. I counted them out. There were ten Holey Dollars and a dozen Dumps. After confirming I had reimbursed the treasury, I counted out that amount for each of you. It is slightly over three pounds each. After Mary Reibey's comment, I wonder about the wisdom of making the small coin fifteen pence instead of twelve, but hindsight is always twenty-twenty. It's the value of the silver, so they won't be melted for jewellery for profit. Perhaps I can source small coins and make them into pennies. Time will tell about that. You may spend these if you wish while here, but remember, once offshore, they will only be collector's items."

He turned to the two youngest men among them. "Manning, Ryan, I'm sorry you were not here to be involved in this project, as I'm sure you would have loved it. However, I have an uncirculated mint pair for both of you as a token of appreciation. Ryan, I am truly grateful that you may have provided me with direction for farming in the colony. Your expertise in wool is invaluable. We shall encourage the endorsement of Elizabeth Macarthur's wool clip. Australian Merino wool will make the most incredibly soft fabric. Large Tweed mills here will be something that will one day come to pass. Governor King's small woollen mill, run by George Mealmaker, is good but supplies only fabric for our needs. A larger commercial mill will not be built during my governorship, but it's on my list. In the meantime, I need to work with you, even from afar. I plan to open new farmland over the mountains for extensive sheep farming, as our whale oil industry is not enough to sustain us."

Marcus nodded. He had long talks with the governor about his father's woollen mills and how he could help the poor villagers who worked in them. He had good ideas, but his father did not like them. He now had a contract with Mrs Macarthur, but he was unsure whether her husband would honour that deal when, or if, he returned from England. He foresaw another trip in years to come. Reverend Marsden's flock was not as lucrative a prospect as it was coarser wool.

Lachlan then turned to the new captain under his command. He had already thanked God for having a trustworthy officer to replace his two departing friends. "Manning, when they return home, you will take over from these two. I will assign you to various special tasks as needed. You will frequently be travelling with me. Henry Antill is my security detail, but I will call you in when Henry is busy elsewhere. I have come to trust you in a very short time. Your firm faith saw to that."

Guy bowed in acknowledgement of the honour. He had hoped to be useful upon arrival, but he had no idea it would be as the governor's bodyguard. A smile licked his lips, but he bit them to hide it. He promised his sisters and brother that he would care for the younger convicts. He had heard of some local children who had been arrested for stealing food. Those imps were no more criminals than he was. They were hungry, and that should not be a crime.

Lachlan then walked around the room, handing out the little calico bags to the men. Each small bag held a fist full of Holey Dollars and Dumps. He had special envelopes for Marcus and Guy, which he pulled from another pocket.

While remaining beside Marcus, Lachlan faced the others. "You really have no idea what you have all done for this community. The number of cases of drunkenness appearing in court has dropped significantly since the currency release. Arguments over the various currency values have all but ceased. I expected riots, but none have occurred. The only problem is the outlying free settlers who now have it in for Rudi due to their own laziness in not adhering to the exchange dates."

Lachlan saw Bethany take her husband's hand, squeeze it, then drop it. A smile lit his face. All moroseness was gone from this young man's demeanour. He sighed and said, "The Exclusives had been warned but ignored the advice, thinking it did not apply to them. As Rudi will be leaving with Lance and Marcus, that will no longer be a problem. However, because of his adherence to my edict, his life would be at risk if he remained, so God's timing is perfect once again. I feel that now we have a chance to see this town grow. However, I'm sad you three will not be here to see it."

Lance fingered his bag of coins. He would trade them all for knowledge of Elise's whereabouts. He forced a smile and focused on his boss.

Lachlan exhaled a long sigh. He turned to Rudi and Bethany. "Rudi, you ran with this idea from a throwaway comment. I freely admit I never expected it to be viable. After leaving you that day, Mark laughed. We doubted that we would even contemplate doing it. The idea was beyond our dreams. When you came that night and revealed what you and Lance had discussed, I could see it was viable. No, more than viable. It was feasible, desperately needed, and the solution. Even Mark realised how this would solve many issues in our settlement. It has." He paused and sighed. "I knew from the moment we arrived that a severe lack of currency was a serious problem, but we had no way to fix it. It was why rum and other home-brewed grog took such a hold. The Exclusives are literally growing their own wealth. The grain we needed to eat was fermented, distilled, and sold to unsuspecting or unscrupulous innkeepers and others. It was so potent that many have died from consuming the undiluted hooch."

The many heads nodded. They had all seen the effects of the potent local brews, even Marcus and Guy.

William said, "Sir, you don't know the half of what went on, as men took delight in supplying a flagon of strong spiritous liquor for the female convicts. You can imagine what occurred after many consumed a fresh batch. It's why I refuse to permit Ann to go anywhere alone." He shook his head in disgust. "The introduction of the new currency has reduced this sort of behaviour immensely. Women are still molested, but not as much as before, as alcohol is now too expensive to be consumed in great volumes. However, opium is becoming a problem."

Lachlan had more ideas about future improvements. "I have another thing I wish to tell you. Lance, this is for your information. Perry White has engaged your architects and is initially having them build some small cottages for him. One of them, Francis Greenway, has already identified a glaring issue the builder missed. As you said, God may have sent the person for the next step forward." He chuckled. "I prayed for an architect; God sent three. He never does things by halves, does he? I prayed for a friend who could mingle with the people, and Perry arrived."

Rudi smiled. He turned to gaze lovingly at his wife. He had learned that himself. Only a few days before he met Bethany, he contemplated his demise by walking out into the bay. Thankfully, he had not done that. Bethany may have died if he had succeeded. Knowing her and loving her had wholly revolutionised his life as she taught him so much about a true faith. He was happy now, but her love was only part of what had led to it. He reached for her hand and caressed it with his thumb. He was not her second choice but her grand passion. His expression softened when he looked at her; love was etched on his face.

Ann saw and smiled, as did Lachlan and Lance.

William was thinking about the buildings. He looked excited. "Really, sir, do you know what you will use these men for?"

Having handed out his gifts, Lachlan sat while William spoke, then he nodded. "My Elspeth, Perry, Katy White, and I have a list of things that need building. Phillip Gidley King recommended a new women's prison, and the captain of the *General Hewitt* reported that another hundred or so women would be sent on the next transport. We will start building that immediately. A new girl's orphanage will follow. King left plans, so we even have that to work with. Katy suggested some changes. Public amenities are a must, but we need to include new hospitals, windmills, lighthouses, and public buildings, as well as a proper courthouse and an extensive public library, to transform this settlement into a decent place to live. Reverend Richard Johnson's library will be housed in a new purpose-built building. More tomes will eventually arrive and be incorporated." He knew that the books Obadiah Jensen had refurbished would hold pride of place. "Then there are the numerous other buildings I would love to see constructed, including new government stables that Brenton will run. I have already selected the site for that, and it will begin construction soon. Currently, the horses are out in all sorts of weather." Brenton gasped.

Lachlan's gaze turned to the coachman. "Yes, Brenton, I can confirm a new stone stable block will be constructed a mere stone's throw from here. As the new government Chief Stable Master, you must consult Greenway about your needs. Sketch a box-like design, with a central courtyard, but leave the structural details to him. It will eventually be part of a government building complex that will include a new official residence, though it will be the last structure considered. I may not even be here when that is built. However, we also need solid barracks for convicts and soldiers here, in Parramatta and in Windsor. I would love to see some decent public buildings large enough to host a sizeable function, such as a town hall. There are certain areas where we need watchtowers and defensive structures. The waterfront wharves are crumbling and dangerous, and we need a new wharf and jetty near the salt boilers. Also, Perry has suggested a new military fort on the point near Bennelong's hut. While working in that area, the foreshore could use some reinforcement, like a break-wall with a new, longer jetty and loading area for bigger ships."

Brenton was reeling. He bowed his thanks.

Lachlan fell silent for a bit. Then turned to his minister. "Oh, yes, William, I have a long list of dreams I would like to see constructed."

Lachlan looked towards Rudi and said with a smirk. "My dreams are all your fault, young man." He chuckled at the stunned look on the soldier's face.

Rudi frowned. "Me, sir? May I ask why?"

Lachlan roared with laughter. "Laddie, you really don't know how important your throwaway comment was. Without these coins you fellows have slaved over for the past three years, this penal colony would have remained stagnant. Now, the government coffers are filling with the coins flowing around the place. D'Arcy has even suggested that Greenway review the hospital foundations. He believes it may need to be started from scratch. Placing rubble in the foundations has created a major problem, as the rats have made it their home. For a hospital, this is not a good situation. Do you know that it's being called the 'Rum Hospital' because it's being funded from rum tariffs?"

Lachlan blew his cheeks out in frustration, then groaned. "I wish I could clap my hands, and it could be built already. I want to see it finished." He sighed again. He flopped back in his armchair and said, "Friends, when I close my eyes, I think about what this place will be like in the future. Someday, someone will bridge the harbour, and at some future date, a wide crossing will be constructed. I foresee many houses along the water on both sides of the bay. One day, there may even be steam-powered vehicles that move many people and carry loads great distances. Like the small sailing steamboat we have, tractors at home will soon be everywhere. I expect these steam engines will soon be adapted for use on large ships. I heard whispers of a man experimenting with a steam-powered vehicle that ran on wooden tracks. Change will occur, and we have all been part of the solid footings. Thanks to you chaps, we can build a firm foundation."

No one spoke. All were thinking of what this settlement could look like if someone bridged the harbour. Was that even possible? Would Sydney still be a penal settlement in a hundred years?

Lachlan sighed again. He was upset that he knew he would never see the progress of this infant settlement. "I feel that this town is my baby. I have thrown my heart and soul into this place and foresee great things for it in the years to come. More free settlers will arrive, and with Marcus's help in the future and his contract to buy our wool, we will have a lucrative export that is in demand in England. Unfortunately, I will not be here to see all the progress, nor will most of you. Even the memory of our convict past may eventually be almost forgotten, but one day, Australia will have its own character because of those convict beginnings. We have an equality here that can only be dreamed about in old Mother England. Some may term it a birthstain, but that same heritage will give these people the strength of character to survive and overcome adversity. Many will one day carry that legacy as a badge of honour. Most of those who come in chains are petty criminals. Few are hardened criminals, as they are hanged at home. I feel that this heritage will be etched in the souls of those born here. The currency lads and lasses in Australia will be the making of a new, strong economy. They have something the British lack: the freedom to choose is one of the greatest blessings this land can give. Though I am the governor here, I will still be a nobody at home in Scotland. I was not born with a silver spoon in my mouth, which is why I wish to offer opportunities to those who have worked hard to bring about change. However, it is more than that: this country has a hold on one's soul. There is a peace in this land that I have experienced in no other country that I have been to. Not even in the wilds of my beloved Mull in Scotland, so I understand that sense of belonging to the land! Bungaree and Bennelong both explained how the people here belong to the land. It took me a while, but I do understand what they mean, for I can breathe here."

The room remained silent. All felt his words. Even Marcus and Guy, who had recently arrived, felt the freedom of this vast land.

All were thinking about the growth of this infant colony and its ancient inhabitants. Each person had experienced the deep peace that seemed to invade one's soul.

They each wondered whether anyone would ever be able to design and build a vast bridge, given the harbour's size and width.

James Milson's cottage on the harbour's north side already had a few neighbours. More people were asking whether they could build there. A small ferry serviced the houses, but the land track from their places took them to Parramatta along the north shore past Marsden's and James Squire's grazing land and orchards, at Kissing Point.

Seeing the faces of his friends, Lachlan sat upright quickly and said, "Right! I'm not going to be morose anymore. Brenton, as I said, I envision the new stable to be large and impressive. So much so that I wish you would jot down what your dream stable would be as if money were no object. Think big! Something suitable for a large ducal residence, add crenellated towers if you wish. It will be the main structure for the settlement, so don't skimp on your ideas. Oh, add a dairy as the wooden one is ready to collapse. Horses and carriages will remain the primary mode of transport for years. Ensure you include upstairs staff rooms as well. Steam vehicles will come, and in the future, there will be other modes of transport not dreamed of today, so make the entries wide enough for two carriages and tall. I must plan for the future, which means stable hands on call twenty-four hours a day, and the ability to adapt the use of such a sandstone edifice will be vital. Now, thanks to Rudi, we have a viable future that we didn't have before. I will work as hard as I have ever worked and achieve as much as possible during my time here." His gaze finally left Rudi, and he turned to Lance. "Lance, your idea of stockpiling the sandstone blocks and bricks has been wonderful. It means we can start as soon as we have plans. Perry assures me that this fellow, Greenway, knows sandstone, as his family are stonemasons and builders. This, hopefully, means he has the ability to design some impressive buildings."

Rudi wondered about the other two men mentioned. "Sir, who are the other men? You said three forgers, who are the others?"

Lachlan said, "Ah, yes, well, there certainly are two more forgers. One is Henry Kitchen, and the other is Joseph Lycett. From what Perry said, Henry will be fine with a straightforward build, and he's doing the brickwork on Perry's cottages in Parramatta. However, the other convict forger is an artist. I was thinking of setting him to work and recording the settlement in paintings, as it is now and, hopefully, as it will be when I have finished. Perry suggested that I have Henry Kitchen design another large weir on the Parramatta River. That town is growing, and we need access to more fresh water. However, there is a third architect. He is a soldier, named John Watt, and I will have him work immediately on completing the extensions for Government House out there. The previous work was for staff quarters and the back verandah. However, the new staff quarters are still insufficient for our needs. The main roof will also require additional work, as the new shingles are already leaking. I have two new wings planned for the main house for more guest rooms. Perry is occupying the only one at present."

Rudi opened the bag of coins and tipped them into his hands. On more than one occasion, Lance, Bill, and he had delighted to dive their hands into the chests of freshly minted warm coins. Pocketing as many as they wished would have been so easy, but they all resisted the temptation. Each day, Bill willingly showed his empty pockets, for he had too much to lose if he were found with a single illicit coin.

Over the months, they had each pulled out a ransom's worth of silver dollars and gazed lustfully at them before returning them all to the chests and locking the lids. Each knew that every single coin needed to be accounted for, and now their honesty had been rewarded.

Their job was complete, and the settlement was safe.

Like the other bags, Rudi's bag contained over £3 in mixed, newly minted coins, and he planned to keep them for his children, though he had in mind giving one pair as a gift to someone special. For Bill, that would have been nearly a full year's wage when he was in England.

Lachlan stood to leave when Henry Antill came barging in.

Henry was puffed and somewhat flustered. "Oh, thank goodness, sir. I thought something had happened to you. I was coming to get their assistance to find you." He sank into Lachlan's chair in relief.

Lachlan roared with laughter. "See, friends, I knew my absence would be noticed. Henry, you were supposed to be asleep."

Henry shrugged.

Lachlan turned to the residents. "I will see you all anon. My friends, it's time for bed. I have said what is needed."

The gathering broke up for the evening.

Lance, Marcus and Guy accompanied Henry and the governor to his home as guards.

~

June 1814

After years in the colony, Rudi, with his family, Marcus, Lance, and the two younger maids, set sail on June 2nd on the *James Haye.*

Perry came to town to see them off and to deliver mail for his family, saying he had found Katy. Telling them that Katy had given birth to their son, David, on the convict ship when docked at Rio de Janeiro. Hopefully, their eldest son, Jem, would join them as soon as possible, as they planned to stay until her term expired in six years. He would do as Lachlan asked, becoming his eyes and ears. He had already sourced an old outfit from Marsden's charity bin and donned it for a walk around the penal town out west. Perry valued the anonymity, which he could not have in England. He was comfortable here in a land where many were scarred. At home, he was shunned because of his melted face.

Rudi and Lance were delighted that the Lord had answered Lachlan's prayer. What was even better was that Perry and Katy were currently living with the viceregal couple. Josh had moved into the tollgate, replacing Mark and Cathy, and Perry filled the void in Lachlan's life. Guy had moved into the staff quarters in Parramatta.

As Brenton viewed Lance's cabin on board, he said, "I hope you find Elise, Lance. Surely, someone must know where the family went. If I hear anything, I'll write to let you know if I discover where the Prices went. The only Price family I heard of were out near Windsor. Bill mentioned some bible bashers out that way when he first arrived."

They parted with a brotherly hug.

It was unlikely they would meet again, but they would write.

Brenton and the family stood on the dock as the ship's crew pulled its thick ropes on board.

As Rudi overheard Brenton's comment, Lance finally told Rudi about his lost love. He smiled and said, "God would need to work a pretty big miracle to find Elise now. Who knows where her family went? She is probably married with a few children by now, as years have passed." He sighed, and his heart sank. "They could be anywhere in the world, so I highly doubt it's the family who have been living in Windsor. When I went to see them, they had left."

Rudi put a hand on his friend's shoulder. "God can do anything, my friend. Trust Him. I have learned that nothing at all is beyond God's control. If you are meant to be together, you will find her."

Lance shrugged. He wondered if he could. Where was she? A long, frustrated sigh escaped from his lips.

Two more passengers were now on board, and they joined them at the railing. John Durecott and James Dunn had been booked to travel on the *Three Bees*, but after it burned, they moved to the lower deck berths with the intermediate passengers.

Captain Folger carried a letter of marque from the governor. With two new majors on board, the captain was content to know his passengers were safe and would remain so.

The ship was to head first to the North Island of New Zealand to deliver food to the small missionary settlement there. They also carried an expectant nanny goat, a milk cow, and an unrelated bull calf for the missionaries, amongst other things.

~

Three weeks after leaving Sydney, their first port of call was the Bay of Islands settlement that Chief Ruatara planned. It was in the northeast of the northernmost island of this land.

A young, heavily tattooed man, Chief Ruatara, welcomed them warmly and showed them around the villages. He and the missionary settlers had a healthy wheat crop growing.

Much to the delight of the chief, this was the first grain crop planted on this land. Josh Callan and Lachlan had sent him letters and gifts.

Rudi knew all about this Maori chieftain from Josh Callan. Josh and the chief had arrived from England on the same vessel, and Josh had taught the chief to read and write. A mutual connection was enough to ensure a warm greeting.

Reverend Robert Cartwright, though only recently arrived, was the mission's leader and knew Lance from Windsor. They had not seen him since the picnic celebration in Parramatta.

On landing, Lance had heard from Robert that some old friends from home were living in this isolated area, and Robert suggested they catch up.

Marcus wandered to the top of a nearby landscape and stood, looking at the native pastures rather than the newly cultivated crops. He wandered up to the top of a high point and stood gazing at the grassy hills, deep ravines, abundant water, and clumps of trees for protection. It was a shepherd's dream of an almost perfect habitat for their flocks.

Rudi came to his side. "Marcus, what's up?"

The young man shook his head. "Nothing! Nothing at all; I can see great potential for sheep in this land. I have not found any burrs in the native grasses, which bodes well for the sheep fleeces. Ruatara also tells me there are no large predators, snakes, or lethal spiders. If it's all as lush as this, sheep will thrive here, Rudi. Captain Folger said he has taken a brief look at the southern island and can see considerable potential for farming there as well. From what I've heard from others, its climate is similar to that of England."

Rudi frowned. "Heard from who, Marcus?"

The overgrown boy chuckled. "While you were swapping people's wealth and assigning convicts, I asked many sailors for information about this and other lands. Many of the whalers and sealers frequent that area. To date, I believe that the South Island, or what Captain Cook called *Toai poonamoo,* is virtually uninhabited. I haven't received any reports of settlements seen down there. Even Ruatara said it was too cold for his people, so they stayed away. He told me some island legends, but according to the whalers, the potential for sheep is incredible. Some say it is like Scotland. The climate is similar and apparently just as windy. However, the sheep don't mind that except when dropping their lambs."

~

Only hours after dropping anchor, a whaling vessel arrived in the bay. Captain Folger was busy overseeing the transfer of stores for the tiny European settlement as the newly arrived ship launched a longboat.

Ruatara warned his visitors about these uncouth men and suggested that Bethany and the maids remain out of sight. Bethany followed Mrs Cartwright into the hut and drank tea with her and the other women. A large box of Chinese tea was a treat Bethany had brought for the new mission.

Rudi met Reverend Cartwright and heard about a young lady whose family had come to assist in their missionary work last year. However, her family wanted her to return to London to be with her aunt. Because Bethany was on this vessel, her parents wished her to travel with them. She could occupy the small vacant cabin beside Lance and across the corridor from Bethany and Rudi.

They had yet to meet her, but Lance offered to meet the Price family and arrange the girl's accommodation on board; therefore, Lance vanished on arrival.

The young lady's parents were worried. They wished her to make a fine marriage, but she had no choice of husband in this land. The only men she met were whalers or sealers, who were unsuitable as either potential husbands or travelling companions.

Lance returned to the ship the night they anchored and went straight to bed. The family he hoped to meet was visiting outside the village.

Chief Ruatara proudly showed Rudi, Marcus, and Bethany

around his village.

Lance intended to go on the trip with his friends, but wished to see this man, Mr Price, first. Could it truly be them? Had they really been the family in Windsor all this time? Due to his excitement, he had trouble sleeping. They had been visiting a village to the north, and he had not been able to find them.

~

The following morning, Lance was on shore before the others rose. No sooner had he disembarked than he saw one of the sailors from the sealing vessel manhandle a girl from the missionary settlement. Then, a horrified Lance realised the victim was his very own Elise.

When he saw her fighting in the arms of a filthy sealer who was trying to ravish her, his anger exploded. He ripped the man's clothing from his back as he clawed at him, forcing the filthy felon to release Elise. He then spun the sailor around and gave him an uppercut to his jaw that sent him flying through the air. As the sailor was no small man, this was not an easy feat, but Lance's anger had been unleashed.

The sailor came off second best, but at least he did not lose his life. The situation might have turned out differently if the girl's father had not appeared. The man was soon flat on his back with Lance on top of him and his hands around the filthy sailor's throat.

A hand rested on Lance's shoulder, and the voice quietly said, "Enough, son. He won't try that again."

When he realised who was speaking, he knew that voice well. Lance released his grip and stood up.

Elise watched the anger drain out of Lance's face. She ran to him and threw herself into his arms. "Oh, Lance, thank you so much. I didn't know they had landed."

Lance's arms enfolded his dream girl.

The older man said, "Come, laddie, we need to talk."

After reluctantly releasing his beloved, Lance nodded and followed the pair. He had a suggestion to make to her father. That suggestion was to offer for Elise Price again. She was some years younger than he, but they had known each other since they were young. It was more than that; he still loved her. He had enlisted, and upon his return home, she and her family had left, leaving no contact information or guidance on where to look. Now, Lance had found her again, and his feelings about her remained unchanged. Parting from his long-lost love, the two men entered a small pine log cabin. Lance's heart rate was elevated because of his nerves. This was the second time he had approached Mr Price for his daughter's hand in marriage.

Lance started to speak. "Sir, years ago, I offered for Elise, and you told me she was too young. However, when I returned, you were no longer there. I have hunted for you for years. I am now on my way home to take up the title and step into my role as a viscount, as both my father and brother are dead. I wanted Elise on my arm back then as my wife, and my feelings for her have not changed."

Mr Edwin Price eyed the young man with a frown etched on his brow. "I know, Lance. That you still wish to marry her is remarkable. However, I will not force her. Wait outside for a moment, my boy."

They went to the door of their tiny cottage and called her.

Elise stood before him in a penitent stance. She was fully aware that she should not have embraced Lance after her rescue, but she was so pleased to see him.

Her father said, "Elise, dear girl," he sighed, "I know you once had feelings for Lance, but I don't know if you still do."

She blushed and nodded. "I always have, Papa, but you would not let us wed. I may have been only fifteen, but he is the only man I have ever looked at. Then we left home eight years ago, and I thought I would never see him again, but God has other plans. I planned to look for him on my return to England."

Edwin Price watched the expressions on his daughter's face. She was now twenty-three and even more beautiful than she was as a young girl. Her peaches and cream skin had tanned a little in the sun, and she had a few freckles, but she was even more lovely inside. Her gentle nature had won over the islanders. Her adoration of the village's rounded cherubs had endeared her to the Maori women. She was permitted to come and go from the village as she pleased. Her father smiled. "Elise, he has asked to wed you again."

Her face lit up. "He still wants me? Truly?"

Edwin nodded. "He does. Did he tell you he is now the viscount, now that his brother has died? Oh, my darling girl, are you sure?"

Elise's head nodded. "He's the only man I would marry, Papa. I don't care about the title. I have told you that time and time again, but you would never listen. For him to arrive here on the far side of the world from where we met and still want me is a dream and a miracle. I am surprised that he is still unwed; for us to be reunited again is not only my dream come true, but only God could have made that happen. Please, Papa, let us marry now. Let Reverend Cartwright perform the ceremony so you can both be there. I will be safe with Lance. You know that. Also, it means I will not be a burden to Aunty Myrtle."

Edwin nodded. "I can think of no one better for you, sweet girl. Go and get him."

Elise gave a skip as she left the room. She closed the door behind her before meeting Lance.

Her smile boded well for them. He asked, "Did he agree?"

She knew her father could hear them, so she nodded. "I have been told to get you. Come." She took his hand and almost dragged him inside.

Lance could hardly believe he had found her. He had intended to hunt for her on his return home, but to find her now was a blessing. He would have been on the next ship a year ago had he known she was here. Hopefully, they could be married immediately. He knew Robert Cartwright had permission to marry someone he deemed suitable without further licences.

Captain Folger could also record the ceremony in his ship's log. Robert Cartwright had his own marriage register, but it was unlikely to be registered in England for many years.

The young couple arrived in front of Edwin Price.

Both were nervous and clinging to each other, not wishing to be parted again.

Edwin's eyes dropped to the joined hands, and he smiled. "I presume you have already asked her, laddie?"

Lance's head shook. "No, sir, not until I have your permission. I have never crossed the line in taking any advantage of her, nor will I. I respect and love her too well for that. I have dearly wished to marry her for over a decade."

Edwin watched their faces as he said, "Well, now you have my permission."

Lance's face broke into a huge grin. "You mean it? Truly? Thank you, sir!" He turned to the lovely lady beside him and dropped to his knee. "Dearest heart, will you honour me with your hand in marriage?"

Elise pulled him from his subservient position and threw herself into his arms again. "Yes, of course I will." She pulled his head down for a kiss, totally disregarding her father's presence.

After an appropriate amount of time, Edwin cleared his throat. "I think that's enough. You will have all the time in the world for that soon. Let's go and see Cartwright. I'll collect your mama first." He walked to the door. "You have one minute, Lance, but congratulations to you both."

Mr Price let the door bang behind him.

Lance again took his long-lost love in his arms and wished to devour her.

With only one minute until they had to join the minister, he wasted no time. He drew her into his arms and kissed her again.

That minute passed in a flash.

The sound of approaching voices broke them apart.

Florence Price was a jovial, bouncy woman who entered, threw her arms around her daughter, and kissed her cheeks. "I knew sending you on that last ship was wrong. You would have missed Lance."

Without fully releasing her daughter, she turned to her daughter's new fiancé. She had known him since he was a lad. "Look after my girl, won't you, Lance?"

Lance came to her side and said, "I will, Mrs Price. With everything I own, and while I live and breathe, she will be my reason to get up in the morning. I cannot remember a day when I have not loved her."

The four people exited the dark timber cottage into the cooling winter sunshine. They went to find the minister and hoped he would perform their union as soon as Chief Ruatara returned with Rudi, Bethany, and Marcus.

~

At four that afternoon, the Reverend Robert Cartwright and his family, William Hall, John King, as well as the entire group from Ruatara's village of *Rangihoua* in the Bay of Islands, the whole crew from the *James Haye*, many from the sealing ship crew, including one contrite crewman with a black eye and swollen lip, and the group of stunned friends from Sydney, attended the nuptials of Viscount Lancelot Upcroft and Miss Elise Price.

After years of waiting, the happy couple were finally married.

Lance, like Rudi, only wanted to marry for love, but he never expected to see his first and only love again. To find her holed up in a tiny settlement of fewer than twenty Europeans at the end of the earth was a miracle. Now, they were husband and wife.

Rudi congratulated his friend, saying, "See, Brent and I told you God had it in control."

Lance nodded with a silly grin plastered on his face. He let out a deep sigh of contentment, lifted his eyes, and thanked God. "Yes, you did."

~

Lance and Elise spent their first night as a married couple in a recently finished cottage in the village.

Another family was moving in soon, but for the moment, they

had the blessing of a nearly week-long honeymoon before they had to set sail for England and a new life. This was because the winds had dropped. The whaler had left hours after the wedding as the sailor had made their presence unwelcome. However, their ship, the *James Haye,* was becalmed in port.

Elise had to pack and prepare to leave her family. Although she knew that she had to go, parting was hard. At least now, Lance was beside her. Wherever they travelled from now on, they would be together.

~

Eight days after dropping anchor, the ship's capstan, manned by a dozen crewmen, wound the anchor aboard. The fresh breeze caught the first of the square-rigged sails, and it ballooned. Other sails followed it, and soon the heavy ship was moving away from New Zealand.

The vessel was homeward bound, and now the brig carried an extra passenger. Elise's farewells to her parents were difficult, but the Prices were thrilled to learn that Brenton and Carol were in Sydney and that they could stay with them if they needed a place to stay upon returning for supplies. Regular food shipments and a few sheep would be helpful if Brenton could source any for the settlement.

Lance was sure he would send supplies whenever a ship was due to call at the mission. Lance wrote a letter to Brenton to share his good news and to express that God works in mysterious ways.

As the sealing ship was heading south to find whales, the next ship heading to Australia would carry a letter to Sydney. Lance's prayers had been answered, and he had found Elise, and he wished to let Brenton know. He also added a list of things he saw they could use, including regular food drops.

~

During the week ashore, Lance discovered that the family had been some distance from Parramatta and had been living in western settlements for several years. They had no idea Lance was not in France, so they had not looked for him.

Lance was surprised they had never met. The Prices had stayed with the Cartwrights for over six months.

The name Price was common enough not to draw his attention. However, God's timing was, once again, perfect.

Chapter 20 Going Home

1815 England

Married life took on a new meaning for Lance.

Elise was quite content to move into his small cabin on board, but Marcus juggled rooms and took the other empty cabin further up the corridor. This left his larger single room for the newlyweds and Lance's old room to use for their sitting room. It also meant that he did not have to listen to the conjugal sounds penetrating through the thin bulkheads from the newlywed's cabin.

With the coming months, they planned to make this an extended honeymoon. Elise's excess luggage was stored in the storeroom next to Lance. Her trunks were used as seating, and extra bedding was pulled from stores as soft furnishings.

~

The *James Haye* sailed eastwards and reached Cape Horn on their one-month anniversary. The winds behind them were kind, and the voyage was not too rough.

Surprisingly, Rudi had not been seasick.

However, as they rounded the southern tip of South America, things changed.

As the seas started bucking as they sailed around the cape, Elise woke one morning and needed to be sick.

This continued sporadically throughout the following days.

Lance wasn't too worried until she woke up on the third morning with the same nausea. Today, Elise was too ill to rise.

The foul weather meant everyone was confined to below decks.

Between bouts of illness, she was well enough, but wished to sleep much of the time.

After a few days of sickness because of the unstable deck movement, Lance gingerly walked to Rudi and Bethany's cabin to seek Bethany's help and advice.

Bethany went to speak with her new friend and shut the door on Lance.

With the excitement of their quick wedding, Elise realised she had not had her monthly flow in the eight weeks since the ceremony.

Bethany confirmed that she was probably increasing. She sat her new friend down and discussed the enjoyable benefits of being in the family way. As they were on their honeymoon, they regularly indulged in the newly discovered delights of marriage.

Bethany said that while she was increasing, her desire for her husband was heightened.

Elise giggled. "Considering the frequency of our current activities, that may be difficult."

Bethany smiled and said, "It's so enjoyable with someone you love dearly. Just remind him not to use soap below the waist. It contains lye and burns ladies' private parts."

Elise's hands flew to her burning cheeks. Her voice dropped. "Oh, I couldn't tell him that. So my itch is not my fault?"

Bethany shook her head. "No, dear girl; men think they are doing the right thing by washing themselves with soap, but they are unable to wash it all off, and even tiny traces are enough to cause us irritation. Only hot water below the waist for both of you, and all shall be well. I shall get Rudi to mention it to Lance."

Meanwhile, next door, Lance and Rudi waited in the adjoining cabin.

Lance paced the small area between the bunk and the washstand. He said, "What's keeping them? What if I lose her just as I've found her again?"

Rudi had his suspicions about Elise's condition but stayed silent. It was not his place to mention the possibility of a child. One conversation he did have was about soap. "Lance, neither of us played around before we married, and there was much I did not know." He swallowed nervously. "One thing was about soap."

Lance spun around. "Soap? You wish to speak to me about soap now, when my darling Elise could be dying? I have only just found her."

Rudi watched his friend pacing the length of the cabin. He nodded. "I do because I have my own suspicions about what has caused her illness, and I am guessing it is related."

Lance frowned and almost threw himself on the small, unmade

bunk. "Go on."

Rudi did. "Soon after we married, Bethan drew away slightly from conjugal activities, and I noticed her discomfort and saw her scratching her private parts. I was rigorously cleaning myself each day to prepare for our frequent activities. However, I did not realise the soap I used was burning her. This stuff contains lye and carbolic acid, or something similar. Actually, I'm not quite sure what's in it, but it burns them. I know it certainly hurts my eyes. No wonder she did not wish to have marital relations as often. I had no idea that I was the problem. I never use soap below the waist now. Consequently, let me put it this way: it works in my favour if I refrain from rigorous cleansing." Rudi's cocked eyebrow made his friend gasp.

"You mean I could be causing her pain?" Lance groaned and collapsed on the mattress in frustration. "I thought I was doing the right thing. I know men pick up diseases from street women, and I presumed that it was related somehow. I shall take your advice. Only a true friend would broach such a sensitive topic." He paused, deep in thought. "Would that make her sick, though?"

Rudi, thankfully, did not need to reply. He could have asked him about her monthly courses, but he doubted Lance would understand, as his sisters were too young when he left. That was something Bethan did not need to explain, as he knew his sisters had called it 'Eve's curse'.

Bethany gave a gentle knock and entered. "Go and see her, Lance."

Lance needed no second invitation. He was gone in an instant.

Bethany pulled the door closed and walked into Rudi's arms.

Although they had only been parted for minutes, the privacy of the small cabin meant they could enjoy a long and loving kiss without interruption from the maids or children.

A shout of delight from next door answered Rudi's question. He said, "So she is with child?"

Bethany nodded. "But she sore too; she doesn't wish to tell Lance about the soap."

Rudi chuckled. "I just did. Like me, he had no idea."

After another long kiss, he drew her onto the bunk and sat cuddling her as the seas were too rough to remain standing.

Rudi said, "Over the years in Sydney, Lance mentioned Elise a few times, followed by a mournful sigh. I figured she must be dead. I never realised that he had proposed to her, and her father rejected him because she was so young. Elise was from a neighbouring estate to Usher, Lance and their sisters. When Gareth and Brenton moved into the Upcroft estate, Elise was already best friends with Lance's sisters. The nine young ones were frequently in each other's company. Then, something occurred when Elise was about thirteen. Lance didn't go into details about what, but his eyes were opened about his feelings for her. He had to wait until she was fifteen to propose to her. He did, but her father said no because she was too young. Lance was only a second son, and he needed to establish himself. It was her father who suggested that he enlist. He promised to return after two years; when he did, they were gone. Lance has never looked at another woman, so causing her discomfort would crush him. He'll listen to my warning about the soap."

Later that day, Bethany had Elise sit in a salt bath to ease her discomfort. A cup of black tea first thing in the morning eased her sickness.

~

The ship entered Rio de Janeiro harbour only days after this discussion. Captain Folger warned them they would need to get their land legs and be careful as they disembarked. He said, "The land will seem to be moving. Close your eyes at your own peril."

The group of travellers alighted, and the first thing they looked for was a grassy common area where the children could run around. After being cooped up on the ship for two months, they were aching to run and play, chasing each other.

~

They spent a week in port restocking for the final leg of the journey. The captain traded some of his pearl shells with merchant stores and purchased goods readily saleable in London.

Two major requirements for this port of call were, firstly, sourcing and loading fresh fruit. Second, Lance and Elise sought a doctor to confirm whether they were having a child.

The Portuguese doctor confirmed Elise's condition and advised her to walk as much as possible, by going round and round the deck or up and down the corridor as she grew larger. This would assist with the birth later.

They had another eight weeks or so until they reached England.

Elise was thrilled to have Bethany on board to ask questions. Her own mother would not have been as forthcoming in answering the intimate questions.

~

At the beginning of September, a cry came from the crow's nest on the mainmast that he had sighted land.

England's shores were finally within sight.

Lance forgot that the captain was unaware of their illustrious status. They were travelling under their new rank rather than their new titles. An overheard comment put paid to that.

Lance said, "Rudi, when we reach home, I suppose we will not see each other much. With me in West Sussex and you in Dorset, we will only meet when we have an official function or political vote to support in Parliament. We must don our titles and dance to society's rules."

Unaware that Captain Folger had taken over the wheel on the deck below them. They missed the captain spinning around to gaze up at them with his mouth open.

Rudi sighed and replied, "I have no idea what a viscount even does, let alone how to be one. At least you know what your father did and are returning to a familiar house. I don't even know what state Buckridge House is in." His groan signalled to Lance that he was stressed.

Lance nodded. "I understand your anxiety, but Rudi, we have both learned to trust God. He will ensure that you have the right people to support you." He paused and frowned. "I've just had a thought. Gareth is learning the ropes of estate management from his father. He'll know enough to come and oversee setting your new estate to rights and choosing a trustworthy agent for you. I won't let him leave permanently, as I will need him myself soon enough, but he could come and set you on your feet. How about that? He or Mr Wright may even know or find someone to fill that position."

Rudi grinned. "That would be wonderful. From what Bethan said, the house only ever had a skeleton staff. I would be surprised if Prinny has done anything since it was returned to the crown, but miracles happen. If Gareth can at least instruct me on how to be a viscount, that would be great. If he understood the bookkeeping, that would also be brilliant."

Lance chuckled. "I need to learn that as well."

A strangled choking sound behind them made them both turn.

The first mate had taken the wheel, and the captain had come to join them. Captain Folger's jaw was open. He swallowed and said, "You're both viscounts? Really?" The two men nodded mournfully.

Lance replied. "We are, and that's why we're returning home. Our siblings' bereavements have meant that our new titles have been thrust upon us." That wasn't the entire truth, but close enough.

The captain nodded. "I heard you mention West Sussex and

Dorset. Would you like to disembark at Portsmouth rather than London? I'm in no hurry to reach the capital, and this would cut the distance of travel to your homes by half." A quick consult and both men agreed.

Rudi said, "That would be wonderful. It's halfway between both houses. Lance's home is between Petworth and Selham, and my new place is north of Warmwell, not far from Dorchester. However, I must first collect my three nieces from Vice Admiral Hunter at Portland Harbour."

Captain Folger's eyes nearly popped. "You know Vice Admiral Hunter? How?"

Lance chuckled and murmured, "This will be interesting."

Rudi explained the tenuous connection. "Uncle John took my three nieces to live with him when my brother died. I must collect them as soon as I can."

The captain muttered an oath. "Cor, sirs. I had no idea you were so well-connected. I apologise for any untoward comments my crew or I may have made earlier in our cruise."

The friends nodded and grinned. Lance said, "Captain, your reaction is precisely the reason we kept the titles and connections quiet. We both prefer to be known by our rank and not our title or bloodline. Can you keep it so for the remainder of the journey?"

The captain's head nodded so vigorously that he had to grab his hat. "I can certainly do that, Majors. As I mentioned, I'm not in a hurry to reach port. However, I must inform you that the Vice Admiral is now in Portsmouth, not Portland. He was promoted to superintend the payment of Naval men some time ago. So, sirs, we will dock at Portsmouth as I suggested. I know Vice Admiral Hunter's niece Penelope is caring for him. I heard about some children who came to live with them last year; I just had no idea they were related to you."

Rudi nodded with a smile. "They are my nieces. Captain, would it truly not be inconvenient to divert?"

The captain bobbed a bow. "No problem at all, Major." He gave orders to the first mate, who turned the wheel slightly to the port side in a gentle tack. The crew trimmed the sails to catch more wind. The captain waited until the sails filled, then said, "We should be there the day after tomorrow, Major Greenwood." He bobbed another bow to each man and returned to the helm on the deck below.

Rudi's family, the two maids, and Lance and Elise would disembark in Portsmouth, after which the vessel would continue to London. Marcus had not yet decided.

~

Portsmouth

Vice Admiral John Hunter was at his desk overlooking the harbour, watching the ship's sails drop one by one, then draw into the bay. He loved the sight and never failed to pause when the square sheets of a new vessel came in sight. He sighed with the utter frustration of having his wings clipped by age. He refused to retire until his honorary nephew returned, and although he was pushing eighty, he retained full mental faculties and intended to work as long as he could.

John watched as the unknown merchant ship pulled into the naval dock and tied up. His bushy brow rose in wonderment. Few vessels ever did that without his express permission. He wondered who had arrived. It flew a naval flag, but was not a navy ship. Who dared dock without permission? Who did she carry?

~

Less than an hour later, John was surprised to hear a knock on his door. A messenger brought word that his family had arrived.

John's face creased with delight. Rudi had returned.

The messenger noted the twinkle in the old gentleman's eyes.

John sent the messenger home to Penelope to prepare the adorable little girls for their uncle's arrival. And another for a wagon to meet them at the dock. Work for the day was set aside. He shut his office and meandered to the dock to welcome the young man home. He had yet to meet Rudi's wife and their children.

The ship was still being processed, and passengers had to receive medical clearance before disembarking. He sat on a bollard and waited. Rudi appeared and stood waving with both hands. John could not wipe the smile from his face when they finally met. Gone was the moody and grieving young lad who had left. Here was the smiling young man whom he had known in his youth. John greeted Bethany and the children as if they were close family. Lance, Elise, and Marcus were welcome to join them. Both ladies received a big hug and a double-cheek kiss. The men were warmly greeted.

John then said, "Come, dear ones, let us go home. Penny has everything ready for you." His excitement was tangible.

Marcus had decided to leave the ship here and travel to his father's Brighton house. His luggage would require him to hire a vehicle, but that could wait. He knew the wool clip could be unloaded into the London warehouse, and he planned to send messages to prepare their storeman to ready space for the numerous bales of high-quality wool. He did not need to be there to see it unloaded.

While Rudi met his nieces, Marcus, Lance, and Elise offered to take care of the Greenwood children.

John's smile lit his ice-blue eyes. He had a spring in his step for the first time in a long time. However, with Rudi's return, he knew retirement was imminent and did not look forward to it. He knew he had to hang up his military hat and move to his new flat in Hackney, London. It sat empty, like a grave waiting for his body. To him, it would be a living coffin. His duty to the Navy was now done. He pushed that thought aside. Today was here, and he would not spoil it with thoughts of what tomorrow would bring. He would delay that evil hour for as long as possible.

Marcus departed the following day, as his luggage had been on top. Lance and Elise also collected their possessions from the small cabin and hired a carriage to carry them home. They parted company from the Greenwoods with many hugs and promises to visit each other.

Rudi remained in town only long enough to give John the letters he carried and to give him something he wanted him to have. He extracted a Holey Dollar and Dump from the small pouch of coins to give to his mentor. "Uncle John, if you had not pushed me into enlisting, I probably would have died in the fire that night, as well. I thought you were pushing me away, but my eyes are now open. Because of you, I found what I did not even know was missing. I found how to fill that void in my heart. It wasn't with Bethany or our children; you told me to look higher. I didn't understand what you meant until I was so down that the only way to look was up. It took nearly losing her for me to understand your words. God filled that void so neatly that I am now complete. Because of that, I can look beyond myself to help others."

John's light blue eyes gazed at Rudi as though peering deep into his soul. With a caring hand placed on the young man's shoulder, John said, "Son, you were hungry for something I could not fix or fill. I tried to talk to you about my faith, but your ears and heart were closed to it. Know that sending you away when I so dearly wished to keep you close was hard, but you needed to get away from Malchus and your parents before your brother destroyed what remained of you. That boy only ever thought of himself, and his money-hungry wife was no better."

Rudi nodded. The last of the scales of rejection fell off.

Seeing relief on Rudi's face, John continued. "I did not weep when news was brought to me of Malchus and Lavender's deaths. No, I immediately sent Penny to collect the girls from their over-fancy mausoleum, and I wrote to Lachlan and you that day. Before the accident, I had moved here to be close to the girls." His head tipped as he watched Rudi for his reaction. A sigh escaped from him, but he smiled. "Your brother would have hated knowing that you now have a title that outranked him in every way." His deep rumbling chuckle was heard. Rudi nodded, and this was followed by a knowing grin.

John then added, "Rudi, I will come and stay when you are settled, as a few days are not enough for me to catch up on all the news. I was offered retirement, but I declined until your return. I will set that in motion. I hope it will take many months to finalise. Age has finally caught up with me. I must pass on my baton of leadership. That means training a new chap." He sighed. "I'll take my time doing that." He chuckled. "I am sure the good Lord has more for me to do, but, as yet, I do not know what that is. My flat in Hackney is close enough to St John's church that I can see touches of my time in the colony. Obadiah Jensen's beautifully bound Bibles and hymnbooks remind me that even the least of us have skills unknown to many. He was a convict who recently returned with Phillip Margate, whom I believe you knew?"

Rudi nodded. Phillip had been based in Parramatta, but he was one of Lachlan's trusted soldiers. Rudi knew Obadiah in passing.

John explained, "Buddy, that's what Obadiah is called now; his wife, Emily, who is Phillip's cousin, as well as Phillip and his wife Phoebe, have moved north to Phillip's small estate."

Rudi knew that the soldier had left, but did not realise that he had married or taken his cousin and her husband with him. Lachlan trusted Phillip and had mentioned his departure, but he presumed it was alone.

John was still talking. "Each Sunday, I see the crypt where Connie and Will Waterson lived. Other children are still there. I see the graves of the reverend gentlemen whom I came to know and love. Reverend Phineas Brackenridge and the man who followed him, Josiah Winchester, are both interred there. George McGillicuddy is now the minister, and I like his style. George's wife, Ellen, would have liked life in Sydney, but they have their work there." John sighed and said, "Now, tell me about what you did in Sydney. I glean all the information I can, but you can't beat first-hand stories. Tell me about Crispin, Helena and Jasper Milroy, the Brays, and Osbornes."

Rudi handed over the letters from the Bray, Osborne, Milroy, and Rosedale households while sitting next to John and filling him in on the two families. After some time, Rudi held out his hand. Two coins sat in Rudi's palm. "Lachlan gave each of us who worked on the project a small bag of coins. It suddenly struck me that the Holey Dollar was like the void in me. The small coin, the Dump, no longer fits the confines from which it was struck, as it has been heated and re-stamped, much like me. I willingly admit the heat got to me in Sydney to the point of nearly ending things. I gave up and nearly walked into the harbour. God sent Lance, and two days later, I met Bethan. So, Uncle John, these two coins are a token of our appreciation for you. Lachlan also sent you a lengthy update on the latest developments in town. But I did as you suggested, I looked up. for my heart is also filled and has grown." He handed over another envelope containing the governor's lengthy dossier.

John took the coins and thanked him. He placed the bulky document beside him. That could wait until he read the news from his friends. Rudi continued. "Sir, Lance and I plan to work with Mrs Elizabeth Fry and her brother, Joseph Gurney. They are assisting convicts on this side and facilitating their transportation. No one cares about these felons, and we must begin to make their path easier. It would be better to supply their needs here before they become desperate enough to steal. Many steal for hunger, some because they need to escape poverty."

Rudi saw John's face light up, so he continued. "Thanks to you and your words to me about watching for girls like Helena, we've found many convicts caught up in the mire of life, facing the consequences of merely trying to live. We discovered that the soldiers guarding them are often worse felons than those they watch. Our first outreach will be to our maids' families. Both girls are still convicts, but their families will be offered a new life with us. If we can train them, then we can train others."

John smiled. "I like the way you think, laddie, but then again, you always did think beyond yourself. Please let me know how I can assist you, as I'd be happy to sink my teeth into this project. I would like to meet with Mrs Fry and her brother to supply additional information. Come and visit me at my new flat in Hackney, London, when you can, and we'll set up a meeting. Mayhap that will be how God will use me there."

"Willingly, Uncle John." Rudi adored this gentle man even more than he had as a lad. Things and conversations from his past now made sense. His uncle's soft Scottish lilt reminded him of Lachlan. These two Scotsmen had been pivotal in his life. In many ways, they were similar. Both had a gentle but genuine faith. Uncle John had been sent to live with an uncle in Norfolk when young, so he did not have as thick an accent as Lachlan. Rudi could see now what the beloved old man wanted him to learn. His eyes had been blind to what was offered to him when he left. Uncle John was correct. He was now complete and content.

~

After meeting Rudi's nieces, unloading their furniture took a few days, so the Greenwoods moved into Malchus's luxurious but uncomfortable house a few miles away. John and Penny accompanied them on their first visit. They had yet to sort out transport for their possessions on the ship. That issue with the luggage wagon was quickly resolved when Rudi visited the carriage house. It was stuffed full of new vehicles and luggage wagons.

As expected, Malchus had enlarged and redesigned their old house during the rebuild. It was now ostentatious and vastly uncomfortable. It was built to impress. Even the golden sitting room chairs were designed to impress visitors rather than for comfort.

Another thing Malchus had done was to build and stock a vast library. This surprised Rudi, as Malchus had never shown any interest in books of any sort. Then he noticed that the thousands of new books had been placed on the shelves by colour and height. He groaned. This would be a mammoth task to sort into the various genres.

The three little girls were happy to leave as they had few memories of their parents. Penny and Bethany's hugs had already eased their sadness. Penny explained that the first time she hugged them, they stood stiff and frightened. After months with Penny and John, the girls now sought the loving care they had grown accustomed to. Freddy, Georgie, and Etta had hardly ever seen their parents, who were often selfish. Malchus and Lavender had spent most of their time in London, galavanting in society. So the girls' grief was not as profound as it could have been. Bethany's loving hugs had been the first they had had for some time, other than Penny's and Uncle John's.

The three girls adored their small cousins. They were intrigued that four of them were twins. Malchus's three girls were older than their cousins, so they mothered them. Andy and Benji objected to the numerous hugs forced upon them by the older girls until they realised that Freddy and Georgie could read; story time drew all of the children together. Thankfully, Uncle John had purchased every child's book he could, and the girls loved story time with Penny. Etta let that cat out of the bag and insisted that Freddy read them the bible story of David and Goliath. Wide-eyed, the boys sat and listened, enthralled as the two older girls took turns in doing the character voices.

On checking the estate books, Rudi discovered that Malchus had milked the family estate dry. What was worse, his brother had not provided for his girls at all. He had probably hoped for a son. This ghastly new building would be sold to provide dowries for the three girls. The house may hold the family name, but it would never be home for Rudi.

~

Ten days after arriving in England, the now extended Greenwood family travelled the seventy miles to the new viscount's grand estate just out of Dorchester, rather than remain in Malchus's house near Portsmouth. Their furniture had been sent on, and the ship had finally left the port.

John accompanied them for a quick visit soon after Rudi brought his family to see Buckridge House. That was more to ensure the house was fit for occupation. He and Penny only remained for two days. Duty called.

Rudi knew that Buckridge House was a Georgian mansion that the old miser had let run down. However, while the crown was in care, the roof was replaced, and maintenance staff were employed to keep the grounds under control. It took their breath away when it came into view. In truth, it was lovely.

Bethany gasped. "Rudi, it's been fully restored to its former glory. It looked nothing like this when we visited. I wonder what that new wing is? It wasn't there when I was here last time. My great uncle always wanted a ballroom, so I wonder if that is what he built."

~

There was still much to be done. Soon after Lance arrived home, he sent Gareth to help Rudi get things into shape. Gareth sourced some staff from his local area and brought them with him. Some were injured soldiers, and others were children of the Upcroft staff. One was a wounded soldier, Gerald Fitzgerald, the son of Lance's butler, who knew estate work well. The man not only had one arm and a limp, but also the voice of a cannon. The bevy of new footmen who arrived with him ensured that his orders were followed to the letter. His authoritative voice carried weight. None dared to disobey. Gerald was thrilled to be accepted, given his disabilities. Having grown up in a big house, he knew what was expected. He was an excellent butler.

Rudi discovered that this man had friends who were injured ex-soldiers; all wanted to work but could not find positions because of their disfigurements. After discussions with Gerald, Rudi contacted his butler's regiment, and many able-bodied scarred men were offered positions as footmen, gardeners, stablehands, and similar jobs. All twenty-six were taken on as staff. Many brought their families. Each assured work for their ability. Any additional staff with the necessary skills were sent to Malchus's house to prepare it for sale. All of the old staff, except two longtime retainers in the garden, had been sacked. They were the grandfather and the grandson who had taken Rudi to London. For some reason, Malchus had kept them on when he inherited the estate.

Lance's house was not far away from Malchus's place, so he offered to watch over the new staff for the squire's estate. Lance set one man with no legs to sort out the library catalogue. An able-bodied soldier with partial vision assisted him. The younger man could get books from the shelves, but could not read them. Together, they made one able-bodied workman. Both were employed in good jobs.

Rudi didn't care if his butler had a limp and was missing an arm; helping him and his friends was the beginning of a new purpose in his life. The footmen respected their old sergeant and obeyed him even to the smallest command.

The new staff were settled in before Vera and May's extended families arrived. After the girls contacted their parents, the parents sent messages to Daisy and Ivy's families.

Thankfully, the latter two sets of parents refused the invitation to relocate, although Daisy's sisters willingly accepted the offer. Rudi had not wanted Daisy's vile, abusive father living with them, but intended to rescue the remainder of her family. Thankfully, she had no sisters who refused their offer.

~

Rudi sent four carriages to collect the two families and Daisy's two sisters. Vera and May went with the vehicles to ensure the correct people were collected. Two carriages were sent for each family. The carriages were loaded with food, pillows and blankets for the journey.

Rudi presumed they would have luggage, but the dozen or more people who arrived wore rags. They had nothing at all. Vera's family had recently been forced out of their rooms and were living on the streets. She found them around the corner from their old room. The reunion was joyous. May's family were extracted from a tiny attic room. Seeing the glossy carriages made their eyes pop.

On arrival at Buckridge House, the new families could not believe what they saw.

Bethany welcomed them all with a warm embrace. She arranged bathing facilities for them all and then went hunting in the attic for something decent to wear. She knew her mother and grandmother had stored their old clothing up there.

Attire for all of them was easily found. The old miser had thrown nothing away, nor had the royal staff. There were cases and cases of outdated clothing from the old man's childhood, as well as Bethany's mother's old apparel and discarded items that had been stained or torn. There were cases of old uniforms from a bygone era, including those of the old miser's housekeeper.

Bethany and the new staff set about remaking these items into serviceable garments for anyone who needed them. Fortunately, many of the new women were soldiers' wives who could sew. The new ballroom was turned into a sewing hub. Long trestle tables lined the room, and the numerous chests of clothing had been unpacked, washed, and sorted. Lace was cut off for later use or sale. Obsolete monograms were unpicked and removed from pockets. Everything was recycled. Once decently clad, Vera and May's mothers set about learning how to manage the housekeeping for a grand estate.

Vera and May's fathers and older brothers tackled the overgrown gardens with the assistance of a few injured soldiers. All the younger sisters became scullery maids when they weren't learning to read and write in a class Bethany had started.

One of the old soldiers had been a teacher before enlisting. He could hardly walk, but he could still teach. Any children who wished to work were permitted to do so, provided they attended class. The soldier's wives were to train Daisy, Vera, and May's numerous sisters as housemaids and kitchen staff, and Vera and May oversaw them all. Carol had taught them well. Both were now excellent cooks and imparted their knowledge to whoever was assigned to assist with meal preparation for the growing household. However, neither girl felt willing to take on the role of a full-time cook. Their little sisters loved preparing the large volumes of food, as up until they arrived, eating had almost been a luxury.

~

Rudi was thrilled when Lance sent a cook. This lady had burns from a kitchen accident on another estate. She had been replaced by her employer rather than kept on while she healed. She was the sister of Lance's own cook. Mildred Dorsett was a perfect fit for the unusual household. Her cooking skills were incredible, and she adored teaching those who wished to learn. Her buxom physique was used to embrace any weeping woman or child. Their lives had changed, and all settled quickly.

Bethany adored the kind lady and was delighted to have a motherly woman among her staff to turn to.

Chapter 21 A New Work to Do

1816 England

John refused to retire until he saw their new home. He was delightfully surprised by how large the new house was and by its excellent condition, and he promised a much longer visit once he was settled in London. When John retired from Portsmouth, he requested to depart by sea for London. He asked Rudi and Lance to accompany him.

Being a Vice Admiral, John was given a naval fanfare and a farewell fit for the king. As his ship hauled the ropes aboard, guns fired as a farewell. This voyage would likely be his final time to dip his toes in the briny ocean while in uniform, and he would not miss that for anything. He had the sea in his blood, as he had made his first voyages with his father when he was only a child.

Rudi and Lance remained at his side for as long as the cold weather permitted. The slow ten-day journey gave John quality time with Rudi.

The two young officers probed John for his early recollections of the colony, from his first glimpses of the barren land in Botany Bay to the people he knew. Bennelong was one name mentioned often.

John mentioned many names they had heard while in Australia. Connie and Nigel Bray at the mill in Sydney, Colin and Aggie Osborne, the potters in Parramatta, and the Milroys and the story of how Helena's father, Linus Rosedale, had taught the colony to farm the virgin soil.

Other names John mentioned were familiar to the young officers. However, they had not met Marquess Oliver Quilpie and his wife, Annie. Annie Gentle, as she was known, had been on the First Fleet with Connie, her husband Nigel, and Colin and Aggie. The Quilpies had returned home before either soldier arrived in the colony, so they did not know them.

On returning to England, Annie discovered John at a function in London and made directly for his side. She greeted him with a big hug. It was her first outing after the birth of their twins, and John had been in London for a Naval function. Seeing a familiar face in a sea of over-preened society was a delight for them both. The Quilpies promised they would visit John whenever they could. With John being in the south of England, that had not occurred.

Though Lance and Rudi had assisted with his move, they didn't remain long. After escorting him on the journey to his new home, they returned to their own homes.

John knew that he would never command a ship again, but he would travel by sea whenever possible. Having the lads with him made the sad journey bearable.

Once in London, he finalised his retirement and felt settled. However, John had no intention of staying in one place. That would occur later when he became too old to travel. He did not look forward to being confined to his flat. He laughingly called it his living coffin.

John's favourite chair had come with him on his final journey, and Rudi carried it up to the flat. Lance carried a special set of crockery and a mug that Colin Osborne had made for him. This small crate contained other special trinkets and gifts from friends and family. A small red jasper rock was from Jasper Milroy. John had instructed Penny to return it to Jasper with the notice of his passing. John used it as a paperweight on his desk. All these were memories of his past.

~

Three months later, Buckridge House was ready for visitors.

John was settled in his flat, already hating it. He felt frustrated at being shackled to his apartment.

After telling Penny, John packed as fast as he could. He stayed with Rudi while Penny attended several events with her family, as London was already oppressive.

Penny now resided with her family in London rather than with John. He missed her bright, cheery face, but she had discovered a young man in need of assistance. John now had a maid come and clean for him, and a young Frenchman moved in to act as a footman and carer for the ageing officer.

John felt an instant rapport with the young lad who reminded him of Crispin Milroy. The young man had escaped from France with nothing and moved into John's London flat the week John did. The lad was an excellent cook and had some nursing experience, should it ever be required. Wishing to see some of the country, he escorted John to Rudi's house and cared for him as his valet-cum-companion.

John had also purchased a sizeable apartment in Leith, Scotland, near his old home. He installed one of his widowed sisters there on the condition that she keep a room for him.

Having eight siblings, he had many visitors when at both abodes. Many used his flat as a base in London or stayed nearby so they could visit often. He hoped to spend some of each summer with his sister in Scotland during the frivolous season in London. He planned to take this trip by sea if possible. If he were not in London, he didn't need to attend any functions.

John knew he would always have a room with Rudi if he wished to leave town, and he planned to use it over the winter. Although he loved the worship at St John's in Hackney, he hated the bleak, smoggy, London days when the fog hardly lifted. The smell of the Thames River assaulted his nostrils, and the fresh farm smells at Rudi's place were a delight. The trip to see Rudi's family was much shorter than the journey to Edinburgh. Warmwell, being only a short distance from Weymouth, he could travel by sea. Rudi would meet him at Weymouth and drive him the twelve miles to Buckridge House.

It was at Rudi's house that John felt he was home. He adored the children's noises and laughter, and they all adored him. John was the loving grandfather figure they never had. However, he knew he couldn't remain with them; Hackney was his base. It was in that flat that he planned to see out his days. A wave of depression wafted over him each time he returned to London. He hated not being busy.

The minister, George McGillicuddy, visited John when he could not attend church. Even as John's legs began to fail him, he made the effort to attend at least one weekly service. George's sermons, though not fire and brimstone, were uplifting. His faith was genuine and strong. He preached the faith of Christ, and John could ask no more than that.

John was stunned to discover that George's lovely wife, Ellen, was a duke's daughter. She had married George, a foundling, without her father's permission.

~

August 29th, 1817

Upon returning from each jaunt, once John was settled again in his new apartment, he wrote numerous letters to family members and friends, inviting them for a visit. He was used to having people around him, and the small apartment was sometimes claustrophobic for a man who had spent his life on the rolling seas breathing in the salt-laden air.

Finally, the Greenwoods accepted his invitation. However, this time they would arrive with others. Rudi planned this to coincide with a special day.

More than a year after returning home to England, a carriage travelled from Warmwell to London. Lance and Elise were collected en route. The Upcrofts now had a son, Lachlan John, and Rudi and Bethany's latest baby, tiny Jennifer Carol, travelled with them. Her twin, Isabella Penelope, had been stillborn. Hence the delay. Bethany had needed time to recover from this twin birth. They had put off the long trip as travelling in a carriage with a heavily expectant lady was no easy feat. However, travelling with tiny babies was equally challenging. Dealing with wet and soiled flannel napkins was difficult. Thankfully, they had brought a large pile of clean ones.

Elise and Bethany insisted on visiting John, which meant the new babies came too. Stops were frequent, but they had more than a week to make the journey.

Vera and May remained with the older children and the new staff, which now included a nurse, the two maids' parents, their families, and numerous other personnel to watch over the boisterous children. Overall, they kept them occupied and safe.

The large house was a rabbit warren of adventure for the imps. Benji was usually filthy, lost, or hiding. One of the footmen was assigned to watch over the lad's every move.

Cook knew each child's favourite treats and promised to spoil them in the parents' absence. With that promise, saying farewell to their parents was a cheerful experience.

Knowing that Malchus died on a similar journey, their driver reduced speed.

Rudi had already made provision for all the children.

This trip had dual purposes. Rudi, Bethany, Lance, and Elise travelled to meet with Elizabeth Fry and discuss how they could help. They were also to give her news of Perry and Katy's situation in Parramatta and of the delight at the couple's reunion.

Over the past months, many of their friends had spoken about Mrs Fry's work amongst the convict women. Being so distant, it was not until the esteemed lady's brother, Joseph Gurney, came to visit the local prison that they were confronted by having done nothing about following up on their idea to assist.

Inspired once more, plans were made to join John in London.

Rudi wrote and made a large booking at a nearby accommodation inn in Hackney. He was looking forward to catching up with his uncle again. They planned to be with him for his eightieth birthday.

John had just returned from Scotland and wanted to catch up with Rudi.

Though they had spent the first six months visiting often when the admiral was still in Portsmouth, Rudi knew his Uncle John's time was drawing to a close. He kept busy and was involved with his church. As he was about to turn eighty. John was now an old man, and feeling his age, but he remained as kind and loving as he had always been.

Penelope remained by his side whenever possible and cared for him with great love and affection. She had devoted her life to him and didn't regret a day of it. She escorted him to church each week and spent the afternoon with him, talking or writing letters for him.

John's body had aged dramatically since relinquishing his post, but his mind was still sharp.

Unbeknownst to Rudi, John arranged a special meeting while they were visiting London. He had arranged the meeting with Mrs Fry at his flat rather than at her home.

John knew this new work would mark the end of his involvement with the colony. If he could help get it off the ground, he would do what he could. All those he invited had a unique connection or involvement with the penal settlement. They had insights into the colony that Mrs Fry and her brother needed to hear. At this meeting, he would pass on the baton to the next generation.

Bethany and Elise came to give Mrs Fry an idea of the activities women could participate in during the voyage out.

However, John had a surprise in store for them all. Someone he knew from his time over there had also been invited. He had not mentioned them to anyone.

The meeting was arranged at his flat to ensure complete privacy. Mrs Fry had a houseful of children, and so she arranged for her brother to bring her and a friend.

From Rudi and Lance, John knew they hoped to begin extending the work amongst the poor of London to their nearby ports. Convict vessels were departing from various ports around England, and Portsmouth, in particular, was a harbour that housed convict hulks.

From John, Rudi learned that more felons were loaded onto these derelict vessels each week than at most other ports.

Rudi had been to Hackney and knew John's large sitting room would easily accommodate at least ten people. As they approached, voices could be heard from within.

Their knock brought a uniformed maid to the front door. "Welcome, Mr Rudi. Vice Admiral Hunter is in the sitting room and looking forward to your visit." She dropped her voice. "I have made a cake for his birthday, and he is unaware that we know it is today." She moved aside so Bethany, Elise, and the babies could enter.

Rudi and Lance closed the door behind them. Thankfully, the maids had not used their titles. They still did not like them and never introduced themselves using them.

On entry, there were three unknown faces.

A tall, handsome, middle-aged man stood as they entered.

John made the required introductions

Bethany's face lit up when she realised who these people were. She looked at the lady. "You're Connie's friend."

Annie nodded and came to her side. "Any friend of Connie's is a friend of mine." She greeted Bethany with a hug.

The couple were Oliver Quilpie, Marquess of Bowbelle, and his wife, who had been Annie Soames, or Annie Gentle, as she was known when she was sent to the colony as a convict. Connie Bray had told Bethany all about them. Annie arrived on the *Lady Penrhyn* in the First Fleet with Connie. Some years after Annie's arrest, the Marquess, Oliver Quilpie, followed her out there, married her, and brought her home. The marquess's first wife was responsible for the false accusation that led to Annie's arrest, wrongful conviction, and transportation.

The third stranger they were introduced to was Mrs Ann Dumaresq. Mrs Dumaresq was a philanthropist who wished to learn more about Mrs Fry's work. She had powerful social connections and wanted to do all she could to aid the less fortunate. She had heard about Rudi's desire to help through some of the injured soldiers who had been in her husband's regiment.

As they were introducing themselves, another couple arrived. Elizabeth Fry and her brother entered.

Everyone stood again, and the men shook hands.

John hauled himself to his feet. After introducing the newest arrivals, he addressed Mrs Fry. "I may be old and grey, but I am determined to see this new work of yours be as effective as possible. I saw the condition of the poor wretches, and their clothing was threadbare. If there is a way to alleviate this, I will do what I can to make it happen with the Navy. I am retired, but as a Vice Admiral, I still have clout at Admiralty House. They will listen to me. Once done, I will consider that I have passed on my baton to you all."

John officially welcomed everyone.

They took their seats once more, but one empty chair remained unfilled. Rudi wondered who his uncle had invited.

John remained standing for a while. Ignoring their titles, he said, "I invited Oliver and Annie Quilpie here as they, too, have first-hand knowledge of the condition there, albeit some years ago. But Annie can tell you of the conditions on board a convict ship which none of the others can. Rudi and Lance have just returned from the Antipodes with their wives. The men worked as soldiers, but employed some of the younger lassies who needed protection. With the collective knowledge in this room, I'm confident we can establish a firm foundation to assist the individuals being transported. I prefer to find a way to assist them before they are arrested, but I feel that is a job beyond us."

Joseph Gurney said, "Thank you, Vice Admiral. I have been touring various prisons across the land and have found only one I could call tolerable. That one is in Glasgow. Many of these lockups are privately owned, forcing prisoners to pay for basic sustenance. For example, Bristol Gaol is privately operated, and felons must pay for their imprisonment. Many are there due to poverty. They are housed according to their ability to pay, ranging from a private cell with a cleaning woman to lying on the floor with no cover. Food is vile gruel, not fit for pigs." He sighed. As Joseph spoke, another knock was heard, and Rudi saw the maid move towards the door.

Joseph continued. "Prisoners can also pay to have lighter manacles fitted. I find this intolerable. All felons have a right to decency. Each one should be provided with nourishing food and warmth. The slops they are fed are disgusting. Yet these same people are expected to thrive on this pig's swill. Most are in there as they are starving. I wish to see them be offered a chance to leave the tragic situations they have found themselves in. My good sister and I will do what we can to make that occur. As a banker, I will do my best to finance her work, but I agree with Viscount Rudi. Rather than give them clothing, let them learn to make it themselves. I'm sure we can supply damaged fabric from the various mills. Knitting wool and needles to make things will also occupy them on their voyage."

Surprisingly, Marcus Ryan was ushered into the room and warmly welcomed by his travelling companions.

With another round of handshakes and introductions, all the men took their seats once more.

Marcus said, "I heard the mention of knitting wool when I arrived. I can supply that by the bale full. Our wool mills have numerous spools of rejected yarn lengths. Some have burrs that are easily removed, but it is not worthwhile for us to fiddle with small amounts. Many hanks of yarn are end-dye lots and other unsellable skeins. If you can use it, that would save us from paying for disposal after we write it off. We also have bolts of cloth with strings attached that you can have."

Elizabeth Fry's head was nodding at the young man. "We certainly can, sir. But what do you mean by 'strings attached'?"

Marcus chuckled, then apologised. "When a flaw is discovered in the fabric, it's marked by putting a string on the edge. A certain number of flaws are passable, but if there are too many, the bolt is discarded. It is what you can have. It's perfectly good for home crafts and apparel, but not for sale. The number of strings on the one-hundred-yard bolt immediately tells us the quality of the fabric. So if it has 'strings attached', it has issues."

Elizabeth was delighted, 'Sir, we will take as much of anything you can supply. Any hanks of yarn that are immediately usable, some of our group can make items to sell, and we can use the money to purchase what we need." She gazed at him and saw something in him that she liked.

Ann Dumaresq had been silent until now. "I can certainly muster a group of helpers. I know many women who are keen to assist the less fortunate. Many would be willing to roll hanks into balls and de-burr the yarn."

Elizabeth Fry turned towards the elegant lady.

Ann said, "Please take no offence, Mrs Fry and Mr Gurney, but with both of you being Quakers, many in society have held back from assisting you. If we can each challenge our friends to follow Christ's teaching to 'visit those in prison,' I'm sure more will join our cause."

Elizabeth smiled and nodded. "None taken, Mrs Dumaresq. I have been feeling this way for some time. The only way this project can grow is if Joseph and I step back and bring others on board. My children will like that. All assistance is willingly accepted. It's too great a job for just two people."

For Rudi, those words brought back memories of William Cowper's bible studies. Yes, this was a way for them all to help those in prison. This was how they would follow the path God set before them. He smiled but remained silent, listening to the sub-conversations among the others. He caught the eyes of Lance and Bethany, then grinned. All remembered that one particular life-changing discussion around their kitchen table.

The meeting reached a plan of action.

Rudi called the maid and asked her to bring in the prearranged tea tray and cake.

The group of friends celebrated a very surprised John for his eightieth birthday. John had no idea that any of them even knew it was his special day. Rudi had remembered and planned for him to be surrounded by those who loved him and his work. His friends from Australia had sent special letters to celebrate the day.

John's eyes twinkled with delight. "What a wonderful celebration. I could not imagine a greater gift than knowing my work with the downtrodden will continue. I thank you all." The big man surreptitiously wiped a tear from his light blue eyes. His heart was full.

The group would act on the report that Mrs Fry suggested. She had seen children living on the street, and their plight was on her heart. She arranged for the children in the gaols, along with their mothers, to learn to read and write. Often she took these classes herself at Newgate Prison.

They all knew there was much work ahead, but this meeting began to expand the work and spread the word.

Vice Admiral John, Marquess Oliver, and the two viscounts agreed that spreading the philanthropic work among the nobility would be beneficial, as it would challenge others to become involved. Knowing how society worked, they planned to challenge the uppity lords and ladies to out-give one another in their charitable endeavours. They knew Perry would assist when he returned in a few years. In the meantime, his father, Duke Percy, had already written to say he wished to support the cause. They could use every available worker. Mrs Fry wanted every port that exported convicts to have teams of helpers.

Rudi and Lance had already decided to begin their efforts with the local county lockups.

Rather than being upset, Mrs Fry and her brother were delighted.

There were gaols and county lock-ups across the land, and each one would need volunteers to assist the prisoners. They planned to start with the women and children, but they would not forget the men and boys. Mrs Dumaresq's offer to contact her various friends would be utilised. As bank owners, Joseph Gurney and Elizabeth's husband, Joseph Fry, had influence amongst London's businessmen and in other major cities across the country.

Marcus Ryan would willingly supply the raw materials and, if possible, source fabrics and notions from other factories. He intended to find other like-minded industrialists to assist him. His eyes flicked from Rudi to Lance. He could finally see how meeting these two men fitted into God's plan for his life. His father had only told him last week to get rid of the backlog of discarded wool and cloth. Now he could do so at no cost to the business. With the money allocated for the disposal, he planned to supply the first crate of accessories they would need. Another nearby factory made knitting needles. He knew the faulty needles were thrown away. That would be his first visit when he went north.

John watched the youngest lad's face. Their eyes met, and a smile lit Marcus's face. It went all the way to his eyes.

John mouthed, "Thank you so much."

Marcus returned the smile. He softly replied, "Thank you for inviting me."

For another two hours, each person contributed ideas for how to assist. Many took notes, as they were unlikely to meet again until next summer.

Rudi spoke up when someone suggested selling the items the convicts made with donated materials and permitting the convicts to keep the coins. He explained, "A throwaway comment from me led to the manufacture of a new currency for the colony." He drew out the small bag of coins Lachlan had given him. Placing a Holey Dollar on his hand next to a shiny Dump, he said, "These have the value of fifteen pence and five shillings, but more small coins are needed. We have discussed the idea of convict women selling their goods, but if we could also send them a small handful of low-denomination coins, it would eventually feed through to the settlement. I have discovered that the Bank of England pays £5 to any female felon convicted of passing forged banknotes, as an acknowledgment that it should have made its paper money more secure. However, if this money could be given in small coins rather than pound notes, New South Wales would benefit. The women are unable to use paper money on board anyway. They could use coins for small purchases. That alone would be incredibly useful in Sydney."

Many had heard about the colony's new, unique holed coinage, but none of the others had seen it.

Rudi tipped out the rest of the bag.

The shiny silver Holey Dollars and Dumps were passed around the group, and the story of their manufacture was discussed.

Marquess Oliver picked up the empty bag and asked, "Why did you bring these back, young man? They are useless here, are they not?"

Lance and Rudi caught each other's eye and smiled.

Rudi explained. "When making these, the utter delight of

plunging our arms into the chests of warm, newly processed coins was wonderful. Even the governor had the pleasure of doing it. It took us a year and four days, from the coins' arrival on 26th September 1812 until the release of the bulk of the new currency on 30th September 1813. Had these coins been gold, we would have felt like Midas. As it was, it was like hearing the sound of pirate treasure clinking. The original coins may have even been just that, as they had different dates in the late 1780s and 90s. The temptation to stuff our pockets was certainly there, but none of us succumbed. We know, as all coins were accounted for."

As the coins passed from hand to hand, Rudi continued his story.

"Shortly before we left Sydney, Governor Lachlan Macquarie met with us all and presented each of us with a calico bag of coins such as this. He had done as we all did, plunged his hand into a chest of mixed newly minted coins, and pulled out what he could in one fist. He then counted the same for each of us who had worked on the project. He reimbursed the treasury from his own pocket, so it was all above board. He wished that we keep some as a token of thanks. I gave Uncle John two, but the rest will be for our children. They are not just tokens of our time abroad, but they represent a significant change in my life. I kept a few more that were in circulation, but left the same value in smaller English currency. We produced a shade under eighty thousand coins in total. I'm sure that a few missing ones won't matter."

Everyone passed the unique coins back to Rudi, and he put all but one Holey Dollar back into the bag. He chuckled as he tossed the large coin in the air and caught it again.

Rudi turned to Bethany and smiled. "Uncle John, to celebrate your special birthday on this day makes my heart joyful. Every person we help will remind me of you and your charge to me. You told me to look higher, and I did. Although I found my faith over there, I also found something far better than a mere fist full of Holey Dollars. I found my own priceless treasure and brought her back with me. She taught me to trust God, and because of that, we are now gathered here today. We each have work in front of us, but with God behind us, it will get done. We know that Christian denominations are man-made. In heaven, there will only be believers in God, and they won't be divided into sects. We all come from different walks of life, but God has called us to love others. He didn't differentiate in any way, shape, or form. He commanded us to love everyone and tell them about Him. This is the work we are called to do."

All their heads nodded.

John's face showed the pride and adoration he felt for this young man. He was positively beaming.

Rudi reached out for Bethany's hand and, taking it in his own, upturned it and kissed her palm. "Yes, Bethan is my God-given treasure. One that makes my heart full. We will work together as we have been called to do, but God has changed and moulded me. I am like the once-rejected dump that no longer fits the hole it was cut from. I have been put through fire and stamped with God's love."

Bethany's eyes shone with her overwhelming love for this Godly man. He was the husband of her dreams and the delight of her heart.

Rudi caught his uncle's loving grin and relaxed. A smile hovered on their lips as silent understanding washed over both men. Wrinkled blue eyes twinkled with delight as they met Rudi's grey orbs. John's heart was full of pride in his beloved honorary nephew.

The End?
No, just the beginning of a new life for many.

Elizabeth Fry's work eventually involved 20,000 helpers assisting British prisoners, which led to the Prison Reform Bill.

For more about some of the characters,
you can find their stories in:-

Annie and Oliver Quilpie, *"Gentle Annie Soames"*
Colin and Aggie Osborne *"The Emancipated Potter."*
Connie and Nigel Bray *"Paternity Unknown."*
John Hunter's governorship *"When Upon Life's Billows."*
Mark and Cathy Duffy, Josh and Jenny in "*Tuppence to Pass.*"
Marcus Ryan in *"No More, My Love."*
Guy Manning in *"Jam or Marmalade for Tea."*

Honest reviews of my books help bring them to the attention of other readers who are more likely to read something from a new-to-them author if it has more reviews (even if it is not five-star).
You can quickly and easily leave a star rating or a short review on Amazon.

The Holey Dollar and Dump, Info.

The dot in the middle of the words "Fifteen" and "Pence" is the "H" maker's mark that William Henshall added.

Note:

The history behind this story is true. William Henshall was a convict who was tasked with converting 40,000 Spanish Real coins into a new currency.

Very few remain as they were eventually melted down and made into other coins.

NSW had a population of about 13,000 men, women, and children in 1813.

John Hunter was one of nine children and was sent to live with an uncle in Norfolk in his youth. He spent his retirement in his flat in Hackney when he wasn't travelling to spend time with his sizeable family. He never married or had any children. His strong faith from his youth stayed with him until the end. John was a member of the congregation at St John-at-Hackney in London, England, where he is buried. He died on 13th March 1821.

John's friend, Reverend Richard Johnson, died exactly five years later, in 1826.

Lachlan Macquarie was the man for the job to turn around the drunken and disordered troops that were in control of the colony when he arrived. He named the land Australia, and his grave bears the inscription "Father of Australia."

Elizabeth Fry and her brother, Joseph Gurney, worked with Mrs Ann Dumeresq and 20,000 other peers to assist convicts, both in prison and during transportation to Australia. Ann's daughter, Eliza, and her husband, Ralph Darling, later went to Sydney as the 7th governor.

Many, if not most, of the other historical characters are real.

Rudi, Bethany, Mark, Lance, Marcus, the Quilpies, and other convicts are fictional, as are the other names mentioned in other books of mine.

Sydney town in 1808

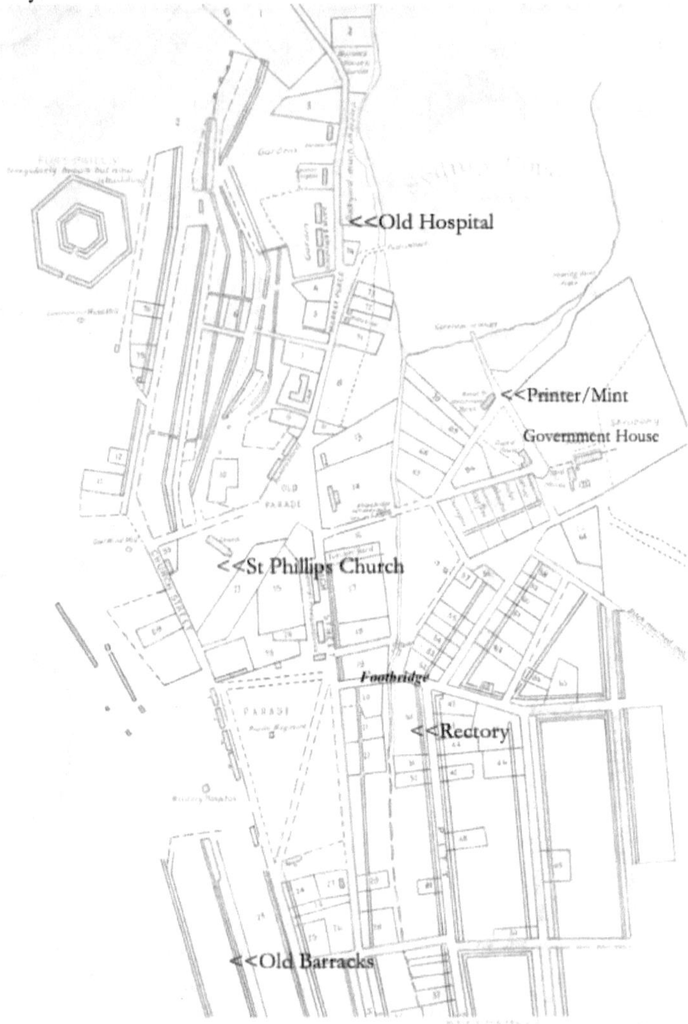

James Meehan's
Map of Sydney
1808

Holey Dollar History

Governor Lachlan Macquarie set out to secure a reliable supply of coins for the colony. A special shipment of 40,000 Reales arrived in the colony from Madras aboard the *Samarang* on 26 September 1812. These coins were Spanish silver eight Reales, known as "pieces of eight," and they were commonly used as an international trading currency.

Macquarie set the value of the Holey Dollar at five shillings, with fifteen pence for the Dump. These new coins entered circulation on 30th September 1813 and were replaced by sterling coinage in 1822. The National Museum's Holey Dollar is one of about 300 in existence.

Convicted forger William Henshall was chosen to cut and counter-stamp these coins. Henshall worked as a metal plater and cutler in England. On an 1811 New South Wales muster list, he was listed simply as a 'convict', without reference to his trade. It is believed that Macquarie probably learnt of Henshall's metalworking skills by reputation. Henshall was granted an absolute pardon on 12 September 1812, six months before his sentence was due to end and just two weeks before the coins arrived.

Macquarie provided Henshall with a workshop in the basement of "The Factory" to make the Holey Dollars and Dumps. This building, used by government printer George Howe, was located at the corner of Bridge and Loftus streets, on the eastern bank of the Tank Stream. It was effectively Australia's first mint, with Henshall as Australia's first mint master. It was across the road from the old original Government House.

Macquarie initially anticipated that converting the 40,000 Spanish coins would take three months, but the project ultimately took over a year to complete. Henshall had to experiment with developing the necessary machinery, a process that proved difficult. It appears that a drop hammer, rather than a screw press, was used to strike the coins, but little can be confirmed. The Dump is the nation's first widely circulated coin and the partner to the 1813 Holey Dollar.

William Henshall had to cut a hole in each silver dollar, creating two coins from one. His reward was emancipation and the reunion of his family. Most of the holed coins were over-stamped around the edge of the hole with the date 1813, though some were dated 1814. The value of "Five Shillings," and the issuing authority of "New South Wales." It became the unique Holey Dollar.

The silver disc punched out of the centre was not wasted; this became the Dump. This disk was imprinted with the issuing authority "New South Wales" and the silver value of fifteen pence. This became the equally illustrious Dump, widely used. Most coins have a tiny 'H' as a maker's mark.

While the original intention was to create 40,000 Holey Dollars and 40,000 Dumps from 40,000 silver dollars, spoilage and the dispatch of samples back to Great Britain resulted in a slightly reduced number of Holey Dollars and Dumps - 39,910 of each - being released into circulation.

Today, approximately 800 Dumps are available to collectors, with perhaps 200 held in museums. The best thing about Dumps is that each coin is different.

The small Dump, valued at fifteen pence, circulated widely in the colony; the extreme wear on most Dumps suggests they saw considerable use. The Holey Dollar, being a higher-value coin at five shillings, was less widely circulated. So, while the Dump may seem the diminutive partner of the Holey Dollar pair, the reality is that top-quality Dumps have great value. They are extremely rare, in fact, far rarer than their holed counterpart in the same quality level. As such, Dumps are highly valued.

Historians have drawn on Bank of New South Wales records to support this view. Official records show that in 1820, the bank held 16,680 Holey Dollars and only 5,900 Dumps. Given that 39,910 of each were released into circulation, the figures indicate greater circulation for the smaller denomination Dump. This is useful information if you are buying an 1813 Dump. It is an interesting exercise to examine the availability of Dumps and their current market values, acknowledging a vast price difference between a well-circulated 1813 Dump and one in the upper echelons of quality. However, our research clearly shows the reasons. Top-quality Dumps are exceedingly rare. 1814-dated coins are even rarer.

Edge milling was used as a deterrent against clipping, in which unscrupulous individuals shaved slivers of silver from the coins, reducing their silver content to approximately 80%. Coins in other lands were clipped. Milling the edges stopped this practice. Earlier coins contained a much higher percentage of silver.

Is there evidence of the original Spanish Dollar design?

While the Holey Dollar clearly shows that it is one coin struck from another, in a less obvious way, so too can the Dump. There is no doubt that heat was involved in the creation of the Dump. When the disc fell out of the centre of the Spanish Dollar, it still bore the original dollar design of a four-quadrant shield, housing a lion and castle in each quadrant. And the shield's cross-bars. High temperatures obliterated the original Spanish Dollar design from most examples. Those Dumps that retain the original dollar design elements are highly prized.

Is the elusive "H" for Henshall present in all coins?

Mint Master, William Henshall, declared his involvement in the creation of the Dump by inserting an "H" into some - but not all - of the dies used during its striking. Its presence on the reverse, between the words "FIFTEEN" and 'PENCE," is highly prized.

The Dump – not as simple as it looks.

No one really knows how the Dump (and the Holey Dollar) were actually manufactured. No documentation as to the method has ever been found. It is safe to assume that whatever machinery was employed was hand-operated, as the first steam engine did not become operational in the colony until 1815. It is also unlikely that Henshall would have worked unsupervised.

The likely production options were the screw press, drop hammer, or hand-held punch, with the drop hammer method onto a pre-heated plug generally regarded as the most likely. The edges were milled with a 'fiddle press'.

There is no doubt that heat played a role in the formation of the Dump. The high temperatures also caused the metal disc punched out of the dollar to expand once the new value was impressed into it, which is why the Dump is always larger than the hole in the Holey Dollar.

The haphazard, obliquely grooved edge milling on the Dumps indicates that a "fiddle method" was the final step in the production process, in which a roll of Dumps was rotated under pressure against a grooved cylinder to mill the edges.

At least four dies were used for the 1813 Dump coins. Only some have the "H" mark. This makes me wonder whether Henshall had permission to use this simple mark.

Have you noticed the Macquarie Bank logo? It's the Holey Dollar.

Characters

Fictional Characters

Captain Rudolph (**Rudi**) **Greenwood** 73rd Regiment ex 102nd Regiment of Foot
B 1784 *(older brother Malchus. Parents and five younger siblings died in a house fire, 1806 Phillip, the youngest boy, aged 3)* Made *Viscount Buckridge* from Feb 1814.
m 10th Nov 1810 **Bethany Edwards** (dark hair, violet eyes) B 1789
1st husband, ***Andrew*** *Edwards, died May 1810.*

1 Andrew James Sydney ***(Andy)Edwards*** *Sept 7th 1810, twin*
2 Amanda Elizabeth ***(Manda) Edwards*** *Sept 7th 1810, twin*
3 Benjamin (**Benji**) Phillip Gabriel **Greenwood** 22 Oct 1811, b in church
4 miscarriage 4 months 26 Sept 1812 Charlie (either Charlotte or Charles)
5 David (**Davy**) Rudolph **Greenwood** 27th January 1814 twin
6 Elizabeth Bethany (**Bet Bet**) **Greenwood** 27th January 1814, twin
7 Isabella Penelope Greenwood - Stillborn twin to Jennifer 1815
8 Jennifer (**Jenny**) Carol **Greenwood,** early October 1815
9 Katherine (**Kitty**) Caroline **Greenwood** September 1817
10 Louisa (**Lulu**) Ann **Greenwood** April 1819
11 Macquarie (**Mac**) Lachlan **Greenwood** July 1821

Malchus Greenwood b 1780 d 1813 M **Lavender** Myrtleford
3 daughters: Fredericka (**Freddie**), Georgette (**Georgie**), Henrietta (**Etta**),
Captain **Lance** Upcroft b 1782 (2nd son of Viscount Boulderson, Father d 1813) *bro Usher d 1812 (elder bro & father John died in Jan 1813, 2 young sisters, Mother still alive.*
M 16th June 1814, **Elise Price** in New Zealand (parents Edwin & Florence Price)
Child 1 Lachlan John Upcroft
Lieutenant **Tobin** Jeeves, a soldier friend of Lance and Rudi
Brenton Wright - a convict coachman, July Cert of Freedom. Sept 1813 exonerated
(Brother Gareth - who will take over as estate manager at Lance's home)
M **Carol** *6 children,*

1 Joseph (Joey) 1798
2 Alfred (Fred) 1801
3 Herbert (Bert) 1804
4 Jemima (Jemma) twins b 1807
5 Charlotte (Lottie) twins b 1807
6 Catherine (Kate) 27 Jan 1814

4 convict maids, **Daisy, Ivy, Vera and May,** at Greenwood's house in the *Canada*
James Callan - M to Cathy
Cathy Callan b 1780 - 2 children 1 **Josh** Callan b 1795 2 Jenny Callan b 1799
m2 Sept 1808 in Cape Town, South Africa, on the way out.
Mark Duffy, b. 1772, Captain in the 73rd Regiment.
Children 4

1 **Gideon** Mark Duffy June 1810
2 **Rosemary** Catherine Duffy 1813
3 Elizabeth (**Eliza**) Duffy April 1816 (twin)
4 Jonah (**Joe**) Lachlan Duffy April 1816 (twin)

Reverend Cowper's staff, Mrs **Delia** Gordon, **Molly** Marchant, **Fred** Morgan
Phillip (**Phil**) Thomas **Tindale** - Blacksmith in Parramatta
M Joanna 2 Children

1 Thomas Tindale - Parramatta Blacksmith (see ***Lockleys of Parramatta)***
2 Caroline (Caro) Joanna Tindale

Marcus Ryan, aged 22 in 1813, b 1792 (see ***No More, My Love***)

Kate Harrison/Katy White & Perry White (***A Lady in Irons***)
Captain Guy Manning (see ***Jam or Marmalade for Tea*** - 2025)
Elise (Elise) Price - missionary's daughter - from Bay of Islands, NZ.
Oliver Quilpie, Marquess of Bowbelle and his wife Annie (see ***Gentle Annie Soames***)
Obadiah "Buddy" Jensen - covered the books (see ***Buddy's Promise*** *{2027})*
Colin and Aggie Osborne, Potter in Parramatta (see ***The Emancipated Potter***)
Connie Waterson m Nigel Bray (see ***Paternity Unknown***)
Wil Waterson - Connie's brother (see ***Paternity Unknown***)
Reverends Phineas Brackenridge, Josiah Winchester & George McGillicuddy. 3 *ministers at St Augustine's/St John's in Hackney. (See* ***Paternity Unknown*** & ***The Breeze Gently Shifts*** *{2027}*)

Real People

Lachlan and **Elizabeth** Macquarie & son Lachlan Jnr (Lachie)
Real servants:- George Jarvis (Indian-born manservant),
Robert Fopp (*butler*)
Joseph Bigg (*coachman*) (liked a tipple)
Mrs Ovens (*cook*)
Mrs **Jones** (*waiting woman for Elizabeth Macquarie*)
Mrs Elizabeth (Betty) Eccles - the governor's emancipated housekeeper in Parramatta.
Later, she ran the Government Dairy at Salter's Farm. She died aged 105
Doctor **D'Arcy Wentworth**, Senior Assistant, partner Ann & children.
Doctor William Balmain
Major Henry Antill
William Cowper - a Reverend working under Samuel Marsden, b 1778, d 1858
m1 Hannah Cowper d 1808 Children 4, Henry, Thomas, Mary & Charles
m2 m Jan 1809 **Ann** Barrell d Jan 1831
Children 1 William **Mac**quarie b 1810 d 1901
Robert Cartwright and family (see ***Tuppence to Pass***)
The various missionaries in New Zealand. (see ***Tuppence to Pass***)
Chief Ruatara (see ***Tuppence to Pass***)
Doctor **William Redfern**
William Henshall arr on *Fortune*, and *Alexander* (dep 31/12/1805 arrive 12/7/1806)
George Howe, Government Printer.
Lieutenant Richard Lundin - the *Indian*
Deputy Commissioner-General David Allen
Captain Percy Earle, captain of the *General Hewitt*
Captain Folger of the *James Haye* dept June 2nd 1814
Elizabeth Fry
Joseph Gurney (Mrs Fry's brother)
Mrs Ann Dumaresq (her daughter, **Eliza** and **Ralph Darling,** 7th governor of NSW
Reverend Richard Johnson, d 13 March 1826, wife Mary
Mary Amelia Harlow & Catherine Lattimore (*Wanstead 1814*)
Thomas and Mary Reibey, the first bank in NSW.
Francis Greenway, Henry Kitchen, Joseph Lycett and John Watts, Architects

Indigenous people named

Arabanoo - Kai'ymay clan
Bennelong - Wanagal Clan, Eora/Dharug language
Abaroo (she became Bennelong's 3rd wife = Boorong) - Burramattagal clan
Nanberry - Renamed Andrew Snape Hamond Douglass White. Gadigal Clan.
Bungaree Garigal, Broken Bay clan; and his wife, Cora Gooseberry -Eora clan,

Bibliography

Holey Dollar and Dump

https://www.nma.gov.au/explore/collection/highlights/holey-dollar
https://www.nma.gov.au/defining-moments/resources/holey-dollar
https://collection.powerhouse.com.au/object/293529
https://coinworks.com.au/1813-dump

The Dump - centre coin

https://coinworks.com.au/1813-dump

Hammer press video

https://www.youtube.com/watch?v=ZFOA6pbI6r8,

***Speke (1)* 1808** *(185-day journey)*

https://www.freesettlerorfelon.com/convict_ship_speke_1808.htm

Governor Bligh's aftermath

https://www.sl.nsw.gov.au/stories/terra-australis-australia/overthrow-and-aftermath#:~:text=In%20May%201810%2C%20Bligh%20finally,comfortable%20farming%20life%20in%20NSW.

William Henshall

https://convictrecords.com.au/convicts/henshall/william/106447
https://www.nma.gov.au/defining-moments/resources/holey-dollar

William Cowper

http://www.cowper200.com.au/william_cowper.html

Government House Parramatta

https://www.parrapark.com.au/public/assets/Shaping-the-Domain-brochures/Shaping-the-Domain-The-Macquarie-Legacy-1810-1821-Parramatta-Park-Brochure.pdf

James Meehan, 1807 map of Sydney

https://nla.gov.au/nla.obj-229911438/view

***Samarang* Coal fiasco - September 1812**

https://navyhistory.au/the-infamous-conduct-of-captain-william-case-and-the-crew-of-hms/

Proclamation about new coins by Lachlan Macquarie

https://trove.nla.gov.au/newspaper/article/628721/7060

Macquarie Bank Logo

https://www.macquarie.com/au/en/about.html#:~:text=Today%20Macquarie%20Group%20is%20a,invest%20for%20a%20better%20future.

Regimental uniforms

https://www.wtj.com/games/republique/uniforms/infoto_uk_line-inf.htm

Government Stables by Francis Greenway, now the Conservatorium of Music

https://dictionaryofsydney.org/media/3332

Sir Robert Peel

https://en.wikipedia.org/wiki/Robert_Peel

If you loved this book, you may also enjoy these similar titles.
(All are stand-alone stories)

First Fleet Convict Era Trilogy 1788-1800

Gentle Annie Soames

Her dreams lead to unexpected outcomes. An Australian First Fleet story.
A First Fleet story with the descriptions taken directly from the Journal of Doctor Arthur Bowes Smith was the doctor on board the Lady Penrhyn.

Annie Soames is a girl beloved by the community but not afraid to voice her desires. That leads to trouble, illicit love, and a world turned upside down.

Oliver Quilpie, the newly married Marquess, finds his arranged marriage unsatisfactory; he is irresistibly drawn to his wife's companion. Unfortunately, he can't keep his hands off her. In retaliation, Annie copies his every move while riding, dressed as a highwayman. However, she has now fallen in love with him. This ultimately leads to her arrest and banishment to a distant land.

After some years, Oliver's wife dies, and his thoughts turn to Annie. He seeks to find her, but she has vanished. He is horrified to discover she was transported to New South Wales as a convict on the *Lady Penrhyn.* Will Annie want to see him?

ISBN 9780645441574 ISBN ebook 9781923097063 LP ISBN 978-1923097346

Long-listed in the Historical Fiction Company Competition 2024

The Emancipated Potter

Sydney Cove 1788 to Parramatta 1795

Not all felons are convicts, and not all convicts are felons.

Colin Osborne's serene life as a talented potter is crushed by a self-important peer. A single punch sends Colin across to the other side of the globe.

Aggie Gibbs is a young convict girl being hunted by a wayward soldier. The two find themselves in a town of criminals and lecherous men.

Captain John Hunter is Colin's mentor, and he paves the way for a new life for his young friends. Then disaster strikes, and he must leave.

Can Colin keep Aggie safe? Will they fulfil Captain Hunter's wishes to build a decent life for the convicts destined to live out their lives in the penal town? Will John ever return to New South Wales? Paperback ISBN 9781923097476 ISBN ebook 9781923097483

Paternity Unknown

Sydney 1788 - 1800 The Aftermath of the First Fleet landing.

Can forgiveness be that easy?

Connie Waterson is traumatised after she became one of the victims of the attack when the convict women were landed on February 6th, 1788. She finds herself expecting an unwanted child. Along with her friends, she must learn to cope with the challenges of their new environment while protecting the life growing within her.

Nigel Bray is a young convict who almost instantly regrets his carnal actions on the day the prisoners from the *Lady Penrhyn* landed. Knowing that Connie is the unwilling recipient of his base desires, Nigel does what he can to ease her path. He is racked with questions: is the child his? Will she ever forgive him? What must Nigel do to win Connie's trust?

ISBN 9781923097438 ISBN ebook 9781923097445 LP ISBN 978-1923097452

The Hunter to Macquarie Collection 1795-1822

When Upon Life's Billows

Sydney 1795-1821 - Governor John Hunter

Keep your friends close, and your enemies closer.

John Hunter loved his life at sea. The wind blows where no man knows, and John is caught in a storm. His ship, the *HMS Sirius,* was wrecked in 1790. Five years later, he became the second governor of the rough and filthy penal settlement of New South Wales. From a place he once loved, he now seems to be in the wrong place at the wrong time, trusting the wrong people.

Helena Rosedale is not your typical female convict. She fiercely battles to prevent the men from abusing her, earning her the nickname "*Helena the Hellcat.*"

Crispin Milroy, alone in the world, serves on the new governor's security detail. Can he win the fair lady's heart? Life in 1795 in Sydney Cove was harsh at best. Food is scarce, and disease often ravages the settlement. Life throws everything at these three, yet somehow, they manage to survive. Why does John trust this young couple when others betray him? What trials must Helena and Crispin endure to make their new lives in this unforgiving town bearable? How can John ease their path?

ISBN: 9780645783339 ebook ISBN: 9780645783346

The Saddler's Song

London 1790s to Parramatta 1840s

The Strains of Starting Again.

George Ellis is the son of a tanner, living on the outskirts of London. Alone and hurting after a disease takes his family, he seeks a new life, setting up a business in New South Wales. His beloved violin is his most treasured possession, and his talent for making music is hidden from all but a select few.

Ben Parker, a saddler, is also heading to the colony. Combining their skills to start afresh in a new world, the young men find accommodation with a family. Two of the daughters steal their hearts — but how will the business survive in a stock-starved land where access to leather is limited? What is the saddler's song, and why is it so special?

ISBN: 9780645783353 eISBN: 9780645783360

Tuppence to Pass

London 1800s to Parramatta 1820s

An Unlikely Partnership

Josh Callan never expected much from life—just enough to get by in the gritty backstreets of London. But when he's caught stealing from the very man who murdered his father, Josh finds himself branded worthless by a sneering judge and sentenced to a distant, brutal world: the penal colony of Sydney. Arriving just as **Governor Lachlan Macquarie** takes charge, Josh steps into a colony on the cusp of change—and into opportunities he never dreamed possible. As he earns the powerful governor's respect and becomes a trusted confidante, Josh begins to forge a new path not just for himself but also for his family and his beloved.

Can a boy dismissed as nothing rise to become something more? And what will his unexpected friendship with the governor cost or gain him in the end?

ISBN : 9781923097070 eISBN: 9781923097087 LP 9781923097544

His Majesty's Pageboy

London to Emu Plains, Australia, in the 1800s

Jack Turner, raised in privilege and known as Lord John. However, at age nine, his true identity is revealed. He struggles with society's immorality and shallowness. He finally meets a pure young woman he feels he could love, but because of his chequered background, he is unable to pursue her. Then, his life takes another turn.

Martha Alexander, daughter of a wealthy shipping merchant, met Lord John while at a society ball in London. She is expected to marry well, and she has feelings for John. But her father's drunkenness led to the loss of everything he owned, including Martha, dooming her to a forced marriage. How do these two young people end up as convicts in Australia?

Paperback ISBN 9781923097308 eISBN 9781923309792 LP ISBN 9781923097568

A Fist Full of Holey Dollars

Sydney Cove 1810+

The Holey Dollar and Dump Story

Captain Rudi Greenwood is a solitary man, trapped in a pointless job in a colony where alcohol is currency and rules are easily ignored in the pursuit of wealth. He is on the verge of ending his monotonous life.

Bethany Edwards, a grieving widow expecting her late husband's child, slowly begins to change from her grief because of her encounters with the handsome but brooding soldier. As she turns to Rudi for help and support, she must face what she truly feels. Will her faith reach a man who believes in nothing, or will his lack of belief keep them apart?

Drawn to Bethany, Rudi is forced to question his cynicism and imagine a different future. When **Governor Lachlan Macquarie** asks for his help improving the colony's roads, an offhand remark from Rudi sparks an idea that could reshape the settlement: a new currency to challenge the power of alcohol. Will Rudi accept the governor's challenge—and what bold choice will make him despised by both the exclusives and the free settlers?

Paperback ISBN 9781923097407 eISBN 9781923097414

Coming 2026

Far From the Whispering Sheoaks

Set in Australia in 1817+

Fanny Little was in the wrong place doing something she thought was legal. Her actions led to her arrest, trial, and banishment. She was assigned from the female prison to ex-soldier Gordon McKenzie and soon found herself in the despicable and humiliating situation of being sold in the public marketplace.

Phil Bentley is a man running from his jealous uncle. He is seeking safety on a secluded farm half a world away. With the community backing them, can Phil save Fanny from Gordon's vile abuse? Why is their relationship destined to spark controversy? And who is Jas? Why does Gordon wish to harm the child? Will they ever escape the shadows pursuing them?

Paperback ISBN 9781923097315 eISBN9781923097322

Coming 2026

Bound Down in Iron Chains

An Australian Historical Tale, set in the Boys' Orphanage in Sydney in 1818+

Smuggling, Rum and Ructions

A gripping tale of betrayal, courage, and survival in colonial Australia.

When honest London bookkeeper **Howard Marlow** is wrongly convicted and sent to New South Wales, he's assigned to the **Sydney Boys' Orphanage**, where corruption runs deep, and the accounts don't add up.

There he meets **Naomi Buckingham**, a convict girl hoping for safety—but facing danger instead. As the two uncover coded ledgers and a smuggling ring tied to the colony's elite, they must risk everything to expose the truth.

In a brutal world built on power and fear, can two convicts bring justice to those who have none?

Paperback ISBN 9781923097353 eISBN9781923097360

Coming 2026

Buddy's Promise

From the Shadows of London to the shade of the gumtrees

Raised on the streets of London, **Obadiah "Buddy" Jensen** hides a fierce loyalty behind a tough facade. When a dying boy begs him to protect his little sister, **Emily Bolt**, Buddy vows to keep her safe—never expecting she'll become the love he can't have.

Exiled to Australia as a convict, Buddy builds a new life, but when Emily reappears years later, everything has changed. He is married with a child.

She was six when he found her. She was lost when he left. Torn between past promises and present choices, can they find their way back to each other—or will fate keep them apart forever? An emotional historical romance of love, loss, and redemption across the seas.

ISBN 9780645783384 eISBN 9780645783391

Coming 2027

More titles are coming.

Unlikely Convict Ladies Trilogy 1792-1840s

Dancing to Her Own Tune

Co-authored by Sheila Hunter and Sara Powter

Sydney 1790s to England 1830s

Annie White is released after serving seven years as a convict in Sydney. She has a visitor who helps her start a baking business. Annie is then asked to assist another ailing man, **Sam Corbett**. She nurses him back to health, and a relationship blossoms between them. They settle into a life together, barely making ends meet, when she realises she's expecting a child. Sam's past is laid bare, and he must come to terms with the revelations. They both must confront their accusers and discover that the answers to their questions are not what they anticipated. Their life experiences seem to cling to them, and, unable to shake them off, they end up back in England. They must face their ghosts and recognise they are not who they think they are. How can they transform their anger and spite into love and forgiveness? The Dance of Life goes on.

ISBN 9780645110715 ISBN9780645110722

Long-listed for the Historical Fiction Company Competition 2022

Amelia's Tears

Parramatta 1828 – England 1840s

From Tears of Sadness to Tears of Joy.

Amelia Westaweller awaits her assignment in the Parramatta Female Prison. Forced to leave the relative safety of gaol, she is assigned and now faces her worst nightmare. A foul man claims her and makes her life a living hell. Then, her world goes black. A glimmer of hope arises when she hears from her brother, Jim, who has enlisted a friend to help her. She writes to Jim, pouring out her heart and telling him of the horrors of her new life. He encourages her to stay firm in her faith. All she can do is pray. When Major **Ned** Grace, her brother's friend, enters her life in Parramatta, he starts to ease her path. Things have changed, as now she has a child in tow. How can Amelia forge a new life for herself? What man could want her with her background and a child at her side? Who is the gentleman who turns her tears of sadness into tears of great joy?

ISBN: 9780645110739 eISBN: 9780645110746 Hard Cover ISBN 9798420617953

A Lady in Irons

England 1800s - Parramatta 1808+

Katy Harrington is mourning the death of her husband after he died in a shooting accident. Barely coping, she awaits the birth of their child. If it's a girl, she must hand the family home to her husband's brother. The day after giving birth to a daughter, she and her daughter are left on the side of a road. She collapses and is found by someone she thought had died in a fire ten years before. **Perry White**, badly scarred himself, nurses her back to health. They marry and move in with her widowed friend, Mary.

After some years, she discovers her husband and friend in each other's arms. Now living in a love triangle, she flees. Grasping the only straw available, she intentionally gets arrested and is sent to a colony far away. By doing this, her marriage can be annulled.

What happens in the Colony is different from what she expects. Governor Macquarie comes to her rescue, but what of Perry and her children?

ISBN: 9780645110784 eISBN:9780645441505

The Convict Birthstain Collection 1820-1840s

NO MORE, MY *Love*

Hunter Valley, NSW, 1820s

Jess Elkin is distraught when tragedy ravages her family. Now widowed, she becomes the victim of a carriage accident and is nursed back to health by the driver.

Marcus Ryan, a hard-headed woollen mill owner, was not expecting to fall in love. Yet, when Jess's fortunes suddenly turn for the worse, Marcus must decide how far he will go to pursue her. Years after following her to Newcastle, Australia, Marcus vanishes. Jess is left wondering if he will keep his promise to return to her... Will she ever see him again?

ISBN: 9780645441536 eISBN 9780645441581

Long-listed in the Historical Fiction Company Competition 2023

The Vine Weaver

Hawkesbury River area 1820s+

New Beginnings and Old Threats

In the 1820s, on a secluded farm by the Hawkesbury River, **Joel and Hetty Walker** create a quiet refuge for young convict women. When troubled **Fran Rea** is brought to Hetty's attention, she is taken in and, under Hetty's guidance and the kindness of farmhand **Hector Macdougal**, helps build a small cottage industry that supports a growing community of vulnerable women.

As Hector's gentle wisdom and compassion begin to heal old wounds, threats from Fran's past resurface, endangering both her and the fragile peace of the farm. The vines that bind their work and land together come to symbolise the bonds between them, bonds that must hold fast as buried secrets and future revelations test their courage, loyalty, and hope.

ISBN: 9780645441512 eISBN: 9780645441529

Long-listed in the Historical Fiction Company Competition 2023

The story continues in "Scotch at The Rocks"...

Scotch at The Rocks

Glasgow, Scotland, early 1800s to The Rocks, Sydney 1830s

Orphaned children Brodie Stewart and Heather Anderson live on Glasgow's streets. Although hungry, they somehow manage to survive and stay out of trouble. Heather finds a job and looks to be settled; things go pear-shaped for them both. Eventually, they marry by declaration, but even that gets complicated, and they are both arrested soon after exchanging their vows. In 1838, they were transported to Sydney as convicts. Heather arrives within weeks of Brodie, and they are assigned close to each other. They are now living in the docklands of Sydney, known as The Rocks. They now have to forge a new life halfway across the world from their homeland.

Adventures abound, and Brodie gets press-ganged. While he's away, Heather's life changes and soon, she's officially selling Scotch Whisky at a shop in The Rocks.

You can take a Scot out of Scotland, but where did the Scotch come from?

ISBN 9780645441550 ebook 9781923097001 Large Print 9781923097254

Waiting at the Sliprails

The Bathurst Road 1830s

A Convict's Tale

Bea Dawes's term of conviction nears an end, and she has few options other than marriage to a stranger or going on the street.

Jack Barnes, the hired drover, wants a wife. Bea accepts his offer; then, she discovers that he could be gone for months, leaving her alone with **Billy and Netty**, part of the tribe of an Aboriginal tribe who live on his secluded farm. Bea learns to love her husband and also this wonderful Aboriginal couple. Drought ravages the farm, and Jack must hit the long paddock with the flock. In his absence, a visitor arrives, threatening to destroy everything she has worked so hard for. Can Bea touch her heart? Can she cope? Will the drought ever end? And when will Jack return?

ISBN: 9780645441543 eISBN: 9781923097032

PenCraft Award Winner for Literary Excellence, Christian Historical Fiction 2024

Convict Shadows of the Past

Two Jennifers, two hundred years apart

The colonial history of cheese in Australia

When she discovers her convict family history, eight-year-old Jenny Kellow learns that she was named after a convict from nearly two hundred years ago. Inspired by her grandfather's stories, she delves into her ancestors' convict past. From him, she hears tales of bushrangers, convicts, and life in the early colony of Parramatta. She embarks on a journey to retrace the footsteps of her convict great-great-great-grandmother to honour her. Jenny's quest begins with microfiche in the 1960s, where she discovers a small tin mining town in Cornwall and the production of a cheese that set London alight. She uncovers that her ancestor, **Jennifer Kellow,** brought her cheese-making skills to Parramatta, where she taught others the craft. Echoes of the past can still be heard if you know where to listen. Who was the first Jennifer, and what does she have to do with cheese? Why is she so elusive? Did Jenny's ancestor, Jennifer, ever see those two small crosses carved into the bricks of the Female Factory? Would Jenny ever uncover her ancestor's story?

ISBN: 9780645783315 ISBN ebook 9780645783322

A NaNoWriMo 2022 book winner

In Defence of Her Honour

London 1800s to Parramatta 1819

Will the real man of quality please stand up?

Bill Miller was raised and educated alongside the family's sons. The youngest, Bert Edison-Browne, had been his best friend. However, jealousy intervenes when Bill's excellent schoolwork begins to curtail their friendship. He wins a scholarship and enters Oxford University. When Bill's father dies unexpectedly, Bert insists that Bill take over as butler, but it's more to oppress him. Bert's jealousy grows and festers. He is now looking for a way to rid themselves of their new butler. A ruckus ensues, and Bill is arrested for assaulting Bert.

Molly Ross, the housekeeper's daughter, will vouch for him. It's too late; Bill has been arrested and is soon to be sentenced and transported. With Bill gone, Molly now fights to defend herself from Bert. After hitting him with a pan, she, too, is arrested and sent to Sydney. Bill and Molly arrive with letters of introduction and compensation from Bert's father. Soon, they will be running the best inn in Parramatta with an endorsement from the governor.

ISBN 9780645441567 ISBN ebook 9781923097049

Long-listed in the Historical Fiction Company Competition 2024

I Can't Stop Tomorrow

Irish Famine 1840s to Avoca Beach, Australia

Escaping bigotry and prejudice in Ireland, the O'Shane family lives on a secluded farm on the west coast of Ireland. The potato blight soon decimated their farm. It's always darkest before dawn, and the two remaining girls cling to the hope of a new life. With the kindness of strangers, the eldest girls, **Clare** and **Kerry O'Shane**, head to their cousin, Sal Lockley, in Parramatta, Australia. A new, wonderful life awaits them both. **Shéamus Connor** is the annoying teenage boy who reluctantly draws Clare's affection. However, living in a convict town means ruffians abound.

John Moore is a bad-tempered and troubled Irishman who is content to live alone on another secluded farm until he discovers Clare and two other lads need rescuing.

Can John protect her from the pain inflicted by an evil world?

Can Shéamus find his lost love, who has fled?

ISBN: 9780645441598 ISBN ebook 9781923097056

Madeline's Boy

England 1830s to New South Wales 1840

The race to protect an Orphaned Boy

All is not straightforward when money and titles are involved.

Orphaned, afraid and on the run, Chip must flee.

Madeline was his mother's best friend. Maddie now needs to keep her charge safe and alive. She must give up her life to protect the boy she has loved since birth.

Months after Chip's parents' demise, Maddie sets out to deliver Chip to his Uncle Humphrey, who lives in Sydney. Through him, she meets Chip's uncle's friend, Tim, who falls for Maddie —but will they find happiness?

The menacing presence soon finds Chip, and Maddie needs to hide him again. They are relocated from hidden farms to secret valleys, ultimately ending up in an Aboriginal encampment.

Can Tim find a way to be with Maddie? And if so… Will Chip ever be safe?

ISBN: 9780645783308 ISBN ebook 9781923097094

Long-listed in the Historical Fiction Company Competition 2024

Jam or Marmalade for Tea

England 1820s to New South Wales 1825 (Governor Brisbane Era)

Martha Hamilton is the eldest of four orphans struggling to survive on their own. She is caught stealing, tried, convicted, and transported to New South Wales. With her family gone, she becomes despondent. Life holds no meaning for her, and the ocean waves look inviting.

Captain Guy Manning is a frustrated and injured redcoat soldier returning to Sydney for a new assignment. He notices Martha trying to jump overboard and rescues her. How do two cats bring them together?

A convict ship is no place for romance, and she's far too young anyway, isn't she?

Can Guy save her and forge a life together for them? What connections does he have to try to save her siblings? Why is marmalade important for their future?

Paperback ISBN 9781923097933 eISBN9781923097285

A NaNoWriMo 2023 book winner

A prequel to 'The Lockleys Parramatta' series

(Free novella with newsletter signup)

Unshackled Lives

Set in England &Australia in the 1800s

Australian historical fiction of early colonial days

Ned Lockley is the second of four sons of the Duke and Duchess of Gracemere. As his mother's favourite, his childhood years were blissful, but he needed to grow up, and quickly.

A whirlwind romance is followed by a loved one's betrayal. The following emotional turmoil is particularly challenging for Ned to cope with, especially amid a collapsing and immoral society.

Ned can't stay as his family is falling apart. His mother's words to remain true to himself and his faith make him leave everything he knows. How did Ned end up in New South Wales in charge of placing female convicts? Will he ever find happiness or discover who Charles is?

ISBN 9781923097377 eISBN 9781923097384 LP ISBN: 9781923097391

A 100-year, six-part Australian Colonial series

The Lockleys of Parramatta 1800-1900

Hands upon the Anvil

A blacksmith's life and love are more than work

Parramatta 1830s

Eddie Lockley's parents were transported for their crimes. Can a steadfast lad rise above his origins and guide others to succeed in a land of opportunity?

Ten-year-old Eddie longs to help his mum and dad. Living in a convict town with his family, the keen youngster has been working with the local blacksmith since his sixth birthday. But when a lieutenant doesn't stop abusing his older brother, the young boy yearns for the day when he can stand up and end the torment. Though he's thrilled when his mentor offers to send him off to learn his letters, Eddie fears he won't be around to watch his siblings' backs. But as he takes on the biggest adventure of his life, the brave believer soon discovers that God is looking out for everyone he loves. Does this young man in the making have what it takes to change everything for the better?

ISBN 9780994578235 Ebook ISBN 978-0-9945782-5-9 Hardcover 9798496177368

Out Where The Brolgas Dance

Gold is found, and so is love
Parramatta 1840s
How can a question change so many people?

It's the 1840s, and discoveries across the Blue Mountains continue. Major Mitchell's new road is complete, and towns are planned and being built. Abundant land is available for those who want it. Eighteen-year-old **William "Wills" Lockley** has laid a solid foundation for a respectable career as a blacksmith, but the Lockley lust for adventure flows deeply within his veins. He dreads the monotony of work at the blacksmith's forge and yearns for adventure in a new frontier. Wills meets six Englishmen (*Coping with what is now known as PTSD*) who have the means to make his dreams come true. What they discover changes the Colony and their lives forever. Gold fever ensues. While in the West, Wills must deal with an uncertain romance. Does Cathy even want him?

ISBN 9780994578242 Ebook ISBN 978-0-9945782-6-6 Hardcover ISBN 9798755445504
LP ISBN 9781923097155

Diamonds in the Dirt

Diamonds, love and money… but there is much more to life.
Parramatta 1850s

The youngest Lockley son, **Luke Lockley**, has completed his university education, and his life lacks direction. No job, no money, and no love. Desperately alone, he prays for guidance. How can Luke trust that God has a plan for him if he can't even find a job? He does the only thing he can … he prays. Within a week, life has changed … oh, how it has changed as his brother Wills turns up with a suggestion. Would Luke be interested in joining the expedition with John Evans? **Reverend William Clarke** needs assistance with a government mineral survey. The challenges, adventures and finds are life-changing for many. However, it gives Luke meaning, purpose and direction. The condition of his heart problems also takes a turn. Can he walk away? Will she wait for him?

ISBN: 9780994578273 Ebook ISBN: 978-0-9945782-8-0 Hard cover ISBN 979-8788011141

The Earl's Shadow

Who or what is the 'shadow'? How does it affect so many?
Parramatta 1860s

Charles Lockley, the Earl of Coxheath, spent his youth as a convict in Parramatta, unaware of his noble birth, with limited education and few social skills. Now, after a near-death experience, Charles must decide how to live the rest of his life. He is thrust out of his comfort zone in London. There, Charles discovers his purpose. He delivers a speech in parliament—an action that will reshape the empire.

His eldest son, **Charlie**, shares many of his father's shortcomings. However, the past continues to haunt Charlie.

But how does **Jim Leslie,** the Cobb and Co. coach driver, fit into their story? And what exactly is 'The Earl's Shadow' that he mentions?

ISBN: 9780645110708 Ebook ISBN 978-0-9945782-9-7

Once a Jolly Swagman

An old black Billy Can contains the secrets of an incredible life
An Australian Historical Novel Inspired by the songs of The Seekers
Set in 1870s Parramatta and Kent, UK

Rick Lockley, struggling to escape his family's expectations, runs away to find himself. **Jack**, a jolly swagman, takes him under his care. Even after years together, Rick knows little about the old man.

On his death, Jack leaves Rick his precious billy can; the contents reveal Jack's identity. Stunned, Rick must travel to England to finalise Jack's wishes. There, he uncovers Jack's life of love, betrayal and a link to his own family. Rick also discovers there is much more to learn about this enigmatic man.

ISBN 9780645110753 Ebook ISBN 978-0-6451107-6-0

Jonty's Journey

Gems, Love, Artists and a Golden Lion

Australia and South Africa 1880-1902

Sydney Jeweller **Jonty Evans's** passion for gems takes him to Africa at a volatile time. There, he finds the diamonds he wants and is given a lion cub. However, Jonty is all but kidnapped. His experiences in the Transvaal plunge him into questioning everything he knows about life. Soon, nightmares haunt him. (This is now known as PTSD.)

Upon returning home, he nearly ruins his chance with **Lottie Lockley** before it even begins, and he finds adjusting hard. Lottie's father, **Luke** Lockley from Parramatta, takes him under his wing and directs him to someone who can assist.

Jonty is then called back to Africa as a liaison and reunites with his lion, Chimbu, after saving the life of his security detail. His life journey introduces him to remarkable artists, politicians, poets, rebels, and the scapegoat soldier, Harry Breaker Morant. Can Jonty lay the past to rest and find his lost peace?

ISBN 9780645110777 HC ISBN 9781923097124 Ebook ISBN: 978-0-6451107-9-1

Released Feb 2023

More books are planned for a new trilogy, but they won't be released until 2027 & 2028

Fools Gold Trilogy

The Breeze Gently Shifts

The Silver Thimble

Knots Behind the Tapestry

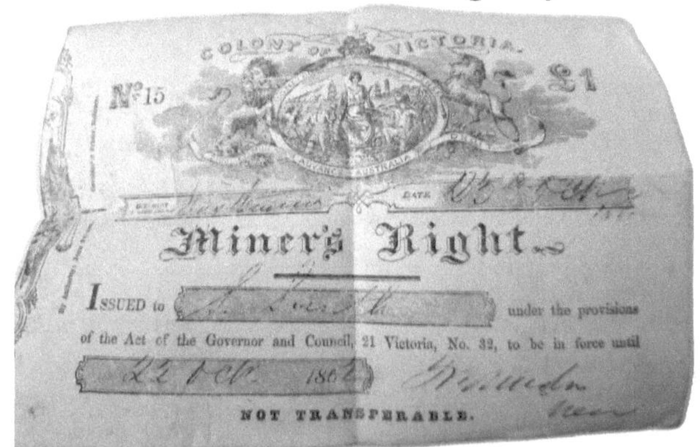

COLONY OF VICTORIA.

No 15 £1

DATE

Miner's Right.

ISSUED to under the provisions of the Act of the Governor and Council, 21 Victoria, No. 32, to be in force until

NOT TRANSFERABLE.

Sheila Hunter's Australian Colonial Trilogy 1840s

Co-Winner of 1999 NSW Senior Citizen of the Year, In the Year of the Senior Citizen

The Story of an Australian Convict Child
An Australian Historical Story inspired by real Life.

An orphaned child, Mattie, is convicted of petty theft, sentenced to seven years, and sent to Australia. She meets another convict woman who, at her death, gives Mattie a chance for a new life. She makes the most of everything that comes her way, earning her freedom, falling in love, marrying, and becoming a mother. But life is not kind to her. She meets bushrangers, moves to Bathurst's gold fields, and opens a store. Yet, she is the kind of woman who made Australia what it is today. Can she survive alone in a man's world? She is a remarkable woman who breaks down all her barriers.
Her faith is what keeps her strong. Can it sustain her through everything life throws at her? ***(Mattie's story continues in The Lockleys of Parramatta - bk 4 & 6)***
Much of this novel draws on family history, including the baptism aboard the convict ship. This occurred to Mary Amelia Harlow on the "Wanstead" in 1814.

ISBN 9781503252370 & ebook AISN BOOTTEDBTO

(The story continues in The Earl's Shadow & Once a Jolly Swagman)

Ricky

A boy in Colonial Australia

Ricky English and his mother immigrated from England to join his father in the new Colony of Sydney. Upon arrival, there was no sign of his father. Ricky's mum uses the little money they brought to secure lodgings in a run-down building. Things go from bad to worse when his mother dies; he is thrown out of the hired rooms, and the caretakers confiscate all their possessions.
Ricky lives on the streets of Sydney Town as a street waif. Ricky finds safe places to sleep and befriends freed convicts who can help him survive. One day, he encounters a lost child and helps reunite her with her family. These people try to help him, but he insists on doing things his way because of his stubbornness. However, he has found a mentor and confidante. The story follows him through his life. He survives and turns his life around, helping others along the way. Ricky's firm faith keeps him strong, but will his new friends ridicule him because of it? ***(Will's story continues in Jonty's Journey)***

Paperback ISBN 9781500770570 Kindle ASIN: BOOMLYN6IG

The Heather to The Hawkesbury

Four Scottish families brave a new life in a strange land.

Torn from their homeland by starvation, four Scottish families are forced to leave the Isle of Skye and seek a new life in Australia. **Mary Macdonald**, her husband **Murd**, and their family, her brother **Fergus** MacKenzie, sister-in-law **Caro** MacLeod, cousin **Alex** Fraser, and all their loved ones are compelled to emigrate from Scotland because of the Potato famine and Clearances.
The story follows these families as they journey from Scotland to the New South Wales colony in the 1850s. Mary struggles to cope with the changes and losses in the first months of settlement. Although the other women rely on her, she is nearly overwhelmed. Mary can't settle in this fierce land and pines for home.
Together, the families endure hardships such as accidents, loss, floods, and relentless work, ultimately forging a strong bond with their new homeland. Trials, tribulations, and triumphs mark their saga as they establish themselves in Australia.
Will Mary ever find peace and contentment where danger and sickness have taken loved ones? Can her love for Murd sustain her through life's turmoil? Will their faith keep them together? And what becomes of the brooch given to Mary as she leaves her mother?

ISBN 9781503251434 ebook 9781923097025 Large Print ISBN1533473641

Available on Amazon/Kindle & Large Print

Sara's Author Bio

Sheila Hunter and Sara Powter were a passionate mother-and-daughter team of amateur genealogists. As they collaborated on their family tree, they made many fascinating discoveries. Their most significant finding was the discovery of four convicts whose perspectives on colonial life sharply contrasted with those of the military personnel. Transported to Australia between 1792 and 1814, these four felons lived during the peak of the convict transportation era.

Before her passing in 2002, Sheila adapted some of these histories into enchanting stories, later published as her Australian Colonial Trilogy. Sheila also left a fourth, unfinished story, inspiring Sara to complete it. Before taking on that task, however, Sara first created the 'Lockleys of Parramatta' series to ensure she could honour her mother's work. She completed the first two books in that series before attempting to finish 'Dancing to Her Own Tune'—for which Sheila had written the first 30,000 words.

Vividly evoking the Colonial Era, these books delve deeper into the theme of overcoming adversity in Colonial Australia, exploring how it emerged, the demise of the Convict system, and the discovery of mineral wealth. Sara skilfully intertwines precise archival data with a captivating narrative to craft a collection of stories about faith, love, loss, and redemption.

Two hundred years after her family arrived in Australia, Sara continues the Australian Colonial stories that start with *Gentle Annie Soames,* a saga about the First Fleet. Her *First Fleet Trilogy* is now complete. Following this chronologically are *The Hunter to Macquarie* Collection, the *Unlikely Convict Ladies* Trilogy, and The *Lockleys of Parramatta.* The *Convict Birthstain Collection*, set in the mid-1800s, follows. All the stories are stand-alone novels.

See Sara's web page to keep up to date with more stories.

An online store offers signed copies.

https://www.sarapowter.com.au

(Australian Postage only)

Amazon Aus QR

Feel free to email me at

saragpowter@gmail.com

FACEBOOK

https://www.facebook.com/profile.php?id=100063887262514

Would you like ***"Unshackled Lives"*** *for free?*

Download from Book Funnel after you sign up.

FREE Newsletter signup

From my web page.

www.ingramcontent.com/pod-product-compliance
Lightning Source LLC
LaVergne TN
LVHW091030080826
845145LV00002B/433

* 9 7 8 1 9 2 3 0 9 7 4 0 7 *